Taking Heart

Taking Heart

Lynne Alexander

FOURTH ESTATE · *London*

First published in Great Britain in 1991 by
Fourth Estate Limited
289 Westbourne Grove
London W11 2QA

Copyright © 1991 by Lynne Alexander

The right of Lynne Alexander to be identified as the author of
this work has been asserted by her in accordance with the
Copyright, Designs and Patents Act 1988.

A catalogue record for this book is available from the British Library

ISBN 1-872180-38-8

Typeset in 11/12pt Garamond by York Typographic Ltd, London

Printed in Great Britain by Biddles Ltd, Guildford

Acknowledgements

More people helped in the writing than I can name. I am grateful to Dr B. T. Marsh for talking to me about his transplant operation; to Dr Bruce Heischober, Dr Valerie Anderson and Dr Jim Morris for their technical assistance; and to Dr David Gorst for his medical knowledge, his facilitating of the Harvey research, and for his enthusiasm and belief in me throughout the writing of the book.

My appreciation to Michael Wheeler and Richard Dutton for their useful suggestions; to Alison Easton for being there when I lost my way; to Vic Gattrell for showing me around the Harveyana at Cambridge, and to Ron Pyatt for showing me the way to my own heart.

My special thanks to Giles O'Bryen for teasing out my meaning, and for his encouragement and patience; and to Dr Stanley Lependorf for reading the manuscript at the last minute and adding some psychoanalytic refinements.

To Paula Day, Pat Urry, Kathleen Marsden and Marilyn Martin-Jones, whose friendship and support made it all possible, my love.

The poem referred to on page 34, and the extracts therefrom, is by Sharon Olds, 'Outside the Operating Room of the Sex-Change Doctor' (*The Gold Cell*, New York, 1987).

A strange grey distance separates
our pale mind still from the pulsing continent
of the heart of man.

D.H. Lawrence, 'The Heart of Man'

PART I

Every affection of the mind that is attended with pain or pleasure, hope or fear, is the cause of an agitation whose influence extends to the heart.

William Harvey, *De Motu Cordis*, 1628

Why should a man who was considered so brilliant and successful have taken up analysis unless his head or his heart had some part in it?

Sigmund Freud

One

The heart: *heorte, herta, herte, hirte, hart, hiarta, hjarta, hierte, hairto, herza, herze, herz, hrid, sr'd'ze, serdze, szirdis.* 1. A hollow muscular organ contracting rhythmically and serving to keep up the circulation of the blood . . . 2. Seat of vital functions. 3. Seat of feeling, volition, intellect. 4. Seat of one's inmost thoughts and secret feelings. 5. The soul, spirit; intent, will, desire. 6. Seat of the emotions (*Mine eye and heart are at a mortal war*). 7. Intent, will, purpose, inclination, desire; obs, except in phrase after one's own heart. 8. Disposition, temperament, character. Obs. *In faith Lady you have a merry heart* (Shaks, Much Ado). 9. The seat of the emotions generally; the emotional nature, as distinguished from the intelligent nature placed in the head. 10. More particularly, the seat of love or affection (*to give, lose one's heart (to), to have, obtain, gain a person's heart; near, nearest one's heart,* close or closest to one's affection. The *verie instant that I saw you, did my heart flie to your service* (Shaks, Tempest). 11. The seat of courage, especially in *to pluck up, gather, keep (up), lose heart. You put heart into me again.* 12. The seat of the mental or intellectual faculties. *O fooles, and slow of heart to beleeve all that the Prophets have spoken.* (Luke, xxiv, 25). 13. The moral sense, conscience. 14. A term of endearment, often qualified by dear, sweet (see sweetheart), etc.; chiefly in addressing a person. *Alas when shall I mete yow, herte dere?*

Hello? Are you there? Are you taking all this in, these tenuous *italics* and bold **bolds**; these imaginative, historical, mythological and philosophical; these medical, metaphorical and allegorical, these imagistic, semiotic, linguistical, romantical, poetical, etc, *hearts*?

The heart. A power-noun, an adjectival bazooka, a veritable verbal ventricular goldmine with its variations and ramifications, its nuances and conceptual possibilities. Moreover, they go on; one, two, three, *five* pages of *heart-affecting, -cheering, -dulling, -easing, -freezing, -fretting, -hardening, -holding, -melting, -moving, -purifying, -quaking, -shaking, -sickening, -stirring, -swelling, -tearing, -warming, -wounding, -wringing* . . . And this is only the *shorter* OED!

My wife Ruth has just come into the bedroom. She wants to know what I'm doing up to my armpits in dictionaries and old medical books. I think of Freud buried in a pile of discarded manuscripts and letters saying he felt like a Sphinx drowning in drifting sands until only his nostrils were sticking up above the heaps of papers.

I tell her I'm looking up definitions of the heart. Quite fascinating, I add. I don't believe it, she says, and walks out, bouncing gently in her nurse's Nikes.

What am I looking for? Illumination, wisdom, an analysis, a way forward, something, anything; perhaps like the young Sigmund Freud, 'to inscribe myself in medicine'. Ah, but there is a difference – namely, that he was inscribed as doer while I shall be *done to*.

Me: So what is to be done?

Cardiologist: I'd say a transplant is your only option at this point.

Me: What if I don't have it?

Card: When is your next birthday?

Me: In about three months.

Card: You won't live to celebrate it.

Me: I see. Thank you.

Think of it as a divorce, he said cheerily. *Decree absolute?* Tell me, I gently enquired, how many times have you been divorced? Twice, he said, it's no big deal. You? Never. Well, he said, there's always a first time.

The seat of love or affection.

I close the dictionary and try to picture the heart as the Seat of Love. One of those private booths like they have in North Beach Italian restaurants, complete with velvet curtains on brass rings, from behind which come sounds which press the pulse's button. Or a throne, an overstuffed rocker, a chaise longue, a beanbag. But these give way to a broken down old porch-type swing from which His dimpled feet dangle absurdly, into which His snuggly bottom and bow and arrow and silvery wings have been ignominiously stuffed. He is looking distinctly put out – his latest victim hasn't turned up.

My mother sat in her old maple nursing chair facing the sea as if expecting my father to rise up out of it and come to tea, quite dry and without fish leaping from his breast-pocket. He is said to have disappeared into it, the sea, during the war. When my clients fail to show without giving twenty-four-hours' notice, they pay for it.

I am a psychoanalyst.

But we were talking about Love's seat. It ought to be soft, roomy:

4

a *fauteuil* for the comfy canoodling of our cute little critter, where he can act out his *sturm und drang* routines in high style and privacy.

Where do we find such a custom pouffe?

Ah, here is a salesman with a polka-dotted tie to help us out. *Step right this way, folks, and you will find the love-seat of your dreams: cloud-soft when you're tired, fibre-firm when you need bucking-up; cool in summer, warm in winter; converts into a double bed, a queen, a king . . . and in the shape of a heart! Folks, I urge you not to miss this special red-sunset opportunity . . . Can't you just smell the smell of new foam and cotton?* Picture Love at Home snuggling his rolls of cellulite into one of these, stoking up with popcorn before his next delightful onslaught, patting the empty seat next to him.

I find I'm patting a cold sheet, and thinking about a patient who left me knee-to-knee with an empty chair half-way through her analysis.

If you want to know, I'm taking the cardiologist's advice, passing the time of day until they find me a heart. 'You'll need to do very little, Frear, just wait I'm afraid. Relax, take it easy, try not to worry.' Try not to worry? Fine. As a sensible man I'm obeying orders – tucked up in bed entertaining a number of my old medical textbooks including the Willis translation of William Harvey's *Motion of the Heart,* 1653, and *Stedman's Medical Textbook,* 1949, leftovers from my days as a medical student. I open the Stedman to **heart** and find:

armored h.

bony h.

frosted or icing h.

hairy h.

irritable or soldier's h.

movable h.

pendulous h.

tear-drop h.

tiger h.

heartburn.

heartmobile.

heartworm.

Isn't it wonderful, this calcareous, fibrinous armed Panzer division; this fatty, degenerated striped feline, this weeping woolly mammoth, this parasitic nematode worm! Indeed, you are I hope as impressed – delighted, cheered in my agony – as I am by so much

5

quaint scientific misapprehension, this evocation of hearts frosted, hairy, droopy. As for the heartmobile, what is this? Some bloody cardiological Batcar, driven by the one, the only . . . Heartman! I can just see him in his red plastic Lolita glasses, his red cape, his T-shirt emblazoned with the Heart, Lung and Chest Fund insignia.

Forgive me, I'm not well. In fact, I am in pain and in doubt of my life. My heart fails me. I could say it has flown from me in the way that the Greeks say the *psyche* does after death. I am left blank, unprogrammed, undefined . . . *suspended*. The heart, to quote my cardiologist, is 'nearly inert'. Dead-beat with the strain of living or not living, a pouchy, shapeless enema bag, in the end not worth saving. White bits of marbling in the meat, crunchy stuff in the coronaries.

Heart transplant: an operation in which a heart from one person is transplanted into the body of another; similarly of two animals; a heart so transplanted; also *attrib.* and *fig.*

Where has my *fig.* heart gone?

Forget the figurative, what I need, and soon, is a heart as in: a hollow muscular organ contracting rhythmically and serving to keep up the circulation of the blood.

Dictionaries, you see, have their uses.

Forty minutes away at the Stanford University Hospital Transplant Center they are on 24-hour alert for a blood, tissue and size compatible donor heart. As soon as one shows up on their screen they'll bleep me. The bleeper is clipped to the heart-pocket on my pyjama top. My bag is packed and waiting.

This has to be the rendezvous of the century.

Two

Donna Cautlin. She was a patient for approximately three months, hardly long enough for an introduction. She went through phases from the manic to the depressive to the regressive. She was on that last occasion barefoot and near-catatonic: she needed some chivvying merely to get through the door. Even her ringlets seemed afflicted with melancholia. *The door, if you wouldn't mind . . .* She tiptoed across the floor like a small child trying not to wake the adults and curled herself into my high-back leather armchair, an Alice shrunk to an alice. Not easy for a near-six footer. But she was a good player and I her willing – professional – audience. She put her thumb in her mouth; I took out my pipe. Thus we got through the session in companionable orality.

An expensive silence. Not that it mattered to me, or Donna herself for that matter, since it was her mother, who lives I gather somewhere down in New Mexico and is quite well off, who was paying for all this.

All this. She once arrived on her hands and knees, having crawled from backyard to backyard, apparently quite unable to walk upright. Even getting into the chair was too much for her. That's okay, I said, sit where you are. So she flopped down with her legs in a V and beat at the floor. What is it? What do you want? I coaxed; she whimpered. Out it came: pea-nut-bu-tt-er. I could smell Johnson's Baby Powder. Her neck was white. I put my fingertips together thinking, This is no problem for me: we have all the time in the world.

All that has changed. She has time, my other patients have time, my family and friends have time – but I do not. What I have is two months at most, according to the cardiologist. What other condition could reduce a person to sitting up in bed with a five-pound dictionary on his chest, rehashing sessions with a former patient with rather hysterical corkscrew curls (sometimes yellow, sometimes henna, and sometimes a most unnerving purple). And the eyes. Maybe Sigmund Freud was right about not making eye contact with patients – or they with him. The eyes seemed to change along with the hair: presumably only an effect. Or she may own a set of multi-coloured contact lenses – designer eyewear for the schizophrenic?

I invited her to reflect on her situation, to cast her mind back to when she was a child, to her first/last memories. What I didn't want was the dumb rabbit routine, which I found exasperating. Do you remember your father? She opened her mouth and her thumb fell out, coming to rest on her lower lip. For all her enthusiasm, I might as well have been reading from *Stedman's Medical Dictionary*.

I am reading from it.

After the heart attack her other self turned up at the hospital, greedy for gore. She wanted to know all about it: where did I collapse; did I hit my head on the windshield (blood optional); did they have to break the window to get me out; were a lot of people standing around watching (helping/hindering/gossiping); did they have to give me oxygen/the kiss of life/kick-start my heart. And then: did they throw me onto a stretcher and rush me to the hospital (in a heartmobile?); hook me up to various gadgets; operation (standard/tricky/delicate); damage (minor/limited/extensive); did my family stand around biting their fingernails/didn't show up until it was over.

Enough. It brings it all back just when I'm supposed to be into forgetting and relaxing. Rosemann and Friedman, old-timey hoickers of the Type A 'coronary prone' personality (easily bored/irritated/impatient/uncommunicative/workaholic, etc.) advise 'cultivating the ability to say no to demands . . . that are going to cause you to feel overburdened'. So, no – sorry, but no more reminiscence work today. They would, on the other hand, approve of this 'stress diary' – very therapeutic. 'Don't be afraid to admit your limitations,' they counsel. 'Never be shy about seeking help and advice.' And finally, 'If you worry unduly about chest pain, imagining that it indicates "a bad heart", make a quick visit to the doctor: you will probably find that there is nothing to worry about.'

All that Type A/Type B nonsense has been debunked.

No, I don't want to tell you about it any more than I did Donna. The point is I must not, much as it compels me, be urged by the craven need to please. This is my life, not the plot of some sleazy medical thriller. It would be so easy to make it all palatable, saleable; to begin, *There she was sitting astride me on the office rug wearing not a lot, when she . . . when we . . . when I was gripped by a pain which ripped into me like wild horses in the desert . . .* Your eyes widen, your breath quickens. In less than a paragraph you're hooked on engorged hearts and genitals, not to mention flaring filly nostrils. More more, you say, crunching another corn chip.

'It still seems strange to me,' wrote Sigmund Freud at about my age, 'that the case-histories which I write read like short stories.' In other words they lacked, so to say, a serious scientific character. This worried him so much that he forced himself to concentrate on concrete problems, ruthlessly suppressing the yen for abstract speculative thought.

What else did he sit on? Quite a lot but never mind about that now. Our interest here is in lending simple strength to the fragile yet purposeful details of male scientific discourse over duplicitous female fantasy; of fact over fiction; which I admit is getting harder and harder to disentangle in this Golden Gated abode of ours, populated by the transplanted, disoriented and schizophrenic.

I am witness to so much: artists of the imagination who carve for themselves life-plots as intricate as a Baroque altarpiece complete with undulating grape clusters, rippling flaming hearts, twisting chubby cherubs, upwardly aspiring vegetable matter, and the whole lot topped with a Dove of God, flapping uncontrollably. I am not a religious man. Such constructions are monstrosities.

In my bottom desk drawer I kept Donna's gear: a rag doll, a stuffed rabbit and several jars of Skippy's. The peanut butter routine ran as follows: I'd give her the jar. She'd dig in, obsessively and methodically scooping up fingerful after fingerful until the jar was empty. She'd use her nails, her tongue. Then, staring into the licked-clean picked-clean jar, she'd look up at me and blink and the tears of loss would slide down her face. Occasionally she'd wind herself up to a full-blown tantrum. Then it would end in vomit on the rug.

What are we to do about all this? All this. More more more: oh the greediness of the sick. The empty jar syndrome. You fill it, again and again and again, and still there is never enough.

What does this say about transplantation?

There is only one non-surgical solution: the head must take charge of the body. The Good Policeman, bobbing up and down up there, must take over where things are out of control below. This is not just Freudian, you realise, it goes way back to Plato. According to him, the body is a sort of bipedal plinth for carrying the head: *so the head might not roll upon the ground.* O noble sphere.

According to Donna he was a jerk. That was her succinct and eloquent assessment of one of our greatest philosophers. You could use a lesson in the appreciation of mathematical and geometrical order, I informed her. I found I had doodled: (1) a triangle; (2) an upside-down triangle or pyramid; (3) a heart symbol; (4) ditto with curly hair. The last resembled a piece of crude adolescent graffito; the symbolization of desire, ho ho? No, not great art. She wasn't interested in my solutions.

I felt under pressure to do something, and quick. It brought back memories of my maiden session with Donna, which was in itself awkward and virginal: so keen was I to do it well that I failed to find a way in. This time – Donna's last – I tried a different strategy, leaning further and further back in my new chair. My fingertips had trouble finding one another. And then, according to some exaggerated system of perspective, my knees grew great and through them I saw D's head shrunk to a hairy dot on the horizon. It will be better next time, I promised myself. How was I to know there wouldn't be a next time?

Her parting words were typical of her:

—'How many shrinks, she posed, brightening up, does it take to change a lightbulb?'

I shouldn't have engaged with her but I did – she caught me off-balance. I said,

—'God knows. A whole convoy – or none. By the time they finished analysing the situation it would be daylight and the light-bulb no longer necessary.

—Wrong, she said. Only one. But the lightbulb really has to want to change.

Ha ha, I went. I really did think it funny, you see. But then the next thing I knew she was saying see you around and I was holding a box of tissues out to an empty chair.

Three

The attendant waves me into the track: *another inch to the left — yo — stop right there.* I shut the engine and apply the handbrake while he swabs at the hood and trunk with a soapy mop, strategically missing out the dollops of bird diarrhoea. Off with the brake and the car rolls closer to the washing contraptions. Brake on. It sets off a bell. Here we go, now very close to the jungle of machines, the lashing soapy tendrils. My heart contracts and forgets to release: it wants out of this thumping hole.

The steering wheel is an insufficient shield against the swish-swishing forces of darkness. My face, if you could see it in the rear-view mirror, would show my womanish terror. Why 'womanish'? All right, scratch that. The point is that it was an irrational fear, some turbid thing roiled up from the muddy depths of the unconscious. There was nothing to be afraid *of.* By the way, you know 'hysteria' goes back to the Greek word for womb?

But to continue.

Stuffed doll arms flail at the windows, trunk, doors. She's after me. I cover my face with my arms. The whole doll, like some kind of enormous fertility figure, straddles the front windshield and starts to dance, her crotch inches from my face, her hula skirt made of black rubber straps slapping back and forth, *floop, floop.* Soon she will crush me and my car between her blubbery thighs. And she can do it, I reckon, with one scissor-like motion. This is no Car Wash, this is Kurtz country and I am done for. No help for miles around. I grab my chest as she squeezes harder still. It's not my nether organ she's after either. *Oh I will wring your heart yet!* She increases the pressure of her obscene cuddle. Only when I slump over sideways does she let me go, and then not without a final slap on the arse to dry me off. I feel a bursting sensation, I see light, hear the honking of horns.

So there you have the story of the heart attack. Now are you satisfied?

An attack of the heart — the realest thing that has ever happened to

11

me. As real as – what shall we say – this notebook, this Papermate pen, with its double heart insignia, that goes *click click*.

So why did it happen? Was it something I did (the broken diet) or failed to do (disobey the laws of summer and you'll be punished with an injury to the heart)? Or did it have nothing to do with me: merely a combination of genetic predisposition and rotten luck?

It is tempting to think of ourselves at the controls, twiddling the dials, screwing up the loose screws, balancing up the old humours – hot, wet, dry, cold – keeping the microbial hordes and pathogenic worms and what-nots at bay. Good health, great, another pat on the back, take another bow. On the other hand, when one of the major parts blows, what then? Who've we got to blame? No one. *Mea culpa.*

You can see the flaw in such a system.

It was William Harvey, I suppose, the guy we call the Father of Modern Medicine, who demonstrated finally and conclusively that the heart is a pump and not a secret hideout for angels and devils. And that the body is a complicated bunch of interconnecting machinery whose parts can and do from time to time break down for no apparent or at least no *self-inflicted* reason. And so the burden of blame was lifted from our poor chests. *Whew.* Not my fault: a breakdown in the system, thus I am absolved. Bless you, O Father of Modern Medicine, wherever you may be.

Not that it works, of course. I mean, we may want to put the blame 'out there' but in the end the psychoanalytic stethoscope, that nosy insinuating pickup, moves in with terrifying, Geiger-counter-ish accuracy on the faultline. What evil lurks in *there*, hmm? What ancestor have I neglected? What gods have I angered (Sigmund, are you there)? Have I indeed broken the Law of Summer? And what if – curse of all curses – my sickness is a sign that I have lost my soul; then to what sorcerer of the psyche do I turn to ask for its return; with what acts of propitiation, what use of magical powers may I seek to overcome the loss? Is there a Lost and Found Department out there?

It's called the Transplant Unit.

Four

Disease, Divorce, Death. When it comes to the big Ds we have permission from the world and its pop psychologists to be thrown. In fact, if we don't behave like curveballs for a while we're reckoned to be in big trouble. But it's the small, hiding-in-the-closet jobs you want to watch out for.

Take the morning of 'the episode'. I went to my closet, got out my Nikes and padded into the kitchen to put them on while I got the Mr Coffee machine going. I bent over, put on the left sneaker, then set to repeat the action with the right one. Except there wasn't a right, it was another left one. I took off the left one and tried putting it on the right foot only it wouldn't go. Yes, that's right, it was also a left one. I examined both carefully. No doubt about it, two identical left Nikes, grey with blue chevrons. I put down the shoes and looked at my feet: one right, one left as per usual.

That was when I got thrown. I began to think: something has happened out there and I don't know about it. Right feet have been banned. Sometime between yesterday and today the order went out while I was preoccupied with one of my screwier patients and nobody bothered to tell me.

I took a last look down at my feet. I wouldn't have minded if both had been rendered left – at least I could have gone jogging, at least it would have been a *solution*. Then I closed my eyes, took a deep breath and looked once more at the Nikes, almost praying by this time that they'd been restored to their usual rightness and leftness: the cosy couple nuzzling together under the table, instep to instep, big toe to big toe. No such luck: they were *ipse dixit* both still incorrigible lefties.

—Ruth!

In due course she came to the rescue, having figured out that I had picked up one each from a new pair and an identical old pair. Had I examined them carefully I would have noticed one was more worn and more faded than the other.

The world was a nervier place that day. I didn't jog (by the time we'd got a viable pair of Nikes sorted out it was too late). I drove

13

down the hill to meet my first patient. I listened and attended, made notes between sessions, knocked my pipe on the edge of my waste-paper basket, crossed my legs, and so on. I may have been distracted by the window cleaner. I may have done a few extra swivels in my swivel chair.

I felt beleaguered, it's true, more annoyed than usual with patients expecting solutions from me. I give them tools, why can't they figure things out for themselves? Who do they think I am, Big Daddy, *God*? Doctor, doctor, tell me what's wrong with me . . . make me strong . . . make me understand so it won't happen again . . . make me not be a victim . . . make me lovable . . . make me change . . . take away the pain . . .

And what, in my heart of hearts, do I say to all this? God save me! Impossible! What feelings? What change? Who cares!

There, I've said it, the unforgivable. At least you can't accuse me of ellipsis.

Doctor, doctor, will I die?
Yes, my dear, and so shall I.

And then Donna Cautlin showed up late and flounced herself down. All right, jeans don't flounce, but the gesture was a 'flounce' all the same. And she proceeded to do what all the other perpetual patients couldn't. It should have made my day.

—I quit, she said.

Or words to that effect. I sat back, smiled, said *ahh* in the standard-encouraging way and invited her to look at what she'd just said.

—Fuck it. I don't want to 'look at what I said'. I said it. I've had enough bellybutton bullshit, I'm taking off on my bike – heading south.

—South. I see.

—Maybe go spend some time down in the desert, Baja, Mexico, who knows, maybe keep going till I get to the end. What's at the bottom, Doc?

—Patagonia.

—Great, I'll go there. When I've had enough travelling, I figure I'll be ready to go back to school.

—I see. Would you like to tell me what's prompted this sudden decision?

14

I felt I was clicking my pen a lot.

—No.

That was when she shut her eyes, clicked them open. It made me think of Cartier-Bresson's remark about Kertesz's photographs: 'Each time André Kertesz's shutter clicks, I hear his heart beating.'

—See you around, doc, take care of yourself.

—Uh, just a minute . . . Do you really feel you've worked out your, uh, problems sufficiently to embark on . . .

That was when she told me the lightbulb joke. I laughed. It was a reprieve. I thought we would go on. It seemed to me she looked tearful so I leant over to get the box of tissues and when I looked up she'd gone. I sat there with my hand on my heart thinking about what virtue there was in the orderly coupling of shoes when she stuck her ruffled head back in the door and said,

—By the way, I found out Freud was a coke junkie.

And threw me a kiss.

Five

When Olga Knipper, Chekhov's paramour, asked him, *What is life?* he replied that that was like asking what is a carrot. Next to my bleeper is a mug of carrot sticks. *Munch munch.*

Donna came to see me in hospital, brought me an over-the-hill gardenia which I suspect she'd stolen. She was in one of her nutty phases. I thanked her for the flower and wished her luck on her trip but she continued to sit there asking compulsive questions leading up to a full-blown cross-examination. *The heart doesn't just freak out in a car wash all of a sudden . . . What did you do . . . Was there something wrong, who did you see just before?* And so on. Yes, it made me tired. The shrink gets a taste of his own medicine eh? That may be. I shut my eyes and waited for her to be gone.

Okay, let's look at the situation. I'm quite fit and lean. I jog at least three times a week, going round and round the old Blind School track where I can observe the dynamics of fog and calorie burnoff. Other days I play tennis at Hearst courts or work out on the torture machines. I don't smoke (not really, I just suck; yes, oral I know); my drinking is moderate. Occasionally I break my diet: a pat of butter here, a piece of pesto brie there. But nothing really out of line. Neither am I having an affair with a sexually aerobic nineteen-year-old. Was that the problem? Did I want to? None of your business.

Unfortunately, this healthy lifestyle is no guarantee. There are statistics which lead us to believe that if we watch our weight, our diet and our exercise (and no extra-marital sex), we will live in health to ninety. But it's too easy to fall off a statistical table onto your face. In short, that isn't Life. People have heart attacks for all sorts of reasons.

Attack, arrest: the words are interesting. They portray the heart not as villain but victim: the dramatic arrest of the heart. By whom? Some female goddess-of-darkness symbol who comes to us courtesy of Sigmund Freud, Inc., and who lurks exclusively in car-wash places, prepared to pounce, manacle and squeeze? Come come: not even I am that party-line-ish. My dreams may be Freudian but my life is more

16

than the sum of my repressed sexual parts. Not even Freud, as it happens, was that much of a Freudian.

(By the way, if you fancy that creature was Donna, forget it: you give her too much credit.)

You think we create our own illnesses? Like the woman who swallows her screams for twenty years gets cancer of the throat; the man who accuses everybody of being a pain in the ass gets cancer of the rectum; the shrink who is unable to sustain a pose suffers an infarct; and so on?

Oh these pat pop theories. Medically speaking, the body is such a complicated thing . . . too complicated. Take 'heart attack' itself: a much abused expression. Did she, Donna, care to know what actually happened?

For some reason, she took my hand while I was explaining. The heart monitor did not fail to register this event. All right then, I told her, there was a coronary artery obstruction, a build-up of what is called atheromatous plaque, or a furring up of the tiny arteries leading to the heart. Think about a tube of macaroni, you're looking down the hole, only there is no hole, it's solid durum wheat. That's what it's like: calcified. When you try to slice it with your scalpel it crunches (funny how one remembers these things). Blood can't get through so the heart starves: no food, no oxygen – kaput. And so, the classic 'attack': the pain in the chest and so on. Actually it was in my throat (angina means choking). Later, in casualty, I started to gasp: the onset, I suspected, of heart failure. I was right. The lungs, water- and blood-logged, backed up. A bloodjam ensued and the ventricle went into fibrillation. A dreadful confusion of electrical impulses. The pump stopped pumping.

They pounded me and brought me back to life.

End of biology lesson.

—But *why?* she cried, dropping my hand. Still she had the nerve to persist. Exasperating child!

Christ! It happened because it happened, because of some genetic disposition; because I was overworked and underslept; because I abused it over lunch with an abnormal slab of blueberry cheesecake; because my daughter told me I was a rapist at heart; because I couldn't see my wife through the pile of books on my bedside table; because I was having trouble with my chapter on loss and longing; because of the damned Nikes; because my last patient . . .

It doesn't follow that it proceeded from any one thing. Not even

17

the cardiologists know what causes heart attacks. In fact, they especially don't know. If I were to tell you the car wash set it off, you'd smirk. Well, smirk away.

Finally, in desperation, I said:

It was most likely the 'Sex on the Beach'.

—Oh yeah?

I knew that would get her attention. Well, of course, to some extent most middle-aged men suffer from sex-death terrors, worries of heart attack in mid-act. A seductive scenario: there I am wallowing in sand, suntan oil and bodily juices, heading nicely towards the orgasm to end all orgasms – when *pfut* go heart and penis simultaneously. A lapsed heart, a gritty foreskin. Eros meet Thanatos. But no, it wasn't sex did me in.

—Sorry to disappoint you, I told her. 'Sex on the Beach' is the name of the coffee I drank at lunch.

—What kind of coffee is that?

—Kenyan flavoured with chocolate and rum with a hint of cherry.

—Yuk, she said.

—My thoughts exactly.

—Then how come you had it?

—Good question. And I poured cream in, no less, and sat there watching it go round and round.

—Weird, Dr Frear.

One could argue, I suppose, that the symbolism of the car wash – the entering of the tunnel with its teeth and whips and lashes – is crudely sexual: the archetypal male terror, and so on. Not to be denied (by me, anyway) but I simply have no such fear in the everyday world of women or their parts or the graphic or technological symbols of their parts. It makes no sense to me. I love *that* tunnel, the suction, the scrub-a-dub-dub, the sudsy baptism, the little sucking sounds of female reception, the in-and-out teasing before penetration proper, the rush of blood that turns me all warm and cosy – I could stay in there forever. As a matter of act I am convinced that that, *that* – the touching, nuzzling, poking and prodding of parts – is one of the best medicines, aside from a merry heart, known to man.

But who, you are wondering, is the recipient of all this joy of curative sex: nurse, secretary, librarian, jogging partner, the young

18

woman at Cocolat with eyes like her rumballs, one of my patients? Listen, in twenty-five years of marriage I have not once succumbed. Innocent flirtations, fine. I find they have the same cardio-respiratory effect, last longer and do not disintegrate into depressing post-affair slumps or slanging matches. Beyond that I have acted professionally: I patted hands, shoulders, allowed myself to be hugged on occasion but mostly kept a safe distance; offered tissues when needed.

I have watched with dismay as my medical and psychiatric colleagues fell in succession. You could see it coming. I remember a skiing lesson up at Tahoe, the classic situation. There we all are at the top of a steep slope. Our instructor, a Norwegian called Gunnar who actually looks like Edvard Grieg, is encouraging a precariously-balanced snowperson to push off. So *sloosh*, off she goes and lands in a heap at the bottom. Number two ditto; also three, four, five . . . Now there's a bloody crater and I'm number six. What do you think happened? An elegantly manoeuvred detour, precisely so. It earned me a round of applause too.

Besides, my wife serves up the safest sex in town.

—What am I supposed to do now? I asked the cardiologist.
—Go home and wait.
—For what?
He didn't need to answer. A heart or heart failure, whichever may be the first. So that is why I am here in bed surrounded by my books and my carrot sticks and my beloved bleeper. Ruth accuses me of staring at it, as she says, like some long lost lover. A watched bleeper never bleeps? As a matter of fact, when she's not there it gets worse: I have been known to address my hopes and fears to it.

Which is all very embarrassing; and why I'm propped up here scrawling away like some Marcel Proust of the psychiatric world. Ruth is on nightshift, my daughter Claire is at the library studying as usual. Except for Willy our dog, I'm quite alone.

This notebook, by the way, is blue and spiral-bound. Normally I use a word-processor for everything from case notes to grocery lists, so this is something of a re-claimed experience. When I was three years old I decided to become an author (that was before the cardiology lark). Putting my ambition into practice, and copying my mother's rolling-stock script, I filled half a dozen school notebooks with fast-travelling but sadly inscrutable loop-de-loops. What's all this? she asked, looking over my shoulder one day. Stories, I said proudly. I still have those notebooks, and I sometimes think that if only I could decipher them I'd be a better man. Or do I mean person?

Dr Michael Brodsky at the Irvine Med Center in his recent JAMA report, has concluded that people can die of heartbreak.

The new Proust biography, which Ruth has bought for me, is quite heavy, though not as heavy as the OED. A fascinating man, Marcel. It seems to me as a reader of books that most novelists fix stories in time. Like shrinks, they like to play God, concocting a set of circumstances that lead to a neat dénouement. They arrange things with the precision of a formal dinner party under a chandelier with a centrepiece when, alas, chandeliers and maybe even dinner parties have gone out of fashion. The cause and the effect of something like a heart attack for example can be more than chapters apart; may indeed never match up. I think Proust would have gone along with that.

The biography is of the current demythologising sort: the great Proust is seen 'flogging the bishop' to such excess that it's a wonder he has any strength left to pick up a pen. He's also portrayed as an asthmatic masochistic homosexual for whom writing becomes an act of sacrifice and sacrilege against his mother: *Albertine slipped into my mouth, in making me the gift of her tongue, as it were a gift of the Holy Ghost, conveyed to me a viaticum, left me with a provision of tranquillity almost as precious as when my mother in the evening at Cambray used to lay her lips upon my forehead.*

A powerful narrative thrust, has this new biography. It gives us insight into the psychological quagmire through which Proust toiled towards his goal. He begins with the eating of a madeleine and goes on from there as if he had all the time in the world. I begin with a carrot stick and a photo-replay of my mother laying her hand on her heart, knowing full well I may never get beyond this single remembrance.

Munch munch.

Six

My mother's hands: broad, the knuckles like Crinkle Crags, the skin tough and patchy, the veins prominent. I tried poking at them – *go away* – but they wouldn't budge. Later when I learned the trick I instructed her: Wave your arms over your head, Mum, and they'll shrink. But she just stared as if she hadn't heard or it took too much effort to raise them. The fingers were not smooth and tapered. The nails were as big as a man's and stained with nicotine. I liked sniffing them.

Other mothers read stories out of books, *Winnie the Pooh, The Wind in the Willows*. Mine made up wandering tales of wandering heroes, who no matter what other adventures befell them always wound up under the sea. This was because my father had done exactly that. It was during the war. I was around three at the time. But since there were no precise details of his death, she was free to make them up. It gave her great scope, there at our window overlooking the sea; perhaps too much, for the beginnings, middles and ends of these stories rarely tallied. Our hero might begin in the desert like Valentino playing Lawrence of Arabia, but end up fishy-eyed. I pointed this out – *Mum, it doesn't make sense* – and, when she wouldn't stop, put my hands over my ears. But I knew in spite of all that that they made a kind of sense underneath.

Fishing for father? First lessons in free association? Perhaps.

She named me Valentine. She would. Now it's no longer a mere embarrassment – like Slim for a fat man or Pee-Wee for a muscle-bound giant – it's a crucifixion. The sort of name only a sadist, a simpleton or a fantasist would give her child. My mother, in other words, who passed on to me the pricetag of her idolatry. The heart-throb Valentino: handsome, charismatic; a Fascist (he was buddy-buddy with Mussolini). After the war he renounced his Italian citizenship, a betrayal for which his fellow Sicilians never forgave him – as who should blame them? But to my mother, in his spuriously exotic headgear bending over Agnes of the well-oiled eyeball, he was catnip. He could do for her what my absent father could not. I'm being harsh. Not only did it rain a lot in the north of

England but it must have been lonely for her saddled with a small child and nothing to do but cook Brussel sprouts for lodgers and stare at the sea.

The other kind of instruction I received at my mother's chest – it was more bony than maternal – was in the language of the heart: a language with no translation. Heartbeat, flutter, throb – these words do not do justice to what went on in there. Nothing can. It was like a garbling animal or one of the more hysterical of the Chinese dialects.

I loved and hated it. For a year or two, while I was still young enough, I'd come home from school and lie in her lap, my head on her chest, and suck on a bottle filled with chocolate-flavoured milk and listen to her heart as if it were some kind of semaphore. The soporific song of life, breath, mother earth? Hardly. I suppose at times its beat was steady but more often it sent out blooping SOS messages, so that I sucked up a fear-taste with my sweet sweet milk.

Sometimes when I got home from school she'd look flushed and then she'd tell me how he'd been with her that day: in uniform or in civvies, always handsome and smiling, if pale. Then one day it dawned. Why doesn't he wait for me? I charged her with this. Because, she replied. Because *why*? Because . . . He doesn't have a lot of time. You mean like an amphibian? She managed to smile. Some days I contrived to stay home – my own heart would join hers in playing-up – and we'd wait for him together. Well, where is he?

Science, my saviour. One could grab hold of a fact, as of a rock ledge or outcrop, and know one was safe. So I shimmied up up up: to the top of the house, to the fell-tops, symbolically to the heights of my learning from which I was able to look down and analyse what was what with her. A manoeuvre which, among other things, allowed me to distinguish that wondrous but unreliable organ from my own.

Seven

And now I shall tell you about the heart. Where shall we begin? From which angle do we attack it? Sorry, I didn't mean to sound like a dog about to ravage a bone. (If it's one thing I won't tolerate it's roughness, particularly in shrinks: men who push their patients around, leave bruises on the mind if not the body.) I mean, of course, how shall we describe it? What *perspective* shall we take: historical, embryological (developmental), anatomical or physiological; electrical, chemical, haematological, and so on. You see the problem.

Perhaps you don't. Perhaps you've never thought about it. Why should you? The heart – one of its claims to fame – goes willy nilly. Mine has stopped claiming.

I did once meet one. It was my first post-mortem, and to be honest it was a bloody mess. You don't know where to begin, or having begun, what it is you've found. Where in the midst of all those quishy giblets is it? Where? I nearly cried out – not the done thing in medical school – as I poked around with my surgical scissors. The lungs presented themselves while the heart played hide'n'seek: find me if you can. Where? There – *there*, stupid. *What's got into you, Frear? Losing your nerve?* Of course not. Of course I knew where it was. Only for some reason it seemed to be eluding me.

Suddenly I was all at sea in my mind: and when I came to I made the decision to switch to psychiatry. It was the second time it had happened; the first was after a hysterectomy. Would you like to hear about that? No? By the way, I didn't really faint dead out, not like some. I merely wobbled. The feeling passed.

I was going to do cardiology because it was 'where it was at' professionally. And also because of my mother. Her heart was always there under her hand like some poor quavering animal, only she believed it was threatening *her* for god's sake, with its palpitating. I never believed her. Clocks went dicky, not hearts.

Cardiac hypochondria, or AIB (abnormal illness behavior) as it's now referred to in the psychiatric literature, is a well documented phenomenon. But the distinctions between the actual and the imagined condition are not necessarily distinct: they are slimy,

23

fobbery, slippery like the innards *in situ*, not labelled and neatly arranged on laboratory shelves. She may have had a bad heart or she may have dreamed she had one: is there a difference?

It's a jolly good thing I didn't become a cardiologist.

Every organism worth its salt needs a heart. Above a certain size and degree of complexity, simple diffusion of goodies in and waste out just won't do. A system of tubes in which all the consumables come dissolved or suspended right to your door is what every little cell and tissue needs. At no extra cost (why run back empty?) all that nasty trash can be discreetly excreted. Now all you have to have is one of our patent longlife/lifelong pumps. Our design team suggests that you have it installed early: even four millimetres is big in ontogenic circles. We take those old-fashioned dorsal aortas, simply join them up, kink the tube back on itself and then just a little fusion and rearrangement of septa, a final half-turn and you have a heart you can bet your life on. Our cardiac muscle cells have built-in contractility so that even before the pump is fully assembled and operational, it is beating steadily away. The Purkinje Fibres (recently patented), excellent electrical conductors, keep things flowing in the right direction, as do our gentle, translucent valves. You can now install our organs regardless of size or sex of recipient in perfect safety.

What is this, Heart-Throb Advertising, or what? You're right, I must stop messing around, this is a serious business. Perhaps I could show you a laser photograph of how it looks inside, rather like a *son et lumière* cathedral.

Or: It's a five-letter word beginning with 'h' and ending with 't'.

How about a diagram? A doodle, mind you, not a masterpiece – I'm no Gray.

—Ruth! Get me some felt-tipped pens!

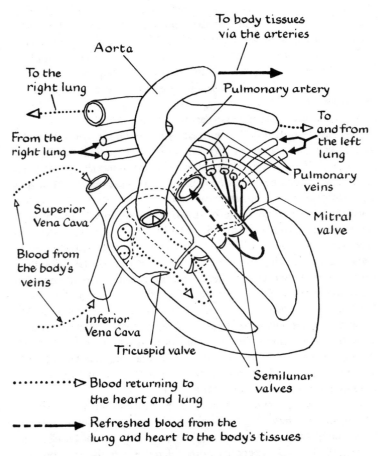

To body tissues
via the arteries

Aorta

To the
right lung

Pulmonary artery

From the
right lung

To
and from
the left
lung

Pulmonary
veins

Superior
Vena Cava

Mitral
valve

Blood from
the body's
veins

Inferior
Vena Cava

Tricuspid valve

Semilunar
valves

••••••••••▷ Blood returning to
the heart and lung

– – – ➤ Refreshed blood from the
lung and heart to the body's tissues

Now you need to know what goes where when.

We'll start on the right side. The blood is returning from its tour
round the body through the venae cavae and pulmonary veins back to
the heart. Here it comes, dark, slow, low pressure, a bit exhausted,
trickling into the heart's entrance hall, as it were, called the atrium
(welcome). The atrium contracts, squeezes it through this valve here
and on into the ventricle. By this time all kinds of pressures are
building up. The heart gyrates, turns pale, goes tense and ker-*thump*,
the blood is on its way to the lungs.

We know all about the heart; it's been discovered, mapped, all
wrapped up. You can relax: the heart does so every other beat. Now

there's something to talk about, something I can tell you about – how the heart comes to relax and unrelax and then relax again. The official theory before Harvey was that the heart filled up like a syringe from the liver, overflowed into the veins, shrank, sucked in a new supply of blood, re-expanded, and so on. The heartbeat, they asserted, occurred when the heart became engorged and powerful. The natural conclusion.

Which teaches you to trust nature.

Anyway, the point is that when it's gathered up into a tight ball – rather like Donna as she sat curled up in my leather chair but ready to spring, with her sweater wrapped round one fist and the other in her mouth – it is during this period of contraction or *systole* (which means 'a putting together') that the beat beats.

Got that? Good. So while all this is going on in the right side, a more agile variation is going on in the left. Blood, much welcomed back from the lungs, gets muscled along to the left ventricle. From there it goes squirting into the aorta, causing a shock wave along the arterial walls which causes the pulse, and sending blood careening round the body.

When does it relax?

Ah. It relaxes when the atrium and ventricle are filled with blood returning to the heart through the great veins. This is when it's biggest and most relaxed (*diastole* or 'a drawing apart'): when it collapses, becomes dark, full, spreadeagled.

I like the thought of that filling and emptying.

Another thing I like is the idea of the heart's capacity to *give*; in other words, to vary its force of contractility on a beat-to-beat basis. By virtue of this law – it's called Starlings' Law of the Heart – the miracle of the heart keeps pumping. I tell Ruth about it but she glazes over; she doesn't want to know any more medical details for one day (she's a nurse, by the way). She wants to know if I'm tired, if I want some soup, how I am.

How am I? With reference to Starlings' Law of the Heart, I tell her, I feel like a man who's broken the law.

Eight

—A transplant, he repeated.

—Come again?

—A heart change: cut on dotted line, snip out old pump, re-connect plumbing, a little solder – and Bob's your uncle.

—Bob is *not* my uncle.

This will give you a further feel for the 'little chat' I had with the cardiologist – coincidentally also British: one of the pink variety with an accent to match, and a smile like a whole package of Philadelphia cream cheese which he flashed at me at significant intervals. He never once looked me in the eye, preferring instead his own socks; which was just as well since mine were odd – which shocked me as much as it did him. It might indeed have counted against me, for getting a heart was not unlike an adoption procedure in a time of scarce babies. One's worth is easily disproven.

We called each other 'doctor', only his 'doctor' and my 'doctor' were subtly different: mine being buttered liberally with respect while his was on a low-cholesterol diet. The psychoanalyst, you understand, is not a *real* physician.

He did so enjoy doodling on his prescription pad! It looked like the Los Angeles freeway system attached to a balloon. But at least we could dispense with the technical language (aneurysm of the left ventricle, etc.) and those unfortunate expressions like *flaccid sac*. He could be perfectly straight with me: your heart is nearly inert. He flashed the cream cheese. That was when he told me to go home and wait for the new heart. What he meant was an old heart: a recycled, a second-hand heart; a heart that was young and healthy but whose host was no longer needing it.

—When? I asked.

He sucked in breath.

—Ooh, could be anywhere from three days – paused nicely – to three months before a suitable heart falls into our hands, *surfaces* as it were.

I pictured hearts floating like oil blobs on water, or falling from the heavens like manna and landing *plop* into his clean pink hands.

27

And then, the whole time I was watching this performance I kept thinking: to be a cardiologist you have to be *good*.

True, Freud had trouble with father-figures too.

But let's get back to the issue at hand: a person cannot live without a heart. Mine is so weak it is essentially non-valid. I couldn't give it away; a Third World Salvation Army heart bank would not take it; nor an ailing monkey. Why should they? Instead of being recycled it will be cut into bits and examined. The pathologists will label the bits, mutter *humph* to themselves and carry on pickling the leftovers. They will go home that night and over their gin-and-tonics say conversationally, *Boy did I cut up a beaut today. It was riddled, muscle-shot. You should have seen that aneurysm. How that guy went on living is a miracle.* I can hear the ice tinkle.

Go home and wait: fine. And in the meantime? Regrettable.

That's how it is, I'm afraid. Of course. These things take time, there are a lot of people waiting for hearts. Of course. Patience, rest, relaxation. Bless you, O Cream Cheese.

So that is the prescription: nothingness. No sex, no cheesecake, no pipe, no wine, no exquisite love, no passionate hate, *nada*. Don't consume too many calories, don't burn energy or release too much heat. In general, keep cool. No *whoomph*. Take a little thin gruel in the morning like Emma Woodhouse's father. Life on hold till the bleep goes. I seem to be reading Conrad interspersed with Austen for light relief. Proust, Freud, Stedman, Gray, Updike . . . I shuffle them around the covers like faceless interchangeable cards. I can't concentrate. Ruth says it's not surprising. I expect too much of myself. She's brought me a bunch of shiny mindless magazines: *Cosmopolitan, People, Psychology Today*, for god's sake. You must be joking, I tell her.

She's right, of course, I need some levity.

Where was it Donna said she was going? I flip open the *Cosmo* and there's a travel feature on Baja. That's it. I picture her lying on the beach wearing a few strings, panting after a swim. Some hulk rubs oil into her back. What hulk? So far as I know she's gone alone. None of my business anyway. The more I try to banish the image the more it gets rubbed in. *Rub rub rub* . . . shoulders, belly. Oh groan. Why does she take up with such creeps? She once told me about a guy who sold her blood up and down the state for money.

How can I sit in bed at a time like this? I can't relax. I can't do anything. What do I say? Hang in there? Each time I turn a page I prepare for the terminal pop. Not beating the bleeper begins to seem like a more profound tragedy than whether or not whatshisname and his party reach Kurtz in time. And anyway, everybody knows how *Heart of Darkness* ends, so why bother.

That damned bleeper. It used to be about other people's emergencies. *Dr Frear, Mrs X has cut her wrists again . . . Miss P the anorexic is on a drip and she's screaming for you . . . Mr B has OD'd on the hard stuff this time – it looks bad . . . D again, she's curled up outside the back door like a baby, she's been there all day waiting for you . . .*

I get up and go into my study. I fiddle, observe my fluorescent desk light. It's old. It has started the hum and flutter. If the heart flutters it's called fibrillation, a fancy word for a simple condition. Instead of contracting and relaxing in a repetitive, periodic way, the heart's muscle tissue writhes helplessly. It cannot pump blood; the steady waves are broken up. In its confusion it can neither contract nor release as the half-alive muscle around the dead bits starts to dance and trip it up. Some parts seem to be working, yet the whole system goes fatally awry in an uncontrolled, ineffectual frenzy. The classic image for the fibrillating heart is a bag of worms. It is known as the Feigenbaum phenomenon: when the electrical activity of the heart suddenly turns anarchistic. If shock treatment is not provided within a few minutes, death occurs.

By now I am busy addressing my prayers to the bleeper. Please go off soon. Save me. With a new heart I could live for another hundred years, run the Bay-to-Breakers marathon: Super-Transplantman.

No, don't go off; not yet; not tonight. I'm tired, I would never make it to the hospital. What if I perish on the operating table? *He's gone . . .* The surgeons snap off their rubber gloves. *Shit, seven hours of labour down the drain.*

It's too much effort to hold a book. I'm not interested in the food that's interested in me. A ride in the car with Ruth up to Inspiration Point, but my attention remains fixed not on the Bay but on my bloody inspirational bleeper. I think of writing a letter to Donna, but where? Anyway, it's not on professionally, and anyway now she has her own life and doesn't need me to spray her messes in front of. I could talk to Ruth but what would I say? I'm afraid, I'm afraid, I'm afraid? It doesn't bear repeating. I could listen to Ruth's soothing words – don't worry, don't worry, they'll get one soon, everything will be fine . . . But I can't believe her, it's not in her gift. I can hold on to her for dear life but where does that get me, since it can only be

29

gingerly, fraternally — you understand what I mean. Ruth, when she's here, can't sleep at night because of my wakefulness and breathlessness but I won't let her leave me, it's too risky. What if the bleeper goes off in the night and she doesn't hear? What if I don't have voice to call her? What if I pop off in my sleep? What if the lightbulb gives out while I'm sitting here watching – will old *lup dub* follow suit? *In extremis*, the medical model fails and magic takes its place.

The facts: I am on the acute list. They are doing everything in their power down at Stanford to locate a compatible heart short of bumping off one of their own staff. I'm not blaming them. But that doesn't stop me feeling irritable, impatient, vexed, yes, all right, *impotent*. What are they doing, marking time until they get the heart of a genius? Computer-matching me? *Are you blond? Statuesque? Do you like to ski? Are you under twenty-five? Have you ever read Sigmund Freud?*

Bloody hell.

What do I *do* meanwhile? Answer: I sit here at my desk playing Russian roulette with a lightbulb. I'm tired of watching it; I'm cold, I think I'll go back to bed.

P.S. The lightbulb died peacefully in the night.

Nine

—Val, what are you doing – it's the middle of the night?

—I'm just listening to your heart – do you mind?

She looks doubtful.

—What, can't you sleep?

No, she doesn't understand. Perhaps I'll try the dog. Here, Willy, good boy, up on the bed. You see? He construes it as affection. The cat? No way: she guards her heart with her claws.

What leather-covered heart will Donna be listening to?

The healthy young heart. A myth, of course. Even a heart as young as Donna's will show electrical arrhythmias with breathing (exacerbated by smoking, drugs, junkfood – a generally unhealthy lifestyle). As for the mature (relatively healthy) organ, drenched in hormones, subject to nervous influences, it registers a ventricular ectopic rate as labile and mad-brained as the tide.

When I was a boy I used to watch the comings and going of the tide. Twice every day, the times varied, there was high tide. At new moon it was at its highest, usually about nine metres; it happened around the fifth or sixth of every month. The regularity was comforting. I was also tuned into currents. Strong south-westerly and westerly gales had the effect of increasing the velocity of the current; easterly winds had the opposite effect.

Last week I was in the middle of shaving the underside of my jaw (I still use an old-fashioned razor) when I thought the bleeper went off. I nearly cut my throat.

I have just seen a newspaper article about a chicken which was decapitated by a Connecticut farmer and thrown into an unlit incinerator. Next day when the farmer opened the door, out jumped the headless bird which 'lived' for a further three-and-a-half days before finally expiring. No, it could not have 'lived' without a heart. What does this prove? Absolutely nothing.

My mother used to put me to bed with a clock in my cot. Not that it worked: I'd already learned to read the hieroglyphs of her heart, got fixated on the musical irregularities of her ticker, the syncopations. My favourite timepiece is that American railway clock that hangs in

31

our kitchen downstairs. Oak. I bought it at a fleamarket for three dollars when I first came to this country. It goes rarely and limpingly; and then of a sudden the hands will fly around backwards to the accompaniment of a kind of jazzy *choo-chuk-a-choo* beat.

I have recently unplugged it.

Now my hands fly – to my heart. I need a steady beat. Where is it? Not on the left: another of those common misconceptions. Most of it lies in the middle, a good third on the right, and maybe a small piece pokes up to the left. Or you can curl a couple of fingers under the heart-spoon, that sweet depression just under the sternum. How does it say? *Lup dub* is what the professors said it said; what we therefore heard as students listening through our stethoscopes. But what does it really say? Mine is confused; I can't distinguish the *lup* from the *dub*.

Antlike? Wormlike? Wavelike? Does the pulse fade? Easiest to feel in the groin area, just at the crux of leg and crotch.

Wormlike is his Bish here curled up asleep. Scratch that. I did not mean to lead you under the covers; indeed, nothing could be further from my thoughts. I was talking about feeling for the *pulse*.

Mine is shrink-like.

You may not realise it – what with so much hype about male mis-uses of power and so forth – but we psychoanalysts are also vulnerable to the advances of sexually aroused female patients. The famous Anna O for instance, who called the cathartic method of treatment a kind of chimney sweeping of the mind – meaning of course she wanted *her* chimney swept. Poor Sigmund, backed into a corner like that. All right, it sounds risible, but what is one to do, given that one has a need to be liked and an innocent desire to reciprocate?

As for Donna, do you call all *that* innocent: clothes big enough for a Barbie doll, the way she wound her corkscrew curls round and round her finger, the way she'd stick out her bellybutton like a three-year-old, the finger- and thumb-sucking routines, even *banana* sucking for god's sake? And all under the guise of infantile regression?

Don't misunderstand me. One would hardly be tempted by such naked neediness. On the other hand, it wasn't easy. On the other other hand, it was my job to encourage her to revert to such ambiguously helpless states as a fundamental part of the transference process.

She had had no father.

Nor did I for that matter – but there is a difference. Without a

32

father I was forced to become my own father, to set careful watch over my behaviour. Whereas Donna developed no controls whatever. This is what I wanted for her: to face her life as I have faced mine. Because it pained me to see her running after a chimaera, gunning her Honda, looking and looking for something, someone, she'd never find. The absent father? Don't tell me, I know all about it. I dealt with it in the prescribed way: interpreted the dreams, analysed them, wrapped them up and put them away – thus facing the loss – and got on with my life. This is the present I wanted to hand her.

—Keep your presents.

She gave me the finger.

How could such a bundle of symptoms dream of going back to school? Immature and masochistic behaviours, affective psychosis (mania), schizoid tendencies . . . Not to mention learning disabilities (dyslexia, poor concentration). I mean –

We were just beginning to break ground when she zoomed off into the sunset.

How could she think of leaving me at such a time?

Answer: she didn't *think*. Thinking was not her strong point. She just *did it*.

Does it mean anything at all to her that I am effectively immobilised here?

No. Somehow I don't think she appreciates the seriousness of my condition. Milan Kundera would. I read in the Sunday papers that he likes Renaissance music because there the heavy foot of the beat is softened. Does he also, I wonder, suffer from a heart?

Mine has become dead-beat, hard-boiled, sclerosed; and I rotten-hearted and riddle-hearted. In fact, it will kill me if I don't get rid of it soon.

It may kill me to get rid of it.

How does one throw away a heart? I was born in the north of England where one threw nothing away. My mother saved old love letters, old Hollywood magazines, sweaters out at the elbows, a one-eyed teddy, buttons. I had a rubberband ball which I wheeled out for company. If the waste of a piece of aluminium foil was a crime, what of a heart?

You think that sounds flaky? Well, so be it. Inevitably one sees the old pump as beautiful, if broken; compares it to an ageing woman; the greater accumulation of wrinkles to her credit.

As for the donor heart – the hard, shiny plastic ingenue, perfectly

33

V-shaped and of an unnatural red – throw in campy false eyelashes to give it the right tacky finishing touch as on certain Valentine cards: that one I resent even though I know – I am told – it will save my life.

Naturally my sympathies are with the evictee and against the incomer. Why must so many things experienced and imperfect be replaced by the flawless and foolish? In spite of the fact that it is trying to kill me I am rooting for it.

What would Donna say to this?

This has to be the lost cause of the century.

Heartless girl.

She's right of course, this nostalgia is untenable when applied to a factual organ. Everything can be replaced; everything *is* in due course replaced. Who should know this better than I? And yet we fight against substitutions as we do against death. We say, don't throw me away, don't leave me – these mini-deaths. And to death itself: don't, you mustn't. By the way, did you know that psychiatrists rate highest amongst medics on non-authoritarianism; and that there is an inverse correlation between authoritarianism and fear of death?

Take the time to figure it out – it's worth it.

But mostly we hold on: and that in itself is exhausting. Better to join an exercise programme.

So I am lying here waiting for a new heart, reading this book of poems Donna gave me. It was kind of her to think of me. Here's one about discarded penises lying around after a spate of sex-change operations. The penises, on a tray, are holding forth. They say things like, *I am a weapon thrown down. Let there be no more killing . . . I am a caul removed from his eyes. Now he can see . . . I was a dirty little dog, I knew he'd have me put to sleep . . .* One of them weeps, crying, *Father, father!*

Thus inspired, I think, what about hearts? After all, if a base penis can talk, a lofty heart should sing. I picture a bunch of them on a tray, my own reject amongst them. I know of course that they will not be set out like hors-d'oeuvres any more than penises, but what matter: the world of dreary fact is already beginning to fade.

So I listen and the hearts' laments assail me: Italian arias, country western twangings, French chansons, German singspiel, wailings of the blues: *Papa papa I'm bleedin'/How could you turn me away? I was a fool not to care . . . Oh me, oh my, wonder what will become of poor me . . . When I see you I just go coo coo coo . . .*

But pity soon palls of course; and guilt fails to sustain. Hardened by rationality, one eventually comes to terms with one's situation: in fact I have no choice. The way forward is now clear and I begin to entertain the thought not of an enemy but a friend: my bright young thing, my user-friendly replacement part, my entertainment for life. And it takes! it catches! Indeed, soon I am eager, fervent even, for the installation of the new *lup dub* in my bosom.

Can anyone out there understand?

All life oscillates, vibrates. The heart, which has a right and a left side, contracts and releases. Systole and diastole: nice rhythmical words. How to choose between them? You don't. You ride and rock with the waves. You give up your old heart to make way for the new and experience a sense of relief as exciting as it is shocking. It's being alive instead of dead. Your heart as it pumps knows that. Can you feel how it draws together, draws apart? Mine isn't sure.

Cold, shivery. (*What will become of poor me?*)

I crawl into bed behind Ruth who turns her back and whispers, 'Spoon me.' This puts me in mind of the 'piggy-back' transplant: the donor heart is placed alongside the recipient's own and joined to it in such a way that blood can pass through either or both. The two hearts then pump blood at their own rate without adversely affecting each other's performance. The cardiologist would not commit himself as to whether or not he will do me a 'piggy-back' (heterotopic) or orthotopic transplant. In due course all will be revealed. Meanwhile I am curled up, my arms threaded round my wife's waist, my sick heart lullabyed by her thrum.

Ten

I am almost never bothered by pains over the heart or in my chest.
I have a good appetite.
I am being followed.
I like to read newspaper articles on crime.
I have diarrhoea once a month or more.

I get a raw deal from life.
I think of things too bad to talk about.
No one seems to understand me.
I am seldom troubled by constipation.

Evil spirits possess me at times.
I sometimes welcome the thought of death.
Someone has it in for me.
Often I feel as if there were a tight band about my head.
I cry easily.

I have often wished I were a girl.
I do not always tell the truth.
Sometimes I hear very queer things.
My soul sometimes leaves my body.
I have had no difficulty in starting or holding my bowel
    movement.

I am strongly attracted to members of my own sex.
My hands have not become clumsy or awkward.
I would like to be a florist.
I am afraid of using a knife.
I love my father.

Everything tastes the same.
It does not bother me particularly to see animals suffer.
I love my mother.
I like to talk about sex.

Strong odours come to me at times.
I liked *Alice in Wonderland* by Lewis Carroll.
I often think, 'I wish I were a child again.'
I have no difficulty starting or holding my urine.
I have liked fishing very much.

I feel hungry almost all the time.
Sexual things disgust me.
I like repairing a door latch.
I am fascinated by fire.

I am not afraid of mice.
I used to like hopscotch.
I love my wife.
I am a special agent of God.

Oh . . . oh oh oh oh *oh*. Stop, please. Enough. I can't take any more.
Don't they realise an excess of hilarity could be dangerous to someone
in my condition?

How – I ask this in all seriousness – how can the psychologists here
(quite sophisticated persons, I presume) expect somebody like me to
waste his time on such idiocy, such brilliant, transparent nonsense?

This gift of unintentional poetic-psychological mirth, this ques-
tion-and-answer test, this collection of 556 bizarre and potentially
self-incriminating, riotous but deadpan statements of dubious
intent, redolent of interpretation to which I am instructed by a girl of
about twelve to respond True, False, or, by virtue of a blank, Don't
know. My responses to these simple utterances could mark me for life
as a liar, a paranoid schizophrenic, a homicidal maniac, a fearful
psychopath, a manic depressive; in short, a man unworthy of a heart –
this heaven-sent diversion comes to me from the Psychological
Corporation, New York. Thank you O Corporation of the Psyche!

I flourish my pencil and begin. I make black dots on a separate
answer sheet: T for True, F for False, nothing for Don't Know.
(Frankly, I have not enjoyed myself so much in years.)

Let us start with the easy ones:

37

I cry easily.	F
I do not like repairing door latches.	T
I never liked hopscotch.	T
I would like to be a florist.	
I am not afraid of mice.	T

And now for something a little trickier: I am an agent of God. Of course I am! What psychoanalyst isn't? Every time I shine my torch of wisdom and clarity onto someone's problems my beard grows a little thicker and more grizzled and the muscles knot up around my neck.

A number of factors may account for it. First, the analyst's position of psychological power and social prestige may attract narcissistically oriented people to our profession. The condition of being 'in the know' while the patient struggles to make sense of his or her life may be implicitly appealing to those who seek reassurance of their superiority. Second (and related), the helping role may appeal to those who have been exploited narcissistically by their families of origin (see Miller, 1981). Third, the practice of analysis reinforces whatever grandiose fantasies we may have, in that we constantly experience ourselves as at the centre of each patient's subjective world. Fourth, it may be that the work of analytic therapy is so difficult and its strains on our normal self-esteem and exhibitionism so great, that analysts need narcissistic restabilisation more than other people do, and therefore take advantage of the transference relationship to be bigshots.

Enough. I'm beginning to feel a tight band about my head. True or False? Back to some straightforward ones. Alice in Wonderland? Frankly, I preferred *30,000 Leagues Under the Sea*, by my Mum. No, I have never wished I were a girl, although female solidarity seems a powerful experience to which I as a male am barred. I also think, quite reasonably, that if I were female I would not be in this particular pickle, given that heart disease is much less prevalent in women. As for my soul leaving my body, I suspect it never took up residence there in the first place. I am not a religious man.

The point of all this dot-crunching is to establish whether or not I'm a good psychological, or more importantly, economic bet. No point in installing a costly heart into some clown who turns around and throws himself off the Golden Gate the following week.

Do I hear queer things? Titter titter. I am beginning to founder, chew my God-like beard; I am leaving too many blanks. Why is there not a 'Sometimes' category?

Do peculiar odours come to me? Yes, but that's because the practice is near a Japanese restaurant. Most peculiar. Does Johnson's Baby Powder count as 'peculiar'?

Am I being followed? Perhaps Donna would like to answer that one.

Do I love my father? I never had a father!

Fascinated by fire? I have always been interested in fire. I seem to remember Donna commenting on the number of candles around my office, to which I responded with some off-hand reference to phallic symbolism in order, perhaps, to divert her from the scent.

No, I do not have a back covered in scar tissue, nor did a loved one go up in some awful conflagration. However, I did once mistake a burst of sunlight on a faraway ship's window for a blaze. I let my imagination carry me away to the extent that I heard and saw the fire engines. I even announced their arrival. Look, look! I cried jumping up and down. It was only when the sun went down that my foolishness was revealed in all its flame-free glory.

Why do I tell this story? Because I am interested in warmth but chary of the fantastical. Prove it, I would say after that. Prove it. I don't believe you. Like Freud before me, I felt it necessary to curb the sparks of my imagination; to install, if you like, a kind of sprinkler system of the heart, controlled from the higher faculties. Thus at the age of ten a reluctant, even suspicious, imaginer was born – although the inclination, the temptation to see a world so ignited and beautiful that it would make my eyes burn and something inside my head dance was still there.

With the weakening of my pulse, everything catches again. The old capacity for creating fire out of nothing is restored. Everywhere I look there are potential blazes. And although I know it is only the effect of sun striking glass, the hee-haw of the fire engines is louder than ever. Help me, Sigmund.

Fascinated by fire? Obviously I cannot put a T or I will be taken for a dangerous pyromaniac. Do I hear queer things? Well yes, quite often as a matter of fact – but if I say so they'll send me to a psychiatrist (anything but that). If I agree to the tight band about the head they'll whip me in for a brain scan. And if I admit to not always telling the truth that will mark me as either a nit-picker or a mental defective. Or are these items actually measures of untruthfulness? Is the assumption that none of us has really loved our parent(s), so if we put a T, then we are lying? On the other hand, if we put an F, are we taken to be social deviants?

What psychoanalyst does not like to talk about sex?

This is mad. Psychologists are bananas! I better simplify like crazy, hedge my bets, punt. Play my False do wisely.

I hear queer things.	F
I like to talk about sex.	T
I am being followed.	F
No one seems to understand me.	

There. With any luck I will have created a balanced, reasonable self, made up of certainties, likes, dislikes, and a sprinkling of uncertainties and fears, but not too many. One does not willingly gamble away one's heart.

Do I love my wife? Dear Psychologist-in-Charge-of-Scoring: I'm sorry, I just broke the point of my pencil so I cannot answer this question.

I feel hungry almost all the time. This was true when I was a child. It was still rationing time, so we had to make do. We made do, and I came out of it believing, along with the rest of the British population, that (a) I probably had it coming (the internalisation of guilt); (b) hardship — if it doesn't kill you first — is a great character builder. The word, by the way, for this apparent contradiction — some sort of positive reaction to one's own misfortune — is contrition; or in psychoanalytic terms, reparation. Quite a useful defence mechanism. What was I guilty about? Take your choice: my father's death/the war/my mother's heart/rationing/our having to take in lodgers/secret sexual explorations/some of the above/all of the above.

I feel hungry almost all the time.	F
I love my wife.	

My pencil is poised half an inch above the T dot. All I need to do is lower it, make the blob and be done with it. But how can I be sure? Now it hovers over the F hole. The words had always stuck with me whereas Ruth could burble them out like seltzer bubbles. *I love you I love you I love you.* She still can. I'm thinking about that visit just after the heart attack. Did Donna happen to notice, I wonder, the seltzer bottle Ruth was carrying when they passed each other in the hospital corridor? No, it was probably bagged. Naturally Ruth noticed Donna. Who was that? she wanted to know. A client, I said; an exclient. Did she upset you? Of course not. No I'm fine. It was kind of her to come. On the way out Ruth told Reception not to let anyone in except family or close friends. My protectress.

It *was* nice of Donna to come, to bring me that illicit blossom, though I wanted to say: I'm not dead yet! Of course to her I am: the relationship is terminated, the analyst terminal. May he rest in perfumed peace. She wished me luck and moved on, if buzzing off south on a motorcycle constitutes moving on. Congratulations, wherever you are, for claiming your freedom – even if it was rather previous. Of course you know you can always come back if things don't pan out for you. As for this, don't give it another thought. Your fault? Good heavens, child, you do have delusions!

I often think of taking a motorcycle trip.   F

It was so nice to see her – Ruth I mean. And the seltzer. I was moved by the simple, thoughtful gesture; the realness of her. Donna, in contrast, was wearing her pretend eyeglasses: red plastic frames. Look Ma, no glass. Poor thing, they made her feel grown up. Then she blew it with those why-why-whys of hers. Not to mention the suggestion that, after all, the attack was necessary, even a *damned good thing* and *about time*; that I needed something to shake me up, to make my heart go *whoomph*. She even used – misused – the word 'catharsis'.

I took Ruth's hand; so real, so warm. Unlike Donna, she will always be there. Other women may pass in and out of my life, my office, my heart, my bed even, but they will never replace Ruth. I picture her now as she came into that ICU room, smiling bravely and holding up the bottle of salt-free seltzer like the Statue of Liberty and I thought: now there is giving. Whereas Donna looked at me with that worshipful gaze through her glassfree glasses – but her earrings, I noted, turned before she did.

There is the other side of course: that phrase *I love you*. Ruth could proclaim it in the drug store, over a bowl of grape nuts. Maybe by sheer repetition it lost potency, though I still kept coming back for more. Feed me, love me . . . Mum, I'm hungry . . . I love my wife. Tricky, resonant phrases.

Don't tell me, I know all about it. After years of analysis, what do

41

you expect? That emptiness, that insufficiency. Which Ruth in her turn fed and stoked by stroking, holding and reassuring me as if I were a child. Of course I love you, of course I won't leave you, why can't you accept you're lovable? Each time was like another injection straight into the heart, which would fill with love, for myself and for her for loving me. And then it would unfill and need another refill. Absorb once or twice a week for twenty-five years. It's a lot of repeat prescriptions.

They've brought me a new pencil. Go on, I tell myself, move it half an inch to the left. One blob, it's easier than saying it. There, you see? You love your wife. Congratulations!

The psychologist has admitted the test is only a formality. Good, I tell him, because it's psychological drivel. He laughs nervously, turns defensive, explains it's useful in the more extreme cases. Then why bother with me? He shrugs – a kind of 'let's not quibble' attitude. We understand one another, don't we? Do we? We discuss philosophical uncertainty and hospital rules. What, I ask him, would you have put for 'I love my wife'? Fortunately, he replies, I don't have to take the damned thing myself.

We part amicably. He assures me that he will add his recommendation to my file. The report will go straight through. I am, he says, the ideal transplant candidate: but for the heart, perfectly sound in mind and body. Perfection at last!

Eleven

—See that? – that's your heart.

The technician is pointing to the echocardiography screen, a graph of the changing frequencies of red blood cells converted to electrical energy. Mine makes a sound like an old-time washing machine: occasionally it goes *pp-shoiing* like a bullet hitting a rockface in an old Western. Old images, sound effects: everything old. Old me. Older at forty-five than Coniston Old Man (a mountain I climbed as a boy in the Lake District).

—It isn't squeezing: no action. See, she says pointing, this here's the left ventricle: sluggish. .

The word alone makes me feel like retching. Try it: *sluggish*.

—And see that thing going flap-flap kind of loose-like? That's the mitral valve.

I'll tell you an amusing medical-students' game. Take one heart post-mortem. Fill your palm with water and pour it into the atrium and watch it trickle through the valve into the ventrical. Here you have to imagine gazing down into the heart as if it were a sort of chalice and you're pouring in a libation; and as you gaze in awe and wonder, the flaps of the valve come together in the shape of a mitre: open, close, open, close. Though the heart be dead, the valves go on doing their thing. A small but neat miracle, no?

The technician is now getting quite excited over what she calls 'curvilinear multifrequency bands'. Mitral valve prolapse vibrations.

See that? She says pointing to a wake of parallel rows of signals. That's the von Karman vortex trail.

—How interesting, I say.

The so-called Doppler principle on which all this echocardiography stuff is based goes back to a fellow called Christian Doppler, one of Freud's contemporaries at the University of Vienna.

—An interesting case, I tell the technician, who happens to be a striking young Japanese woman.

—Is that so?

—Interesting but tragic, I say.

—Somewhere along the line his creative juices ran dry. He spent

43

his time working out riddles and was unable to publish anything of scientific significance.

She looks sad for him.

—Oh gee, that's really too bad, I mean why was that do you think, Dr Frear?

—Well, I say, I'm no expert on the subject, of course but Freud traced it to his unhappy marriage and a psychic conflict around a young girl he was strongly attracted to.

—So why, she asks, didn't he leave his wife and marry the girl?

Why? (Why . . . why . . .) The echo of our questions – are they not the most interesting thing about them?

She repeats the question.

—Well there were moral reasons ·. . . rectitude. She looks blank but soon brightens up.

—I guess things were a lot more complicated back then.

So this is how it is. The technician hears musical precordial murmurs; my mother heard scrabbling animals; my wife's tick is as steady as a metronome's; Donna hears the *broom broom* of a Honda. Mine? I try to encourage it by recalling that clock that lay beside me in my cot, but hear nothing. A hole, a gap, a tunnel, a cave, a crater, a thoracic amnesia, a bit of limbo under the breastbone. Listen to that silence. *No man can hear his own tune.*

I need a heart. Each night when my head hits the pillow I dream of getting one. *Give me thy hand, and with thy hand thy heart.* That is what I intone each night to my beautiful new bride, my saviour, as I lead her, or the remains of her, by the hand away from the accident. And now . . . obediently she reaches inside her gaping chest and offers it me. It's still warm, beating. I am moved; I take the sticky gift. I am eager of course but so is she. Like a woman who always carries her diaphragm around with her, you know she's willing.

Yuk, I hear Donna saying, that's sick.

Forgive me, I can't help it. I'm like Bela Lugosi, you see: repulsive, ghoulish, waiting in his laboratory for his next victim, prodigious eyebrows twitching at even the faintest heart-rending clunk of metal on metal. If I open the bedroom window in the direction of the freeway I can hear the sound of traffic in the distance. I listen for crashes, explosions; I wring my hands, get excited, drool at the reports of fatalities from far and near. I do not exaggerate. I mean the victims of these accidents no harm of course, but they are my life. I have need of a heart, any he᷄ ᷄t.

You raise a Lugosi-like eyebrow at the bent of my fantasies. Why, do you expect more seemly behaviour from a middle-aged psychoanalyst? Do you think *we* don't get carried away? Do I disappoint you? I hate to tell you this, but we are the worst patients in the world.

So I conjure them, my child-brides – teenagers on motorbikes, college kids in sports cars, young marrieds in battered old pickups – their lungs punctured, their kidneys ruptured, their brains dead. But their hearts, ah, their hearts . . . A cop shines his flashlight down down down into that dark hole into a sudden undamaged radiance.

I taketh possession of hearts; I swalloweth.

Like Marlow's savage fireman, my teeth are filed to fine points. I send creatures out to do my bidding. Catch 'em, I snap. Bring 'em to me. To you, huh? laughs Donna. And what would you do with 'em? I see myself devouring that which I had created, giving instructions that my victims be cut open quickly but nicely so that I may have the thing still alive and dancing. Eat 'em! I cry, sniffing my prize.

Twelve

I'm considering writing a paper on the Everyday Pathology of Bluejays. Except for their brutish squawks (who says Nature is perfect?), there's a pre-op-ish quiet about the morning. It puts me in mind of Freud's Vienna before the Anschluss.

I should imagine that an operating theatre during a transplant is one of the least silent places in the world. I do imagine: the clumsy clatter of surgical instruments, the cursings under the breath; the chug-a-lugging, gurgling near-hysteria of it all. And you may think the jangle of nerves is silent, but I bet you it's not: nor *it*: the *lup-a-dubbing* donor organ. (Perhaps I'll write a story called *The Telltale Transplant*.) But then I'll hardly be in a position to make bets, will I: not a peep, nor the flicker of a bluejay. The little death of the anaesthetic.

Ruth, on her way out, tells me Anna-Claire is coming over later in the morning.

Have I told you about my daughter Claire? Her name will tell you something to begin with. Anna-Claire, but known as Claire. You can imagine the fuss over 'Anna' (Freud's daughter's name.)

—Who the hell do you think you are, Sigmund Jerkoff Freud? And me – what do you think you've created, Dr Frankenstein, some devoted little Anna: daughter, patient, nurse? Well no way.

She knew she had me. So we made a deal to banish Anna; and although in moments of forgetful tenderness 'Anna' escapes my lips, we more or less honour it. Ruth, exempt from the prohibition, quite often calls her Anna-Claire and gets away with it. But then women do in Claire's system.

Anyway, it's not a bad name, Claire; and unlike her unfortunate friend Venus – a distinctly un-pretty girl – with Claire at least there is no obvious discrepancy. It may even suit her. By which I do not mean that she is acne-free (which she is) but that she is as clear-headed as a High Sierran stream run off a recent snowfall. Have you ever swum in such? I remember once – it was just over a pass, a hot July sky and fields of snow nicely juxtaposed – I took off my boots, everything: *Geronimo*! It was one of those numbing life experiences.

46

My daughter Claire, that is to say, takes second place in *sangfroid* only to Sigmund Freud, whose greatest cultural achievement according to Reich was a capacity for curbing the instincts (thus his great fascination with Michelangelo's Moses). Actually this is a false comparison; indeed, poor Freud had no *sangfroid* at all. I always picture him as he is in that cruel Steadman cartoon: bursting from the page, smoke coming out of his nose and ears (and no doubt elsewhere), the ubiquitous, phallically pugnacious cigar stuck in his gob; whereas Claire according to Steadman would be balancing on the half-shell like some feminist Botticelli Venus in a pastel-coloured boiler suit, mouthing the most blood (and everything else) curdling curses from out an angelic pair of lips. Freud's demons hung around haunting him all his life, whereas Claire's have been evicted; and will be kept out, by court order if necessary.

There was the point, post-pubescence, when things got a bit tricky. Not that it *hasn't* been so since, but at least we know what to expect now. Then it was the shock: one day she walked into the house clutching her biology book to her chest, saying, Dad, I don't understand this heart circulation stuff, can you explain it please; and the next she flung it across the kitchen and called me and her teacher 'Pig' or more precisely *'Peeg'*, telling me she didn't want my help – the patriarchal opprosor had had his say for long enough. Ruth got accused of collusion: Why do you put up with this *shee-it*, huh, man? When Ruth tried to answer, she made further derisory remarks in this vein. He exploits you, uses you, man. *Shee-it*, it makes me *see-ick*. It made us sick too. When I queried the word 'man' in such a context she threw the book at me.

Of course the worst insult she ever hurled at me was 'You *Freudian.*'

That weekend Ruth and I went up to the Russian River. Everything was under water: cars, bridges, people, trees, beds, even the rescue equipment. The next time we visited there were no visible signs of flood damage. The sun came out, birds did what birds do: it was lovely. I said it was like the stages of development: Claire's *woosh* would pass. It didn't. Now birds remind me of my heart.

I would rather not, at this stage, get into an analysis of my own daughter: it wouldn't be healthy and in any case, it's against the rules. Of course Freud often failed to obey his own injunctions. Not only did he analyse his own daughter over a period of several years, but he chatted away about himself and his family when he was supposed to be the transferential smoking blank-screen. 'The trouble is –' here he beat his fist on the head of the couch on which H.D. the poetess was lying – 'I am an old man – *you do not think it worth your while to love me.*' He broke his own rules, but what you forget, like everyone else who criticises him, is that it was he who invented them.

Claire. She got the highest marks in her class but quit high school before she graduated. She joined a women's commune. She works as a waitress – wait-person if you please – at Chez Panisse, where she makes good money in tips. When Ruth and I go there, which is infrequently since the food is not to my taste – too rich, too elaborate – she makes sure not to serve us. I think many of her conclusions about heterosexual marital behaviour, for example, come from observing couples under her direction. A very skewed sample, as I tell her, of the human race: bourgeois and bored with one another. I also think it odd that a vegetarian should want to work around all those killed birds and beasts.

She reads widely, magpie-ishly. Since she works nights, she has plenty of time during the day to spend at the library. She has a visitors' card for the U. C. Berkeley library, so she spends most of her time on campus. She audits classes, mostly in English literature and women's studies but occasionally she drifts further out into things like philosophy or even religious studies. I think if she'd been registered, she'd probably have several degrees by now. Fuck degrees, she says. Yes, as a matter of act I do find her language offensive. I also find it ironic that in adopting many so-called 'masculine' behaviours, which includes 'bad' language, she is taking on the role of the perceived oppressor. I also worry that she can take neither her principles nor her ideologies to the cash counter at Wells Fargo. Frankly I do not understand why she is subverting herself like this. To which she'd say, Frankly, Valentine, I don't give a fuck about what you don't understand. You see how she proves my point?

Her current obsession is with the sisters, wives, mistresses, grandmothers, aunts, great-aunts, nannies, governesses, cooks and godmothers of the great writers. Scratch that: the word 'great' is a male construct; quality is itself an irrelevance when you stop to consider that the one was striding about the landscape waxing poetical while the other was ironing his socks.

She's here.

—Hi, Dad, how are you?

—As you see.

—Did you sleep last night?

—Like a log.

—You sure about that?

—Claire, you should be studying law.

No reply.

I remember once sitting on the sands at Hest Bank – the tide was out, I was very small – with my legs in a V, digging between them – for China I suppose. I dug and I dug, methodically, tirelessly, creating a sort of mini-Stonehenge around me. My mother left me there – I was happy in my work. It got dark. I didn't find China but perhaps it didn't matter. When another boy kicked all my neat piles into messes, I am reported to have thrown up my hands in despair and cried, How can a man live like this?!

The tide, in due course, smoothed all over.

What I'm trying to say is that there are similarities between us, Claire and I. I often tell her she would make a fine lawyer. But she will insist on using those minesweeper talents of hers to examine texts. You root out the emotions, she says, I go for the hidden meanings, the sub-texts, the contextual and historical significances. Claire: she doesn't read *books*, she examines *texts*. My daughter the literature surgeon. It's all a bit discouraging, to tell you the truth. She was a rather gay child. I mean it in its old meaning: carefree, light-hearted, and so on. But now – sometimes I think she has the heart of a mercenary, the brain of a nuclear physicist and the hands of a surgeon. You go in with the knife and come out with . . . Forget it. The imagery is getting unpleasant, mixed up. The point is that if it were that simple – a matter of aiming the knife, *zip zip*, and out comes the rotten bit – well, fine.

But I doubt it. Part of me was glad when Claire seemed to be rejecting all that *mentation*. The id rejoiced for her; yes, the id (banging his pail with his shovel) did a kicking-up dance in the sand. Oh to make messy piles, to *not* dig compulsively, to *not* have to follow tortuous routes to heaven but to lie in the sun, to make revolting peanut butter messes. In short, to enjoy. Enjoy? What is this word?

Question: Is it possible that Donna, for all her fuck-ups (the aptest expression around), understands it better than we do? (Claire is *determined* to enjoy her life.)

Answer: Freud's pleasure principle concerns itself more with the avoidance of pain than with the pursuit of pleasure.

God (or someone) be with her.

My daughter, in between exploding textual minefields and serving *coq au vin*, goes for long improving hikes in the wilderness in boots the size of monoliths. What have we here, a finely-turned ankle? But let me not be provocative nor disobey House Rule No. 1: Do not describe a woman in such a way that it bites off bits of her, dislocates her, reduces her to a naming of parts. Therefore I shall tell you of neither knee nor of nostril, nor of how lovely she is even in scruffy or minimalist or deconstructed clothing. However, I *shall* tell you, freely and without a stitch of guilt, that she is tall: for being tall, you see, makes her woman-proud. It also means I look up to her, she's bigger than I am.

I do so now.

She stands at the foot of my bed, tries to smile, flips her straight hair off her forehead.

—What's that? I ask, pointing to the book she's clutching.

—*Philip's Phoenix*, she says. It's about Mary Sidney, Philip's sister, Countess of Pembroke.

I hope I manage to look interested.

—The title's a reference to one of his poems. The phoenix is of course a resurrection symbol. After Philip died she mourned for a couple of years, then she rose out of his ashes, as it were, like the Phoenix.

As it were.

The little woman behind the great man? Pah! Shakespeare's sister, Wordsworth's sister, Sigmund Freud's mother – bring on the girls! forget the boys! The great man was a sham, a front, a ventriloquist's dummy, a brainless mimic who merely followed the great woman round the kitchen hanging on her apron strings and words in his coat or armour or his fluffy slippers or whatever, taking notes.

—It's a sexist conspiracy, Claire announces. They're all busy trying to show how Mary couldn't have written *The Dolleful Lay*. They attribute it to Spenser. Percy Long says it comes closer to imitating Spenser than Keats or Shelley, thus implying the improbability of such an achievement by a woman. Herbert Rix shows how it uses sophisticated techniques like anaphora, allegory, personification and so on. To write such a poem, he argues, assumes a rhetorical training similar to Spenser's – which she didn't have of course – and anyway he says she didn't have the discipline. And Pigman argues –

—Pigman?

—Pigman – she manages to laugh. I kid you not. G. W. Pigman the Third, *Grief and English Renaissance Elegy*.

What does one say – Pig . . . *Peeg* . . . Simply *oink*? Suddenly I'm too tired to play feminist Old Macdonald.

—Pigman (she's getting into her stride) argues that *Astrophil* has two hundred and sixteen lines (twice one hundred and eight) and *Lay* has one hundred and eight, the same as the number of sonnets in *Astrophil and Stella*, and one for each of Penelope's suitors in the Odyssey. Such cleverness, he concludes, can only be attributed to Spenser and, by extension, not to a woman. All the contextual evidence is ignored.

Horrors, I say, and so forth.

—But tell me, granted she inspired brother Philip and did a jolly good promotion job after his death, and assuming she wrote this doleful ditty or whatever – we'll give her the benefit of the doubt – it sounds like at best it was a good sub-Spenserean imitation. The question still remains, at least in my mind: Claire, was she any good? (Notice I did not ask if she was as good as Sir Philip. That would be invidious.)

Silence. Take note, that this is no idle, passing-the-time-of-day question. This is a question which I know full well must provoke at the very least a cascade, a Niagara of feminist/literary abuse; a lecture on gender, religion and politics in seventeenth-century England and the role of women therein. Her pronunciation of the words alone (male, patriarchal, sexist . . .) are enough to make a strong shrink shrivel. Was she a *good writer*? What's your historico-cultural context?

But she says nothing, studies her Penney's workshirt with Renaissance concentration. Finally she says – and very gently,

—Dad, I don't think you heard what I was saying.

I insist I did but still she says nothing; looks at me; doesn't pursue it.

—Forget it, okay?

What choice have I?

I remember playing checkers with my mother. I was maybe six years old. I let her win. Partly I felt sorry for her and partly I was afraid if she lost she'd stage one of her heart attacks.

How fearfully intellectually talented we are, my daughter and I; how quickly we learn to psych one another out. So this is it, then, I

51

think, another of those beastly cross-circulation devices: daughter 'married' to father in order to keep his heart going develops sudden brain slowdown and concomitant failure (softening) of will. In other words, we may never play for real again.

Thirteen

What happens when one 'feels sorry' for oneself? How can this be explained? Answer: by arguing that people have the capacity to detach themselves from themselves and their situation; so that that detached 'other' appears to be looking on and commenting on one's plight. It is in this frame or rather frames of mind, for example, that one says about oneself 'poor you (me)' or 'why you (me)' or (what have you (I) done to deserve this?'. It is also in this 'split-off' condition that one may cast around, often quite shamelessly, for someone to give one's misfortune or affliction to. For instance, why couldn't it have been that dumb Cream Cheese Cardiologist instead? One feels oneself to be undeserving of one's illness, and in such 'self-pitying' (and related states) one may achieve notable levels of ignominy. This seems to be particularly true when confronting disease.

I gaze encouragingly at the bleeper: *bleep*. Then I stare down at my chest: which of you will surprise me and go off first? The bleeper with its low-pitched, come-hither noise – siren of sirens; or will it be you, my heart, king of beasts, grabbing me by the throat and tearing me to shreds from the inside out?

The question is, how long can it hold out? Another week, two, a month at most? I have been waiting seven weeks and four days. Three months is my limit. That means roughly another month to go. At most.

I am no mathematician.

Of course, how one experiences an event depends upon one's situation. Take the example of a lost five-dollar bill: is this a tragedy? For most non-destitute adults in most contexts it would probably give rise to a cognitive state of, say, mild regret. For a child it could elicit a fear emotion. For a bag-lady it could be the tragedy of a lifetime.

What is this crumpled note in my fist?

Okay. We'll talk about anticipatory excitement. Take the case of a young man waiting for a date. The girl in question is quite pretty, to him ravishing. He suffers from the delusion that without her he cannot live. He awaits her arrival: feeling an optimistic surge, he begins to whistle (. . . *it's only a heartbeat a-way-a-ay*). Now he begins to think about what will happen when she arrives: the movie, the kiss, the feel of her breasts. New life, new heart. He looks once more at his watch and now his whistling dies away. He is sweating. Oh god, what if she doesn't show? (i.e., anticipatory excitement has turned to concern or worry). As the prospect begins to loom larger, it turns to resignation, hopelessness, and disappointment. Notice, however, that the undesirable event that constitutes the object of this concern is that the earlier anticipated desirable event might not materialise. In other words, initially he reacts to the prospect of her arriving but later he reacts to the prospect of her *not* arriving. The situation is quite symmetrical. If one experiences a fear emotion with respect to some prospective event that is undesirable to some degree, then the absence of that event will be desirable to the same degree. If one fears something that is extremely undesirable, one will consider it extremely desirable that the feared event not happen and, of course, if one reacts to this latter prospect, the eliciting conditions for a hope emotion are satisfied. Thus, in so far as hope and fear have complementary objects (an event occurring and not occurring), the contribution of desirability to the intensity of the two emotions will also be the same, so that one might expect the intensity of fear and of hope to sum to a constant for the occurrence and non-occurrence of any prospect event.

At some point 'fear' becomes an inappropriate label for the emotion: 'dread' is much better. Whereas 'fear' focuses on the possibility that the feared event will occur, 'dread' seems to presuppose that it will.

What are we talking about here?

Anxiety is a manifestation of undischarged sexual energy. Of course, that was only his first theory . . .

Cut the bullshit, Frear.

Okay. The thing we most fear in the end comes to get us, so we might as well let go.

Flutter flutter goes my fiver.

Now let's look at this thing rationally:

(1) There's a shortage of spare organs.

(2) The Jarvik-7 – one of those off-the-shelf plastic spare part jobs – is a dismal failure. Here, have a look at this old magazine. Witness that poor shnook Schroeder smiling bravely from his wheelchair while his daughter carries his heart-driver over her shoulder.

He looks like a man who has lost his heart.

My daughter would not carry my heart over her shoulder.

(3) Schroeder was born on St Valentine's Day.

(4) He lived for six hundred and twenty days. Better than nothing?

Easy for you to say. The point is, it wasn't quality time. He spent his days and nights in some twilight state of infections, fevers and strokes. The stroke alone would have killed a normal-hearted man but the dumbheart Jarvik-7 kept thumping away. Schroeder should have asked to be put out of his misery. Barney Clark did.

(5) They're now working on a nuclear-powered model: a sort of mini-reactor using a tiny capsule of plutonium-238 to drive the mechanism.

The problem is radioactive contamination.

There's a dreadful buzzing going on in my head. I think I'll get some rest now.

Jeremiah in the Lamentations says, *From above he has sent fire into my bones, he has made me desolate and faint all the day . . .* He's talking about emotional stress – he's mourning the destruction of Jerusalem – but he feels it, the pain, in his bones.

I can't sleep – that buzzing. I'll have to read.

It has taken me nearly two months to reach page 147 of *Heart of Darkness* where Kurtz is lying, as Marlow approaches him with a candle, in the dark waiting for death. His features change. His last words are expletive, repeated. We all know what they are: *The horror! the horror!*

According to Ruth, who has come running in like a prophetess in flames, that buzzing noise is my bleeper.

Fourteen

I'm ready, my bag has been packed for weeks, a squashy bag which Ruth carries out to the car. We're ready to take off, seatbelts fastened. No, not yet. I make Ruth go back up to the bathroom. What for? Dental floss, I forgot the dental floss. She gives me a funny look but obeys.

On the way to the hospital we pick up Claire.

The journey from home to the hospital usually takes about forty minutes, allowing for traffic. The green down jacket was a Christmas present from Ruth. I put it on thinking I'll keep my heart warm for its last few hours in my employ. When the car heater comes on full blast I start to gasp. I crave air as I crave a heart. Claire, leaning over from the back seat, helps me to rip it off.

—Val, Ruth says, I told you you were overdressed.

—Now I'm cold, I say. Where are we going Ruth?

She is very matter-of-fact, that's her way.

—We're going for your transplant.

Like we're going to the movies – that cornflakes-soaked in-milk voice, usually so comforting.

—I'm thinking about the heart, the donor heart.

—What about it, she says.

—It can only live for a few hours. What if it dies – stops beating – before we get there . . . Ruth step on it.

—Don't be silly, she says, it'll be there before we are.

—How?

—Don't you know anything? They bring them by Lear jet.

A jet plane carrying my heart! As we speed over the Dumbarton Bridge, I picture an iron strongbox on a plumped-up red cushion in the middle of the empty hold of a plane, guarded by a soldier with a machine gun. Or do they transport the entire body? Surely 'harvesting' does not literally mean the medical team pulls out the heart like a beetroot from the ground and leaves the body gaping and bereft on the freeway verge?

Ruth explains how they take the body to the nearest hospital where they harvest the heart. It is then put into a plastic sack and transported in a bright plastic carrier – they come in red and yellow, not unlike our picnic hamper at home. Quite jolly, really.

—Wait a minute, what if it gets there too soon? Will they give it houseroom in the chest of a convenient ape?

—Val . . .

—What if it gets there too late – they remove my heart and the replacement part doesn't arrive in time?

—Val, they wouldn't do that and you know it. Just relax, they wouldn't have bleeped you if they didn't have a heart for you.

—That's true. Yes. Of course.

We have done dry runs a dozen times at least but now that it matters we get lost. We wind up at the Menlo Park V.A. Hospital, turn around and skid off the wrong way down University Avenue towards the Bay, make another steamy illegal U-turn and floor it in the right direction, following signs to the Med Centre.

—Jesus, Ruth, be careful.

Note: when normally cool wife loses cool, husband starts worrying.

We wind up in the shopping mall. Ruth stops the car in front of Niemann Marcus, rolls down her window and yells at a lady to tell her the way, quick. The lady does a T'ai Chi revolution, smiles and shrugs. It's a good thing we don't keep a firearm in the car. We stop at a bus stop. Claire gets out and shakes the guy waiting there. Listen, I hear him say, I don't live around here . . . She waits for the bus. When it comes she practically assaults the driver. He gives her directions.

The main entrance of the hospital. Ruth bursts briefly into tears but quickly recovers. I am my usual self. *In the heart of ancient Sparta was a temple dedicated to Fear.*

—What did you say, Val?

—Nothing.

—You okay?

—Fine.

Actually, I'm not so sure. Those red oleander hedges; that ginkgo tree reaching out its arms for me, the concrete paving done in haemal shades . . . *A formal yet welcome approach . . . the new entrance is designed to reflect an atmosphere of peace and dignity.*

Hang in there.

—Hi there, Dr Frear.

A warm welcome from the nice (pregnant) transplant counsellor. How kind, such a nice smile.

—Don't worry, Mrs Frear, we'll look after him.

Ruth and Claire hug me hard and run.

—So here you are.

—Yes. Is my heart here?

—Well, not quite, but we've been in contact, it's on its way. By the time you've been through the pre-op cooldown, it'll be here.

Do I look doubtful?

—Honest, she says, I promise. Don't worry.

No.

—How do you feel?

I look at her. Such an earnest question. She has nice eyes. She takes my hand and I say I'm fine. Alarm, as opposed to non-specific anxiety, is triggered by an obtrusive event in the environment and commonly occurs when an animal is in a strange and disorienting milieu, separated from the supportive objects and figures of its home ground. Ruth? Claire?

—Of course you're tense, Dr Frear, it would be unnatural if you weren't. But you know the surgeons know what they're doing, their track record is proven.

Skinner says emotions don't exist. 'It has not been possible to show that each emotion is distinguished by a particular pattern of responses of glands and smooth muscles.' Skinner you're a jerk: *myocardium* is stringy, unlike the bowel which is smooth (and which has just given way). The nurse helps me to the bathroom: embarrassment is the worst part of all this. I apologise.

—Don't think of it, she says.

At least I am excused the dreaded enema.

The faster the heart pumps the greater the blood-flow through the coronary arteries. If that flow is impeded for any reason, we feel a rapidly developing pain in the centre of our chest and a tightening or constriction while the heart goes through its violent activity. There are documented cases of terrified patients who died immediately before surgical procedure or during induction of anaesthesia. A number of reports concern patients with heart disease who succumbed in situations of fright or excitement, including during ward rounds, watching a wrestling match, and upon administration of last rites.

She hands me over to the transplant nurse.

—Good luck, she says.

—Thank you.

—If you'll just step in there, Dr Frear, and remove your clothes – here, you can put this on.

One sock off one sock on, diddle diddle dumpling my son . . . My son, where are you going? Where am I going? Far far away, to America, to study. She put her hand to her heart. Shirt, sweater, pants, underpants, socks, all bedded in the green down of my jacket, a tidy pile like a gravemarker of the old me. These treasures that I may never see again. The rabbit perhaps knows anger and sadness but can it be wistful or melancholic about its discarded clothes, not to mention the bit of me I've come to have removed? Will I go home with a doggie bag? Emotional range is in fact a good gauge of the nervous system's (and the mind's) complexity. A jellyfish's repertoire of emotions is very limited compared with, say, the above rabbit's. His instinctive response to danger is to run; other animals battle it out – the well known fight-or-flight syndrome. *Hysterical Neurosis, Dissociative Type.* The *Diagnostic and Statistical Manual of Mental Disorders (revised edition)*, states, 'Alternations may occur in the patient's state of consciousness or in his identity, to produce such symptoms as amnesia, somnambulism, fugue, and multiple persona-lity.' Dissociation, here, seems also to refer to a change of speaking and acting such that one is confused about the self. A 'fugue' – literally 'flight' or 'escape' – refers to a psychological or even physical wandering away.

—Don't even think about it.

—What was that, Dr Frear? You okay in there?

—Yes, fine, be right out.

I think this gown has shrunk – or I've grown, Alice-like. *Did you like reading Alice in Wonderland?* Oh yes. *Hey- ho, the shrink is shrunk, the wicked shrink is . . .* Wicked, Dr Frear? Would you like to tell us about that? No. I'll tell you about regression. Regression is a form of escape by acting as one did in problem-free situations such as by acting as a child. *When I was a boy with ne'er a a crack in my heart . . .* This should not suppose that one actually becomes like a child but rather that one . . . Keep making those sand piles. Oh but why? Look, when the moisture in them dries up they start to crack. What am I doing this for? Shut up and keep digging, kid. Metaphysical definitions of regression such as, 'The ego attempts to return to an earlier libidinal state,' should be avoided.

—Oh there you are, Dr Frear. What was that you said?

—Sigmund Freud was really a very fearful man.

—You don't say. I'm afraid you'll have to give me that gown now – it doesn't do a lot for you anyway.

He saw chaos everywhere he looked. Of course *fin-de-siècle* Vienna was a pretty awful place. Outside the Vienna Parliament, on the Ring stood statues of charioteers. They were supposed to represent man's ability to control his urges. (According to the Platonic parable, the soul is a chariot from which the mind must direct the horses or passions.) But inside, as both the young Hitler and the middle-aged Freud noticed, endless ugly scenes were being enacted, in which various delegates 'hurled themselves on one another, fought and roared like wild animals'. Fact is, he saw us as part-human, part-animal in the process of tearing ourselves and others to pieces. Also he saw the individual as a state: the 'id' is the lowest level of the state within each person, or in political terms the urge of the peoples of the provinces to embrace death in war, civil war and rebellion . . .

—Could you just shift a bit, Dr Frear? There, that's fine, we just have to get this cool mattress in place for you. Okay?

Naked. She wipes me down with a cool washcloth. that's very kind of you. Now she gently guides me onto a slab. The mattress is freezing, wet. Why are you doing this to me? Do you want my heart to fail right here and now so you can save your valuable person-hours and go home to a tortilla dinner in front of the six o'clock news? Don't tell me, cool-down procedure to decrease the oxygen demand of the body, reduce stress on the heart I know I know, but it is so unkind.

Fear is in the mind but, except in pathological cases, has its origins in external circumstances that are truly threatening. 'Landscapes of fear' refers both to psychological states and to tangible environments. What are the landscapes of fear? Ask some of my patients about their fears: of children with muddy shoes, of strangers, alien beings, hospital corridors, wind and rain; a phallic army of flutes, fish, worms, pigeons, dogs, garden hedges . . . enough. I have six file drawers full of them, in fact one of my favourite patients – yes we do have favourites though it's not done to admit it, even to ourselves – this one was afraid of bicycles and horses – sexual of course. In the end she bought herself a motorcycle . . . yes, a great success. Hysteria, as you probably know, goes back to the Greek word meaning 'wandering womb'. Oh where is my wandering womb tonight? It is of course

60

more prevalent in women than in men (have I said that already?) Anyway it can take some extraordinary forms: paralysis, uncontrolled weeping or laughter, young girls often have it . . . sex again . . . there's even the case of the woman who kept going in for operations.

—Dr Frear, I've just checked with the team and they're ready for you now. I'll just wheel you along, okay? Just relax.

—What's that whining noise?

—That's the helicopter just coming in on the landing pad up on the roof – with your heart.

Oh. A couple of white-coated attendants running down the corridor with my heart in a plastic picnic hamper. Am I supposed to believe this or have I got tangled up in the filming of a medical soap? I hear one shout to the other,

—How was your trip?

—Fine, no hitches.

—A good heart?

—The reply disappears down the corridor with him. Wait . . .

—This one's for real, Dr Frear. It was touch-and-go there for a while but now it's here you can relax. They'll be ready for you in just a minute. Everything's fine, nothing to worry about now. The anaesthetist will be here right away. You okay there? You ready?

I've been ready for a long time.

This is it. They come at me with a buzzing shaver. Then the jabs and the hookups: respirator, pressure monitor, anaesthesia machine, catheter up my penis. Of what am I to be delivered? Ask a stupid question. Shaved, parted and entered.

The green tiled walls are closing in. Lights: three flying-saucers that resemble breasts in which I can see myself reflected, greatly distorted and magnified. Action: bring on the surgeons. Blue masks and paper hatties, hear hear. Tell me, is God watching? Is He (She?) angered by this vain intervention? Does S/He mean me to die young like a tree with heart-rot, vertical, proud, thickening, just earning its rings but quietly decomposing within, falling to earth without warning from its great height while people flee and cry *tim-ber!*? Does S/He not denounce the tampering with a heart in its shrine which even in its failure is sacrosanct? Can't I just go away and lick my wounds?

Gentlemen, you are hereby dismissed.

The chief surgeon introduces himself.

—Hello, Dr Frankenstein, I say.

He has no idea how serious I am. You are my creator, I your monster. I shall pray neither to God nor to Sigmund Freud before I go under, but to You.

Now my front is exposed I'm no longer cold; the hot lights warm my poor heart. Without any prompting from me – its last dance? – it winks and dimples and pumps enough to amuse everyone on the team. My own expression is deadpan.

What is that noise, that repulsive smell reminiscent of dentists and butcher shops? Ah, the breastbone, how inconvenient of it to be where it is. Sternum in the way, boys. Well, nothing else to do but saw through. A pretty little thing, a lady's saw you might say, excellent, indeed, a precision tool made especially for bone. Tell me, doctor, where does the bone dust go? Not up your nose, I hope. Did you know, by the by, that according to Sigmund Freud the nose, the heart and the genitals are inextricably linked? I'll tell you about it when you're not quite so distracted. Perhaps there are little vacuum cleaners to suck it up? What do you think about while you're sawing? Is it boring? Do you keep up a steady rhythm or do you make progress in little excited spurts? Ah, there we are, the impediment of bony hymen removed, your way is clear, doctor . . . Except not quite, those ribs, what is to be done with those ribs? *Get me the rib spreader.* Eyes bright over the mask. No, no, anything but the rib spreader! Sorry, no choice. Hand on the lever, cranking my chest open. Just a little wider, ah that's good, we'll just bend that heart-spoon out of the way.

Excuse my laying my heart open to you. Do you know who said that, doctor? The male patient, in a position of abject weakness, competes with the surgeon by exercising his brain muscle. It was Thomas Mann, as a matter of fact, in one of his letters. Thomas who? Oh I forgot, you guys are glamorous but not over-bright. A pity doctor, and very short-sighted of you. Or do you prefer to read Mrs Mann, like my daughter Claire? I myself am a reader. My daughter takes courses in literature at Berkeley. Of course she has a special interest in *feminist* literature – texts that is – yes, very clever she is, if a bit headstrong. But psychoanalysts, I don't mind admitting, are always looking for answers, the perfect solution. So we look between the covers of books. That's because we secretly believe it's only in literature that we get the Real Truth. Even Freud knew about that, Goethe, Shakespeare . . . Shakespeare's sister . . . You don't agree? The heart is merely a squishy transferable bit of meat? What an extraordinary thought. Imagine if Shakespeare had seen it your way. Instead of saying, *What rare present is this?* he would have gone, *Gee whizz, there goes another whopper!*

Forget it, Frear.

Oh. What's that?

There it is: the stretched and fibrous muscle, the puffed out pouchiness that is, was, the court of me. The surgeon considers the offending organ, points with his knife-tip. Ooh, me too, show me, I want more than an abstraction in beet, salmon and butter, the colours still wet and glistening. Shit: why did I eat all those pizzas? Too late. Forgive me. For the moment it seems a tranquil bundle, rather peaceful, sufficient to an insensible body. Yet a pity to lose it now, alas.

This time the surgeon goes smartly to work – Vincent Price in one of those grade Z horror movies. His eyes over the mask are dementedly wide as he slaps the hand of one of his assistants.

—No, no, you fool, not the liver, it's the heart we want!

Just stop right there, gentleman, I have something I wish to say to you. Put down your knives and forks and listen for a moment. They cross their arms over their chests and smile politely. Well now. As you know, we psychoanalysts are encouraged to know everything, every secret, every fantasy our patients are capable of dreaming up, yet to have no horror, to give nothing away; in other words to keep possession of our souls. What do you have to say to that? Nothing. These guys are strong silent types.

They hook me up to the bypass machine. Blood chases the knife as he slices and snips the aorta, the venae cavae, then sticks a holding tube into their gaping maws. The heart and lungs are short-circuited: not needed on voyage, not so long as the big box of tricks keeps them going. Dr Frankenstein turns to wash his gloves again. The suction machine – welcome to babydom – slurps and gurgles. And now . . .

Wait.

Give it up, Frear.

No. *To give nothing away.* Didn't you hear what I said?

Hah. Even Faust couldn't manage that.

Oh. So long then.

And without further ado Little Jack Horner puts in his thumb and pulls out a piece of plumbing that looks like an old red girdle dangling its garters in mid-air – oh what a good boy you are! – and passes it along with tweezers for everyone to see.

—Here, hold this thing a minute. Not too much water in the cavity, there.

—Help, what's that smell?

—Nothing to worry about, it's only the small bleeders being cauterised; everything is going smoothly, the veins and arteries are quite happy in fact in some ways it's quite good being without a heart in fact bypass machines are highly reliable, more so than —

But wait, what's this, can it be . . . Yes, ta ta, the new . . . Drum roll while it is removed from its pink and yellow picnic hamper. Using calipers it is passed from hand to hand. Wait, I'm not ready yet, I have to . . . What? There isn't time for introductions, we have to work fast, don't you understand? Yes, but . . . No buts, Mac, this is it. But I need to know — can't anyone hear me? — I mean, what sort of heart is it: meek or adventurous, carefree or laden with sorrows? Or what? *Behold the ears of my heart are set before thee; open thou them, O Lord.*

—Gee, such a little heart in a big hole.

—Yeah, the disproportion is enormous, the old heart was so swollen.

—This is the critical time, you guys.

They have seventy-seven minutes to get it sewn in properly. Flip, stuff, into the hole, jiggle it about, got to get it right. Massage it, get it warmed up and comfy in there, con it into thinking it's just like the old place. Sing *There's No Place Like Home*. Reconnect plumbing with connectors that will eventually rot away, steel thread where necessary. Close up ribs, replace breastbone, smooth skin over all. And with that the curtain falls on the last act; the old heart is dissected and forgotten, and history begins now.

Listen. The atmosphere in the room is hush-hush, followed by a controlled sort of hoopla. Wait for it.

—Pulse rate good, pressure good.

—Sounds like a good start.

—The heart's beating at ninety-five beats per minute.

Well done, Gentlemen.

Happy Birthday, Valentine.

PART II

They have seene me and heard me, arraign'd me in these fetters, and receiv'd the evidence; I have cut up mine anatomy, dissected my selfe, and they are gone to read upon me.

John Donne

One

I open my eyes, try to focus, cannot. Where are my contacts? I hear voices, can't make out the words. I try to smile, can't; nod, cannot. Someone takes my hand, I squeeze it.

—Dear God, thank you, but oh, the pain.

What do you expect after being sliced open and sawed in half?

—Go ahead and cough, I'll hold your ribs. Nurse, another injection for Dr Frear.

—Please, can I listen doctor?

He hooks his stethoscope to my ears and the cold paddle receives and transmits the beat. *Lup dub, lup dub.* Fast. Let that much sink in. Why so fast? I ask him. Because the vegas nerve – vagrant, vagary, vagabond: a directionless ambling nerve that traipses down from the brain into the heart; the laid-back Mogadon nerve, the shock-absorber, the peacemaker, the hushing nanny – has been cut. My heart now beats at roughly a hundred per minute.

My heart? Whose heart? What does it feel like? It feels *fast*. I'd expand on that only there's a tube in my mouth and I'm choking to death.

—It's only the respirator. It's to help you breathe for the first few days, he says. Don't let it worry you.

A small thing all things considered. Go ahead, Valentine, thank the doctor for your new high-tuned heart.

—Thank you.

—Don't let it worry you.

Wired up like a space monkey to a breathing tube, immune system suppressed, pain-martyred, doped to the eyeballs, don't let it worry you. Neat little paper electrodes taped to the skin above my heart. *My* heart? *Whose* heart? Don't let it worry you. *Don't let it worry you.* It's like the refrain of a song. They watch the monitor. They say I'm doing fine, just fine. I'm in an isolation cubicle. I don't feel fine. The oxygen mask irritates. Cold water condenses in the system. The nasal tubes irritate. They are stuck up there for hours on end. Not to mention the thin, supposedly weak elastic supports that are actually as sharp as razors which slip over my ears and cut into the flaps.

67

I close my eyes, try to imagine my daughter, my dog Willy, my wife. Where are they? Instead I see Donna mounting her motorcycle; I see Sigmund Freud, leering; I see my mother on her nursing chair; I see myself riding on her stomach; I see my father, whom I have never met, riding a surfboard . . .

Saved. Look, my real family – there on the screen of my protective pericardial bubble. It is like watching them on TV. Or rather, it is they who are watching me. They may not breathe on me nor comfort me with apples neither. Do I dare eat a peach? Certainly not, for their fruit baskets will be riddled with morbific beasties from the outside world. I am raving, forgive me. Call it a drug-induced dream-state.

Perhaps I haven't explained this thing about the suppressed immune system. The drug Cyclosporin – which stops the heart rejecting – also suppresses the immune system, which means in turn that I am vulnerable to all kinds of weird and wonderful infections. They give you a heart – begin now – you worry.

Whose heart?

Who cares.

Don't you want to know who your donor is . . . was?

No. What does it matter. Maybe.

You could ask.

Not now.

Why not?

I haven't the strength, you fool.

Intellectual curiosity is a sign of wellness.

Well, I am not well.

Besides, once I know, the knowledge will become a burden.

You could invite the burden in. You could ask the nice pregnant transplant counsellor. Think about it, Valentine.

I don't want to think.

There she is.

All right, shut up.

—Excuse me, miss, but could you . . . my donor . . .

—Of course, Dr Frear, I understand. You want some information about your donor, perfectly natural. A good sign in fact.

She smiles, flips through my records.

—She was nineteen, killed in a motorcycle accident. That's about all I am at liberty to tell you right now.

—Did you say *she*.

—Yes.

—A woman?

—Well, a girl – a young woman. (Embarrassed giggle.) I know it's weird, she says, but if you think about it rationally (oh I do, I do), they're all the same, hearts, it's just a matter of matching size and blood type and so forth. Of course you're a doctor, Dr Frear, I don't need to tell you, but we get lots of people getting real screwed up about these things; a black guy doesn't want a Caucasian heart, a Catholic refuses a Protestant heart, and so on. People are real funny. But you can't let it get to you. As far as the body is concerned a heart is a heart, a pumping organ, the rest is in your head. I mean, look at little Fay down the corridor; she's got the heart of an ape and she isn't growling and growing fangs. Is there anything else I can do for you, Dr Frear? Just hit the buzzer if you want me.

I want you. I don't understand. Tell me again. The great man with the snip-of-a-girl's heart? Or the snip-of-a-shrink with a great girl's heart? How is it possible? 'Cardiac compatibility' means her chest cavity must have been more or less equal in size to mine. Claire would like that. No she wouldn't. It's not equality she wants – she'd rather see me cut down to size.

Look, Claire, I'm cut.

Freud comes and goes, talking of Moses' Michelangelo; mumbling the word *suppression*.

My family come and go, talking of nothing I can make out. They are the other side of the glass. You want to know what it's like being oogled and ogled? Go to the Seattle Aquarium. If you sit in the middle while the sea creatures swim around – giant California octopi, dogfish, turtles – it will give you some idea of what it's like. The quarantine unit. My family and other sharks watching me, the leggy, hairy creature of unmotility, while I in turn watch them – when I am sufficiently *compos mentis*. I keep thinking the PR department should lay on a prerecorded message: 'Here in this cubicle is our five hundredth heart transplant recipient, *Valentinus Frearus*, still alive after (fill in the blank) days.' Sound effects? Tape of the heart? Splendid idea. Sell like hot cakes at the Nature Company along with the tapes of whale moans and hooting owls and the beat and sloosh of puerperal wombs. Why not? Get people in the mood, susceptible; *lup dub, lup dub*. Call it the Edgar Allan Poe living exhibit.

—Dr Frear, excuse me – the pregnant transplant counsellor – how are you feeling today, I mean about it being a woman's heart and all?

—The heart is a pump; read William Harvey.

—Yes, I know, but emotionally, you know, how does it feel now you've had some time to let it sink in?

—You really want to know?

—Sure.

What I feel is panic, outrage, a confused combination of the two, scratching inside my chest. A woman's heart? No! Dump it out, get rid of it, send it back to its donor, its next of kin, whoever. I don't care what you do with it, just get it out of here. Restore me to wholeness, to *regulation*.

—Fine, I say.

—Well, if you ever want to talk about it, I'm here. Okay?

Yes, all right, yes. Valentine Frear – ego-identification, remember? Where am I? Maybe it should have come with a government health warning? 'DANGER: This heart may cause doubts, fears, night terrors, qualms and other irrational female longings.' Female? Okay, scratch that. But it *nags* for god's sake in the morning; later on it does its washboard routine *lup dub, lup dub* . . .; at lights out its like the little engine that couldn't. How do I proceed from here?

I am rendered different, *not me*. The pink meat of a woman's heart . . . No, it isn't rational. How can I tell Claire this? Go ahead, throw something at me. Better yet, let the heart do it for you; a just punishment for a life of male sin. Let it shame me, mortify me, curse me like a strawberry mark as it has cursed women from the beginning of time.

What was it Plato said? If you behave badly you get reincarnated as a woman.

Serves me right.

Serves Plato right.

Which? I don't know. I don't have the strength to work it out. Where were we? Who are those people out there?

—Dr Frear, your wife and daughter are here.

—Thank you.

Ruth and Claire, posing for an old *Saturday Evening Post* by Norman Rockwell. Hands to hearts they blow kisses that go *splat* and dribble like soap bubbles down the partition instead of wafting through as kisses should. They pass tissues to each other, wave them, laugh snottily. A sticky business all round.

And he? Husband and father, subject of their dumb show? He is risen, praise the Lord! He is, in fact, a pretty poor specimen with a droopy crooked smile and a one-inch tube sprouting from where his heart used to be. The smile is crooked because of the tube in his mouth. There is another up his nose. In fact, he is festooned; this the drip and suck of his existence. Bring on the soft plasticated nasogastric endotracheal octopus man! *Hnnnnh* he says. The tube scrapes his windpipe and he starts to choke; that in turn causes a small earthquake in his chest – any second he'll bust his stitches and the whole mess will open up and spill indecorously out. He tastes sour plastic. He desists from speech, raises his right arm with the rubber hose attached to it, and waves. He negotiates the simulacrum of a smile around the tube, and does his best to look alive – which he is.

Apparently. Yes. A miracle. Thank God, and so forth. I keep thinking I should be cheered seeing my wife and daughter looking patriotic, but instead it irks. Why are they mouthing those dumb monosyllables: *How-are-you?* I am also touched. I lie back and watch them, my teary-eyed but stiff-backed, germ-proof, hug-proof family, American Gothic pledging allegiance. You can just about make out Claire's pitchfork.

Two

Dad. A statement. A greeting from my daughter who manifests herself at my bedside with a face untrammelled but for two clawmarks above the nose. Did I say my daughter – *my* daughter? Oh no, not mine – Ruth's perhaps – but certainly no man's; no *snool's*. The snool (def.: an agent of phallic lust) is hereby denied that which he lusts after with all his heart (the rights of possession) and quite right too. You see how insidious is the snool, how by anticipating criticism, by throwing down his weapons, by admitting his sins before he has even committed them, he has learned to get away with anything, to worm his way into the closest of kernels? Not a man but a gentle-man. Bullshit. The gentleman is a rapist. The therapist is known in feminist circles as the rapist. The analyst is one of the arch-snools of this world. Snools maintain and perpetuate the sadostate.

—Dad, she repeats, grabbing the end of the bed.

What does one say now, at this moment, to the *presence* of her? Why are your knuckles so white? Why those shades? Why do you hang back like that as if I were the Big Bad Wolf hiding in Little RR's bed? Come a wee bit closer, hmm, the better to see you my dear . . . You know; I take it, about Freud's famous patient, the Wolf-Man? No? In that case you are in for a treat. Are you ready? Sitting comfy?

Once upon a time there lived a Russian who was unhappy because he'd caught the clap from a servant girl. He also had a few obsessional symptoms. So he trots along to see Dr Freud (he's now living in Vienna) and tells him all about it. Hmmm, ve-ery interesting, says the good doctor, sucking his cee-gar. And now it is the doctor's turn to talk. So he explains to Serge (his real name) that (1) what he wants is to be screwed by his father; and (2) the two wolves which he keeps seeing every time he closes his eyes are his dear Mom and Dad screwing on a hot summer's night, Mom down on all fours, Dad taking her from behind. This explains, says the wise man, your lust for squatting woman viewed from behind . . . which all goes back to the servant girl scrubbing the floor . . . In other words, round and round we go. End of analysis.

Where were we? Oh yes, I am tucked up in bed with only my snout exposed and my daughter is clutching the edge of my bed giving voice to the magical word 'Dad'. Why magical? Because it was a word that I never got to say myself. Anyway, that particular word seems to throw this patriarchal plug-ugly into confusion so that he finds himself scooting further down the pillows. He is not normally at a loss for words but now he hesitates for the possibilities. That is, in answer to her implied question (How are you, Dad?) he could say, As you see; alive, for the moment; quite happy; juddering with terror; and so on. He could snap his wolfish teeth and say, Fine and dandy, and how are *you* my dear? Or he could confess to being no man at all.

In short, he's thinking about whether or not to reveal what they've gone and put inside him. How he's been given a chance to do it over, for his daughter to cheer; redemption through transplant! The erstwhile hard-hearted male, her own father, welcomed into the fold. Mother and father in one, Hermaphoditus of the dual nature, neither male nor female but both at once; the androgyne with newly-functioning tearducts and burgeoning breasts (a Cyclosporin side effect). Like the de Murano painting of Christ showing his wound where Mary's nipple used to be; *Harlequin Breastfeeds His Son*; Benignity, Justice, the milk of creative inspiration – in a word: perfection.

No, it's too embarrassing. You see how cowardly is the snool?

The fierce grip relaxes, she scrabbles in her bag and comes up with the notebooks I asked her to bring, one red, one blue. She tosses them into my lap.

—You writing a book – *The Heart-torn Son of Freud* – or what?

—Save the sarcasm, it's just for making random notes. A simple convalescent's diary.

She has also brought me a study of Victorian marriages, and a book of poems, light verse from a welter-hearted daughter for a feather-hearted convalescent.

—Thank you, I say, sticking my nose into the marriage book, and while it's safely there she asks the question:

—Dad, how's the heart?

My answer is writ for me by Hilaire Belloc: *I said to Heart, 'How goes it?' Heart replied; 'Right as a Ribstone Pippin!' But it lied.*

—Fine, I say. As you see. Working away. Fast but efficient. Quite the mini-miracle, what?

She looks away. Is that a tear I spy, or merely a bird-bright eye? Oh, that's a good one – the all-in-one gesture that tidies hair from forehead and at the same time manages to brush away any telltale moisture such as might dangle embarrassingly from the tips of female eyelashes. Be gone! Be as you were: composed. Above all be not bamboozled by a father's change of heart.

—You heard?

—I heard.

—And?

—And what.

She's not going to make this any easier.

I lie with my arms laid down at my sides. Look how thin and pale we are, they say. Don't they move you, my daughter – these bumpy but inadequate veins? No? My phallus – who's talking about that? Okay, that too I lay down. You come in peace; so do I. I'm sorry, I didn't invent the language. I come, you come, we all come: *pace* for once, Sigmund. Come, embrace the old wolf, for he may not be with you much longer. Lay down your own weapon (that pretty pink tongue) and forgive the heart-torn snool. No? Well, perhaps not just yet.

Can you not see the struggle going on in that WE CAN DO IT breast, those hands, that worn-torn mop of hair? Oh the body speaks (screams, squawks, hits high Cs) even as she stands there at the end of my hospital bed. And don't think I don't also see myself as she sees me: a distinctly unattractive male animal resembling in fact more the Rat than the Wolf-Man; greying with stick arms and legs, rather remarkable ears through which the light shines pinkly, sharp teeth. And that other pink-tipped appendage, the bulge under the blanket just *there*. Oh god, why does it have to show? I should have instructed them: would you mind removing that too while you're about it? Here, I'll put the book over it, how's that. All gone, see? You were so easy to please as a child. Come, I promise, I'm harmless. We aim to please, to do no harm (the physician's oath).

The promises of a snool are worth beans. Bully and cringer cower together under the blanket.

—Hey Dad, you've lost so much weight your ears stand out.

Little Englishwoman. Hypocrite. Why do you edge away like that? Where has all the openness, expressiveness, *thinking through the body gone*? I present you with a body and you look away. What is this, Claire? Are you happy to see me alive? I'm happy to see you. I have no gun in my pocket, the war is over, capitulation's a foregone conclusion. Come, you win, shake my hand: merely a hand, see? – quite clean, marked like yours with a headline, a lifeline and a heartline. How does the heartline read? Interrupted, I dare say.

—Look, about the heart. I try again.

—What about it?

—Well, it's in there and it isn't mine and . . . well, I was wondering how you'd feel about it – I mean, do you find it as interesting (small British understatement) as I do? You know, the symbolic stuff and the gender thing of course, all mixed up in there – very powerful – confusing too of course, I mean I haven't figured out exactly what's going on here yet, but . . . (Spit it out, Valentine.) Claire, you do realise I have a *woman's* heart?

—So?

Flatness, silence. I'm thinking about what writers write when they want to describe touchy situations. She flinched; she blanched; she looked sick; she froze to the spot. She *does* look sick, she *is* frozen to the spot at the end of the bed. Awful, I'm thinking any minute she's going to fling off the blanket, tear open my pyjamas and rip it out of me. HOW DARE YOU!

But she just stands there. The bed is enfolded again, her knuckles have grown bigger than my ears. My poor daughter, what is it you cannot bear to hear? How can I help you, how can I fix it for you so it isn't all so awful, so it doesn't hurt so much? You don't want me to fix it, I know. How dare I? The *fixer*? God help me, I can remember changing her diaper. One night I noticed the lips of the vagina were stuck together so I applied some vaseline and gently manipulated them. She howled, I gulped back tears. I did that several times a day until the labia stopped trying to fuse. She whimpered, I gulped back more tears. The tiny parts were beautiful; I wanted them to be flawless. They became so, florally open, chubby segments of a rubber plant.

The psychoanalyst *fixes* his patients up but good, the father *fixes* his daughter's boo-boos, the husband *fixes* his wife.

Is this how it is to be forever, this contracting, this not getting together, this getting too close and then ducking apart; these seemingly unbridgeable differences? But what about the boggling similarities. The sharing of things no one else can possibly fathom?

—Claire, I thought . . . This girl's heart –

—This *girl's* heart?

75

—Claire –

—And now, presenting, the Man Who Got a Woman's Heart. He rises from his bed of guilt and goes out into the world to Do Good and Feel Love and generally end up a bigger and a better –

—Claire –

—Or are you writing a sci-fi novel – feminist science fiction is real big these days. *The Female Man* by Dr Valentine Frear: the all-time, living, breathing androgynous feminist hero!

—Claire –

—Or is this *Tootsie Part II*, complete with handbag and eyelashes? I mean, what are you trying to do here? Do it over, do it better? No more female fuck-ups – I can do anything better than you, including being a woman. The all-time Jesus, Dionysus, Tootsie cheap makeover . . .

—Enough. Claire, this is a travesty. It's not what I meant at all. I saw it as a chance, a possibility, transformation. I felt I'd been given –

—What you mean is you've *taken* – appropriated, annexed, stolen, cannibalised – some poor girl's heart. And now you want me to get down on my knees and –

A sudden dash round the side of the bed. Cheek glued to mine. It has all happened too quickly. What is my daughter doing down on her knees?

Three

—Lunch, Dr Frear?

The nurse brings a tray of quiche and salad, so many fresh colours and textures; low fat yoghurt for dessert which goes straight to the libido (that creaminess sliding between the lips . . .) For a time I feel quite cheerful. The sound of lettuce crunching in my ear distracts me from the noise reverberating in my head: like a Walkman screwed to my ears and on it a ghastly tape with only a bass beat and no melody 'composed' by Glass or Reich or some other sadomasochistic composer with *delirium cordis* who wants everybody else to share in his suffering.

—What do you mean *take heart* – what kind of nonsense is that?

The word *proprioception* has popped into my head. It means something like 'muscle sense'. But it's more than that. It implies a sense of what is 'proper' about one's own body; you are my 'property', I own you, I accept you. So now, do I take this heart to be my . . . I don't answer. My what? May I report that at last sighting it was observed jutting pugnaciously from my Gucci hospital gown, gathering itself up into a ball like some angry infant getting ready to go *pow* with its fists. So the answer is: No. Whatever is in there has nothing whatever to do with me. I disown it, I know it not. Or how about: I've lost my symbolic affective 'imago'? There's also Potzl's syndrome or *somatophrenia phantastica*, a sort of preposterous and often comic madness in which patients disown parts of their bodies. Nurse, take away this foot immediately! Or, Nurse, would you mind just removing this heart – you can put in on my tray next to that piece of leftover low-fat quiche.

—Oh, didn't you like the quiche, Dr Frear, I thought it was pretty good myself.

The transplant counsellor.

—It was fine, I'm just feeling a bit queasy.

—How about if we try shifting the focus away from your body, Dr Frear. You could tell me about what else has been on your mind.

—Uh, what mind did you have in mind? Listen, it isn't easy. Life as a patient is not what one would like it to be. Day merges into night, the nights go on forever. It is quite astonishing how one loses track of the date, of an overall time-scale. The drugs add to one's confusion: sedatives and hypnotics and so on, on top of all the pain-killers and anti-rejection drugs. Sedated in the morning, awake at night, a vicious circle.

—I'm sorry, I didn't mean to whinge. I'm trying to keep clear-headed. Actually, what I feel about my head is that it could fly off at any moment. I once had a patient who was half-strangled as a baby and left for dead. She had no memory of the event – only learned about it later from a newspaper clipping she found in her mother's underwear drawer. Yet she had trouble breathing, and as if the strangulation had actually occurred, her head – she demonstrated – felt loose. 'Unscrewed' was the not unsignificant word she used. Which is why she tended to rely – again the acting out – on her body. Compensation, as I explained.

—Dr Frear, I hear her asking, are you in pain or something?

—Pain is partly a matter of perception. That is, when some major physiological event occurs, a barrage of nocioceptive input is gener-ated, ongoing perceptual configurations of body integrity are broken down, and a state of tension exists until a new perceptual whole is formed. An adjustment to one's altered physical requires the addition of new information. By observing, touching, understanding certain physiological processes, the patient gains more information about the injury and this permits the restructuring of perception so that the catastrophic event can be translated from confusion and surprise into a meaningful, albeit unpleasant, configuration of experience.

—Dr Frear, are you in a *lot* of pain?

—I think we really have to define what we're talking about when we talk about pain.

—I thought it was something that hurt.

—Pain is certainly an unpleasant experience and one which we primarily associate with tissue or other damage, or describe in terms of that damage – but that's precisely the point, that the *perception* of pain is subjective and dependent on the influence of psychological, emotional and somatic variables. The literature suggests, for exam-ple, that the meaning ascribed to the word 'pain' (as in the case with all words of course), is ascribed during childhood in the family context. Parents may use actual or threatened pain to shape the behaviours of children. In this way, pain becomes associated with punishment and the explanation of guilt. It's often the parent who is *in pain* who provides the model for identification. My mother, for example. But the point is that the suppression of emotions generally (and anger specifically) may predispose to the development of pain.

—Dr Frear, you just had *major surgery*.

—I am aware of that. Look, no one is denying the organic basis of pain, but Freud observed how patients often used, increased or maintained their pain in different ways. His patient Elizabeth Von R, for example, suffered leg pains. She, he observed, had 'picked out from among all the pains that were troubling her at the time, the one particular pain which was symbolically appropriate'.

—Is there one particular pain with you, Dr Frear?

—The chest – it pulls across my chest. I can't move my arms.

It's useful to see how our various innate drives play a part in how we perceive our pain – sexuality, aggression and dependency, preeminently. The relationship between pain and aggressive feelings is pretty obvious. Pain is often the end result of aggression, either inflicted upon others or inflicted by them on oneself. But the relationship is a complex one since pain may lead to anger as easily as anger to pain.

—Are you feeling angry at your body, Dr Frear, or the doctors, or somebody else for causing this to happen?

—Look, please try to understand that I'm not talking specifically about my own situation. I'm trying to look at the psychodynamic aspects of pain in order to avoid making simple causal connections; trying, that is, to focus on the *interactive* role of the pain experience in psychic functioning. And that requires a consideration of pain in the context of the Freudian metapsychology. Thomas Szasz points out that the individual may react to his body as he might to another person. Indeed, attitudes may be projected onto the body as they might be projected onto others. Thus pain may be perceived as a hostile attack emanating from the body in much the same way as hostility may be perceived to emanate from another person.

—Dr Frear, what exactly are you afraid of?

—What am I afraid of?

What is anybody afraid of? Look at Donna. She takes off on Highway 1 and never looks back. What about head-on collisions; fog, getting smacked from behind by a Mack truck; from above by a two-ton falling boulder; did she stop to think of the possibilities?

Look at my drug regimen. I'm on Persantin (for life), Nuseal Aspirin (for life), Imuran (for life), Cyclosporin (for life), Acyclovir (three months), Vitamin C (one month only), Multivite (ditto), Ferrograd (ditto), and of course Prednisone, the infamous mood exaggerator.

—At night I hear coyotes out there, whole families of them.

—There aren't any coyotes in Palo Alto, it's a suburb.

—No, I realise that.

—Look, Dr Frear, it's only been three weeks since the operation, you're still adjusting. You need to give yourself time.

—I know.

Look, I can wiggle my toes, write in this notebook. Major accomplishments. You wanted to know how I'm feeling? I feel like I've been hit by a Mack truck, okay?

Four

And now – welcome to cardiac kindergarten!

First we crawl up the stairs on our hands and knees, then down again.

Now we sit on the side of our beds and pedal a wooden contraption.

And now we go up on our toes and down again; and up and down.

And then we walk, or rather shuffle.

—Very good, Dr Frear, says the physiotherapist.

—Thank you, I say.

So you see, I am following my nose, although the nose's itinerary is necessarily rather limited given a basic dependency on the body's more mobile divisions, which are unfortunately not very mobile.

—It will come, she says encouragingly.

These things take all one's concentration.

Donna, zooming around on her bike down there, will have no idea what I'm talking about – this basic physical struggle to get around, re-learning how to twiddle one's toes, a daily existence whittled down to bone and muscle. Aching bone and muscle. Of course the staff here do understand, especially my friend the transplant counsellor, who comes round a couple of times a day to sit with me even though she's terribly busy – I hear her being paged constantly. It doesn't matter that she is appallingly poorly read (I badger her about that). I don't think she's married.

Yesterday the surgeons came round and shot me full of hypnovel, then threaded a canula down the right jugular through the valve and pinched up a piece of ventricle. Sipping my heart through a straw, gentlemen? They enjoyed that. Humour: a good sign. The pressure was terrible but the results were worth it. Heart muscle, they said – I held my breath – in good nick, you're out of danger. As soon as we get this damned cold licked you can go home.

I coughed my gratitude. The transplant has saved my life. What kind of life? A limited one, but a life. I have a puffy face and a rather sinister Hobbit-like sprouting of hair on my fingers and toes (another Cyclosporin side-effect, nothing to worry over). The cold doesn't help. I'm afraid of rejection.

Do you know what happens when the valves shut down or the muscles give out? You foam like a horse at the mouth: pink froth. The threat is there. Such a dangerous contraption never beat in man's breast.

But today I have made great progress. Of course I have to keep track of how far I've gone because I have to be able to do the same distance back. Once I got stranded in Geriatrics, had to lean against a wall until a nurse came running with a wheelchair. But today I even made it down to the restaurant for a coffee (decaf.), came back up in the elevator, had a chat with the librarian and fetched up back at Transplants with my nose pressed to the glass of the isolation bay where a new heart-lung recipient about two feet long was sitting in the middle of a double bed gnawing on his bear's snout. I managed to engage the transplant counsellor in a discussion of his case. The psychoanalyst, so it appears, must stick his nose into everything, like a hound-dawg on the scent of something like a cross between a warm sheet and a ripe Camembert.

I am much exercised (note avoidance of the word 'obsessed') with noses at present.

I am disappointed about not going home, but also somewhat relieved. Here I can cope; there, who knows? Here has become my home: it's safe, the nurses accept me as I am. What am I? I told you, a kindergarten pupil. Good morning Valentine, how are we feeling this morning? Wretched.

Of course I'm looking forward to being back with my wife; and yes she's been to see me, every day as a matter of fact; and no, my failure to mention this fact is no Freudian slip but a slip-*up* – the Freudian slip being a much over used and misunderstood concept.

What else would you like to know, Nosy Parker? Who was Nosy Parker? I haven't the vaguest idea. My wife's nose? All right – since she has no feminist objections – it's a medium-sized probe, slightly retroussé and with a sprinkling of freckles. Lickable comes to mind.

And now you accuse me of coming down with a cold in order to avoid going home. How dare you. Listen, it would be a feat *not* to come down with some infection or other, especially in this place where germs are flying around like unconscious libidinous drives. Mine by the way – I refer to my nose – looks like a blown-up condom, strawberry flavour.

'I would have a lot to write about the nose and sexuality.' So wrote Sigmund Freud to his pen-pal Wilhelm Fliess, the Nose and Throat man. In fact, it was a subject close to both their hearts. As Jones says in his biography, they took an inordinate interest in the state of each other's nose, 'an organ which, after all, had first aroused Fliess' interest in sexual processes'. They harboured the theory that the nose swelled and became turgid during genital excitation.

I'll tell you a story. Once upon a time, it was a dull winter's day in February, Fliess was sitting in his bath and a man entered the room to inspect some piece of gas equipment. As he bent forward, the man wobbled. He held onto the wall, wiped the perspiration from his brow. Fliess wrote, 'For me the diagnosis was clean.' Seating the plumber under a lamp in his consulting room, he found a considerable swelling in the lower part of the septum of the nose near to the tuberculum septum. One application of cocaine and, poof, the vertigo and sweating ceased. His diagnosis was confirmed: the nasal reflex neurosis was born.

No schnozz was safe from Fliess. Soon he got excited about looking up ladies' noses – especially those with dysmenorrhoea (painful menstruation) and those who'd had repeat abortions – and what do you suppose he found? Correct. A swelling of the turbinate bone. And what do you suppose he prescribed? Correct again: nasal applications of cocaine. And then what do you think he found? 'G' (genital) spots! Then he wrote a monograph, *The Revelations Between the Nose and the Female Sex Organs*.

The male ones came next. 'I will only mention a recent case,' he stated, 'in which a typical neurasthenic episode associated with ophthalmic migraine caused by onanistic abuse, the nasal membranes were very much swollen.'

Yes, it strains one's credulity rather, but you'll be glad to hear that Fliess's writings have been consigned to 'the realms of psychopathology'. He had by this time gone bananas, potty, left reality behind. He began to see noses and genitals everywhere and every variety of neurotic symptoms and sexual irregularity he traced to his 'nasal reflex' theory. As for Freud, he bought it all. And paid through the nose? You could say so. His nasal symptoms got worse, which may or may not have been due to a chronic sinus infection, or to smoking; or to . . . ? He suffered from migraines, fainting fits and bowel trouble. Emotionally he was in a mess: he was depressed, he underwent a personality change, his moods swung from extreme exhilaration to profound depression and twilight states of consciousness.

What was the nosogenesis of all that? *Herzinsuffienz*, of course.

83

20 April, 1895
My dear Fliess,
I would like you to be right in thinking that the nose has a large share in it, and
the heart only a small one . . .

Sigmund Freud

He took more cocaine. The heart got worse. The nasal symptoms
got worse. Fliess made him give up smoking which drove him nuts.
He wrote, 'I shall follow your prescription painstakingly [he used the
word *peinlich*; literally 'painfully'] as I did once before when you
expressed an opinion on the subject (while we were waiting at the
railway station). A severe [scratched out] acute cold has not made
things any worse.' He kept taking cocaine for his headaches. The
Herzinsuffienz got more acute. Fliess eventually diagnosed 'nervous
cardialgia' of the nose.

Yes, Donna was right. Freud was a junkie.

But this was only the beginning. The plot thickens (so does the
mucus in my nose). You sneeze? I suppose you know about the
correlation between the sneeze and the orgasm? Now I will tell you
about a Freudian plot to transplant emotions.

The seat of the emotions, Freud claimed, is not in the heart but in
the nose. (Dr Freud's Nasal Emporium: Ladies right up and have
those emotions aborted while they're still in the foetal stage!).
Actually, I think there's something to be said for a humane resettle-
ment policy. All that emotional broo-ha-ha in there does the heart no
good at all, causes quite a lot of expensive damage. All right, so he
went a bit over the top, had rather strange visions of noses and
genitals; but that's no reason to throw the baby out with the Oedipal
bathwater. Are these not after all, as Jones tells us, the harmless
peccadillos of a man of genius? You think not? You think it's all quite
sinister: a first-class snorter employing the formidable nasal route and
doing so regularly; and not only a junkie but a pusher too? Beware,
twentieth century, you have been *fliessed* again!

I don't know. A few grains of morphine – the doctors don't see
why not. It's called pain control. My cold has worsened. Had to
phone Ruth and tell her not to bother coming this morning. Come
the weekend, with any luck – if it doesn't rampage into pneumonia or
worse – I'll go home. No, of course I'm not smoking. How could I?
I'm not doing *anything*, that's the problem.

Freud's smoking problem was another story. He wriggled, he

84

became ambivalent, he swore to Fliess he felt better *in spite* of his intensive smoking. In the end, he gave up giving up. 'I'm not obeying your smoking prohibitions; do you really consider it such a great boon to live a great many years in misery?' In other words, is it worth it? Is it? How the hell should I know? Smoking is the least of a long list of 'thou shalt nots'. To tell you the truth, I haven't even felt like it. The pain I presume is finite, but even that may be no bad thing. Freud found it quite stimulating: in the sense of invigorating, like a cold shower. Listen to this: 'One evening last week I was hard at work, tormented with just that amount of pain that seems to be the best state to make my brain function . . . and I had a clear vision of . . .'

Of what do you think?

Noses? Right you are!

No, I am not dreaming. I rarely dream, or if I do I don't remember them. Dr Freud, on the other hand, dreamt quite a bit and had perfect recall. He dreams of women; women and doctors; women who get sick; who have the nerve to die. In one of his more fabulous dreams he sees his patient Irma who develops more and more symptoms including a vagina growing in her mouth. He sees 'some remarkable curly structures which were evidently modelled on the turbinal bones of the nose'.

A whole parade of patients began to haunt him, patients he killed (by cocaine overdose), maimed or failed to cure. He sees himself (or his Doppelgänger) in his dreams, and that guilt-ridden double worries. He worries about the drugs he's prescribing. Even more he worries about the effects of psychoanalysis. What if it's all a big mistake? What if it doesn't work? What if?

And his answer? He reassures himself (and the world) that what he is up to is not therapy but science; and that his intention is 'to govern, to educate, and to psychoanalyse'. He does not pretend to have the means at his disposal to change the world, he merely offers a *dose of reality* (snort snort), calling it 'the transformation of hysterical misery into common unhappiness'.

Which means that once you stop being a nut you can see the stark brutality of your life. What he offered was awareness not happiness.

A few other things besides my nose are troubling me.

When one lies around alone as much as I do, one is inevitably subject to fantasies. I'll tell you mine. One is that the pregnant counsellor is going to name her child after me. Actually, she said if

85

it's a boy she's going to call him Alexander and I said, what about his middle name? She hadn't thought about that so I said, how about Alexander Valentine. She liked that. Well, everyone wishes for immortality. And then, as I was thinking along that vein, I began to imagine a grandchild also with my name and my nose. There I am whispering quiet, important things softly into his head from somewhere, wherever I am, and I say to him things like read books and don't worry about material things and forget about possessions and go ahead and risk yourself and love with all your heart.

It must be the drugs.

Five

—Hi, what are you reading?

Ruth. Late.

—You're late. Freud's letters . . . heart trouble . . . birds of a feather and so on.

—What's this?

—A book Claire brought me on Victorian marriages. Classic studies in female repression.

—I brought you some magazines and videos. Give yourself a break.

—I can't.

—How are you, Val?

—Terrific.

—You've developed an infection, they told me. Some sterile atmosphere. I think you'd be better off at home. What do you think?

—I don't.

—What are you on? You sound drugged to the eyeballs.

—Oral antibiotics, a few other things. Nothing wrong with my eyeballs.

—I'll talk to the doctor.

—I shouldn't bother if I were you.

—Don't you want to go home?

—Of course.

—Are you comfortable?

—Like a pasha.

—You know what I mean – reasonably comfortable.

— The bed is solid concrete.

—I brought you a rubber ring and this special orthopaedic pillow. How's the rear end?

—Sore.

—Turn over, I'll massage it.

—That's nice.

—The skin isn't deteriorated.

—High up, the sacrum.

—How are your bowels?

87

—I'm constipated, does that please you?

—Here, organic figs from the health food store. Did Claire upset you, or what?

—No, I upset her. We talked about the donor business.

—What donor business?

—I'd rather not get into it again.

—Anyway, it's not what you need to think about.

—What do I need to think about, Ruth, tell me.

—Val, I'm going.

—No, wait, I'm sorry.

—It's your heart, not hers.

—It was hers.

—Well, she blew it, didn't she. It's not your fault she killed herself on a stupid motorcycle.

—Quite right, very sensible.

—If you go on being snide, I really am leaving.

—Tell me why she should have been killed and I should be here having my back rubbed.

—Listen, that girl didn't die because of you or for you or anything at all to do with you. I'll wring Claire's neck when I see her.

—This has nothing to do with Claire.

—Oh sure.

Val, she died because she was riding around on one of those death buggies and after the fact you happened to benefit. If you hadn't been given the heart, either somebody else would have gotten it or it would have been buried and rotted away with the rest of the body.

—Oh wonderful, I love it. Ruth, you are a treasure. Lo and behold, it is not only morally defensible but ecologically sound, the right-on thing to do, like recycling bottles and cans. My wife, how is it you can turn anything into good behaviour.

If you feel bad about the girl, why don't you do something practical like offer a scholarship in her name (The Harley Davidson Prize, Ruth?) or make a donation to the Heart Fund. What do you think?

—That's a very useful suggestion.

—You don't like it.

—I think you don't really understand what's going on, Ruth.

—Val, you may just have had major surgery, but you're a turd.

—Funny you should say that. As a matter of fact, I have started a bowel diary in which I wax creative on the quality of my turds, or bemoan their absence. This morning I wrote – here I'll read it to you – *1 a.m.: I strained my heart with bearing down and nothing came. Disappointment overwhelmed me. I was close to tears.* Don't you think that's poetic?

—I think it's pathetic.

—You mean bathetic.

—Don't tell me what I mean, Val, please.

—Wait, just listen to this. *A small but definite success; light brown, a touch of yellow, a floater!* Really, it could be a poem – *Ode to a Turd Recollected in Tranquillity.* I mean, so simple and yet so essential; a subject you Americans scrupulously avoid, and why, when it is basic and at the same time universally symbolic?

—Fine, go sell it to a publisher. What's the matter?

—I need to cough.

—Go ahead, I'll hold your ribs.

—It hurts like hell.

—Okay?

—Thank you.

—Val, I cut out this quote by Virginia Satir. She says, 'We do not cope the same way when we're riding the bottom of the wave as when we're riding the top of the wave.'

—What's this, back to the womb on a surfboard?

—Val, I'm trying to help. All it says is, just because you're in a rough place right now and not feeling on top of things doesn't mean you aren't coping.

—Who says I'm not coping?

—Well, I wish you would stop working out on me.

She picks up the book on Victorian Marriages Claire brought me.

—How is it?

—Quite interesting.

—Is that so?

She isn't listening.

—One of the chapters is about John Stuart Mill. He's the Englishman who wrote about liberty – and equality between the sexes.

—I thought it was about marriages?

—Yes, well, this was a 'liaison'.

Now she's listening.

—He and Harriet Taylor had what they called an 'anti-sensualist union': sex-free.

89

—What did they do?

—Do? They talked about not having sex: passionately, sensually, orgasmically on Harriet's side, and on Mill's logically, coolly, with relief. I find the lust against lust rather fascinating, the prohibition itself a kind of higher romance spinning off from ordinary life.

—You would. I'm going to the bathroom. Be right back.

Would I call ours a Victorian marriage?

If you mean sexless, no. But if you mean passionate, also no. That's how it is in these long-term sentences. You achieve, if you're lucky, a companionable sort of mating. Ruth, for example, likes it when we hardly move, presses me in the small of the back to slow me down; sometimes we stop completely to give her time to relax and feel me inside, and for me to wind down. Of course it varies; over the years we've developed a wide repertoire from cuddling to coitus that has stood us in good stead through parenting and sickness and busyness and boredom. There have been fallow periods too. When I was distracted by other women her body knew it and she kept well over on her side of the bed (the joys of a king-size bed), steaming quietly to herself. When my heart was 'returned to its senses' (nothing to do with me), I'd gather her back in the thrum's fold where she'd snuggle with some relief.

And now? *The transplant recipient should be made to understand that full sexual intercourse is equivalent to the climbing of two flights of stairs.* To hell with the joys of companionate sex. I want to leap whole staircases in a single bound.

Need, commitment, devotion, safety, security: these are the tepid words I keep using in relation to Ruth. Whereas that other word hangs in the atmosphere like hospital disinfectant disguised as air freshener. The word gets up my nose. It is of course in a very confused state. This is unfortunate. So am I. Of course I love her.

We met at the Medical Center in San Francisco. I was doing psychiatry, she health education. She was sitting on the floor at a student party gazing up at the most effete bag of bones in California. I cracked my knuckles and willed her to gaze at me like that – for hours, years on end. I'd never get tired of it. So what if she got a crick in the neck? She walked straight past me on the way to get him a cheese and anchovy canapé.

Eventually she flowed in my direction, like a drop of exhausted venous blood back to the heart. We drove out to the gold country. We were eloquent, we wrapped our limbs around one another on the forest floor, surrounded by pine needles and red earth. Her heart relaxed for both of us, mine contracted and excited her. She said, I love you; I said, I want you, and other such unoriginal variations on the theme of infantile need. The body, after all, is urgent at that age. Dear life, dear love, transfuse my cold heart with your warm American blood.

She did. It was as simple as that, getting Ruth. I knew I would. She couldn't help loving and I couldn't help absorbing. I lapped it up; I was safe, cared for. I'd won. She would never reject me. My heart became effulgent with love. It triumphed. We were married in the Town Hall. We have stayed married.

Now Ruth's trying to be nursely and understanding but at the same time resenting me for it; and somewhere along the line we are failing to meet in the middle. Par for the course? Well that may be, but here is where it gets tricky; where the fault line under our feet threatens to divide; when in the changing of a heart a crater opens up and you fall in.

Forgive me, I'm being apocalyptic and unfair not to mention ungenerous. Ignore me, it's the sedative, it has a depressive effect. I feel like I'm on an emotional roller-coaster – have you ever been on a roller coaster? I have: the centripetal force whipped the spectacles clear off my nose. I walked around blind for a day. Now I'd be invulnerable – contacts, you see.

Ruth. Now there is a woman who has so much love and generosity of spirit in her she can ride out the rough patches. Hold onto your specs, dear! Did I say love? Of course there are times I think it's merely an overdeveloped sense of responsibility, or fear, or worse still lack of imagination. Rectitude or *gaucherie*, bravery or sheer-shitting terror? What language . . . *The medical man must always express himself with dignity.* Is it any wonder I fled from all that? Ruth and I stay together for the same reason we have always stayed together, because . . . Do you want the whole run-down on separation anxiety or shall I tell you more about *scotoma*? Or about the patient of mine who suddenly left in the middle of analysis; or how I used to wake up in the night with panic attacks not unlike my mother's; or . . .

—Val, you okay?

Ruth.

—Ah, you're back, that's good. Stay with me.

—I have to go to work. But listen, good news, they're letting you go home.

91

—When?
—Wednesday. Two more days. Hang in there.

You see how she copes with all this? Indulges my angst and ingratitude with equal equanimity? Threats, schemes, so-called boyish enthusiasms that would have driven other women off the deep end long ago? There's an old Greek word for the kind of affection that develops between married people: *storge*. Sounds stodgy? Hmm, well. It's about being bonded and intimate; about commitment and caring and settling down. Building a nest and nuzzling down in it with your feathers and featherling(s). Unromantic, inelegant, plodding yet *real*. (Remember that word?) It's about trusting and taking each other for granted, finding each other unexciting but basically likeable. It's about security and dependency and inadequacy and fear. It's about sharing bathtubs and books, about squabbling over who fixes the dinner, about staring at each other over it with nothing to say. Holding hands, holding on in the dark. After a while you don't question it; after a transplant you do.

Ruth knows I'm being ornery because I'm ill. It rolls off her like water off a seal.

Why do I go salivating after the forbidden? I told you how easy it is to lose your tastebuds in a place like this: it gets so you long for something sharper, more intense. Go suck a lemon? Touché. The fact is that I am indifferent to food, exempt from sex and brain-weary. Is it any wonder I turn my attention to chimaerical things? Yes, guilt and love, they get mixed up, didn't you know?

I don't think people know how to cope with the extraordinary (that's why they dream – and come to me). Ruth deals with the whole transplant business as she does with everything else – efficiently, matter-of-factly – whereas I'm going through a major seismic disturbance here. Look what happened with Claire. Nothing definable – she was here no more than half an hour, but at the end of it she was on her knees and I was . . . By re-defining the word 'take' she caused a small ruction in my chest. Take heart? She left and Ruth arrived, and in the changing of visitors the world tilted.

Haven't you got enough on your plate? Ruth said, as she handed me grapes, juicy red grapes. They reminded me of bursting organs. Forgive me.

92

She's gone. Donna is gone. My donor is dead. Forgive me, I'm very tired. I can't keep my eyes open.

We're driving along the coast somewhere down near Big Sur where the road is bendy and the cliff drops down into the Pacific. Ruth touches my arm and says to slow down, there's an accident up ahead. I stop and get out. It's winter, night, foggy. What's going on here? I ask. Motorcycle ran off the road. Bad news? Yup. somebody has retrieved the body, a dripping, bloody mess. I kneel beside it. I'm a doctor, I say. Somebody giggles. A woman appears out of the fog, kneels on the other side of the body and unzips its − her − leather jacket, pulls out the heart, puts it to her ear and, satisfied it still ticks, hands it to me. Here, this is for you, she says, take care of it. And she walks down what's now a hospital corridor. I run after her − wait, why me? She turns, points to my chest and says, You'll be needing it. When I look down there's a neat cookie-cutter type hole, heart shaped. Oh, I say. It seems funny and shameful at the same time so I cover it with the heel of my hand. Truthfully I'm afraid to look inside. But I also have the problem of the heart, which I'm still holding in my hand. It feels like one of those hard rubber doggie toys, warm and slobbery as if it's just come out of the dog's mouth. It's still beating. Better do something quick. But what? Suddenly I remember a pegboard game I had as a child: square peg into square hole, round peg into round hole . . . *plop*, it fits! Now how to prevent it from falling out?

I'm running. Run run run back to our house where I start turning out drawers looking for a needle and thread. Ruth! Ruth! She appears, looks annoyed, says it's late, what am I doing at this hour of the night sewing? I point to my problem. She ignores the jagged business therein, orders me to button up and brings my robe, makes me a mug of cocoa, lights a fire in the fireplace. But I'm shivering something terrible. I know what I know. Pretty soon the fire's blazing, but my teeth are chattering away cartoon fashion. Suddenly I see our house for what it is: a four-chambered organ with an auricle and a ventricle to the north and to the south; an organ that, unable to contain itself, has flung out projections onto the hill; that bubbles and hisses with its own circulating warmth. Nevertheless I'm getting colder by the tick.

Hearths, says Ruth, don't necessarily make warmth.

But, says William Harvey, hearts do.

Six

The polite Englishman rises at my bedside, in so far as his gouty legs will allow, and puts hand to breast – *Cor a currendo . . . ut centrum in circulo . . . principalissima pars* – and bows.

—Your devoted servant, Dr. William Harvey.

What does one say? Not *the* Dr Harvey, the immortal William Harvey? *De motu cordis,* etc.? And he replies with another, shallower bow:

—As you see.

—Please, I say, indicating one of the orange plastic visitors' chairs, sit.

Indeed, what I see before me, or think I see, perching rather as if he didn't quite believe in the chair's reality, is a skeletal character in a black robe-like garment trimmed with mangy fur and splattered here and there with traces of – good heavens – dried blood. From an absurdly receded hairline a few lank grey hairs, that could do with a good washing, hang to his shoulders. The goatee is rather goaty. The skin is pulled tight, the eyes are too close together, the eyebrows are raised, and an expression midway between a sneer and a flinch graces a virtually lipless mouth. Altogether none too fresh, but what can you expect? The immortal may be privileged, or cursed, depending on your point of view, to hang around forever, but not necessarily in good hygienic order.

—Dr Harvey, I say, this is indeed a surprise, an honour, a –

—I beg your pardon, he replies, reaching into a cupboard, but would you mind if I employed this receptacle? The heat is rather crucifying, the gout you see . . .

And with that he fills a plastic bucket with water from my sink, rolls down his stockings and plunges in his feet.

—Of course, go right ahead. I read in Aubrey that you were troubled with gout. Nasty business.

—Aubrey, my biographer? That curious, credulous and unmethodical scandal-monger; yet withal harmless and entertaining – we used to sit in the dark for hours on end telling of our patients. Yes, one must keep cool. But you were saying?

I was saying . . . what? Thinking what? That his seventeenth century feet are oh-so-pale? (A circulation problem, Dr Harvey?) But while I am fixated on his feet, he is glued to the heart monitor as if it were *Dallas*.

—Pardon me, but might you inform me as to the purpose of this contraption mounted precariously above your head like the eye of God gone wild with imaginings?

—Oh that, that's a heart monitor. It's basically an electrical picture of the heart, very stylised of course, shows the state of the muscle. That first blip is the P wave – that's the atrial signal – and the next bunch make up the QRS – that's the ventricular complex. Now it's going wild because it's picking up my voice. It's monitoring the implanted heart.

—If you please . . .

He lifts his feet from the bucket, inspects them one at a time, wiggles his toes and, plunging back in, sighs deeply.

—Forgive me, Dr Frear – 'tis Dr Frear? – but did you say 'implanted'? He has the look of a man daring another man to run him through in front of his wife and daughter.

—Yes, it's quite simple really. Mine, being irretrievably muscle damaged, was surgically removed and a donor heart put in its place. The donor is matched by blood and tissue group and must weigh within twenty per cent of –

He has risen up on his little legs, causing the bucket to overflow.

—Please, Dr Harvey, do sit down, you're creating a flood.

—Fludd! Where? Just the fellow . . . friend of Thornborough's . . . *Medicina catholica* . . . Fludd – Robertus de Fluctibus, a man of Kent like myself. Is he here too?

—No, I meant a flood of water.

—Ah yes, the living water . . . *sanguis itaque est spiritus* . . . the river of life flows round and round. Fludd my defender. 'Why not, you cynics,' he cried. And albeit one of the Rosy Cross and a curer by the powder of sympathy the man is not withal of ill repute but a seeker after a medicine combined with a mystical theology; and let me further add that though 'twas to gain power over the elemental spirit it was not, like Faustus, to gain riches and sensual pleasures –

—Dr Harvey, I'm sorry to interrupt you but I meant *flood* not this Fludd character. The water, your feet . . .

—Oh dear, you must forgive me, this is all rather unsettling . . .

95

The heat and so on . . . Machines for measuring pulsation, the transmutation of hearts –

—Trans*plantation.*

—I fear I am being toyed with; how may I comprehend such things?

No answer springs to mind.

—Tell me . . . (he reads the name tag on my bed) Dr Valentine Frear . . . Curious name – I take it you are a physician?

—Well, not exactly. I trained in medicine – at Cambridge as a matter of fact. Gonville and Caius – they have combined since your time.

—I see. And what specialism, sir?

—First I did psychiatry – mental illness, neurological and personality disorders, and so on – and after that –

—Ah Frear, do my ears deceive me, has human behaviour become a field of medical speculation?

—The psychosomatic interface interests us greatly, though our approach is different from the medics. Dr Harvey, I am a psychoanalyst.

—A good barber does not make a good philosopher.

—Look here, I am *not* a barber. As a matter of fact, there are some who would say that we psychoanalysts are the élite of our profession, except that we cannot be doing with élitism. No, think of it as a sort of philosophy; or at least a system of enquiry; a kind of narrative; a discourse . . . It is, like Christianity, based on a founded system of beliefs and practices; that is to say, neither the identity nor the existence of its founder is in doubt: Sigmund Freud.

—A Jew?

—Yes, as it happens. I mean yes, he was a Jew.

—Dr Frear – he waves a foot – I am not a religious man.

—Nor I, Dr Harvey. This is not a religion, though there are many, including my wife, who occasionally bring this accusation to bear.

—A demonstrable science then?

—Well, not exactly. A theory perhaps, though my daughter would deny its relevance to the social order. It's based on Freud's self-analysis which confirmed certain findings about, uh, resistance and the nature of sexuality, and of course the unconscious.

—I beg your pardon?

—Dr Harvey, imagine the mind divided in two between the

96

conscious and the unconscious. The former you will understand. The latter consists of impulses, thoughts and feelings which are basically unacceptable to the conscious part. This is of course a highly simplified model; in fact Freud came to realise that it was inadequate – that the term 'unconscious' was better used as a descriptive adjective rather than as a topographical noun. However, it will do for now.

—Excuse me, but – I am a simple anatomist – may I enquire what you *do*, sir?

—Yes, well, briefly: psychoanalysis can be described as a technique in which a person, the analyst, encourages the patient or 'analysand' to free-associate; that is to speak out anything which comes into his or her mind. The analyst then guides with the occasional question and certain encouraging noises, and later on, there are interpretations. The assumption is that this will in due course lead to the uncovering of the unconscious or repressed mental contents, which could not have been elicited by any more direct approach; and that their extraction and recognition by the patient will have significant and beneficial therapeutic consequences. In other words, Dr Harvey, a sort of excavation of the mind – or heart if you prefer. Think of Plato's cave.

—It is indeed so that Nature is wont to show her innermost secrets away from the beaten track. But – forgive me, I am no philosopher – was it not in Plato's cave (he blinks as if he has just entered it) that man was imprisoned, mistaking the shadows on the wall for reality?

—Exactly. Now think of it as Plato up-ended, or the cave turned inside-out: the internal truth – if you like, the secrets of the heart – revealed.

—Sir! (He glares.) 'Twas I who at length, after great diligence and having frequent recourse to vivisections and the collation of numerous observations, revealed the motion and use of the heart. In short, 'tis in nowise a cave, sir.

The eyes are dilated. A touch of claustrophobia, Doctor? An instinctive recoil from the darkness within?

—I know, I say, that physiologically speaking it's a pump. As my wife and others around here keep reminding me. I guess we owe you.

—I myself prefer, he says, the term *Sipho* as it may be applied to the pumping device of a fire engine. One such engine which made use of the *Sackpumpen* was well known in London in my time. Warner was particularly interested in the heart as a hydraulic mechanism.

97

—Dr Harvey, in that case, you ought to be able to understand the idea of transplantation

He returns to his foot-and monitor-watching routine. He does not look happy. I see in the face of the father of modern medicine a lost boy:

—Is it truly so? Has it come to pass that a heart of another has taken root in you? My mind, you see, is greatly troubled by this: surely it is not possible?

—Not only possible, Dr Harvey, but routine. They do several each week in this hospital alone, it's one of the largest centres in America. If you don't believe me, you can go up to the top floor and have a look for yourself. I heard the chopper land not too long ago – they bring the donor heart by helicopter or jet, you understand, land right up there on the roof. Barnard in South Africa, about thirty years ago, first broke ground . . . Dr Harvey?

—*Quid illud et qua re* . . . Putting hand to heart (to protect it from being broken into?) he agitates the water with his feet: Dr Harvey as pedallo driver. He is going nowhere in a hurry. We seem to be chasing each other in a circle, both breathless.

—Dr Harvey, surely you must appreciate what transplants can mean for the future of humanity: the culmination, as a matter of fact, of your achievements. You should be proud. I don't see why you're getting so worked up –

—*Shit-breeches!* My achievements, how dare you? he cries, over-turning the bucket and drawing a small but peculiarly sinister-looking dissecting knife.

—Dr Harvey – good heavens, calm yourself – (So this is the famous Harvey temper.)

—The heart, he cries, transposed, sewn into the body of another? Do I believe my ears? I do not.

Why the little hypocrite.

—Dr Harvey, please sit down. I mean, if you want to be anal about it – this is ass-backwards. You were the anatomist, the great dissector, the cold-blooded Aristotelian observer, correct? You were the one who gave it press as a pump.

—You have an unfortunate way of expressing yourself, Frear. I observed, dissected and described the heart. Yea, I exposed the naked plain truth to its very source – but never let it be said that I went thus against nature.

—Nature? Who's talking about nature, Dr Harvey? Listen, if it's

98

a pump, a fire engine complete with 'water bellows' and 'clacks' and so on – with all due respect, I don't see how you can burble on about nature. You prepared the ground, you made it possible. If it's a machine, it stands to reason that it can be replaced. This is the logical conclusion of your work.

—Reason, sir, logic? He stares at the monitor but sees only the Devil's script.

—The heart . . . The heart is married to one body and one body only and that body reigns supreme and there is no question of divorce betwixt them. Do I make myself clear, Frear? 'Tis a connection given and sustained by all things natural according to the principle of final causes. Furthermore, that the heart of one person should be put into another; this operation of which you speak unless it be a fable can only be the invention of madmen. You have created a false idol, a fantasy; fabricated a shadow and a chimaera; a monstrosity . . . It is a crime against Nature, Frear, and there is no higher or greater authority than Nature. Socrates would have poisoned himself sooner; Aristotle . . . Sir, I am not a little disturbed to find that you have impeached and derogated Nature to the role of a discarded mistress. This must not be so. Nature, by the principle of motion and rest in all things; the prime efficient cause of all generation; under whose aegis light things rise and heavy things descend; the spider weaves her web, the birds build their nests, incubate their eggs, and cherish their young; the bees and ants construct dwellings and lay up stores; yea, the very hearts beat in our bodies – to the feet of the Mistress of all this we must bow down and worship. In short, the sun is not to be snipped from the heavens, sir.

—Dr Harvey . . .

How can I break it to him? That not only do we transplant *human* organs but that we use animals' – pig, sheep, baboon – as well as *women's* hearts. No, it can't be done, not yet. Our boy needs handling.

—Dr Harvey, you must try to understand that the heart, in fact the body itself, is to us a more – how shall I put it? – a matter of fact thing. The heart in particular is a piece of equipment that works or doesn't work. If it breaks down we bypass it, or if necessary, as in my case, replace it all together. In a sense – since you are so keen on nature – think of it as a *naturalising* process. I mean, you talk about Nature with a capital 'N' whereas we do not. Call it the *embourgeoisement*, if you like, of nature. (Yes, Plato would have a fit but then he's had rather a bad press lately.) You happen to have re-emerged in an age that is plugged, perhaps unfortunately, into chaos, unpredictability, *Civilisation and its Discontents.* Perfection? We have virtually ceased to worship except perhaps our own inventions. (And perhaps the devil: a squatter in that cave whom we find remarkably difficult to evict.) But the other God and his verities elude us. I mean, once you discover you can manipulate nature to the extent that we have, then the pulling of the forelock becomes, well, we just don't do it. I daresay Sigmund Freud has a lot to answer for. Dr Harvey, are you alright?

He stares ahead, unseeing, slightly cross-eyed.

—There is only one way, he says, to attain to the perspicuous truth and that is through anatomical inquiry with one's proper eyes. We are in grave danger if we believe only what we are told whilst the book of Nature lies so open. *Cum tamen apertus facilisque Naturae liber sit.*

—Are you saying, Dr Harvey, that you don't believe me? (Stubborn bugger.) You want evidence? Fine, have a look at this then (I open my pyjama top to reveal a fine ridged scar and its surrounding mottled purple landscape.) Does that convince you?

He is like Dracula before a crucifix. Can it be that bad? Evidently, for if he was mad before, now he is pitiful. I button away the distressing evidence.

—Dr Harvey, don't get me wrong, the heart is not without spiritual and symbolic significance for us, but we also have this spare-part view of it as well. The two coexist quite comfortably with us – Dr Harvey?

—So this is where all my efforts have led? (Sub voce.)

—I wouldn't be here talking to you if not for the transplant – have you considered that?

—I address myself to the general and not the particular.

—I can understand your reservations, of course I can. And you're right to be sceptical. These things can be dangerous, the modern surgical elixir may be getting out of hand. Where, for example, are we going to get all these healthy hearts? Who is going to safeguard them, their donors, their recipients? Can death be defined? To whom does the body of a deceased person belong? We're not unaware of these things. And yet it is progress, I think you'll agree.

—Progress?

He looks quite lost, standing there on his wet feet, out of all time and place: the great man of heart and blood who thought he knew it all now wet between the toes and reduced to a Latin gibber.

—*Cui bono, cui bono?* Why? Why do they do it? What is the good of it all? Tell me, Frear?

What comfort have I to offer him? None.

—I'm sorry, but you have seen the evidence for yourself. Things have changed: you call it monstrous, we call it a miracle. Now it is we who perfect nature.

God the transplant surgeon and his assistant the psychoanalyst, the re-fashioners of nature. We do a brisk trade. Welcome, Dr Harvey, to the twentieth century.

Seven

Wednesday February 14th: St Valentine's Day. Release day.

Greetings from Valentine in *Herzland*.

11.30 a.m. Packed and waiting to go. Packed and ready to go *for the last three hours*. Ruth and Claire were due at 10.00; apparently there has been some delay.

The hospital waiting room: the place where the well hang out awaiting the sick, and where the sick hang out awaiting the coming of the well. Which is what I am doing. I don't like waiting any more than I like saying goodbye.

The hospital gift-shop – where I went to waste some time – was overflowing, not surprisingly, with Valentine cards: O hearts! O Valentines! Valentines for wives, husbands, mothers, daughters, grand-daughters, fathers, brothers, special friends. Bloodshot hearts and rainbow hearts; dancing, singing, flying hearts; poetic, jokey, crude hearts; biblical and literary; pop-out and pop-up; ballooned, dripping and entwined; hearts bulging out of bodies, hearts on springs, hearts with wings. Pizza hearts, chocolate hearts, cheesecake hearts. Hearts served up on doilies.

Is there no end to the entertainment value of hearts? Evidently not.

Trekked back up feeling rather sick to my stomach and dizzy from a combination of exertion and an overdose of cardiac cliches:

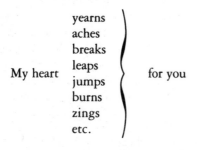

For whom? None of your business.

Looking back – diaries are useful that way – I see that it is a month minus two days since the transplant. Do I feel like I've had a change of heart? 'Change of heart' – an interesting expression. It puts me in mind of a neurasthenic cartoon character crawling his way along a hospital corridor gasping, *help me, Doc, help me* . . . , being hauled off by the scruff of the neck to the operating room *(saw, scalpel, drill . . .)* and bouncing out again, light and balloon-like, whistling and gay, with his changed heart in his bosom. However, I am no cartoon character (courtesy of neither Disney nor Hallmark); furthermore, it was a literal transplant that I underwent; and further furthermore, balloons can go *pop*.

The nurses have inundated me with Valentine cards. *A Valentine for Valentine* . . . It is sweet of them, of course. What they don't know is that St Valentine was a third century Christian martyr portrayed in early iconography with a bloody erection, not to mention crucified, whipped and beheaded. I mentioned it to my counsellor. An interesting transposition, don't you think, I said: from bloody Roman arrows to Cupid's tickly darts? I watched for her reaction. Weird, she said. Perhaps the Christian martyr suits me better than either the love god or the balloon-man. It is raining at the moment here in northern California, not one of those English seaside drips but a torrent: the kind that causes houses to slide down hills. Thus Ruth's delay.

Never mind, my friend the transplant counsellor is here. She bears a prescription for nine different drugs and a nervously parental pep-talk. I understand, I tell her, that without religious adherence to the medicament cocktail the body will go on alert, the heart will be exposed as an immigrant rapscallion and all her cheerleading will have been for nought. She makes a moue. I know you know all this, she says, but you'd be surprised. There are people who say they understand and repeat all my instructions to a T, and then they go home and don't take their pills, plus they smoke and drink and eat steaks and whipped cream. All together? She fails in her earnestness to see that I am teasing her. So I promise to take my pills like a good boy, to lead an orderly, professional life, to not smoke and to lay off the chocolate chip cookies. Already I have lost thirty pounds staying in this gourmet ghetto. My patients will think I've been to a health farm. Don't worry, I add, I'm not going to go squandering it – I'd have to be a mad delinquent to want to ruin two hearts. What else does one say? Thanks for saving my life? I'll miss you, she says. Take care of yourself, I reply, wishing Ruth would turn up to save me from

103

doing something I will regret (like crushing her in my arms, bending an ear to the foetal heart, and so on). My knees, however, remain locked in maidenly embarrassment and my hands rest demurely in my lap, puddled in sweat. A peck to the cheek. The throat lump is considerable.

—Dr Frear – call from the receptionist – we've just had a message from your wife: she's been held up again – the Dumbarton is flooded. She'll be here as soon as she can. She says hang in there.

I'm hanging. The chairs here are upholstered in alternating pink and blue, there's a round card table and magazine rack with copies of *The Economist*, *The New Yorker* and *Encounter*. Next to me is a fish tank. Fish, according to recent medical research, are said to soothe. There is also a coffee machine, a Shoji screen, a sort of stained glass vortex and a clock. The clock ticks slower than my heart; the fish seem infected too. Perhaps they have caught our human apprehension instead of us catching their fishy laid back-ness. Dr Harvey points to a brilliant specimen.

—The fish, he says, has a simple but tenacious inverted heart, with the ventricle above and the auricle, a sort of bladder, below.

—In that case, I say, there is something fishy about me, for my heart is distinctly upside-down too.

He fails to comprehend my metaphorical drift.

—Never mind, I say, have a cup of coffee from the machine. His eyes light up.

—Coffee, Frear?

—Well, it's only instant, I say, tastes like old socks, but you're welcome to try.

Which he does and spits.

—I did warn you, I say.

I am discovering things about him: two, for instance, that have caused him suffering. One, which occurred during his lifetime, was the loss of his notes on insects ('twas the greatest crucifying to me that ever I had in all my life'); the other (running a close second to crucifixion and occurring during his present incarnation) is having been exposed to instant coffee.

There's no getting away from it, our William is a junkie. According to Keynes he was probably the first Englishman to become an addict. Perhaps he'd like to try one of my steroids; or pop a phenothiazine; or a prednisone-cyclosporin cocktail, eh Will? He and his brother Eliab guzzled the stuff (this even before coffee houses were

104

in fashion in London) which was imported by his brothers Thomas and Daniel the Turkey merchants. No wonder he never slept.

Don't you see, my dear Dr Harvey, you were suffering from vaso-dilation. No, no, he's trying to deny it. Yes, yes, caffeine-induced insomnia, it's well known, that's why we drink decaffeinated, it's not bad especially the water-filtered stuff, you should try it. His voice is unsteady with emotion.

—Coffee: *organon salutis*. An instrument to cleanse the stomach. The drink that helpeth the brain and the digestion but above all – he fixes me with a coffee-bean eye (high roast) – comforteth the heart.

—Oh well, in that case . . .

True, he is still a bit addled but he's slowly getting there, his only real complaint as I say being with the coffee. I promise him when we get home there'll be excellent Mocha Java from Peet's. He looks dubious but ever hopeful, wonders if they might not have Sumatra. Certainly, I tell him, anything the old heart desires.

He still tends to waffle on about Nature and about how we need to consult more with sense and instinct than with reason and prudence. He is quite ridiculously contradictory. He speaks of 'weak fools and rickety children, scandals to nature and their country.' 'The Heralds are fools,' he says, *'tota errant via.'* 'A blessing goes with a marriage for love upon a strong impulse.' And a blessing, I think, to be so morally simple-minded, everything clear-cut. But that's what they're like, these medical chaps, and why I never became one of them.

12.00 a.m. Twiddled thumbs. Reviewed Valentine cards for third time this morning. One of them, unsigned, reads, YOU'LL ALWAYS HAVE A PIECE OF MY HEART. Left or right ventricle? A sliver of slippery septum? Rather bad taste in the circumstances. Unless it's from Donna, knowing nothing about the transplant.

By the way, you will be surprised to learn – Valentine's Day being a hetero-patriachal/capitalist invention – that even Claire has sent me a Valentine card. Not that it is without sting. *They were bolde, her herte they tooke.* But lest you think her cruel, she has added at the bottom: *I'm sorry. I love you anyway. Claire.* Which tells you a great deal about her, about us.

The card from my wife? It says, I LOVE YOU STILL on the outside, and on the inside: I LOVE YOU WHEN YOU MOVE AROUND TOO. Typical optimism, vote of confidence in life, movement, the future. Ra ra Ruth. Why am I so unappreciative? I'm not. I think she's

105

wonderful but what happens if I *can't* move around? Or stop moving. If I wobble? Will she run along beside me, holding me from behind?

—Dr Frear, your wife and daughter are here.

—There you go, Valentine, you're a free man.

All I have to do is open the door and go. Or as Dr Harvey puts it:

—*Solvitur ambulando*.

Eight

The body is on its way home. I say 'body' for that is the sum of what I am: embodied, lumpen like a policeman except that it's not the feet that are the melancholy bit of my anatomy. Does the heart, doctor, have feet? Is that the sound I hear, *pitter-pat-paddle-pat,* the toddler-in-my-bosom trying to make a quick getaway? Dr Harvey blinks. The sun is too bright for him, he's sweaty inside his ancient ruff, dopey from the heat.

Ruth drives, Claire sits next to her while I sit in the back with Dr Harvey and all my gear. Our dog Willy takes his usual place in the rear – it's a station wagon – from whence he licks my face. Apparently, he is glad to see me, has missed me.

I can feel it happening all the way home, the gradual deflation like a slow leak. Mount Tam looms up out of its low-lying mist like in an Oriental print, the Bay Bridge is a bunch of tracery against the elusive-vague, water-foggy landscape. It reminds me of some badly remembered lesson.

Ruth's head turns a few degrees in my direction as she changes lanes. I see the compression of her lips. I feel I want to study that face some more, treat it as a foreign country, make discoveries in it. So I reach out and touch her shoulder; she pats my hand and puts it away. Not now, Val (there there, do not distract). That American peanut butter matter-of-factness clots my mouth and respiratory passages until I can hardly breathe.

The Koreans, I gather, are masters of melancholia. They have eighty words for rain, a hundred for getting dark. The vespertine of the heart; dusk. Americans are different of course, they take courage up to the last, wax toothy in the face of contrary evidence they call adversity. With my new equipment I could be one of them, a cheerleader in gold and silver spangles; leave England's rubble and bogs behind once and for all. Or did they make some ghastly mistake, a piece of the old heart left in there to rot like a remnant of decayed tooth that will go on nagging and nagging *ad nauseam.* No, I will spit this thing out in due course. Dr Harvey recommends coffee – and patience.

107

—The traction and propulsion of the muscles, he says, will improve I warrant. Do not despair, sir.

—Thank you, doctor, but the fact is – we've arrived at the house – I can't get out of the car.

I try heaving myself up by my arms but they're too weak to propel me; try a rocking motion but that doesn't work either. Why did I buy a Volvo with a Freudian back seat that sucks like a womb? I need a rest.

—Don't panic, Val, says Ruth, it'll come.

In fact, it's Claire's muscles that eventually get me out of my hole. But I'm wobbly. It seems a long way from car to house. Neighbours and friends have gathered round to welcome me, to toast my health, my new heart; and whyever should they not – a splendid idea – except that the guest of honour, an embarrassment to everyone but most of all to himself, has to be led inside, as Dr Harvey puts it, 'tripping on the toe', 'apologising as he goes' and 'with the movement of a man in delirium and useless and convulsive and irregular as . . . ' That will do, doctor. I must to my bed.

And now I think perhaps he's right after all, that nature had not meant a girl's heart to drive a man's body. However, he assures me locomotion will return. 'Animals,' he points out, 'at first do walk delicately and practise the discipline of local movement just as a man who is learning to play upon the lute is always guarding mistakes; their gait is vacillating. Your heart, once it learns to accompany the blood with the proper continuo will cause the limbs to respond with a more determined beat. Do not give up.'

He has a kind heart.

I have come home, only home no longer signifies.

Give me time.

And now, seeing that we are both somewhat recovered from our exertions and he is in a mellow mood and even beginning to appreciate the possibilities of this transplant business, I judge it time to break the news to him.

—Dr Harvey, you do realise it was a *woman's* heart, a young girl's?

Silence. He looks as if someone had siphoned off the blood and filled his vessels with water, then plonked him in an electric chair. His eyeballs pop, his hair stands out from his head, even the fur on his collar looks like porcupine quills. He stares at me through perfectly centred eyeballs and then, like a statue come to life, he steps forward and the normally well-regulated seventeenth century voice booms out,

—Guard your hearts, men!

—I'm afraid it's a bit late for that, Dr Harvey, it's gone forever.

He calls it a monstrosity.

—A monstrosity?

—*Praeter naturam*, a crime, a contamination . . . *furor uterinus* . . . an abomination, the perfection of man infected with the germ of woman's imperfection, an outrage, a . . . Oh, what is to become of you, Frear? Effeminate males, virago females, these are the natural intermediaries between the perfection of man and the imperfection of woman; oh but the hermaphrodite, the androgyne, these are of the category *monster*. A woman changing into a man perhaps – this is what would have been expected, as what is perfect is unlikely to change into that which is less so – Johann Schenck von Grafenberg says so in his *Observationes* – but this . . . this degeneracy is unheard of: a loss . . . *mollities, consilium invalidum et instabile*. It is, in short, sir, a *chimaera*.

A chimaera?

Once again I am tucked up with my dictionary.

Chimaera: *1. Gr. Myth. A she-monster represented as vomiting flames and, usually, as having a lion's head, a goat's body and a serpent's tail. 2. Any such imaginary monster. 3. A frightful, vain, or foolish fancy. 4. Biol. A mixture of tissues of different genetic constitution in the same part of an organism.*

According to this it could be said that:

(1) my heart, being a motley mix of my own genetic materials and my donor's, is a *chimaera*.

(2) Since I have the body of a man and the heart of a girl (the mixture of tissues) – I am myself a *chimaera*.

(3) My donor, whom I imagine as a sort of she-monster with if not exactly a lion's head at least a lion's *mane* and who is also if not a fire-breathing dragon then a fire-*belching* one (the motorcycle) – is also a *chimaera*.

(4) Dr Harvey – with *his* goat's head and wormlike body – might he not also be a *chimaera?*

109

(5) And Donna, once patient, so-called analysand, swallowed up in coastal fog –

My heart is soft, flaccid, exhausted – lying, as it were, at rest. I quote Dr William Harvey.

Ruth is quite different, real and all-of-a-piece. When she comes to bed I reach for her.

—Come here.

—Val, you're not serious . . .

—Don't be daft, I can't move a muscle. Just hold me.

—Can't you sleep?

How can I sleep? My kidneys twinge, my skin itches, I have indigestion. The transplanted heart goes on announcing itself, tweaking the body in myriad clever ways so that hardly any part escapes, not even the toes.

In no time at all she's asleep and I'm on an elbow watching her. I study her with a Harveian eye, this collection of womb, ventricles, veins and sinews, vertebrae, joints, brain, eyeballs, muscle. The human body; the *imperfect female* human body.

Dr Harvey has crept back in. He tells me about how Leonardo sat at the bedside of a hundred-year-old man. Said the old man: I feel no infirmity apart from the weakness of old age. And with that he died. Leonardo, impressed with 'so sweet a death' immediately set to work dissecting him. After that he made drawings of the century-old ligaments.

So, Dr Harvey, if I fall asleep and die, will you slice it out and – with the aid of my daughter – draw it and afterwards label the offending bit?

Nine

Naturally everyone wanted to know: how is it with the new heart? I
wasn't inclined to tell them and Ruth, doing her wifely bit, shielded
me. I suppose she kept certain people posted. But now that the initial
touch-and-go period (will he make it?) has turned into ordinary
convalescence (looks like he will); indeed, now that I am mobile and
even beginning to resemble the human again, they gather round,
greedy for information. It gets up my nose. Mostly we refuse their
dinner invitations, but this one's in my honour: a celebration, an
official welcome back to life.

—We can't not go, says Ruth, you know they mean well.
Do I? Some take the ghoulish approach. How was the donor killed?
Details please. Others take the Inspector Clouseau tack. Who was
she? Why did she die? Was it suicide, murder, act of God? Who
donated her heart? These folks think it would be 'neat' to contact the
donor family in order to try to piece together the 'puzzle of the donor
heart'. They would just *love* to know whether she had a husband? A
child? What else did she do besides ride a motorcycle? Oh, aren't you
just *dying* to know? (As a matter of fact . . .) How tantalising,
frustrating! (Actually, I have other things to worry about.)

Understandable? Forgivable? Listen, it hurts, it's boring, and it
gets worse: pornographic, necromantic, soap-operatic – you name it,
they've got it on their minds. No, I say, I am not interested in this
sort of meretricious enterprise (one of Dr Harvey's favourite expressions). Why can't they leave the poor girl alone? Besides, there are
ethical considerations.

So then the hotspot is on *me*. If you won't talk about her then tell us
about you. How can the human body adapt to such an invasion? How
does it *feel?* Isn't it *weird* having someone else's heart, a girl's no less?
Can you lead a normal life? What do you eat? Does it give you bad
dreams?

I tell them the tellable things. I say patients react to surgery in
different ways. At first you feel euphoric. I've done it, you say to
yourself, I'm alive, I've been given a second chance. You thank some
deity or other. I describe the feeling of coming alive again, the release

from pain. But then you think, second chance for what? The life of a mollusc? And so on. That period is already over for me. I'm into the second phase of the reactive process, which is about uncertainty and dread. You start walking again, you eat, you laugh, you make love, tentatively (one staircase at a time – the staircase bit causes quite a lot of mirth), you get a taste of the old life returning in all its complexity. But then you remember and sink. I can't last. Why did I bother? How to enjoy the good times when you know they're limited. You feel your pulse, you hear music coming from a next-door car and you fall back against your headrest and close your eyes in weariness and wonder.

When dessert comes, to the accompaniment of oohs and aahs, it is a pastry in the shape of a heart, about an eighth of an inch thick topped with whipped cream and strawberries. I'm sorry, I say, I'd love to but really I couldn't (I really couldn't) and I lay my hand suggestively on my hankie. Aw, come on, says my hostess, it won't hurt you, and hands me a plateful. A primitive, talismanic thing: eat your heart like a good boy and you'll grow nice and strong.

Do they invite their senile fathers to dinner and serve them brains; their blind great aunts and serve them glazed eyeball? Then why for heaven's sake do they think they can make free with the heart? Nor do we stop at eating them, oh no, we drench them with perfumed oils and hang them up in bathrooms, dangle them on our bosoms, stick them through our earlobes, nostrils and for all I know bellybuttons, silkscreen them onto our mugs, our underwear, our . . . The heart has become cheap currency. I begin to fear that it may in the end find itself on the same endangered species list as with the whale; that we shall soon be driving around with bumper-stickers announcing: SAVE THE HEART.

However, I do not spoil the party. I push the heart around on my plate to show willing and eat the strawberries. I try to deflect their attention away from me, from the transplant. I am dismissive, perhaps coy (Ruth says rude but I deny that). I'm learning, I say bravely, to live with it, but no more holidays planned in advance: the heart, you see, is so unpredictable. I try to talk about rejection but get interrupted. – Oh, God, don't tell me about rejection . . .' Unpredictable? Forget it.

—When my husband left me, we'd planned a holiday in Corsica and then he took the other woman instead.

—Being cheated of a holiday seems to be more painful to you, I say, than the loss of your husband.

The remark does not endear me.

But even after my attempts to discourage, they persist. Over the coffee (NB Dr H: Jamaican Blue Mountain), somebody goes:

—But a *woman's* heart – I can't believe it doesn't feel *different* somehow.

—It doesn't, I say, and lift my cup.

But they are watching me and waiting. So I say,

—The heart is a genderless organ. Although it has been invested down through the ages with a lot of emotional-symbolic baggage, say, as the seat of love and so on, it is physiologically speaking simply a pump.

—More coffee, anyone?

Ten

The middle of the night. I troop down to the kitchen and open yesterday's paper.

Heard about the guy who got given a woman's heart? Imagine, it's hard enough living in the same house – but in the same body? Har har . . .

Ruth has followed me down.
—What are you doing? she asks.
—Look at that. I show her the column.
—Stupid, she says, ignore it.
—Ignore it, how?
—Easy, she says, tightening the cord of her bathrobe.
She dumps milk into a saucepan while I scribble my reply:

Dear Editor,
    That was a cheap shot in this morning's paper. As the (male) recipient of a female donor heart I found it objectionable and silly, an insult to both male recipient and female donor; and another excuse for one of your cheap sexist remarks. Sincerely, (Dr) V. Frear.

I hand the thing to Ruth.
—What do you think?
She says she can't read it.
—Drink some milk and get back to bed – look at your hands.
—What's wrong with my hands?
My hands are shaking. I put them out of the way.
—Anyway, I say, no point in going back to bed. I have to get up and pee every half hour.
—Anxiety, she says.
—Thank you, Dr Frear.
—You're not still worrying about this donor stuff, are you?
—Of course not.
—Val, sweetheart, you have *real* physical things to worry about: your gums, your kidneys, that muscular tic. Don't go spinning off

114

into some blown-up guilt trip – it'll undermine the whole healing process.

—On the contrary, I say, it's quite functional. In fact, you should be pleased – it stops me worrying about my body. It's called sublimation.

—I know what it's called and it doesn't make it any better. But if you're enjoying yourself, go right ahead, don't let me stop you.

She hands me a mug of hot skimmed milk with little red hearts dancing around the outside.

—Do we have to have these things?

—It's just a design, we've had it for years and it never bothered you before.

—Precisely. Ruth . . . never mind.

Sometimes I feel like we're two kids on opposite ends of a see-saw: *up, down, up down* . . . Wait, I say, you don't understand. But she's already being flipped up in the air like a pancake while I'm being bottomed out. Only in bed do we occasionally even up, shoulders and hipbones. But as to that other thing, that *design*: I fear those two will never match up again. *It's bad enough living in the same house* . . .

Maybe this guy has a point after all; Dr Harvey too. These are uneasy (unnatural?) contingencies.

Something is wrong here. Ruth is all squared-up while I am hunkered and dishevelled. I feel as if I have entered some sulphurous cave where the surface of the rock doesn't bear touching and bogeys abound. It causes an ache in the sinuses, a rumble in the chest. Ruth says it's the underfloor heating coming on. I am tired of her explanations. The fact is I am beginning to be more at home in this fetid psychic cave of mine, for it is a place where I have permission for once to be as wild as I like: to address body parts, hold conversations with my own circulatory system, summon historical ghosts and historical patients to my heart's (dis)content, not to mention a defunct donor. The comfort of chimaeras cavorting together. The entertainment of the unspeakable?

They have given me one of their neat little ECG portable cassette machines to attach to my belt with wires taped to my chest. This means I can monitor my heartbeat. Do I want to listen to a heart that has been salvaged out of a pile of twisted up metal-and-bone wreckage? When I listen to this heart it goes *bam bam bam* on my chest wall. Who asked to be saved and transplanted? Ruth says don't

115

be stupid, it sounds fine to her. I say, you don't hear what I hear, which is true.

When she goes I try to read some of Forster's *A Room with a View*, the passage where Mr. Emerson pokes his forefinger against his heart and proclaims to the world, 'Here is where the birds sing, here is where the sky is blue!' Well in here it's vulture and buzzard and swirling black fog country. No *tweet tweets* here, no blue sky! Keep out, sweetheart!

I once had a client with a psychosomatic pain in her heart. When I asked her to describe the 'pain' she said she could feel energy all over her body but not in that spot. A sort of dead spot? I suggested. Sort of, she agreed. How can a dead spot be painful? I countered. She said she felt backed into a corner. That confirmed my suspicions of course. She called me a shit.

My therapeutic sessions are (were) models of form, the analysis based on rational structures. To take an architectural analogy: I liked my house orderly, its corners squared up, its floors level, its foundations firm – like the spikes under our deck which go thirty feet into the ground. And if you think there's sexual symbolism in that, congratulations, you get the Sigmund Freud gold phallus architecture award.

If we measure reality by angles, there is something not quite right going on here. I can no longer say that I am at right angles to the floor because the floor itself has shifted, the assumed terrestrial horizontal has been abolished. As Ruth pads away, William Harvey wanders into my field of vision. What is this thing, this column of light before me, of what colour? Neither white nor grey nor neutral seems to fit it exactly. And its voice? Unlike the human, which rolls out with the promise of breath, blood, cavities and tongue, this emanation is more like what is left after the sawing of bone. It distresses my ECG pick-up.

—*Insetti di letto* it hisses.

—Come again?

—Bedbugs?

—*Bedbugs?*

—I suffered them in Rome too, Frear, I came up in welts.

—Well this isn't Rome, I object, and they are not bedbugs but innocent fleas from the cat.

—Innocent? he barks, scratching his thin shin.

A moody spook. And talk about behaviour disorders! Coffee, port

– he swills along quite nicely and then suddenly does a flip into self-denial, nothing but water for days. And the worst part is he thrives on it, gets a sort of glow about him, starts spouting stuff about the soul being 'luminous and aetherial'. Then it goes and he drags himself around like Jacob Marley on a bad night complaining about his mattress.

—What is it this time, princess? I ask him.

—Sir, I am much troubled with a hot-head, and my thoughts working warmly do keep me from sleeping; my way is to rise out of my bed and walk about in my shirt until I am pretty cool, that is, till I begin to have *a horror* and then return to bed and sleep very comfortably.

He means a chill.

—Would you like a drink of something, William?

—Nothing, Frear.

He stares out at the shadows of the tops of trees below us.

—What is it, William. What's on your mind?

He holds onto my chair and shows me his feet. They are the only bit of him that is not luminously white. In fact, they look as if they've been sunburnt: the veins stand out, the arteries throb alarmingly.

—Sit, William, I say, and lower him into a chair.

I soak a dishtowel in cold water, bend down and apply it to his poor feet.

—Frear, he remonstrates, do not tax yourself.

—It's all right, doctor. Takes my mind off my own feet.

—What ails yours, Frear?

—Oh nothing much, just another side effect of the drugs. Ruth says I've got to concentrate on getting back on my feet. Shall I show them to you?

They're swollen and hairy.

Eleven

According to William Harvey, the female of our species is:

1) psychologically 'softer' *(mollities)*
2) sooner tamed
3) admits more readily to caressing
4) less spirited than men (excepting the bear and leopard)
5) softer in disposition
6) unreliable in judgement as well as ethical and moral considerations
7) more mischievous
8) less simple
9) more impulsive
10) more compassionate (easily moved to tears)
11) more jealous, apt to scold and strike
12) prone to despondency (less hopeful)
13) more false of speech (deceptive)
14) of a more retentive memory
15) more wakeful
16) more shrinking
17) more difficult to rouse to action
18) less needful of nutrition

than the male.
How do I feel about this?

Shrinking
Moved to tears
Wakeful
Despondent
Won't someone caress me?
Not hungry

A provolone cheese is suspended from a beam in our kitchen. A friend brought it back from Italy. The size of a fist, encased in a waxy shell,

118

quatrosected by thick string, it puts me in mind of the heavenly organ. It is weighty and yet one flick sets it twirling in its orbit.

According to the good Dr Harvey these 'feminine' characteristics of mine are due to an oversupply of the cold and cheesy (mucusoid) humours. I am suffering, he concludes, from a case of turbid mucus obstructing the pericardium.

What do I think about that?

(1) I doubt if he'd be admitted to the AMA on the basis of that particular diagnosis.

(2) That he's an old curdbag.

(3) That we are two cheesy-hearts.

A simple walk down the street: call it an advanced shamble. Ruth or Claire goes with me, sometimes both. We progress gravely, increasing by half a house each day. Soon we're doing two houses, three, four; by now we're up to a quarter of a mile. I am inclined to overdo it, forgetting that I must get back. Ruth reminds me. I'm fine, I say, straining to get myself uphill. Last week when I got to the top I collapsed next to a garden gnome whereupon its mistress said, 'shoo!' Ruth left my side to go and explain. The woman gawped, then said, 'Well I'll be,' and vamoosed. Another neighbour asked, 'You okay out there?' Oh sure, I'm just doing a little grass testing, like to get the feel of it between my toes. Actually, I was just winded from the incline. My punishment, according to Claire, for a life of bourgeois luxury in the Berkeley hills. Ruth sat with me, talked me down, held my hand and abdomen while I breathed. Then she ran back and got the car.

Today Claire goes with me. She sizes me up.

—Ready for the Bay to Breakers? she asks.

—Not just today, m'am, Indian Rock Park will do me just fine. It's a few blocks away, uphill. So off we go, Claire doing her wide-boy imitation, holding me by the elbow as if I were some doddering old retainer under her protection. Before I can even open my mouth she says,

—Don't give me any facile 'inverted or diverted maternal instinct' crap.

—I wouldn't dream of it, I say.

119

In fact, I'm busy hanging on.

—So, I ask her, how goes it? What are you reading these days?

—Guess?

—Sigmund Freud?

—You got it.

—Know thy enemy – so you can string him up by the nostrils. *Which* Freud, and why?

—The Dora case. I thought it was about time I read him for myself.

—A lousy choice – his most blatant failure, even by his own reckoning. You're better off starting with *The Psychopathology of Everyday Life.*

—I'm already hooked on this one.

—Oh? You mean you *like* it?

—I didn't say that. But the guy can write.

—That's very generous of you.

—It reads like fiction a lot of the time, which I find pretty weird. It's as if he's turned her – her life – into his creation. I find all the hysteria stuff gross, all those men pronouncing on this one young girl. And her father delivering her up to Freud, going, 'Bring her to reason!' Yuk!

—Fortunately, I say, we've done with hysteria.

—Oh yeah? What about all those hysterical nags, hags, bags running around the place?

—I meant as a clinical diagnosis. That case is a mess and Freud knew it – that's why he delayed publishing. You can't construct a decent analysis based on a fragmented and incomplete case history by an unreliable narrator –

—Which unreliable narrator are we talking about – Dora or Freud?

—No one's accused him of hysteria yet.

—Well, in that case, get ready for it.

—Must we?

—Tell me what his diagnosis was based on.

—Oh, you know, the usual Victorian psychosomatic symptoms: the vapours, coughing fits, fainting fits, temper tantrums, head-aches, anorexia, suicide attempts – she was a melodramatic, atten-tion-seeking little pain in the ass, in my opinion.

—In my opinion, she was an intelligent, frustrated young girl being pimped by her father and analyst and sexually harassed by her

120

father's mistress's husband. She was being forced to play a part in a drama concocted by a self-important, self-serving male triumvirate – her father, Freud and Herr K who wanted her – that refused to recognise what she wanted – which was Frau K.

—He failed to master the transference, admitted it himself.

—*Master* the transference? Shit, Dad, listen to how your language – the whole psychoanalytic framework – perpetuates male domination and female submission. He couldn't 'master' the transference because he couldn't put himself in the female role.

—It wasn't that simple.

—Oh no? *You are in love with Herr K and I will prove it to you.* Freud made her yawn, Herr K made her want to barf.

—Vomiting: the somatic conversion-displacement of lubrication from genital area to mouth and throat. He cured her cough, by the way.

—She could have sucked cough drops, it would have been cheaper. Analysis was as irrelevant to her situation as it would be to mine.

—No problems, my dear? Got the world sorted out?

—I didn't say that.

—What about therapy?

—Same difference. It all derives from a patriarchal psychiatric model – individualise the problem, pathologise women and obscure the political reality of their situation.

—Ah, reality. How about lesbian analysts – would you go to one?

—A sellout. I'd go to you first.

—Against the rules.

—How come Freud took Anna on?

—I thought we were talking about Dora?

—I figure he was obsessed with her.

—He got a bit worked up.

—Worked up? The guy was pissing blood over her. He was *hysterical.*

—Touché. Claire, if you're trying to suggest he was in love with her, you're being naïve – and you're wrong: she was a bloody pain.

—Because she wouldn't submit to him.

—She was working out her anger towards men.

—You mean she didn't wet her pants over him.

—She resisted him – it's all part of the theory. You can't overcome the resistance, you can't work. But if you read the case – instead of whatever biased feminist interpretation it is you're reading – you'll

121

see that it was a rather painstaking and brilliant, if foolhardy and erroneous, piece of –

—Bullshit. She denied the whole thing.

—Not entirely. In her penultimate season, she confessed.

—Oh, is that what you guys are into, squeezing out confessions? He should have been a cop or a priest. He steam-rollered her. She was bored, itching to get away, so she let him have it. Okay, Siggie, you win. Shit, that's no *confession*. When he was frothing at the mouth of his dream interpretation – *his* interpretation, *her* dream, please note – she yawned and said, 'Why, has anything so remarkable come out?' I mean, big fucking deal, right?

—A simple act of vengeance, as he pointed out. She was compelled to deny what he or any man had to say. It's perfectly obvious.

—Listen, you want to know what this case was?

—I can't wait.

—A circus; a circus of sickies: the hysterical daughter with the syphilitic father with the paralytic mistress with a sex-starved husband who propositions the sick daughter . . . bring on Sigmund Freud, the sick psychoanalyst being paid by the sick girl's father to 'bring her to her senses'. The mind boggles.

—So do the legs.

—Her father was trying to serve her up to his friend Herr K so he'd be free to diddle around with the wife. What does Freud the objective analyst do? He leans forward and whispers, quite a dishy number, hmm? I mean, what's going on here, an analysis or a pimping session? She was fourteen years old, for God's sake. It's obscene. She wanted not to be betrayed and hurt for a change, she needed people to be straight with her. She was a *kid*, for chrissake, who needed a mother. And then when she kept insisting he didn't turn her on, Freud told her it was proof of her hysteria!

She's really getting into this.

—Where does the guy come off telling her what she felt? I mean, you can just see him waving his fat cigar at her. *When he pressed up against you on that lakeside path, you felt stimulated down there, hmm?* I mean, the guy couldn't even call a cunt a cunt – he called it *un chat* for pete's sake – the great sexologist – just like you, he couldn't say a dirty word to save his soul. That's what it's all about, you guys are all a bunch of Victorian prigs.

—Claire, that will do. I think this is about as far as I can go.

—Dad, I'm sorry, I got carried away.

122

—A small case of hysteria?

—Stop – let's stop here, I mean.

—Actually, I'm glad we can still do this. It's no fun being treated like a flower pot. Yes, let's sit down for a minute. I've got one of those electrolyte muscle cramps.

—Do you want to wait here while I get the car?

—No, I'll be fine, we'll sit on a rock together, contemplate the view. It's nothing serious, don't worry.

—We went too far, I should have made you turn back sooner. Mom will kill me.

—She won't know. Listen Claire, about this Dora case – it stinks. The amazing thing is that he allowed it to be published. At least give the guy credit for that. And we've learned from his mistakes. It was an early case, it only lasted, what was it, eleven weeks, and then she walked out on him. There's been entirely too much importance placed on it.

—Who placed the importance? Answer: Freud. Because she finished with him – he couldn't hack it.

—She walked out on him just when he was getting going, when he was reaching a successful –

—Climax? Analysis interruptus?

—Quite so, very frustrating, I can tell you.

—Oh, has somebody ever walked out on you?

—You know better than to ask.

—Oh right: Top Secret. By the way, do you happen to remember what his 'final solution' was?

—That is a most unfortunate way of putting it. Of course I remember – the famous wife-daughter swap, Sigmund the Swinger. You really picked a winner with Dora.

—The perfect ending to end all perfect endings. Herr K wangles a divorce so he can marry Dora. Frau K is now free to marry Dora's father. Everybody lives happily ever after and Herr Freud gets his commission. I wonder if they've sold the movie rights yet.

—She had done with him.

—Ah, but had he done with her?

—Have you ever thought of becoming a lawyer?

—It's not a bad idea. As a matter of fact, I'm thinking about it – except I like literature too much. Contradictory, I know.

—'In the unconscious, contradictory thoughts live very comfortably side by side.' Sigmund Freud. You see, he has his uses.

—Hmm.

—I suppose to you she's rather a feminist heroine: pre-Oedipal, the denial of female subordination, and so on?

—I like the way she picked up the purse she was supposed to have symbolically masturbated into and told him what he could do with it. Happy New Year, doc – and she was off, end of analysis. That's what got up his nose. She didn't lie down and wave her pretty legs in the air and tell him he'd solved her life and how wonderful he was, ooh ooh. Basically, she thought he was an asshole. He couldn't handle that.

—She took her revenge by deserting him as she believed herself (transferentially) deserted by him. But I think the real act of vengeance, although unconscious, was this case: a remarkable piece of subversion – as you've just so brilliantly demonstrated.

—Dad, I don't go along with it for a minute, but I'm finding it pretty compulsive reading.

—Is that supposed to be some kind of backhanded compliment?

—I think he was probably a frustrated novelist or something. The whole thing is a sort of edifice, a construction – and in that sense it's brilliant, I can see that. But for that reason, it's horrifying. All that influence on our culture, on people like –

—Me? Well, as it happens there's more to being an analyst than following a slavish Freudian line. Besides, it's the clinical practice rather than the theory that's seminal.

—Seminal?

—Okay, I'll cut out my tongue when I get home. Listen, I don't have to defend him to you – and certainly not in this case. But you might be interested to know that the real Dora didn't end up a very heroic figure. According to Deutsch, who treated her years later, she became a frigid, anally obsessed compulsive. He called her 'one of the most repulsive hysterics' he had ever met.

—Dad! I don't believe this. Frigid. Anal. It's –

—Claire, enough. We're going round in circles and I'm knackered. I need to get back, put my feet up and contemplate a stiff gin and tonic. You know, sometimes I think it's the brain that's the exhausted bit of my anatomy.

—Dad, I'm sorry. What can I do? I'll make your drink. I'll take Willy for a quick run before I go to work.

—Guiltwork at overtime rates, my dear? Working off the aggro you can't let out on me?

—That's right, turn it all back onto me. How about you guys: don't you ever get to be the 'case'?

—I'll see what I can do. How about *The Case of the Terminal Heart?*

—Low blow, she says.

Twelve

—Sir, the proper inference from these premises appears to be that it is only the male of the species – *de calido innato et semine* – to whom we may ascribe perfection. He is the efficient instrument; and the female, not less than the egg she lays, the same; however – imperfect. But – you do appear to be not entirely well, Frear. Have you overtaxed yourself, or has your daughter distressed you?

—I'm fine . . . a bit overstretched. We overdid it on our walk. This drug cocktail is the pits. What's that you're drinking?

—Bloody Mary, he says, deadpan. The perfect and efficacious semen – he raises his glass – being concocted from blood. To your health, Frear.

We clink glasses. Dr Harvey and I are sitting on the back deck which looks west over the Bay and the Golden Gate. This house, by the way, was built around 1910 according to some loose and sprawling Italianate model. Dr H likes to sit in the front courtyard early in the day because of the fountain there, which has symbolic significance for him (it corresponds to the heart: fountain in the bosom) and because while it catches the sun (an even more major cardiac metaphor) it is still cool enough to sit out – his need to keep cool having progressed from the prophylactic to the obsessional. He's lucky, as I tell him, this is *northern* California. Oh but the ambivalence! You can see it in the way he is drawn to the sun yet retreats each afternoon to the cool of a north-facing bedroom, the dousing of toes and spirit in darkness. He blinks like a mole as the sun goes down behind Mount Tam. It is no ordinary sun to him, but a cosmic force. Ruth is fixing dinner in the kitchen.

He sits with his feet up on the railing while I sit perpendicularly with my right hand skulking inside my shirt like a neo-Napoleon, or worse still, Mrs Frear the elder. The good doctor is getting juiced up. His voice, accompanied by the distant but ever-present freeway roar, drones on. His subject: what is and isn't perfect on this earth.

—Although females, he begins, are the result of a generative event not carried through to its final conclusion, it is nevertheless true that in all genera, Nature makes a differentiation in the sexes which is

126

necessary for the reproduction of the species. And so the female is not a thing monstrous but is according to the general tendency of nature: *intentio naturae universalis.* Nor, he goes on, do my colleagues and I of the enlightened school of medicine – we, that is, of the *neoterici* – consider her to be a species apart but merely less fully developed. In a word, Frear, less perfect.

—I see. What's missing then?

—Heat, Frear. The hottest created things are the most perfect. Because of a lack of heat in generation, and being of a colder and moister disposition, her sexual organs have remained internal, so that she is rather incomplete sexually and generatively speaking.

—O penis envy! O God! O Father! O Sigmund!

—Which explains her excessive desire for coitus – *furor uterinus.*

—Hmm.

—'Matter desires form as the female the male.' Aristotle's *Physics.* You know it, I presume. In other words, the imperfect desires the perfect: woman seeks completion, that is perfection, through congress with the male: it is the only solution. Perfectly logical. Surely you do not disagree?

—Well, I wouldn't mention it in front of Claire if I were you. By the way, Dr Harvey . . . (Please God, give us something else to talk about.) Uh, let's see now . . . Did you know that this is the epicentre?

—The *epicentrum*, Frear? Without doubt, it lies *in medio* from front to back, right to left, top and bottom. Hence it is the epicentrum.

—I do beg your pardon, doctor. I meant not the heart but the earth. You've got to remember that around here the word epicentre refers to earthquakes. This is one of the *epicentres*; as a matter of fact you happen to be straddling one at this very moment, Dr Harvey, the San Andreas Fault.

—Fault, Frear?

—A weak point, a crack. The fault line stretches through most of the state of California but this right here is the core.

—When one of these so-called quakes occurs, the earth –

—Trembles. Cups rattle on shelves, the teeth in your head, the roots of trees let go. At its worst, buildings crumble. Fire is the major hazard. Then there are worries about the freeways and the bridges.

—But you told me, did you not, that they had – 'give' was the word you used, Frear.

127

—So I did, but whether it's enough we don't know. Let's hope we don't get to test it out.

—An odd place to choose to live.

He shifts himself in his deckchair.

—Nowhere much is entirely safe these days. Anyway, we're constantly taking risks and we reckon it's worth it for the weather, the view, the natural beauty of the place. It isn't really a matter of choice any more, we're here' we're stuck with it. Californians have developed a rather fatalistic attitude, internationalised the danger, so to speak. People take bets on when it will blow. Would you like to place a modest bet as to which will go first, the quake or my heart?

—I am not a gambling man, Frear, he says and looks away.

If he but knew of the *terremoto* in my heart. This morning I received a letter from my donor's mother, written on yellow paper and signed 'Bella'. She has invited me to visit her in New Mexico. Not only that, but she has enclosed a pink stone in the shape of a heart which she says contains an innate warmth. It fits in the palm of my hand inside my pocket. I draw it out.

—What do you make of this, William?

He examines it.

—It puts me in mind of the uterus. The heart was my first love, but I also devoted myself to the study of the womb. A most interesting organ, Frear. I could tell you many things of the womb: how in marriageable virgins 'tis like a pear; how after being distended by labour it recovereth its natural firmness, especially if it is to be compared with the male organ which goes soft and flaccid so soon after coition . . .

And so he goes on singing the womb's praises while I'm thinking that any minute now he and I and Claire will be holding hands and chanting together, of all things female and full of the glory of God (yes, she of the divine uterus). But pretty soon he is describing shoving balloons in, sticking umbrella gadgets up and opening them (ouch; no anaesthetic); and before long we have before us a terrifying animal-like creature, *animal avidum generandi:* gross and clammy, endowed with powers of movement and a sense of smell, consuming innocent you-know-whats if they happen to have the misfortune to be anywhere in the vicinity; in such a frenzy to procreate that if it is not satisfied it wanders round the body like a mad-brained ghost (this happens especially in moonlight):

—And how dreadful are the mental aberrations, the delirium, the

128

melancholy, the paroxysms of frenzy, as if the affected person were under the dominion of spells, and all arising from an unnatural state of the uterus. Look you, how the womb rises out of its place and compresses the heart so that the sufferer falls down breathless in a swoon.

—Dr Harvey, you know it's a damn shame you and Dr Freud couldn't have met. You could have talked wandering wombs long into the night.

—Ah yes, your teacher, as Fabricius was mine. I should have liked that.

—Not that I actually studied with him, of course. But tell me, what in your opinion is the cause of this, uh, 'unnatural state' of the womb?

—Over-abstinence from sexual intercourse of course.

—Of course.

—All things – this is most delightful, Frear – grow and flourish in spring. It is as if, with the advent of this glorious luminary (he makes a sort of prayer gesture to the sun) Venus the bountiful descended from heaven, waited on by Cupid – a cohort of graces, and prompted all living things by the bland incitement of love to secure the perpetuity of their kinds. Or as if the genital organs of Saturn, cast into the sea at this season, raised a foam, whence sprung Aphrodite. For, in the generation of animals, as the poet says, *superat tenor omnibus humor* – a gentle moisture all pervades – and the genitals froth and are replete with semen.

He has worked himself up – how shall I not say it? – into a lather.

—But about your patients, doctor, you were saying . . .

—Ah yes, I had many patients, sir, young women who when they continued too long unwedded were seized with hysterics, or fell into a cachectic state, had distemperatures of various kinds due to the eagerness for offspring. To such a height did the malady reach in some that they were believed to be poisoned or moon-struck, or possessed by a devil.

—I see (pregnant pause). And what did you, uh, prescribe for this condition?

He swigs. Was that a wink, doctor?

—My advice was as follows: let the man anoint the top of his yard with a little oil of gilliflowers and oil of sweet almonds together, and so to lie with her; for this assuredly brings down the matrix again.

129

—I see. (If you wouldn't mind just keeping your voice down, doctor.) And the outcome of the treatment?

—The complexion is improved, the breasts enlarge, the countenance glows with beauty, the eyes lighten, the voice becomes harmonious; the gait, gestures, discourse, are all graceful.

Oh, but did we not see it all coming, see where he was headed and did we not follow quite willingly (nay, eagerly?) towards that Apollonian, that foaming, billowing, sun-humping, frothing consummation? (What was that Sigmund? What the lady needs is a good fuck? Oh no, Dr Freud, that will not do, it will not do at all, for what she needs is not a good fuck, oh no, she needs the all-time *perfect* fuck.)

—Another drink, Doctor? Look, the sun is going down. What do you see, William?

—I see . . . I see it, Frear, and I humble myself before it, that mere bloody point or pulsating vesicle when the foetus is still in the milk or in the guise of a soft worm; I see, when the bones can be distinguished from the soft parts, the organ of life beginning to sprout, a small gourd or goose's egg, or large bean nestled in a child's breast, or sometimes more like a cone or pear when contracted. I see the valves by which blood is thrown into the chambers like closely folded pieces of linen or the sails of dainty vessels; I see the fibres of muscle running hither and thither like the web of a spider or the struts of your lateritious Golden Gate. I see how the arms of the major blood vessels lift themselves up from the shoulders as if in prayer; I see the pores of the separating spine like a bracelet composed of so many amber beads strung upon a thread; I see it wrapt in its double sac from whence I deliver it; I see it opened up, lit from behind as of a California poppy by the sun, like red silk, sweating, glistening, pulsing . . .

—Dr Harvey –

His nose, in the sunset, glows and sweat drips from the end of it. A lopsided smile, the first he has managed to produce, stretches his lips. I lean forward and touch his knee.

—Dr Harvey, I think you have had enough to drink. And perhaps it would be a good idea if you stayed out of the sun tomorrow.

—Yes, yes, Frear.

He looks but doesn't see me, or Ruth coming out with the guacamole and corn chips. He sees only one thing. He stares directly at it and holds his gaze. I want to say, don't stare, it can damage your

130

eyes – the words no father ever said to me – but I too am held by that neon beefsteak: what can it do to us at this stage? It beats. It is alive. It dwarfs the mountain behind which it will soon disappear. Let us not resist it.

And William here, who has plunged his blood stained hands within the breast and severed everything with his gory blade – what of him? He who broke through the outer approaches and threw aside the tottering ramparts until the hidden recess came into view; who held it in his hand and said the seventeenth century equivalent of 'that's it' – a pump, a pistol, a no big deal thing. What then? Did he hose it down, dissect it, say righty-ho and go home to his wife for a fried egg – sunny-side up – supper? Or was there something else? An act not widely advertised?

There was. 'God forgive me,' he said, got down on his gouty knees and worshipped.

Plop goes the sun.

Thirteen

Halfmoon Bay. The three of us, Ruth and I and perforce Dr H are sitting on the sand, watching the waves. Ruth has her skirt hitched up, Dr H has his breeches rolled and is playing catch-me-if-you-can with the seminal Pacific. I give him the nod – the wife and I need a little privacy here – and he sashays off.

I have just come from my three-month post-op tune-up and service at Stanford, including twenty-four-hour thallium scan, muscle biopsy, ECG, arteries – the works. We're here so Ruth can ask me how it went: a place where she can take great gulps of ocean air or burst into tears without people looking at her.

—So, says Ruth. She draws breath.

I throw a stone, it lands three feet away.

—Well?

And another. That's better.

—Val, I'm waiting.

—For what?

—I'm leaving if you don't tell me soon.

—Stay. Everything's fine.

She breathes out.

—I thought so. You're a sadist. What else did they say?

—'Arteries pristine, excellent progress', I quote. They've even skipped me from twice-monthly to monthly ECGs. Rejection complexes less urgent. I can start jogging tomorrow if I want. Anything goes, almost. In fact, they were quite impressed. Wanted to know my secret.

—What did you tell them?

—I said I was being sustained entirely through the office of female generosity. 'That explains it,' they said, 'good home care'.

She puts her arms around me, holds me close.

—That's wonderful news, Val.

We watch the waves together, isn't this nice. If only time and the urge to put the world and its husband to rights could stop right there.

—With any luck, she says, pretty soon we'll be back to the old life, almost as if none of this ever happened.

—But it has, Ruth.

—I know, but still.

—Still what?

—It means you can get back to a normal life.

—What's normal?

—Damn it, Val, you know what I'm talking about. Work, for instance. Did they say you can go back to work?

—Yes, if I want to.

—That's great.

—*If* I want, they said.

—And you don't?

—No. Not yet.

—Oh. What *do* you want?

—Not sure.

—Listen, Val (she takes my hand), this is crazy. I don't know where you are in your head and you won't let me in. What am I supposed to do?

—Be patient.

—How long?

—That's not a patient question.

—Why can't I help you work this thing out?

—Because it's my 'thing' not yours.

—Wouldn't it be better if you had just a few patients a week? Get your mind off your heart, restore your confidence. Otherwise you'll go bananas – if you aren't already.

—Thanks for the vote of confidence.

—Why do you keep shutting me out?

—I'm not shutting you out I'm shutting me in. It's not something I can share with the world.

—I'm not the world.

—It's not that simple.

—I didn't say it was. Why do you have to make everything more complicated than it is? You tie everything and everyone into knots.

—Everything *is* in knots – read R. D. Laing.

—I don't want to read R. D. Laing. I read him back in the sixties. He's old hat. Val, what about us?

—What about us?

—Damn you. Okay, how about if we went away together.

133

—I can't run away from this thing.

—What thing?

—See that up there? It's hanging over me.

—It's called blue sky, Val. Jesus, you really are perverse. They give you the all-clear and all you can think about is dying.

—It's not all I'm thinking about.

—Okay, what *are* you thinking about?

—Flying.

—I see. Not dying but flying. Is this poetry time or what? Okay, I give up: where to?

—Somewhere in New Mexico.

—I thought you said you couldn't run away from this thing.

—This isn't running away, it's running smack into it.

—You're not in any condition to fly yet.

—Yes I am. I checked it out with the doctor.

—All right, but you can't fly alone, it isn't safe. I'll go with you. I'll get us tickets. I always wanted to go to Santa Fe. What about the altitude?

—Ruth, I'm going alone.

—Alone?

—Correct.

—Oh God, don't tell me, you tracked her down, you're going on some wild donor-chase. Am I right?

Plop goes another stone.

—Val, what can you accomplish going after a ghost?

—Her mother is alive.

—Where will that get you?

—I can't explain. It's something I need to do.

—It's unethical, there are laws about these things.

—Ruth, stuff it.

—Val, this is crazy. She's *dead*.

I watch as she runs away down the beach, getting smaller and smaller until she's a mobile dot among the rocks. I throw a few more pebbles, observe the water birds, enjoy the peace. A most exotic, short-legged, stocking-free wading specimen is legging it towards me along the water's edge, his Royal College medals flapping. His narrow chest reminds me of a palette with not enough room for all the colours. Poor William, I think, he must be hot inside those weeds, but of course nothing matters so long as his feet are immersed. He appears to skip like a boy. Eventually he subsides next to me.

134

—Tell me, William, about your wife.

Alarmed at the sudden intimacy of my tone, he shifts a few notches away, digs his feet in. I pat his arm.

—Don't worry, I'm not going to eat you. I was just sitting here thinking about my own wife and that set me to wondering about yours – you had one I believe?

He draws himself up.

—Elizabeth Browne, maiden of the parish of St Sepulchre, Newgate. Tall, of dark complexion.

—What else?

—Daughter of Lancelot Browne, doctor of Physicke, physician to Queen Elizabeth, later to James the First.

—And quite useful as a father-in-law, no doubt, professionally speaking?

The toes and eyes curl.

—There there, doctor, calm yourself. About your wife Elizabeth –

—My dear deceased loving wife, she was mistress of a remarkable pet parrot.

—You don't say.

—I was myself most fond of the parrot and therefore named him Horace, of whom I was also fond. An excellent and well instructed bird, Frear.

—I'm so glad to hear it, William.

—He was sportive and wanton, he would sit in her lap, where he loved to have her scratch his head, and stroke his back, and then testify his contentment by kind mutterings and shaking of his wings –

—Good God, William, if you could but hear yourself! Better yet, if Dr Freud could have heard you. Tell me, what were you doing while wifey toyed with the birdie in her lap, eh?

—In truth, Frear, I always thought him to be a cock-parrot by his notable excellence in singing and talking. For amongst birds, as well as humans, females seldom attain such proficiency of voice or provoke to discourse –

—Please, Dr Harvey –

—But alas, the parrot grew sick, and being much oppressed by many convulsive motions, did at length deposit his much lamented spirit in his mistress's bosom, where he had so often sported –

—So you went and picked him delicately off her breast and whipped him onto your dissecting table.

135

—When dissecting his carcass, to discover the cause of his death, I found in the womb an egg almost completed but, for want of a cock, corrupted. Which many times befalleth those birds, that are immured in cages, when they covet the society of the cock.

—Dr Harvey, we're talking about your *wife* not your pet. You haven't told me anything about her or about your feelings for her.

—I was fond of her too.

—Oh jolly good.

—We married when I was twenty-six years, in London.

—Is that it then?

—There was indeed one more thing to be said of her.

—Yes, William?

—She was barren, Frear.

—I see. And was that a great disappointment to you?

—It was God's will, sir.

We sit in silence. He is busy drawing a diagram in the wet sand with the tip of his dagger. Perhaps while he's thus distracted . . . One last try, I think, to draw him out. For who knows but what passionate and sanguine nature, what heart cicatriced in several places lies dormant in that narrow enterprise? Surprise us Will.

—Tell me, I say conversationally, about Padua. What did you really get up to in Padua?

—Get up to, Frear?

He gazes up at the sky. Eventually – he seems to be rolling time itself back to his student days in Padua – he speaks.

—I sat high in the roof of the operating theatre in the glass cupola through which the morning light did pour down on the corpse below and witnessed the dissections of my teacher.

This line of questioning is useless. One more try, the last.

—That's very interesting, William. But what about afterwards, when you washed the blood off your hands and went out for a stretch and a breath of balmy Italian air. I mean, did you never wander the hubbub-ish streets of Padua struggling against an errant organ?

He smiles.

—I remember buying from the market fish still flopping from the sea. I brought the creature back to my room where I slit open its thorax and watched the last spasm of the creature's heart.

—Dr Harvey . . .

The diagram he is drawing is of the heart. Of course.

After a long while he stops doodling and says,

136

—I remember being lost, Frear, along the Venice road on one of the lagoons that merge into maritime marshes, a sort of no man's land, half drying soil and half fen, not unlike malarious Cambridgeshire, cut through with mysterious rivulets and runnels of water hidden in tufts of grass. (He wriggles his wet toes, then suddenly waves the dagger.) It must be so! The heart is in motion and the blood circulates unceasingly, constantly warming itself in the heart. That is how it is, Frear, just as the earth revolves around the sun: the heart and the blood . . . In a word, all of nature, wherever I looked, corroborated my theory. (He pauses.) It was merely a matter of proof, step by painful step . . .

Ruth is picking her way towards us in the warm sand.

It is getting dark. I look up and see the deep vault of night already spangled with stars, while towards the east there rises a great slice of moon. From one point a glow spreads along between sea and sky: Venice city of romance. On this particular evening there is a great festival. To the light of torches and lanterns there is dancing and the gondolas, like black swans, glide along the canals. A night of enchantment! As for William, he is lost and penniless, tired and arguably ill with incipient gout, yet none of it matters for he holds the secret of a beloved which no one can take from him.

Lucky William, a honeymoon that will never be over.

—What is it, Frear?

—Tell me, shall I buy my wife a parrot as a going-away present?

Fourteen

Ruth. You think me unkind on the subject of my wife? Cheated her of her autonomy? Portrayed her coming and going with medicines, drinks, books, and so on, chauffering me to hospital, taking me for therapeutic walks and acting as general sexual factotem and arm-filler in bed – and little else? A cardboard character? Well there you're wrong: cardboard is a lifeless, flat thing, grey or brown with tripe-like corrugations to give it substance, whereas my wife is more like those rolls of plastic packing bubbles. I once squished a whole roll with my thumb, row after satisfying row, *pop pop pop*, once you start you cannot stop. It came in a box my mother sent me shortly before *she* popped off. It contained my old rubberband ball.

As I was saying, Ruth keeps me alive. She is efficient, determined, professionally cool, yet ever comforting. Her approach is strictly do this do that and all will be well. Her heart is steady, we're a team. Some team, do I hear you say? Claire points out how by the end of each day she's wiped out. I do not deny it. I watch our cat Minna nursing her kittens and find myself thinking not William's frothy thoughts of Springtime and Renewal but: Deceptive Mammary Calm.

How to do this thing gracefully. The cardiologist encourages me to live a normal life. A normal life? I understand, he concedes (remember the cream cheese), it's a matter of adjustment. I see him coming at me with a jeweller's screwdriver: a twist here, a twiddle there to the defective part, *eh viola!*

What is this normal life then? New Valentine, new Ruth; new heart, new home; come and join us as we gather round the harmonium singing *Heart of My Heart* – follow the bouncing ball. Okay, don't say it. But what am I to do with this pretence that nothing untoward has happened? For this so-called normality is becoming more like *nothingness* every day: a slamming of the lid. As for Ruth and her brave little chin-up coping strategies – I should be grateful but I'm not. I want to strike her as I've been struck.

Burst a few bubbles, eh doc?

I'm not really so bad, you know.

138

I am. I'm a real shit.

And now you say. 'Nah, underneath that metal plating there's a heart of gold.'

Perhaps now you will understand why shrinks have such a high rate of suicide.

I'm sitting at the kitchen table practising my normality. I reach up for Ruth's *Larousse Gastronomique* and open to – where else?

Heart, unlike most other offal, is made up largely of muscle, and very hard-working muscle at that . . . Not surprisingly, it is inclined to be tough. The most tender (and tasteless) is calf's heart which it is possible to grill or fry gently . . .

And Ruth – you think she's such a tender morsel? All that cow-eyed giving, what is it but a neurotic need to please, to ingratiate; give give give, endless let-me-love-you-so-I'll-be-indispensible-and-then-you'll-love-me-and-never-leave-me.

Normal life.

Oh, it's hopelessly corrupt. Love is a con just like psychoanalysis: another form of projected need, introjection, distorted cathectic bibble-babble. One takes, the other gives, an unequal trade-fair. We marry people who have what we haven't got and vice versa. We aren't kidding when we say: *Meet my other half.* Monogamy the cripple, marriage the ceremonial toy. Ah, the devil speaks. Ignore him. Oh no, we'll stay together, grow together, merge at vital points, forever and ever and . . .

My head hurts. Ruth asks if I want to see someone. See someone? She means a shrink. You mean someone like *me*, are you kidding? Why not, it might help. Help what? Anyway, I have someone to talk to. Who, she asks, looking worried, but I don't answer. True or false: I am often rude to my wife. Perfectly true. This isn't like you, she says.

Who is it like? A man who sits in a straight-backed chair looking out to the Bay, fingers touching; who has visions of his drowned father jack-knifing backwards out of the water while his mother holds her heart and looks surprised; who holds rather corrupt semi-Socratic dialogues with the ghosts of a seventeenth-century anatomist and a girl with green fingernails. Go to such a man?

Thank you. Ruth has just brought me a cup of herbal tea made with teabags which Dr H reckons are stuffed with denatured weed.

He is still pushing coffee. If only I would drink of the spiritous liquor, my heart would swell and grow fulsome. And what then? Will Old Faithful burst forth with a gush of holistic tofuti fruitshake for God's sake, like some post-modern fairy tale come true? Fine, but what if what comes out – stand back, folks – is more like an oil slick, some terrible effluent? Change doesn't just happen. It's like a scientific experiment – we medical men know all about it – the medium has to be right for the new organism to grow.

It's my birthday. This means dinner with Ruth and Claire at her place of work – Chez Panisse, Berkeley's finest and best, where I get waited on hand and foot. Yet my heart hurts – someone's heart hurts. We drink Ridge Chablis and eat baked Sonoma goat. My wife and daughter raise their glasses to me. I've made it to forty-six, I'm making it, welcome back to normal life.

Ruth is wearing a little white number that makes her look like a schoolgirl, while Claire looks like Whistler's daughter in a long black column of skirt. I compliment her. She digs into the sugar bowl. We sit in the window protected from a traffic-infested Shattuck Avenue by a courtyard arbour. Beyond the foliage however is a defunct Co-Op supermarket. So it is with my heart: one minute corona-ed with spring-like arteries, the next that boarded-up, failed experiment in liberal-socialist supermarketing. To begin, says our waitperson: a ragout of periwinkles, barnacles, little scallops and clams. How does one tackle them? Ruth says they just slide down, you don't have to think about it. William whispers, *Some of them seem to have no heart, for the whole body is used as a heart, or the whole animal is a heart.*

I can't tell you what that does for my appetite, Will.

Claire says eating here is not her scene. She twirls her wine glass, keeps her head down. Ruth listens in on conversations and reports back: real estate, cancer, creative process . . . My kidneys send me running to the bathroom.

Please, no more.

Get back in there, Valentine, they're doing this for you.

Napkin on lap, I tuck obediently into my 'Perfection Squash Soup'. Made from local baby crook-necked squash and zucchini no bigger than your little finger: foetuses of the vegetable world, you might say. My gums hurt.

—Everything all right here with you folks?

—Perfect, says Ruth.

William hisses, *Perfection must be inquired into by and by*, and disappears into the shadow of a giant swiss-cheese plant. I order a bottle of Cabernet Sauvignon. Ruth says I'm drinking too much. Warms the cockles, I say. What the hell are the cockles anyway? asks Claire, who is also getting pissed. I explain – William to the rescue again – they're named after certain bi-valve molluscs of the *cardium genera* whose shell has convex, radially-ribbed valves.

—Here's to the heart as a bi-valve mollusc.

—Cheers!

—Cheers!

Dinner, the theatre: the normal progression of an evening out. We make our way down to the Berkeley Rep. The play turns out to be a new British version of Dracula – you know, the guy with the tacky as in blood (get it?) psyche, the fangs and the oral fixation. Men, women, he's not fussy (see: polymorphous perverse), just so long as he drinks – though he does seem to prefer women if he can get 'em. Not that he can ever get enough, which is of course the problem: mission impossible, and so on. So, Drac old boy, why don't you just lie back and tell old Big Ears here all about it. Didn't your Mama back in Transylvania have enough milk for you? Or was there a traumatic incident with a bitten off nipple, milk inextricably mingled with blood?

He claims two sisters, Lucy and Mina. They arch their necks to meet his embrace. Oh yes, he finds them, over and over again, these more-than-willing sexual blood donors – what greater evidence of *giving* than blood flowing from your own blood-stream? – while he-who-can-never-get-enough can always be relied upon to take the stuff. Our motto? We aim to be pleasured. He turns to us, his audience, his conspirators (*wink wink*) before tucking in. Good to the last drop; home of the never-empty Freudian jugular vein.

Mmm. Yes.

He tears open his shirt, grips his victim by the hair and forces her face to his chest, where a thin stream of blood trickles from the wound. Her white nightdress is smeared with Heinz gore: drink drink, there's a good girl. He throws back his head and gargles, she moans with pleasure. A miasma fills the theatre and my chest.

Oh it's a great shrink's story: all that yummy repressed Victorian sexuality. And Dracula himself, the Romanian Jekyll and Hyde: on the one hand, the cool customer – aloof, brilliant, charming,

141

fascinating and bloodless; on the other, drowning in the hot sauce. No no, yes yes; part saint, part sinner. Oh, that needy, greedy, never-ending oral phase!

And the women who feed him and upon whom he feeds? Who is to save them from their unutterable female weakness? Why, who else but those figures of sanity, wisdom, love, friendship and decency and above all power over the forces of darkness and evil – bring on (*slurp slurp*) the shrinks. Dr Van Helsing, would you like something to drink?

Help, get me out of here! Ruth? Claire? Anyone for a glass of wine, a coffee? At least having to wait at the bar (it's the intermission) saves me from having to talk about it, because really what is there to say that hasn't been said? And anyway, it's hard enough to *breathe* in here. And furthermore, my mind is on other things. So we drink our drinks and the bell rings for us to return to our seats.

What happens after they've put the stake through the vampire's heart and the actor crawls out of the coffin and washes the ketchup off – what happens then? When the theatre clears itself of his pestilence and the streets are safe again (can they ever be) for our wives and daughters? Answer: his heart, pierced, bleeds, proving . . . what? Why, that he has one. We must not take these things for granted, you see. And really, when you think about it (I'm thinking) it's a blessing in disguise: no more sleepless nights, no more fluttering about that unappetising northern English seaside town in the dark and cold, no more AIDS-terror (what are the statistics among vampires?). Of course, extinction is a gradual process (the dodo, I believe, hung on for half a century or more) but eventually (with any luck) we may find him at peace. Freedom, my friend. Daddy, you can lie back now. There's a stake in your fat black heart . . .

And now we are ready for the dénouement, for the moment we have all been waiting for: the thrill of seeing Dracula paying for his pleasure. Ready folks? Here it comes, keep your eyes on Dr Van Helsing (MD, PhD) as he sneaks up on the coffin, prises open the lid and takes aim with his stake. Warning: all delicate flowers (that includes me) now avert your gaze. Claire stares. Ruth looks away.

Aargh.

Fifteen

Dawn. Dr Harvey appears wearing one of those white plastic noseguards. Underneath it the skin has gone raw and peely. He's wearing his Royal College medals. He'd fit in nicely on Telegraph Avenue among the barefoot Counts and Contessas and their second-hand military paraphernalia. He smiles benignly from beneath the noseguard. He is mellowing nicely, the cadaver with the sexy tan.

Actually, he reminds me of one of my berobed patients from the Theological Seminary, who also came to me to discuss matters of the heart, though of a different order. Patient T felt he was a victim, as he put it, of his heart. He had dreams about it growing larger and larger, filling his whole body, squashing all his other organs including his brain. He had trouble concentrating on his work. What he wanted, he said, was to be able to 'get on top of it'. I pictured him struggling to mount a red, heart-shaped inflatable but failing to achieve it and winding up each time underneath. He was told if anyone could help him I could. Leg up anyone?

—I remember, Dr Harvey says, closing his eyes, a strange kind of disease which befell a sensible man of my acquaintance. It was a stout man who did so boil with rage because he had suffered an injury, and received an affront by one that was more powerful than himself, that his anger and hatred being increased every day, by reason he could not be revenged, and discovering the passion of his mind to nobody, which was so exulcerate within him, at last he fell into a strange sort of a disease, and was tortured, and miserably tormented with great oppression and pain in his heart . . . *summaque oppressione et dolore cordis . . .*

—Exactly, Dr Harvey. We can't afford to let our trapped emotions destroy our bodies. What did you do for him?

—The most skilful physicians' prescriptions doing no good upon him, at last, after some years, he fell sick of an attack of the heart and died.

—In other words, zilch.

—Frear?

—You did nothing.

—What would *you* have done for him, sir?

—Well, I'd get him to explore the root of his anger, the denied traumatic event, and so on. Of course, first we'd have to build a strong transferential relationship and a good working alliance.

—In my experience, Frear, in cases where cardio-vascular affection is manifest there isn't time for –

—Screwing around in analysis? A problem, I admit.

I wander out onto the deck, which is enveloped in fog. A voice beckons, my heart goes clackety-clack in my chest.

—So, Dr Harvey, what am I to do?

He appears not to have heard. He is staring at the sun trying to break through the fog.

—Wouldn't it be a fine thing, William, if there were a science of the emotions? Just think if we could lay people out, put a machine down close to their chests, turn a switch and chuga-chuga-chug, the printout would unravel all that emotional spaghetti.

—Spaghetti?

—Pasta – you must have eaten it in Padua. William, what is the cause of all this twisting?

—Aah, Frear. Every affection of the mind that is attended with either pain or pleasure, hope or fear, is the cause of an agitation whose influence extends to the heart . . . and hence, by the way, it may perchance be wherefore grief and love, and envy, and anxiety, and all affections of the mind of a similar kind are accompanied with emaciation and decay, or with cacochemy and crudity, which engender all manner of diseases and consume the body of a man.

—What you're describing is the deep interlocking of the psychic and somatic aspects in the causation of disease. But it doesn't tell us what to *do*. That is our frustration, our curse, our guilt. We practise, we perform, we theorise, we expound, we defend but in the end . . . Is it any wonder we jump off our decks, our Golden Gate. As a matter of fact, I'm in danger of taking off myself.

—Are you embarking on a voyage, sir?

I hand him the letter from New Mexico.

—Monstrous. Be warned, Frear. She would undo heroes, not make them. You must not lose your head.

—What head?

—The divine banquet of the brain, as Plato had it. I see the brain, Frear, being the topmost part of the body and with its defences of hair, skin and thick bone also serving as our defence system and cooling tower.

—Ah, bring on the super-ego! Dr Harvey, the analyst's role is to unblock those lines of defence not shore them up.

—A pity, Frear. 'Twould be to my mind like letting out a herd of galloping wild boar.

—It certainly seems like that at times.

—Why not keep them locked up then?

—I just told you. Besides, you proved my point a while back with that patient of yours with the raging boiling whatsit. Repression, suppression – we believe these are some of the worst causes of mental and physical disease to hit our kind.

—Are these things not more effectively purged through the palate and the nostrils?

—Well, as a matter of fact, we prefer psychoanalysis. It's longer and it costs more but it's less messy.

—One could look deeper into the matter, he says, making as if to peer into my skull. It is quite simple really. Having in the second dissection removed all the bones of the skull, leaving the brain invested by the meninges with its appendages such as eyes and spinal medulla, I see –

—William, if you don't mind. Look, these are mind-body connections we're talking about, not the literal brain. We stopped doing lobotomies years ago.

—Ah, he says, you mean the brain by which we are mad, that we rave, that fears and terrors assail us by day or night. Dreams, untimely errors, groundless anxiety –

—Precisely.

—Blunders, awkwardness, want of experience –

—Mm.

—I do not envy you your occupation, Frear. I was frequently bothered by neurotic patients who did not oblige me by providing an interesting autopsy. Valetudinarians, moreover, are affected and nice in their food and many of them are always complaining. Do you find this to be so in your practice, Frear?

—We have our problems. As a matter of fact, it isn't easy. Between all those 'mms' and 'ahhs' you actually have to *listen* and in the end come up with an interpretation. And then what? They walk out. They climb on a motorcycle and say, So long, it was nice knowing you. They find an alternative obsession. They say they're

145

going to take up meditation, go back to school. They say how much I've helped but I know they're madder than ever. They go jump off a bridge. How would you like to spend your days listening to people who dump their pain and then go? What am I supposed to do then? Carry it around on my back, in my head, in my . . . Then there are those who say they didn't get *heard*. What is that supposed to mean? How can they sit there telling me they didn't get heard when I spend hours – days, weeks, years – listening; when what they brought was a wet, eggy-dough reality and what they went away with was a nice egg bagel which I made especially for them? I mean, you don't throw the stuff into a pot of roiling, boiling water and expect it to come out the *same*, do you? As I told a patient recently, you've got to *roll with it*, sweetheart, you know: *Und so weiter* . . . By the way, Doctor, do you know why bagels have a hole in them? I'll tell you. Bagels were baked to celebrate the relief of Vienna from the Turkish infidels sometime around the seventeenth century. The commander of the liberating troops was a Pole called Jan Sobieski. The locals were so grateful that they rushed forward to kiss his stirrup – *Bügel* in German – as he passed on horseback. Jewish bakers prepared a special stirrup-shaped bread to mark the occasion; the name however has degenerated from *bügel* to *bagel*. What do you say to that, William?

—In my opinion, Frear, the Turks are the only people who know how to order or govern their women, and use them wisely.

—Did you know that women are born with clean hearts? My daughter Claire told me that. An Indian legend.

—I should like some coffee, Frear.

—In a minute. Dr Harvey, there is only one solution.

—Java?

—No, *transference*. Do you understand, doctor? The elemental, here-we-are-in-it-together complementary relationship; the perfect pair, that dynamic duo: analyst and analysand. A relationship so highly charged that it is, as Lacan says, not without terror or pity. In fact, Freud himself made no distinction between transference and love. A source of wonderment, a moving and astonishing experience, an –

—Val, do you want some coffee?

Ruth, my wife.

—In a minute. But do you know, William, Freud's 'fundamental rule'? It is worth reiterating here. Patient and analyst should not have known each other beforehand; they should not bump into each other in predictable places; their only link should be analysis itself, sexual encounters are forbidden, absolutely forbidden. In other words: do it alone, and keep your distance. Refusal, rejection, repression, denial: they are all tools of our trade. Do you see how we deal with the very materials that are causing the problem?

He blinks.

—It is not easy to understand, I admit. But that is where the transference comes into it. A patient comes to me, kinked, knotted, twisted up inside herself. Straighten me out, please, she cries; and inevitably: love me. But do I respond? Of course not. At which point she says: I hate you. You see how it is, how important it is that, although I may bleed, I be no friend, because it cannot be; because once I hold out my hand to touch her, to bump up against her, to soothe, to talk her down – she is a goner. We are both goners. It is only in the painful reverb of our own voices – helpless, strangulated – that we can identify the source of that pain. And on my side in the dreaming, inventing and transposing that I can make sense of it, so that eventually we may achieve wisdom and strength and *distance*. All this, you see, I do for them.

—You have a kind heart, Frear.

—Love? Of course it depends on your definition. You, for example, in so far as this word is applicable to you, you love your brother Eliab, your brother Eliab's coffee, Virgil the parrot – or was it Horace – ice-cold water in buckets, California sunsets, the heart, particularly of certain fishes, and the uterus of the doe. Am I right?

He nods.

—And the patient of whom I spoke? She loves anything that moves fast from bunnies to speedy motorcycles. But this is of course what we call a pathetic fallacy, because a bunny is not a man any more than a pretty cleft-nicked bauble is a heart. And what do I think of love? A protean concept which we psychoanalysts have as much difficulty defining as everyone else. Eros, sexuality – see libido. Instinct theory – see self-preservation. Object theory – see infantile and dependent love. Genital, oedipal . . . Phantasy . . . mania? Dr Harvey, I'm weary. Le Rochefoucauld says, 'It is with true love as it is with ghosts: everyone talks of it, but few have seen it.' I want to see it. Dr Harvey – William – I am in love with my heart donor.

—That is impossible, sir.

—That may be, I won't deny it – but I'm going after her anyway. I've had enough of fantasy, death, nothingness. Call it intellectual

147

masturbation if you must. I must stop this literary *coitus reservatus* and *do something* – yes, make her real by actually going to her not only in my imagination and daydreams. I must do more. She has given me everything, and what do I give her in return? A hymn, a paean, a heartfelt declaration, perhaps a dedication, an *in memoriam*. How feeble! Enough. I shall go and breathe the life back into her.

—Mad, Frear, quite mad.

—I don't care.

My daughter? My wife? Yes, of course they're the realest things in my life and yes of course they should be occupying my thoughts and time and yes they have problems too, yes I know Claire is going up and down like an emotional yo-yo because she's got a new lover and yes Ruth is starting to look like somebody snuffed the life out of her, so where do I come off talking about life and yes I know they both need me and yes I know they think I'm going bananas and yes to all that – *yes* – but this is different and perhaps, no absolutely, more necessary to my well-being. You hear that lup-dubbing?

—Can you understand, William?

—Indeed not. What of the reality principle about which we spoke?

—Fuck the reality principle.

PART III

No one who, like me, conjures up the most evil of those half-tamed demons that inhabit the human breast, and seeks to wrestle with them, can expect to come through the struggle unscathed.

Sigmund Freud

One

Neptune's brain coral, a remarkable piece of mimicry: a lump of rock which resembles the human brain but for a certain unwelcome and unconvincing crustiness: snaking cracked riverbeds, devil's gorges going from nowhere to nowhere; the sort of place where Gila monsters lurk twitching their tails, tongues, little red eyes; where if one fell in one might never get out alive.

I am in New Mexico.

I'm in a taxi headed towards Santa Fe through Albuquerque sprawl, getting the tourist run-down from my Indian driver. The sub-horizon is a flat plain with marching power poles flanking the road. Tin-roof churches, mobile homes, JCBs, a white cross halfway up a hillside; an avenue of spindly trees leading not to a stately home but a racetrack.

—What's the cross about? I ask.

—Guess somebody died, he says.

The Indian Pueblo reservation is demarcated by billboards: SPACE FOR LEASE; SANTA DOMINGO TRIBAL CENTER; DIESEL FUEL.

—At least it's your own land.

He says he doesn't live on the Pueblo any more. Gashes of red earth, extrusions of knobbly rock and pimply looking trees, bushes with guttural Spanish names beginning with 'ch'.

Higher up the horizon are the white and vermilion flat-topped outcrops he calls *mesas;* beyond them mountain ranges that enclose the valley on both sides like parentheses: Sandias, Jemez, further north the Sangres. Sangres – doesn't that mean blood? That's right, Sangre de Cristo, blood of Christ mountain. It's late afternoon, His blood is venous.

The driver wants to know where I'm from.

—California, San Francisco area, but originally England.

—Oh, thought you sounded kinda foreign. We get lots of tourists around here. You down here on vacation or something?

—Or something. Tell me, is it always this hot?

151

—Hot? You kidding? This is nothing, early summer yet, you wait.

—Oh.

What have I done? Left a world of eucalyptus-green cardiac hypnotics and come to the other side of the spectrum, where pounding hoofbeats and heartbeats are already gathering. There's dust clogging my arteries. Even the plants – ground-hogging, water-hoarding cacti – threaten to grab me by the throat like a bunch of mean-spirited gremlins.

Brain coral country.

—Over there's the Jemez range, he says pointing to an ECG along the skyline with some sinister-looking structures lurking in one of its folds.

—Good heavens, what's that?

—Oh, that's Los Alamos, the power station. A lot of people work up there.

—I see.

Excuse me driver, but would you mind taking me back to the airport?

The sky, apparently joining in the general glower, responds with its heavenly dimmer switch.

—Guess we're in for some weather here, he says, turning off the main road towards a place called Madrid – the accent is on the first syllable.

—That's how it is out here, he says, flash storms, flash floods, then it's over, blue skies again, you never knew what hit you.

We're passing through some high, lonely place: a convocation of stony English butlers, altar heaps, mini Jacob's pillars, Stonehengey teeth, magic mushrooms, sacred plumes – glorious three-dimensional inkblots!

—Dramatic? Yeah, you could say that, he says.

At which point the heavens open with a whoop-de-doo and a Somebody-up-there's displeasure. Welcome to the land of the Great Superego in the Sky. I have just failed my first test as a Southwestern human.

—Nah, he says, nothing to be scared of, it's just the way of it around here.

—Excuse me, but would you mind stopping the car for a moment.

—You mean now, mister? Up here? You sick or something?

—Or something.

152

So he stops and I pour myself out and lean over a boulder; and when I'm done and somewhat recovered I walk out, Valentine the Bold, to greet the storm, a human lightning rod in a heart-fund T-shirt.

Right here, come and get me.

First comes the flash and then the crack, and then – wait for it – the boom-ba-boom, BOOM, and then a dazzle and sizzle culminating in a coronary light show: an angiogram in overhead projection. Then – silence and sun – it's gone, leaving no sign of itself except that all of nature, including the rocks, seems to know that something out of the ordinary has happened. The lizards blink, the flowers, whose private parts have been flailed, shiver and nod; the driver drops to his knees.

—What are you doing?

—Sniffing for fire, he says.

I put my hand to my chest.

—Did you see that?

—It would be hard to miss.

—A real mountain storm, huh?

—My people, he says, believe these things are sacred messages.

—Is that so?

—Who knows, maybe that one was for you.

Oh, special delivery from God: GO BACK YOU ARE GOING THE WRONG WAY?

—Well, I say, it's all in the mind of course, a matter of perception and interpretation. You can see signs in almost anything.

—What are you, some kind of psychologist or something?

—Or something.

—You know, sometimes I think you Anglos really are crazy.

—Oh, how's that?

—You think too much with your heads.

—And what do you think with?

—We think here, he says, pointing to his left nipple.

—Oh.

We're off again, bouncing in the ruts: high desert, five thousand square miles of solitude. Apparently it's densely populated but you wouldn't know it. The houses are all dug in; only the invited can find their way, and the sun, who has *carte blanche*. My mouth is dry, my contacts – I have to remove them arc full of grit.

—What's that over there? I ask.

—Oh that's the maximum security prison. Nobody, he says,

153

escapes from there alive. They love it when some jerk goes bananas and makes a run for it in high summer. Then they go collect the picked-over bones to show to the other guys and scraps of bleached striped material for recycling. At midday your skin fries like an egg. My people, he says, call this Land of the Dancing Sun.

—Is that right?

I can think of a few other names for it.

I think we must be getting close – to what? My donor? Hardly. The closest I can come is to her mother. What the hell am I doing here anyway? The heart detective, shielding his eyes, has a bad case of the willies.

This must be it. We bump and metal-grind to a stop.

In the midst of uncharted territory, my movements no doubt observed by creatures watching from the safety of their holes and overhangs, I manoeuvre myself out of the taxi (easy does it) and grope purblind and contact-less across a strip of desert scrub towards what looks like a house carved out of rock.

Bella Cautlin is braced in the doorway like Leonardo's drawing of man and his correct proportions.

Two

—So you're Valentine, I'm Bella – howdy.

Howdy? She puts her hand on my heart – an Indian greeting, she explains. I offer my hand in return.

—Come on in, you must be real tired.

—I am rather. It's the first long trip I've done since the transplant.

—Listen, why don't you just go and crash in that hammock over there, it's real comfortable, and I'll fix some herbal tea, I've got some terrific stuff, good for the heart, speaking of which this right here's the heart of the house, I call it the Sun Room, I'll tell you all about it when you've had a rest, I designed it myself, the Indians say a round space is the most spiritually satisfying, no corners for energy to get trapped in, have a good rest there, heartman.

Heartman? She speaks in run-on sentences. My head hurts. Yet I'm like a fish giving itself up to the fisherman – *plop,* into the hammock. Above me roof beams radiate out from the top of a huge Ponderosa pine pole like the spokes of an umbrella and just out of my line of vision is a round stained-glass window with a sun motif. I'm not so sure about this high altitude.

The next thing I know she's standing over me with a cup of strange-smelling liquid.

—Hawthorn tea, feeling better?

—Oh dear, did I fall sleep? How rude – do forgive me.

—No sweat, heartman – you don't mind me calling you that? You're looking a whole lot better now, drink up, I'll show you around outside, it'll be sundown soon.

We circle the house, Bella points here and there. Adobe is the natural flesh of walls out here, she explains. It has the plasticity to be shaped any how. The bricks are made of sun-dried mud which becomes the walls. It rises up out of the earth. Most of the house is buried beneath ground. For protection, she says.

—See how it huddles against mother rock.

The house is based on an ancient pit house. Back then the first upright stone wall was 'a child's heap'. Gradually, they got better at

155

it, learned to apply mud plaster, soften corners, blend masses, thin out walls.

—It looks real simple, she says, but it's not. 'Course they had three thousand years' experience behind them.

For all I know we could be in Mexico, Spain, Africa; we could be back seven thousand years in Mesopotamia or in *fin de siècle* Mali.

—It's a real organic way of building, she says, a great way of getting in touch with the earth. You learn from your materials the feel of the stone teaches you a lot about all kinds of stuff, balance and precision and so forth, and then there's the energy of the sun. 'Course we had to blast rock for this one, but we did the bricks and the mud-plastering part in the old way and we used sheepskin instead of brushes for the finish, that's what gives it this suede-like texture.

—What makes it shine like that?

—Mica particles, we added them to reflect the light, you'll find potters around here using mica in their glazes too, neat stuff, huh?

I run my fingers around a curved shape, she caresses another. The walls are three feet thick at the base tapering to a foot at the top.

—It's all done by feel, she says, no tool is more sensitive than the fingers. Women, you know – the *enjarradora* – did most of the building.

—And what were the men doing?

—Who knows, the usual, getting stoned, loaded, laid, killing animals, they've turned up scads of evidence from excavations of the old adobe civilisations: women's fingermarks, small shallow palms.

I see an Indian house-mother patting the walls with new plaster, painting them with *yeso:* pattycake, pattycake.

—The daughters didn't ever leave, she says, they brought their husbands home and then they built on another room and another until the house became a house heap.

She runs her thumb around one of its curves.

—I have a real special relationship with this house, she says: symbiotic. They say adobe serves as long as it's lived in, once abandoned it settles back to earth. Every year the weather takes off layers of wall skin, which have to be scooped up and used to patch and heal – man and earth, keeping each other alive, that's what it's all about.

—Tell me – if you don't mind my asking – when did your daughter first go to California?

—Oh, couple, three years back. Went with some jerk who sold

her blood for money and they took off, that was the last time I saw her alive.

—I'm sorry.

—Don't be, she says, her life was bad news, I reckon her death was an improvement.

She turns her back and I follow her down a scrub trail leading off from behind the house up towards a rocky outcrop. She stops to point out wildflowers ('that big trumpety one over there's called datura'), gives me a hand at the steep places.

—This is my magic circle, she says, terrific views from up here, good place to be with the sun.

She hunkers down.

—Good view of the house, too (she points) and its domed roof, actually it's a solar bubble, you can see how it catches the sun. And the other houses, they're dotted around, they're hidden real well but if you squinch up your eyes you can start to pick 'em out, like over there there's that dusty pink one, that belongs to a writer friend, and that one, looks like dried blood –

—Tell me about the colours, what accounts for the variation?

—Depends on what bricks you get, you'll see a lot of different shades around here – anglo flesh tones, underdone pork, ski tans, chocolate fudge, mine is one of the paler ones, which is great – perfect camouflage.

She scrabbles in the dust and comes up with a black and cream pottery fragment.

—Here, that's for you.

I protest.

—Take it, heartman, the place is crawling with old shards.

And Gila monsters and snakes and coyotes and vampire bats and wild boar and rusted beds in the middle of nowhere. And what else, Bella?

—C'mon, let's get back, I'll show you your room.

On the southern side of the house is what she calls a growhole: a greenhouse dug below floor level, lush with vegetables.

—In winter, she says, the heat rises and spreads through the house, a soft humidity fresh with oxygen, in the summer there are lots of dark cool places to go and hide – it's a real energy efficient house, c'mon, we'll go down, you look like you could use some rest.

Deep down. A troglodyte's room; a room lit from skylights hacked

157

out of rock, with walls that, what with the refracted light, take on the lustre of translucent skin.

—It's very beautiful, I say. Amazingly cool.

—There are lots of blankets if you get cold, you can put your things on that shelf over there, anything else you need?

I'm staring at a large cupboard opposite the bed.

—That's locked.

—Was this her room?

—I wouldn't think about that if I were you, heartman, it was a long time ago.

—Are those her belongings in there? Sorry I'm prying. It's none of my business.

She leans both hands on the doorbeam over her head. Her body torques.

—Valentine, if you came sniffing around for dirt or some interesting case material or whatever, forget it. If I thought that's what you were up to I wouldn't have agreed for you to come out here. I was curious, so were you I figured and that's just fine but don't push it, okay, you'll find people around here like their dead to stay buried, know what I mean? Have a good rest, I'll see you later.

—I won't be long – just sort out a few things here, I say, but she's gone already. And now I lie here in this solid smooth room with its mute evidence, trying to fit the pieces together. A house that is said to cuddle against mother rock, a house in which a mother and daughter could snuggle up together around a fireplace while outside the coyotes howl and the wolfish wind scrapes the walls. These walls, as Bella explained, are practically wind-proof. No fear for human kind: a safe place, a burrowing away from wild things, weather and human ghosts.

Oh yeah?

On the wall just beside the bed there's a *nicho* – a shallow arched cave in the wall, a sort of mini-altar where people put their prized possessions: nativity miniatures, masks, ceramic animals, kachina dolls, and so on. This one is bare but for two candles in silver holders and a photograph of the former occupant of this room.

So it was you.

Three

The walls of the left auricle, according to William Harvey, are of an extreme tenuity. A nice word, that, indicating fragility and tenuousness. Whereas the left ventricle is another story altogether. This contains, he told me, the most powerful muscles known on earth for they work by day and night so long as life continues. In fact, so thick are its walls that the actual cavity hardly exists at all.

—You okay in there, heartman?

—I don't know.

—You must have been dreaming.

—I don't dream, I never have.

—You do now, heartman, you were moaning like a coyote, and look at yourself, you're covered in sweat – c'mon and have a bath, I'll show you where it is.

We travel along a narrow tunnel that appears to be covered in white icing that has slipped in places, gone lumpy in others. Bella guides me down a few steps into what must be Part Two of my dream: a bathing pool carved out of the earth and surrounded by tumbling rocks and plants and a ram's skull. Musical sounds trickle down through ferns, the smell of damp earth mingles with scented candles.

—It's based on a natural hot spring, she explains. Hot springs are very spiritual places, heartman, sulphur was considered primal stuff, 'course this is only well water, but we've got lots of good minerals around here – I've made it fairly cool.

She's got her hands in her pockets waiting for me to get in. My foot gets caught in my underpants so that I hop on one foot and nearly fall into the pool, which she thinks funny. I do not. When I manage finally to insert myself, she throws a sponge at my chest and I yelp. (The sponge has no heart for the whole animal is a heart . . .) She touches my shoulder – at least there's no electro-static charge. Could be dangerous in water.

—That must have been some dream.

—I told you it was nothing, I'm fine.

So how come I'm gripping the rocks, half out of the water like some merman about to spring? She eases me back into the water,

159

closes my eyes and makes circles with her thumbs on my temples. Oh. Am I doing my coyote imitation again? Bella, why do you have a ram's skull in your bathroom looking down on me? Her hands smell of chilis, the fumes burn my eyes; her nails, familiarly, are painted green. *Hysterics suffer mainly from reminiscences.* Who would have guessed it would happen like this?

—Hang in there, heartman.

She puts her hand on my chest.

—Just breathe nice and easy, let the breath come, let your shoulders go nice and loose, release your neck, that's it.

—Bella, I'm dying and you're doing relaxation exercises?

—We're all dying, heartman, with every in-breath there's life, every out-breath, death, we recreate ourselves each time – keep breathing, there – as you reach the furthest point of your out-breath you die and begin again, let it happen, stop holding on, we're all flowing and changing and constantly renewing, it's all part of the cycle, the in and out, don't think about it just let it happen, put your head back and let go –

She's gone. Damn her. What am I supposed to do now? Blow soap bubbles, whistle 'My heart belongs to Donna'?

Christ, get me out of here.

This is the core of psychosis – don't think I don't know it. Or I'm dead. In being mad we die, psychiatric lesson number one. We become invisible, disappear, drown – Donna, where are you? No, it's *she* who is dead, not me, that's the point. You see how easy it is to be reborn – the ultimate transference trick. How we can split, merge, re-combine; the body loses its organisation, becomes a bunch of new particles; the loved one is not only invested with trumped-up significance but possessed, *consumed* –

I should have known, put the pieces together, but how? There are no how-to's in this transaction, one cannot prepare: how tiresome is the shock. One holds onto ledges only they're rough rock and one's hands begin to bleed. The heart is tangled up in coronary arteries like bindweed, *lup dub, lup dub,* its squeeze has green nails . . . Who's there? Donna – *my heart.*

The power of the transferential relationship is that it can survive almost anything: the patient terminating treatment, an accident, even death. But *this?* The victim is fished out; as she dries out, her vital statistics (age, weight, size of heart, tissue type) are assessed; a telephone call is made to her mother in New Mexico, the go-ahead given, the heart nicely removed and brought by picnic hamper back to California.

—Donna.

—How you doing there?

Hanging on. In an effort to shore up a sense of reality the psychotic needs to rebuild his world. The reason there's method in madness is that there needs to be; I mean, one can't afford to be sloppy about this thing. The most illogical-seeming delusion thus provides for its sufferer a universe of logical psycho-dynamic relationships; somebody to guide him, converse with him, tell him why. You do for me what I have done for you, even if you don't know you're doing it. God, a patient, what does it matter?

Bella, standing over me, pushes her cowboy hat back with her thumb. This is silly, real people don't wear get-ups like that, only cowboys in old Westerns, not *mothers*, for god's sake.

She doesn't look like anybody's mother.

—Bella, did you know all the time?

—Know what, Valentine?

—Shit, you know what I'm talking about: that I knew your daughter, that she was my patient, that I was her analyst. That photograph in her room –

—It's not there anymore.

—That's not the point, you can't undo the evidence: I've seen it, the damage is done.

—What damage, heartman?

—*What damage?* Bella, do you deny –

—I told you, death is a part of life, Donna died and you're alive, I deny nothing.

—And there's nothing even mildly shocking or coincidental about that.

—Not if you look at it as part of a plan.

—*What* plan, for god's sake?

—Cosmic of course – synchronicity, heartman, these things are meant to happen, you know, parallelism between psychic and physical events, time and meaning.

—No, I do not know. Bella, I have your daughter's *heart*, do you understand? Christ, this is unreal.

She laughs.

—What's unreal? Matter is formed through illusion, the dream is the substance.

161

I should have known. It should have clicked from her letters. I should have known that of all the curses this world had up its sleeve for me, this would be it.

Bella Cautlin is a Jungian.

—The heart, she says, is one of the great archetypes.

She rolls up her shirtsleeve, reaches for the sponge, puts it to my chest and presses. If I were religious I'd cross myself. In the event, all I can do is put my hand over my shifting perspective.

Four

I follow her back to Donna's room and collapse on the bed wearing less than a towel. It's night by now. Bella lights one of the candles in the *nicho* where the photograph was. Its shadows are as alive as everything else in this room.

She tells me I'm not breathing.

—I thought as much.

—Not fully, she amplifies. You're obstructing the breath, nothing can get out if you don't breathe, it's all in there, all that good stuff, that terrific energy – that's spirit you're trapping in there (she taps my scar). She identifies tension in my neck, my shoulders, most of all in my heart – she can tell by the way my chest doesn't move.

—Let the breath out. Empty yourself. Let your defences down.

—I can't.

—You can, says Bella.

Pray do not let the side down.

I let the side down.

I let her sculpt me with eucalyptus oil. First, long, light, gliding strokes for spreading the oil and making, as she puts it, acquaintance with my body. Slow, rhythmic strokes with the whole of her hand down the centre of my legs and up the sides. Then pulling up my legs, one hand after the other overlapping like roof tiles; then kneading and squeezing those doughy muscles as she rocks her own body from side to side. Then the deep friction: circling and pressing down into the soft tissue between bones and around joints. Small precise movements, sometimes she uses the heel of her hand. Then the beating strokes: the light rapid blows using the sides of her hands – except for the heart area, it's still too sore – and finally back to the feathery strokes. She pours more oil onto her hands. Hairy legs need more oil. Those lumpy veins.

Finally, the chest (smooth: the hair has not grown back). She arranges my arms so they flop at my sides. *Before a man attains to maturity he was a boy, an infant, a foetus, an embryo . . . made up of three bubbles, or a shapeless mass or a coagulum . . .* Welcome to coagulum-dom.

—I'm liquid, there's nothing left of me; what do I do now?

—Nothing, just go with it, trust me.

Trust you?

—Let your eyes close. As your eyes close and you feel your body breathing, let your hand, your thumb, press into that point at the centre of the chest between the nipples where it feels so sensitive to the touch. Now, push.

Push?

—Just enough pressure to release all that bad stuff in there, all that anxiety, that stuff that makes you want to jump out of your skin, wish you were dead, all held there, all dying to get out, all denying life. Let it out, Valentine, let it go, rid yourself of the junk.

The great spring clean: you've heard of brain-washing, this is heart-washing.

—Free it up, let the light in.

Ah, Kepler's luminous cheese!

—Imagine – keep breathing – imagine a flame warming you from within.

Ah, all those little *nichos* in the heart, each with a flame of its own.

—All the things that are holding you back, cramping your style, causing you guilt-trips – breathe through it.

Bella, is this the closest you will ever come to culpability?

—Don't hold on . . . Let go . . . With each breath let your heart be filled with light and heat. Be filled with yourself not your pain . . . Focus your attention on that single point of light in the centre. Feel the heart expanding into space, just floating there.

The luminous sponge?

—Go into the centre of the heart. Go deeper . . . Now open its doors . . . Empty it.

But Bella, why is the cupboard locked?

—Take away your hand and fold it across your stomach. Feel the emptiness, the peace, the silence.

The first nurturing environment an infant experiences, writes Sigmund Freud, is its mother.

—Bella, what did you do with the photograph? (She kneads my left shoulder.) Did you lock it away in the cupboard?

—None of your business, heartman.

—But it is my business. I came here to find my donor.

—Well you found her, heartman. Donna – as I'm sure you know –

was too flaky to carry a Donor Card, so they phoned me, I gave them the go-ahead, you can thank me for your heart.

—Thank you.

A middle aged man checks into a swank hotel. He eats a hearty dinner then goes up to his room, falls asleep and is attacked by a witch. She stabs him in the chest and pours his blood into a leather flask, then plunges her arm into the wound and draws out the man's heart and replaces it with a sponge she's found in the bathroom and leaves. The man wakes up relieved to find it was only a dream but when he stoops to lower himself into the sunken bath the wound opens and the sponge falls into the water.

Five

Bella's studio is so far below ground it feels like a bomb shelter or a tomb, or a dug-out cathedral – the effect of dusty light filtering down from a skylight some considerable distance above, and of the Jeremiah boulders leaning over one another. The sun, by the time it gets down here is rendered impotent.

While Bella works, I snoop around among jeweller's saws and blades, crucibles and torches, kilns and pumice pans, mortars and pestles. Even the dust is interesting dust. I lift the lid of a wooden workbox.

—Those are my knives in there, she says. Sharp, watch out.

—What's this, it looks like stiff pink underwear?

—Casting wax, she explains. It's part of a process called 'lost wax casting'.

—Poor wax.

Her hair is pulled back, presumably so it doesn't catch fire from her soldering iron or get dunked in chemicals or lost in wax; her goggles are up on her forehead. I sniff.

—What you're smelling, she tells me, is plating, in that tank over there – cyanide. This acid hood is for protection. It's an electrolytic process. Most people send their stuff away to be gilded, danger of cyanide gas and all, but I like doing it myself. It's not that I'm so in love with the process, I just don't like letting things out of the studio because how do I know what's going to happen, I like keeping an eye on my pieces.

She picks up a gold ram's-head ring, turns it this way and that.

—Truth is, she says, I'm more interested in the end product.

—I've never thought, I admit, about the process of making jewellery.

—Jewellery? she comes at me. Heartman, I don't 'make jewellery', I make art. It's my form of expression, get it, an occult and spiritual enterprise, it's my vision, my vital spirit, my inspiration. It's one thing you need to know about me if we're going to get along down here: it's where I live, understand?

She breathes out, touching her heart.

166

It is also how she earns a hell of a lot of money.

She flips her goggles back down. I wander out to the photographic gallery at the far end of the studio where there are pictures, mostly of Bella and her work, plus some Indians showing their wares.

—Who's this old guy?

He looks like the Geronimo of the jewellery-world.

—That's probably Slim you're looking at, maker of silver, Navajo jeweller from about 1885.

—And this?

Suddenly she's got the soldering torch blistering away. A mother and daughter. They look alike only the woman is dark and all shine while the little girl is as pale as a porcelain mortar. The woman's got her hands on the girl's shoulders, showing off her rings to good effect. It is possible that the nails are digging into the girl's shoulders, but it may be in order to gain support – the girl's expression doesn't tell us. On my way back to the work area I upset an Indian basket mounted high on the wall: a cascade of brilliant ropes erupts from it. Fine gauge wire – delicate, valuable stuff, she warns.

Bella and Donna.

Gold. Soft, weighty, warm, ductile, malleable; it can be shaped without breaking, wound fine as hair or as thin as a leaf, sliced like tenderised meat. Mixed with other alloys, it can change colour, from rose to green to yellower yellow. It can be dull or sparkly or glowing. Like fire, another magical substance, it can transform the very air around it and make people melt with desire for its beauty and radiant warmth.

—Then there's its fiery nature, she says. It resists the force of fire – like never oppresses like, heartman, that's the secret of power. It doesn't lose weight, comes out the same as when it went in, only purer and nobler.

And that's not all. It can be traded, it can be drunk. Gold, fire, sun (the sun metal: symbol of power as well as purity of heart): the holy trinity, the *elixir vitae*. Transformation: common metal into gold, the alchemists' magic substance. In other words, perfection.

—Tell me, if you don't mind talking about it , how did you get involved in all of this, where did you learn to do it?

—I don't mind talking about it, but I'll go on working on these wing sections while I talk. This is one of my eagle pendants, it's for some rich dude down in Dallas, I guess it's for his wife or girlfriend – I studied design and jewellery at the Art Institute up in San

Francisco, then I wangled a Danforth grant and got to travel to museums all over the world, Cairo, Morocco – I even got to see the gold collection in Leningrad, that gave me lots of ideas, I came back with thousands of sketches.

Silence while she polishes between the feathers with her burnisher as if her own take-off depended on getting in there.

—I gather you're doing quite well?

—Yep, too right, and I deserve every penny of it, I've worked my butt off to get where I am. When I got back from travelling I landed my first teaching job down here, that was in Albuquerque in the new craft arts department, round about then I first got into doing my butterfly pieces and then got into eagle and sun shields and custom concho belts and things really started taking off – I got a gallery to handle my work and then an East Coast show and then it was museums and eventually I was able to build this place. And that's been the most important thing for me – sun, rocks, canyons, plants – it's all out there, the organic contours, the rough and smooth textures, the repetition of shapes – feathers, scales, leaves, bones, skulls, horns – it's a real treat living out here if you're an artist.

—I can see that. What about Donna?

—That was pretty sneaky, what about her? Mother abandons baby and goes flying all over the world to study winged forms – how'm I doing? Okay, so I didn't have a whole lot of time for her, how could I, I was busy studying and travelling and living and that's how it was, and there were men in my life too and she cramped my style, so okay I didn't make it as the world's greatest mother but (polish polish) I'm no *monster*. I mean I was young and dopey and I made a mistake and it was before abortions and it was real important to me to make something of my life and if you're thinking what I figure you're thinking, doc, forget it, I don't blame myself for her being so *weird* and – don't look at me like that – it sure as hell wasn't *my* fault she rode her bike into the sea.

—Bella, you needn't be so defensive, I wasn't judging you. Let's go back to the gold: why gold in particular?

—Why gold?

She stops burnishing and swivels round.

—You really want to know why gold, I'll tell you: my father.

—How lucky I didn't have a father. Was he an artist of some sort?

—Definitely – bullshit artist, con artist, you got it. Shit, he wore a

168

Stetson at one end and gold-tooled high-heeled cowboy boots at the other and there wasn't much in between besides belly and prick.

She goes back to hammering.

—I thought he was your inspiration, you said –

—I said he inspired me to work in *gold*, that's different: a yen for sparkle, sure, he passed that on to me, gave me a taste for gold every time he stuck his face into mine. That fucking gold tooth, I still see it in my dreams.

—Oh, by the way, she says, tossing me a chunk of what I take to be gold, before you go to bed drop that into a cup of water, in the morning, drink it.

—Drink it?

—Good for the heart, she says. It's the minerals. I have a friend who practises Ayurvedic medicine in Albuquerque, I told her about you, she says you're a gold-deficient type.

—And what is this type, Bella?

—Let's see (she reads from a book): gold types are cheerful when talking about death, under the delusion that their heart is turning around, lacking in self-confidence; always striving for perfection; oh, and they tend to see spectres, spirits and ghosts hovering in the air.

—Bella –

—Listen, she says, don't worry about it, just try it, it can't hurt and it may do all kinds of good things – it's supposed to strengthen your teeth, make your hair thick and shiny, make your skin glow, and best of all you forget your goddam sexual angst –

What does she know about that?

—Heartman, I reckon we gotta do this thing right, first the transplant and now the transformation. Hey presto (she snaps her fingers): *chen-jen*, true man.

Very pretty, Bella. And tell me, shall the true man/new man awaken with a heart of gold? Or no heart at all?

Six

Twenty-four carats, gold with a difference: of the earth and yet not of the earth, a philosophical secret. Do I believe it? I scoop out the trifle, weigh it in my palm, feel it with my thumb, drop it back into the glass and watch as it swims to the bottom: a tropical heart-fish, a fluttering scarlet bird. I hold it up to the skylight and watch as watery dragons appear surrounded by five dazzling colours and an array of dog's teeth. The dog spits out stalagmites like mid-winter icicles which in turn throw up rocky masses like lava. Warm, spirituous, perfect? Who knows, but it's better than prednisone any day. Glug glug.

Actually, I am feeling much restored, expunged of a vivid New Mexico morning: emptied of all non-essential spongiform-cardiac matter. Let bygones be bygones and semilunars be semilunars, and let all our *nichos* be virginal and the cava of the vena be like unstuffed manicotti and the aorta as a silver flute. And so may our atria be as light as styrofoam and our ventricles as full as the Red Sea for ever and ever, amen.

Keep those candles burning.

More gold dust with boiled water for breakfast, Bella? *Quinoi* – and hawthorn tea? Actually, if you don't mind, I think I'll just help myself to some Sanka (de luxe gold label) and sit here feeling virtuous, soaking up the ambience of bleached pine and bone counterpointed with the dried blood of terracotta – such a nice combination of shades and colours. I practise my Mister Clean of the Bosom deep-breathing techniques. Bella, why are there skulls in different stages of decomposition mounted everywhere I look? Are you doing a comparative study or is this some kind of designer leitmotif to go with the Navajo rugs?

Ghosts, according to local lore, are said to have a 'bad heart'.

Well no wonder. So it's simply a matter of keeping up the good heart anti-ghost campaign: off with you, flick flick of the dishtowel, quick sweep with the broom; it's crowded enough on this planet without you guys coming back to invade us.

Bella says her prayers prone: on her back centred in her magic

170

circle, golden heart and golden thighs open to her all-father Father (the sun), and a great stretching of the arms and a tinkling of gold ornaments and a parting of the thighs to receive the ejaculation of sunbeams. (See Ernest Jones for a discussion of the phallic nature of the sun.)

This is no alternative nostril breathing session.

Last night Bella examined my tongue. The tongue, she said, is the sprout of the heart. Mine is furry: a bad sign. Well, Bella, I told her, the clitoris is the sprout of the womb. Is that so? Quite so, I said: one of those useful little titbits one picks up in medical school.

I am rather puzzled by this problem of the locked cupboard. As a matter of fact, none of it makes any sense. Tell me, Bella, given your belief in and wish for avoidance of returning revenants: (a) how is it you chose to donate your daughter's heart; and (b) how is it you agreed for me to come here? Curiosity? Or is this some kind of spiritual alchemical experiment? I am beginning to feel slightly uncomfortable. Please don't misinterpret this. It was a generous act, giving her heart, I'm grateful. I'm just trying to comprehend.

One has to scrunch up to get through the passageway into Donna's room, but once inside it's like a perfect little chapel: cool, white, bare (except for the cupboard and bed), complete with altar. Never in my life have I seen a shape so white and satisfying (I run my finger round it) framing absolutely nothing. How can there be nothing, Bella? How can the photograph have disappeared? I know it's the way with things out here (flash storms, flash floods: now you see it now you don't), but these mysterious disappearances can become in themselves rather compelling.

I remember a story Claire told me, it was about a nunnery in some hot foreign place of long ago which was famous for its 'picture' gallery of first-night sheets from the Royal marriages. Framed in ornate gold. Oh regal Rorshachs! Oh blood and semen Divine! The story, however, concerns the last of these 'portraits' which was a square of virgin linen, not a mark on it. It was called 'The Blank Page'.

What do I see when I close my eyes? A bare white altar. And after that? I see the Queen of England, empty of function but mighty full of significance. *A meaningful symbol of our time*, amen. Archetype, Bella, *archetype?* Shall we just have a peek in that cupboard now?

Don't push your luck. Valentine.

Seven

Sticks and stones may break my bones and names ('you Freudian flake') may break my heart – but I jest of course. We are made of stern stuff, both heat and Jung-resistant. Which is the problem according to Ma Belle, who listens more or less politely to what Dr Freud has to say on the subject of dreams ('an expression of immoral incestuous and perverse impulses or of murderous sadistic lusts') and then says, I think he was out of his fucking skull. Of course she knows nothing about his theories, or Jung's either for that matter, but her response is that my kind of 'knowing' is about as useful as a sun lamp in New Mexico. The body, passion, gold and the sun are the only things worth knowing about. She turns her goo-goo-eyed gaze up to that great fat slob in the sky with the all-too familiar gold tooth. However, I am barred from speaking my Freudian *craperoo*. Save it, she says, take a holiday from that weird head of yours.

Her inconsistency is extraordinary. *I* don't need, she says, to worship these paper phallic gods of yours. Oh no, yours is made of glowing matter a zillion times the volume of the earth and in a permanent state of effervescence exploding every second from its core where the temperature is thirteen million degrees centigrade, sending fountains of flame shooting out into space. Hot Daddy!

Don't you see, Bella, how it is, how none of us escape? That however you may despise me for my Sigmundolatry, you too have been seen to get down on your knees – or spread them as the case may be – in *worship*? You want to know what I call it? I call it *phallocentrism*. Claire, where are you when I need you? So you don't worship the penis. Congratulations. You worship the phallus instead. Follow the golden tool, eh? You may not know it but you are a good Lacanian. We could argue the issue of *phallo-* versus *andro-* centrism, but we won't. The point is that you are still operating in relation to a Primal Father, a powerful Other, and within that model you cannot escape castration. Welcome to the club.

She tells me I'm spending too much time holed up below, which is what Donna did too and it drove her crazy.

—What are you doing down there anyway?

172

—Filling myself in on a few things, I say.

—You read too much, she says.

—I'm getting into those Indian stories. I have discovered that ghosts, besides taking the form of ravens, vampire bats, dogs and lizards, can also take the form of men, pale, horrible and thin.

William are you listening?

—Forget the stories, she says, try living for a change. Come up into the light, heartman.

The beginning of the world started in darkness. The people lived underground where life was cold and miserable without the sun to warm them. However, First Woman solved it all by mating with the Sun, or rather one of his beamlets, and in due course giving birth to a couple of energetic and forward-looking War Twins who said to themselves (more or less): Gotta be a way out of this dump. Of course we know that First Woman, who was 'sad in her heart as a mother is sad for a sick child', was behind the Twins and their rescue operations.

These twins are known collectively as Ahaiyute, but I'm thinking as I read that they might have been more aptly named Adolf and Benito. Their solution was this: first they set up a ladder out of the underworld. Then they started dividing up the people, red this way, yellow that way, brown over here. The ones who fell down (monsters, cripples, idiots, the sick and the old) they kicked out of the way; or they stepped on their backs, from which position it was of course easier to get onto the first rung and thus into the light.

However, when the Terrible Twins got to the top and opened their eyes, they were in for a surprise because the light from the Sun was so stabbing and blinding that 'they cried out with pain and their eyes watered and their tears flowed'. But as their tears hit the earth they blossomed into sunflowers. Bella has many in her garden.

Actually, I am busy studying the cupboard. An extremely interesting piece of furniture probably belonging to some old New Mexican folk art tradition: four-square, four panelled, stocky, crude, primitive, its legs nothing more than cobbled-on wedges, its side strips nailed together. So what is interesting about it? Its hinges and keyhole, which are curiously ornate, and the fact that it is locked.

The pine is quite old and, being hollow inside, quite resonant, though the sound changes depending on where I tap. It behaves rather like a sounding board, I suppose. The wood itself, when I put my ear to it, has a kind of vibration of its own, and is warm and rather perfumed, though the metal bits are cold and if I put my nose right up to the keyhole and sniff I can detect a musty smell. In the middle of the night I sometimes hear flapping or soft drumming noises coming from within.

Bella, even you must know the effect of an off-limits cupboard, especially on someone in my susceptible condition. We need hardly discuss its symbolic significance. ('Whenever a man dreams of a place . . . and while he is still dreaming says to himself, "this place is familiar to me, I've been here before", we may interpret that place as being his mother's genitals.') Speaking of which, do you know the story of Sigmund Freud and his nanny? Once upon a time, Sigmund Freud lost his nanny − she'd been thrown in jail for shoplifting. Simultaneously, his mother was busy with his new baby sister. So he's understandably distraught: where is my nanny, where my beautiful Momma? he cries. Psst! Over here, his wicked brother informs him, *in the cupboard*. I don't believe you, says sceptical Sig, the precocious scientist (he was three): show me (let's have some demonstrable proof here). So his brother flings open the doors − Voila! − at which poor little Siggie sits down on the floor, pisses his nappy and cries his heart out.

Drip drip drip. It's the middle of the night; but for that maddening drip onto a wooden shelf the house is dead quiet. It can't be rain, where is it coming from?

The patter of bare feet, the smell of a cigar. Who goes there? A cigar-smoking person of restricted stature takes my hand and pulls. The hand is sweaty.

—Come, it says.

—Come where? Who the hell are you, *what* are you?

—Guess. (He blows smoke in my face.)

—What do you want with me now?

— I'm here to help you. The cupboard, he growls, There's only one way to find out what's inside.

—But it's locked.

He smacks his forehead.

—Look, I presume she's keeping it locked for some reason, anyway this is her house and I'm her guest, I have no right to stick my nose in her business.

—Hah! Ha ha ha ha hah! (He holds his sides, drops cigar ash on my bare foot.) Frear, you are a case.

—Leave me alone, I say, I'm going back to bed.

—Do you resist me?

I try to pull away. He's surprisingly strong.

—You want illumination or don't you? Think, *Dum–kopf*! You want to spend your whole life in this cowardly intellectual *scopophilia*? Jerkoff! Get going.

—No, Yes. I don't want to see. Anyway, what about you.

—*Halt den Mund!* You are an idiot Frear. If you do not understand you will be stamped into hell. Is that what you want? Okay, go back to bed and diddle yourself, I'm leaving.

—No, wait.

—Hah! I knew it. Look how excited you are, my friend. You can't wait to find.out: incest, cannibalism, a lust for killing – who knows what wonderful traumatic incidents are buried in there.

—Wait a minute, whose traumas are we talking about, hers or mine?

The cigar wiggles up and down in his mouth.

—Yours of course, you booby. How much longer are you going to live with these desexualised displacements of yours. Eventually they will get the better of you. As I wrote. But now – *we're going in men!* – are you ready, Frear? The hallucinatory wish-fulfilment realised at last!

—Wait – I'm not ready. I need to think about this.

—Think, Frear!? Why are you always *thinking*? Phooey-plunge!

—How? How are we going to get in?

He laughs so loud he starts choking. I slap him on the back. The whole room is filled with smoke.

—She's hidden the key.

—I have my own key. (He digs me in the ribs with his elbow.)

—Where did you get it?

More mirth.

—Look what she's done to you, Frear, turned your guts to fruitloops. So have you forgotten lesson number one? Who else can get into the cupboard but the *father* or the analyst? And how does he get in? Right, with his big *key!*

He takes out his penis. It's not very big but it glows like a torch in the dark.

—So, you ready, Frear?

Drip, drip, drip.

He inserts his key–penis in the filigree keyhole, turn the lock (click clunk) and flings open the doors. One of the panels slips.

175

—*So!* What have we here? One droopy sunflower (he tosses it aside), water dripping from the top shelf. Is that all?

I scoop up a drop with my finger, lick it.

—Well? says weeny Dr Freud.

—Salty.

—Of course, semen, *ja*.

—Wrong. Tears. The beginning of the world.

Eight

In walking the heart seems to shake about as if it were loose; at times a single thump of the heart; palpitation of the heart; violent palpitation of the heart; a kind of restless anxiety, arising in the region of the heart, and driving him from one place to another, so that he cannot stay anywhere.

Gold as a Remedy in Diseases of the Heart by J. C. Burnett MD

I am walking in the desert, placing one foot in front of the other in my lightweight Roots, bought dearly on Vine Street in Berkeley, around the corner from my office where Donna had her 'analysis' and not far from the car wash where I had my heart 'attack'. I am trying to tune in to animals and insects laid low by their all-father Father who are art up yonder and would winkle them out and fry them up for lunch given half a chance.

No, of course I shouldn't be out here at this time of day, but one cannot hide from such a pre-eminence indefinitely. I mean, he *knows* what's what. He crooks his finger with the chunky gold ring and yodels: Come to me, my son.

Yes, Papa.

I obey, and how glorious it is, even though the bastard is charbroiling the back of my neck, arms legs, head (I must get a hat), to be walking. At last one needn't think. Not that it stops me seeing things: Bella slicing into that sheet of gold with her scalpel; Donna slicing her veins until the scar tissue on her wrists is so thick she can't buckle her watchband; my mother's gold heart-shaped locket baptising my forehead as she presses me to her ever-failing heart; Bella's father (Donna's grandfather, whom she never mentioned) presenting her with his gold tooth; Freud's mother also pressing him to her bosom whispering, *Mein goldener Siggie . . .*

There's a rabbit crouched panting under that overhang; thus I am thinking about that most bizarre of all my donor's symptoms, the rabbit fantasy. I thought it was all of a piece with certain of her more vivid descriptions of the landscape out here – its beauty but also potential hazards and cruelties – which, though well done, frankly seemed exaggerated: too juicy, too bloody, too *too* to be true. Now I

177

begin to understand that this place is by definition *hyperbolic*: a dream/nightmare landscape complete with giant blossoms and snakes and tarantulas and dingoes and coyotes running around; with horsetails growing as high as palms; with the sun growing pustulous and blood-shot; with women dripping gold but lacking a deal of maternal tenderness; not to mention men walking around with hearts not their own. In such an environment, to be-think oneself a rabbit is not as lunatic as it sounded once upon a time in my breezy Bay Area office.

What is this rabbit's behaviour then? If not down his safe hole, he crouches panting (as we have already observed) under an overhang. He sees mirages, tries to reach water and cool trees that aren't there until finally he drags himself into the shade of another overhanging rock and crouches *there* panting (yes, a rather repetitive routine but I am not here to *sell* rabbit behaviour, merely to describe it). Look at him. His fur is caked with dust, his eyes ache and his ears twitch. 'Why does He have to be so hot?' he groans. It's all rather cutesy and anthropomorphic, but that's how the story goes. It's called 'How Rabbit Shot the Sun' – one of Donna's favourites. 'What have we done to deserve such torment?' Rabbit squints up at Sun and shakes his ears, 'Go away! You're making everything too hot!'

'Where do I begin? asked my impatient 'patient'. And I answered, Why not begin with a dream? Gaps, hesitations, obscurities, incompletenesses and chronological mishaps – no problems, I reassured her, it doesn't need to 'make sense'. In fact, I expected her associations to be rather rabbit-like. So I sat there and observed (patiently) as she scampered and darted from hole to hole yet found nowhere safe to hide, made wild backward leaps, and even got frozen to the spot. That was all right. You must understand that when our patient's 'get stuck' is when we make our best moves as amanuenses, guides, *ghostwriters*. In rendering that patchy, thin-eared child's tale into smooth narrative fiction complete with beginning, middle and (I hoped, satisfying) end, I believed that I was nudging her on, showing her a way forward. But in the end she somehow failed to be rabbit-like enough, for in telling (or re-telling) Rabbit's story, she threw me off the scent. Because it sounded too much like a story, I grew suspicious and failed to listen to what she was saying.

Rabbit is experiencing murderous feelings towards his father. Running, always running towards the eastern edge of the world, he yells, 'If he doesn't stop shining, I'm going to kill him!' But by the

178

time he gets there, Sun has bedded down for the night. 'Yellow-hearted creep,' sneers Rabbit, or words to that effect.

He hides out, waiting to ambush Him. Ha ha, laughs Sun. He figures he'll have some fun. He rolls away from his usual rise 'n' shine place and sweeps up into the high Oedipal sphere before Rabbit knows what's hit him. Ouf.

By now Rabbit is almost dead from the heat but he won't give up. Day after day he prepares the ambush but Sun always pops up in different, unexpected places. Then one morning He rises in a sort of *Schlamperei* (Freud's term for his self-confessed theoretical sloppiness). Rabbit, on the ready, draws his bow and, *whizz*, the arrow buries itself deep in His side. Ya-hoo! Rabbit goes bananas, rolls on the ground, does cartwheels. But when he next looks at the Sun his heart sinks, for where his arrow has pierced Him there is a gaping wound and from that wound there gushes a stream of liquid gold. The whole world has been set ablaze. Flames shoot up and rush towards Rabbit, crackling and roaring. Oh what have I done? he cries.

Rabbit hides under a cottonwood for a while, but the flames are getting closer. He can feel their breath on his back. He hides under a greasewood tree until that's about to snuff it. He keeps going (*pant pant*) but his strength is failing. His fur is beginning to singe. He dives under a small green bush with thin branches and flowers like tufts of cotton, his eyes shut, his ears flat against his body, quivering. His heart is going like gangbusters. As the sheet of fire whizzes overhead the little bush crackles and sizzles. Then everything grows quiet. Rabbit raises his head, cautiously. The earth around him is black and smoking but he is safe. The little bush is no longer green (it's now called desert yellow brush).

And Rabbit? To this day he's got brown spots where the fire got him on the back of his neck. He tends to exhibit neurotic, even *hysterical* symptoms. Jumps at the slightest noise. Runs and hides if anything comes near him. Blinks, twitches, freezes under scrutiny. Would go careening off a cliff under the right circumstances. A lovable but entirely pathetic member of the Animal Kingdom.

And what about the Sun? Well, just look at Him. You can't? Of course not, that's the point. He blew up. He got so hot and cocksure of Himself that now no one can look at Him long enough even to sight an arrow. He is afraid of nothing and no one, not even His own shadow – which is bad news (see Carl Jung). There are stories that one day He may microwave the world for a snack. In other words, He won. End of story, end of trail, end of the line. *The* end. Oh, except for one thing – he always looks both ways before he heaves his whole body into view in the morning (the snool).

—I knew a mountain once, Donna began (If you look in my case notes you'll find it there) it was up in the Jemez towards Lost Borders down in New Mexico where I lived with my Mom. She's beautiful, an artist, she makes things out of gold. Nothing grew there except scrub, even the lizards hid out. One day I saw a rabbit, which was special because they'd been wiped out by the heat. This one had brown spots on the back of its neck.

There were further closely observed details, as I recall, about the precise way its ears twitched and its nose wriggled; in fact (it comes back) she said,

—I wouldn't be surprised, doc, if rabbits' feelings were in their noses.

—Mmn, yes, I crooned, underlining that one.

Of course then everything began to go OTT, which is when I put my fingers together, swivelled round in my chair so I could get a better view of the sailboats in the Bay and began to dream my own dreams while she told me all about how she brought her Dad up to the secret place to show him the rabbit and he shot the rabbit and raped her, or was it the other way around?

Welcome to the talking cure.

I think I'll just sit down under this overhang.

It is well known that Freud 'reneged' on his seduction theory – that he changed his mind about whether his 'hysterical' patients had been seduced as children. At first – so the story goes – he believed them. He even reported a dream in which he was feeling 'over-affectionate' towards his eldest daughter, then wrote to Fliess: 'The dream of course fulfils my wish to pin down a father as the originator of neurosis and put an end to my persistent doubts.' But soon he came to disbelieve them; and still later he decided they were remembering not real seductions, but their fantasies of seduction. The scene of seduction was a double disguise: pure fantasy converted into real memory. He compared these fantasies to the 'imaginary creations of paranoiacs which become conscious as delusions'. He was bewildered. 'Reality was lost under one's feet.' It was *he* who'd been seduced.

The retraction may of course have had something to do with the fact that it was no longer nursemaids and governesses who were the

180

chief culprits, but these fathers and uncles. But how could so many fathers and uncles seduce so many girls? Katharina, Dora, Anna – impossible! Then there was Freud himself and his own father. And with all those hysterical brothers and sisters in *his* family, would the finger not point? No! It cannot be.

He was consumed with desire for a solution. How he searched – as I search – for a way out of this sucked-dry dreamscape, for the bedrock of an event. What about the long-suspected *Urszene* – the original or primal scene? He searched and searched again, like a detective on the scene, to establish something beneath that reverie, the novelette that comes with the telling and the re-telling of an event, the editorialising of our desires and fears. Did it happen or didn't it? You see how determined we are to find our way – and not just any zig-zag cross-country path through leg-scratching scrub, but a definite and definable *trail* whose outcome is known? It happened, it didn't happen. Who knows? The area is inadequately mapped, the terrain pitted with danger, hopping with ambiguity. The heat is devastating . . .

What's that? There, there a thimbleful of cool pool – the trickery of the sun and one's shimmery eyes in cahoots, the mythical moment where thirst and sexuality meet, where the heart throbs in a kind of primal *Organlust*. A mirage.

This is where one begins to see luminous yolks oozing everywhere. In such a place, I feel I could be walking in his doomed footsteps, scuffling from fantasy to 'psychic reality' until the idea of a verifiable event is as hilarious as a drink of water. Welcome to the desert of Freudian *Fiktion* (no way out). Is that you? No. A delusion, the *ground of reality* gone. I might argue (if my brain were not Cream of Sun Soup) that this hopelessly beautiful but confusingly contradictory landscape, stratified pink, orange and blue – in which one canyon leads to another or where one goes round in circles – is his true and important if uneasy and unsatisfying legacy. Except for the fact that I am hopelessly lost and left, willy nilly, with the curse of his disavowal (the efflorescence of pubertal sexuality).

One sits on a rock with sun-dried egg on one's face.

An Ohio University study of heart disease in the seventies was conducted by feeding toxic, high-cholesterol diets to rabbits in order to block their arteries, duplicating the effect that such a diet has on human arteries. Consistent and unsurprising results began to appear in all the rabbit groups but for one, which strangely displayed sixty per cent fewer symptoms. Nothing in the rabbits' physiology could account for their tolerance to the diet until it was discovered by accident that the student in charge of feeding these particular rabbits liked to stroke and pet them. He would hold each rabbit for a few minutes before feeding it. Astonishingly, this alone seemed to enable the animals to overcome the toxic diet. The experiment was replicated and similar results obtained.

(1) Does that mean that evolution may have built into the rabbit 'mind' an immune response that needs to be triggered by human cuddling?

(2) Is the body, psychoanalytically speaking, a fiction?

Nine

Having been dunked and revived and fed (squash blossoms, jalapeno peppers, strange little deep-fried flour balls called sopapillas) and given a hearty red wine to drink, I am now sitting yoga-style on the floor under the great viga-spokes of the sun room being eyeballed by Bella. And what do we call this little number when it's at home, Bella: the facial Rorschach; psychic laser works – ; Jungian ping-pong; yin-yang transfusion service (bloodless, very clean); anima-animus introduction agency? She calls it Tantric meditation. It looks to me more like a staring contest. Basically you stare at one another without speaking for ten minutes. I must be mad, I have agreed to do it. You have nothing to lose, she tells me, but your Self. Oh, is that all?

—Think of it as a creative journey into the landscape of the face, just let yourself wander.

—I've already done that number. What if I get lost again like today?

—You got found, didn't you?

—What happens at the end of it?

—You'll find out. Stop trying to know everything beforehand or you take all the adventure out of life, and don't forget to keep breathing.

—I'll try.

She sets the timer and we're off.

The fact is if you stare at a face long enough it stops being a collection of standardised hardware store fitments. You know what happened when Freud looked into Irma's mouth? He saw nose-bones, scabby, horrible. When I look into Bella's face I see puma-coloured plains, smooth peach-coloured bluffs. Wind sculptures, pockmarks of pinon and juniper – so far so good. A stone bridge. Cliffs burning red from within. Lava walls that could cut like glass. Grape-coloured shadows. This isn't as easy as it looks. Rock crevices too sharp to grow a tree. Craters too deep to climb out of. Nothing stirs except a rattler. Flicking Indian red pentstemons, fire-weed, lichens, ferns, so-called innocent little stonecrops – how do I get out?

According to Indian legend, the Eagle Person, or First Person, flew higher than anyone else in order to get above it all. He hovered on a warm thermal, enjoying himself, anticipating his pleasure.

But when he looked down, all could see was death.

The all-father Father of the sadistic streak bounces his wares off rock, twisting their flues into pink candy floss, that stuff that disappears in your mouth so you're not sure if you've eaten it except that afterwards you are left with a smear of darker greasier red on your face like the River Chama which Bella calls a heartening colour but, oh, somehow it hurts and why, because my blood feels charged like that river with its red sand dragged down from the mountains; and the light of this place lies on my eyelids like blood; because with the cauterising of the veins around my heart and with the sense of so many heart-liberated children running around the place – everything catches again the way it did that day sun struck glass on a ship out on the Bay and I shouted Fire and there was none.

—Time's up, Heartman.

Ten

Taken medically gold can affect the brain, cause temporary loss of vision, pustular eruptions, tenderness in the nose, foulness of breath, retching, flatulence and icy cold hands and feet; also sexual excitation (the genital sphere is powerfully moved; a long dormant appetite is roused and generally great orgasm of the parts results therefrom).

J. C. Burnett MD

—Bella, it's the equivalent of *two flights* – remember?

—Don't worry, heartman, we'll take it real slow, one step at a time.

Well, there are flights and flights. Some curve so elegantly and have such fine-turned spindles and smooth-to-the-touch mahogany handrails that one doesn't know one is climbing; and at some point there is a turnabout and one is swooping down the banister and the glide is such a gift that one closes one's eyes and puts off thinking about the inevitable crash at the bottom.

I think we have just entered beyond *Beyond the Pleasure Principle*.

—Tell me, Bella, what is the difference between a Tantric meditation and sex?

The sexual act, according to Bella, is to the microcosm as the power of love to the whole cosmos. Two bodies unite, members seeking out like members, in a symmetry of form and a synchronicity of heartbeats that echoes the harmony of the spheres.

Bring on the violins, Mantovani. Bella, a matching of heartbeats even between two *normal* hearts is improbable; between yours and mine – forget it. Nor do our magic circles match up – mine is more like a seamed egg. As a matter of fact, as our microcosmic coddling proceeds, I begin to feel as if I might make a dreadful mess on the Navajo rug: a rich brew of egg-nog, chilis and gold dust.

Bella explains that the libido, contrary to popular (Freudian) opinion, is not limited to sex *per se*. It is about the psyche and its neutral energy: light, fire, the sun, creativity; in short, the life force. Dissolution and creation, emptiness and totality, death to the world and unity with nature; a drowning, a merging with the Great Mother

185

in a world of undifferentiated water. Thus, one 'overflows with emotion', 'bursts with energy'.

There are difficulties. I have not been well. My warrior spirit's feathers are moulting. My kidneys seem to be jiggling about inside me. My gums feel like puffed, deep-fried Indian bread. Wouldn't it be nice to feel, as Galen did, that sexual pleasure softens man's lot on this earth – begging for a moment the question of the soggy mattress.

Sex scenes are notoriously difficult to describe: either embarrassingly purple or embarrassingly euphemistic or simply embarrassing full stop. *I bare my chest. She stares into my eyes and breathes, it's as if we are welded together – just like one of her torso pieces.*

Leonardo, presumably speaking of heterosexual sex, has this to say about it: 'The act of coitus and the parts employed therein are so repulsive that if it were not for the beauty of the faces and the adornments of the actors and their frenetic state of mind nature would lose the human species.'

Poor Leonardo.

Sigmund Freud also had his problems – no sex after forty-one we gather.

As she traced the scar on his chest a spurt of blessed nectar, the condensed cream of Truth, passed from one to the other in a shower of celestial bliss . . .

We seem to be at the bottom of the ocean floor among the primal spongy muck. Enough! Let us kick our heels and rise! *Jouissance! Two flights*, nothing, give me five, ten, fifteen . . . Give me the never-ending staircase and such a rise that only dreams are made on . . . to cloud-capped towers, gorgeous palaces . . . The discourse of sex is the discourse of freedom. Whoopee! Look at poor Doppler who stayed with his dull, unloved wife and turned into a robot, and then compare him with Koch who left his wife for a cute cookie and went on to cure tuberculosis and cholera. What more proof do you want of the beneficial effects of a good fuck?

Eleven

Where to? Bella is taking me to an Indian ceremony on some magic mountain down near the Sunspot Solar Observatory. We're going on her Honda Gold Wing, an absurd machine, a sort of motorcycle version of a stretch; a fat-wheeled bicycle – built-for-two with black padded upholstery and gold star studs. (Donna had the same kind apparently.) The body itself is painted shiny black with thin gold lines, mirrors fly up from the handlebars in a huge V, its innards are exposed under the body, its exhaust is obscenely visible. What I think is: *donorcycle*.

I am remember, a man, who drives a Volvo station wagon – a family car. It's also the first time I have been on a motorcycle! and I must confess to finding the experience even more frightening and uncomfortable than I'd imagined. Exciting, yes, that too.

We're making good time across the desert, wearing goggles, spitting frequently. Hot wind. A café sign sails off into nowhere. Bella says the windstorm won't last. The boulders, like a bunch of heavies lined up along the road – vast chests, pinheads – seem to nod. Amphitheatres of rock, giant mushrooms, an altar with lumpy saints, an operating theatre complete with the body parts of giant creatures including a square-headed whale with eye-hole, a human hand, a rabbit's rump, a camel's hump.

—Bella, do you know how to get a camel to pass through the eye of a needle? Answer: liquidise him first. Your daughter told me that.

Bella says it's time to lay the ghost.

Ghosts are dead persons who are in some sense still alive. They make doors creak, cause sudden illness, accidents, and so on. They may appear as an ectoplasmic shadow or a mist. They seem to pervade the Navajo world after dark, appearing as coyotes, owls, mice, bats, whirlwinds, spots of fire or indefinite dark objects. They make noises – whistling sounds – of birds and other animals. After sunset, fear of ghosts keeps the Navajos inside their hogans.

Will we make it across the desert before dark?

Somehow I don't think all this is credible, except that it's happening. Where are we headed, what for? Ah, to get in touch with

187

those lower-level forces: the Ki, Chi, Hara, belly, and gradually to the very hearth itself. *Go into your heart.* Enter, step right in folks. A tin-roof tabernacle in the desert. If you get thirsty all you do is tear open one of those cacti and suck. Watch out for the spines though.

Is it part of some curative plot (*cura*: anxiety, care, cure)? Well, it won't work, I tell you, because only in a secure place are we cared for and thus without care, and thus free to dance on mountain tops without falling off a cliff. Yet around us I see a place of heightened awareness that encourages insecurity, paranoia; a conspiracy of unhappiness; a desert's beauty and its attendant sorrows dragging themselves across the high domed places like revenants. And if I suffer from negative magnetic forces (from North Pole-itis or what-ever), from living in my head, from denying the Goddess aspect of myself, from an emotional agoraphobia, it is for the same reason that your daughter, Bella, hid out, sucking her thumb huddling against mother rock instead of mother. You get my drift?

Corpses whose lives have been truncated do not rest in peace.

We are headed for a de-ghosting.

Indians, according to Bella, believe the human spirit can pass into the body of another person. So how do you get it out? Answer: you sweat it out. I have never held on so tight in my life.

Twelve

The Temple of the Sun.

The first sunrise, as we know, was terrible to the War Twins, causing a howling and a tearing of eyes worse than after the eating of an extreme chili. I know how they must have felt, for having completed the desert journey by night and arrived in time to watch one of Pop Sun's repeat performances, I'd say he hasn't lost any of his original hot sauce. He's getting hotter. Where are my dark glasses, Bella?

Tipis surround the inner circle, the Sacred Hoop. At the centre is the Sun Dance Pole, about fifty feet high; also known as the Living Tree, except that it isn't living since it's been felled in order to set it up here. Twigs, skins and offerings have been placed in its high-up fork to represent the nest of an eagle.

Q: What would the Eagle Person see if he looked down?

A: A dead tree festooned with scarves.

The place is already crawling with Anglos, Germans, Dutch, Japanese; Buddhists, Rastafarians, Jews, Mormons – a tribe of international spirit seekers in leather, silver and beads. Bella, in gold sunburst medallion and concho belt over a pair of shiny shorts, stands out. Even her hair is like fiery spaghetti.

The dancers have already been here for a couple of days, fortifying themselves with prayer prior to the Sun Dance. Their faces are painted red with black chin circles and nose dots. The younger ones wear juniper wreaths on their heads, while the warriors and shamans wear the Sun Dance head-dress which is hung with ermine tails and crowned with eagle plumes.

The Dance will last for several days. During that time the dancers neither eat nor drink. The idea behind it is that one gains vision through hunger, pain and exhaustion.

Nursing mothers who have brought their babies to be blessed, lay them down at the base of the Sun Dance Pole, the symbolic centre of the universe. *Grow up and be brave. Make your people proud.* Children, it is said, are the guardians of our immortality.

189

Holy men are down on their knees preparing for the first event of the day.

—What's on? I ask Bella.

—You, heartman, she says.

It's the ear-piercing ceremony.

Before leaving her house, Bella presented me with a gift: a fine gold heart earring complete with digital innards. I admired it, thinking, What's this then, back-up lest Donna's should fail? I'm sorry, I said, handing it back, but I don't have a pierced ear. You will, she said.

Bella whispers to one of the leaders and I am beckoned forward. *Now?* Oh god. I lie down on my back amongst the dancers, like the white spoke in a heap of multicoloured pick-up sticks. *Grow up and be brave. Make your people proud.* Something cold numbs my earlobe. I try thinking about the circle, the idea of which is very strong hereabouts. The sky, the great circle that surrounds us. The Earth, the circle that supports us. *Mother Earth in her roundness provides us with the fruitfulness of life.* The sun comes and goes in a great circle. The heart is the sun in the bosom . . . tipis are round . . . the blood goes round . . . *Oh the blood goes round and round, ho ho ho ho, ho ho, and it comes out . . .*

Ouch.

My fingernails are filled with dust. There's blood on my ear, now trickling into my shoulder. Van Gogh cut off his earlobe. I always thought it was the whole ear but it was only a small piece. Still, what's one little hole compared with that? The artist's heart, he wrote, is like a broken pitcher. And what comes trickling out, Vincent, turpentine and a scum of lost love? Look where the sun got *him*.

I feel for my ear: it's still there. A heart of gold dangles from it. *Valentine Frear: He wore his heart in his ear.*

Many of the dancers have already been here for days without eating or drinking. Even after four days they still sweat, which doesn't make medical sense: the body can't survive without water, after a few days the kidneys start to shut down. But they are doing it.

The Indians are no fools; they know blood and sweat must be mingled with light relief. Thus the *Koshare*: the delight-makers, the Shakespearean fools, the clowns, the almost-ghosts. Supposedly

190

invisible, they wind their way in and out of the crowd making mischief: tying shoelaces, untangling hair, mimicking walks. Now they're peering into people's faces, touching chests. Somebody explains that they're pretending to be the ghosts of departed relatives and they're on the look-out for people in the crowd with bad hearts. In that case, let me be gone. Bella has already done a bunk – she went for a smoke behind a tree, but was caught by one of the *Koshare* who is now making terrible faces at her, drumming with a small drum in her ear, generally making a nuisance of himself. She blows smoke into his face.

But the *Koshare* have sniffed me out and pretty soon all three of them are gathered round, bobbing and waggling their feathered heads, pointing at my chest. I look down. Is it leaking? One of them removes his mask and bends his head to listen. Now the head Shaman has shambled over to join the party. Apparently – somebody translates – there is something strange about me: I look to them like 'a luminous egg'. You mean transplant radiation? Donna was it contaminated? The Shaman puts a hand over my heart and says a prayer for me. No translation is forthcoming. Bella, can we go home please?

—Nobody leaves now, heartman. The Pole Dancing is about to begin.

Smaller drums like a pulse in the throat have joined the great drum. A raucous symphony of eagle-bone whistles. Each dancer in turn lies down at the base of the Sun Dance Pole and a holy person makes an incision in his chest or back. A piece of wood is thrust under his skin. The peg is fastened to his spirit-rope and that's tied to the Sun Dance Pole. The pierced dancers stagger to their feet and start on their rounds, wheeling and chanting, their eyes following the sun across the sky. *Heya, heya, hi-ya.*

The dancers will now dance round and round until their spirit comes free, along with a lump of skin.

'Here I shall haunt . . . I shall hear the drums far down in the dancing-place . . . I shall see the Sun Dance on the top of Toyallanne and know what was in the hearts of the men of Pecos . . . ' So wrote Mary Austin, an anthropologist visiting New Mexico back in the thirties, who saw wonderful things in those bared hearts – like the wings of the argemone bursting and floating apart. I see only what the Eagle Person saw.

Many of these ceremonies were considered barbaric and have been banned for much of our century, but four years ago the Pueblos lobbied and the decision was reversed – the Office of Indian Affairs is into revitalising Indian culture. So here we are, the sun beating, the great drum starting up, the chanting to the sun getting going: *We have only you in our minds. If we succeed today civilisation will endure.* I feel for my ear-heart. It really makes me feel quite jaunty. Bella says it looks 'neat'.

There are around a dozen official dancers so far. The rest of us gather round in a great circle to watch. As the drums increase our feet move in sympathy and our bodies sway – though with me it's less a dance than a stumbling. The Pole Dancers seem set, in spite of their bulk, to go on forever. Jiggle jiggle go their overdeveloped male breasts. The orderly functioning of the universe, the grand design of circularity, a oneness with nature, a bunch of fat knees going up and down in the scorching sun, head-dresses slipping down sweaty foreheads. Heart disease is up by thirty per cent on the reservations due to lousy diet, obesity and alcoholism. Where are the funny guys when we need them? I feel for my earlobe and this time come away with blood. *Heya, heya, hi-ya.*

There shall be no rest for the dancers until the skin breaks and the spirit is freed and if any of them stays on his feet until sunset he shall become a medicine man. *I give you this piece of my spirit, give me the peace of your presence.*

And what happens to the luminous egg, Bella? He gets coddled.

—Time for the sweat lodge, heartman.

192

Thirteen

We duck down and enter a low, dome-shaped hut covered with rather mangy-looking skins and with a hearth dug in the centre filled with red-hot stones. There are already a dozen or so people squashed together in a circle around the hearth and I'm thinking this is where I get off, but Bella grabs my arm and pulls me forward. The circle somehow expands for us.

We take our places, knee to sweaty knee. What would Sigmund Freud, who couldn't take eye-to-eye contact, have done with this?

—Relax, Bella whispers, nudging me to breathe.

Breathe what, there's no air. Somebody lights a long clay pipe and puffs, which is even worse. I feel, in what is fast becoming an obsessive gesture, for my earring: what if it melts in the heat? What's the temperature in here? Anybody taking blood pressure? The pipe-lighter coughs, regards his pipe, gazes up at a piece of dangling animal skin, smiles and comes out with an anecdote about some guy called Scar Face who went to a sweat lodge and came out minus his scar. Do we really need the hard sell? I cross my arms over my chest.

—A place where miracles can happen, a place of great energy, he says. At this people join hands so that the energy can flow round without interference. I uncross my arms.

—It's just a question of letting go of that bad energy and inviting the good stuff in. Welcome. Do anything you feel like, he instructs. Talk, sing, share your feelings, be quiet, whatever your heart desires.

Bella nudges me to take off my T-shirt, which is wet-through.

—I can't, the scar.

—So what, she says.

So what? Bella, a fourteen-inch vertical sternum scar is not a thing to bring to a sweat-lodge 'n' tell. Or is this my appointment for spiritual cosmetic surgery; and shall I leave, like Scar Face, a seamless wonder? The pipe is handed on; sweat drips from elbows. It's hard work letting go.

More positive mumble-mumble. *Heya, heya* . . .

The man across from me takes a puff and breaks into what sounds like Hebrew chanting. It is. The Jews, he gets round to explaining, have a similar ritual to the Indians: they bind leather straps around their arms and heads symbolising the connection of hearts and minds to the Tree of Life.

—Since we're talking of *bindings*, I say, let me tell you about the *Geradhalter*, or straight-holder, invented by the illustrious Dr Daniel Gottlieb Schreber back in the last century. A fascinating guy, this Schreber. He created a whole armoury of goodies to discipline the growing child's body: a sleeping belt kept him strapped so that he couldn't masturbate; a shoulder band stopped him slumping; the head-compressing machine, the *kopfzusammenschnurungsmaschine* for god's sake, kept the head from lolling on the neck in its *Schlamperei* way.

People are looking at me. How do I know about this weird stuff? Answer: because Sigmund Freud based a case study on the writings of his son, Judge Schreber. Schreber became a famous nutcase, suffering delusions and visions, and writing his memoirs in the comfort of a Viennese mental asylum. One of Schreber's symptoms, I tell them was the chronicling of miracles 'enacted', as he put it 'upon my body'. Among them were 'the miracle of the eyelids', which he described as little men pulling his eyelids up or down as they pleased with 'fine filaments like cobwebs'. Then there was 'the coccyx miracle' in which 'god-like rays' invaded the lowest vertebrae and made sitting or lying down impossible. And then there was 'the compression-of-the-chest miracle'. He felt the chest wall being compressed 'so that the state of oppression caused by the lack of breath was transmitted to my whole body'.

—So you see, I wind up, from swaddling to strapping, how it all comes round? How what begins as a tenuous connection through a mere filament or cobweb of fine-gauge gold wire suddenly turns into a sturdy harness. How what connects us to the Tree of Life can also bind us to the Pole of Death.

—I'm not surprised he went nuts, says an anonymous sweat-er, with a father like that.

—I guess it depends on how you look at it, says a girl with a droopy feather in her headband. But I thought we were here to let go of all that yukky stuff. Isn't that the point?

I think I must be smiling in a sort of luminous, eggy way.

The Jewish man is for some reason moved to tears.

—Thank you, he says and I know he means it because he touches his heart.

I think I'm suffering from compression of the chest. Before I know what I'm doing I'm peeling off my wet T-shirt. Now my mutual perspirers really are staring at me. The Jewish man asks if he can touch the scar.

—Sure, why not.

Anybody else for a cheap thrill? This is easier than psychoanalysis. Feather girl leans forward.

—May I? Ooh, it's so intense, she says, it's like communing with, well you know, the *source*. Gee, I'd really love to hear all about the operation, I mean it must have been such a *powerful* experience.

Yes, a real knockout and I'd love to tell you all about it, but perhaps another time.

—Where are you going?

Bella leans forward. A drop of sweat from her chin drips onto her sunburst, *ping*.

—The Phoenix, she says in a sort of banana slurry voice, resides in the fire of the heart. Let's remember, folks, that we're here to release the spirit.

The Phoenix, that curious bird, not unrelated to the chimaera perhaps, with the trick of picking itself up out of fire and flying off with only a few scorched wing feathers. But what if it doesn't get enough wing motion going, what if it's too young, its feathers too soft, its muscles inadequate to the exercise? Duh, how do I get out of here, it's getting warm? The flames are nipping at her tail feathers, but she's just not putting two and two together. Go, Phoenix, go! She panics, digs in her claws, and hangs on for dear life. It's not so easy to Phoenix-exit from a flaming heart. No, stupid, up up and away. Flap Flap. At-a-girl. This time she rises up squawking, only not for long and then – *splat*.

—When I was a kid, I tell them, a local farmer gave me a chick and instructed me to keep it nice and warm, so being obedient and literal-minded, I went home and put it in a box and bedded it down on top of the oil stove and turned up the temperature gauge. I would imagine flaming Phoenix smells not unlike cooked baby chick.

—The vibes in here are getting me down, doesn't anybody have anything *positive* to talk about?

—Yeah, me too.

—Okay says pipe man (there's a good sport). This is a sacred place, full of the spirits of beings, animals and human, the energy of imagination; most of all the perfection of dreams. (He sighs.) The

195

feathers tied to prayer sticks outside the lodge frame are like living ornaments blowing wishes. I think we should all make a wish from the heart.

—Yeah.

Sweat, sweat, sweat – so will a healthful flood be opened which comes from the heart.

—Yeah.

I notice they have that communal clammy-eyed look that could pass for enlightenment on a dark day. But *insight* in the Freudian sense? When the sun goes down they will be drinking wine out of jugs and eating spiritual stir-fry topped with toasted marshmallows.

—Lift up your hearts, God exhorts us, offers my Jewish friend.

—Yeah.

Oh yeah? Lift up my heart? I think that's a mighty fine idea, only what did you have in mind, some kind of pulley inside the rib-cage? Something is wrong in there. It feels like a steel ball. What is that line from Shakespeare? *I cannot heave my heart into my mouth.*

Besides, I have other plans.

—Where do you think you're going, heartman?

—To a dance. If you'll excuse me, folks.

I bow out.

The Indians welcome me, a pale scrawny Anglo with a gold heart dangling from his ear and a rather remarkable scar running from breast to belly button. An old man with a chest not unlike a dry stream bed himself puts his hand flat across it and listens through his palm.

—Let the spirit which is fire go out of the body, he pronounces in wise audible tones. Then under his breath,

—You sure you oughta be doing this? That fry-boy up there is a real bastard.

He puts the peg under a flap of skin up near my shoulder. He's afraid to go anywhere near my scar. Then he ties the other end of the rope to the Sun Dance Pole. Peg o' my heart.

—Now all you do is you dance until the flap of skin comes loose. Just like pulling teeth in the old days, ha ha.

He squeezes my other shoulder and says,

—Take it easy there, feller, okay?

Okay. I'm off. I'm dancing and I don't feel a thing, round and round, *hey-heya boom boom*, nothing to worry about, no where-to-next, no what-to-do; just follow the bouncing yellow ball up there on the blue board and when I need to rest my neck and eyes, I follow the red trail on the ground. Good clean fun, *heya, heya, hiya, lup dub ho*, and oh the vultures and the Eagle Persons will be breakfasting well.

My chest is burning, must be something cooking in there, some yeasty brew of the spirit. It feels like Old Faithful getting ready to blow. *From deep underground comes a bubbling muttering sound.* No don't stop me, I'm doing fine, I'm ready for anything; rakish, youthful and shiny-hearted. I have to keep lifting my feet or they'll stick. Welcome to the great melt-down. Round one is for Mother Earth. *We love her the way a new born infant loves his mother's heartbeat. Lup dub, lup dub.* What was that syncope? Where is the sun, where are the other dancers? And what's that roaring noise, that pressure in the throat?

Round and round and . . . I was like one of Plato's perfect little spherical beings who got punished and split in two and was condemned to journey, night and day, pining for his other half, analysing, analysing, round and round, dying of dehydration, exposed in his heart-free state like a half-moon on its back. And then they interrupted this inefficient sport and plopped a heart into its hole and sewed me up – whole again! – a replete, jolly spherical thing, round and round we go.

Round and round, now on this hard dry crust of a volcanic eruption, on the top of a mesa looking down into a canyon so deep it's dark even in sunlight and I see the creamy cup of a datura growing up from between two rockfaces, a breast heaving with gold and the sun looking down and licking his lips.

Go away, Sigmund.

Round and round we go, this round is for memory, everything wiped clean, *locked away in a cupboard* and it is *uncanny* but *boo-hoo* to the uncanny, says Sigmund Freud, it is something that ought to remain hidden but has come to light and it is experienced, *hey-ya ho*, in highest degree in relation to death and dead bodies and as I look down from my high plateau what do I see below me but a hollowed-out cavern which is not a cavern at all but a steep-banked, dark-panelled operating theatre and there at the bottom is – yes, it is he – Dr Freud taking Dr Harvey's place at the dissecting table, lighted by candelabra, yes, showing a bit of tooth (can one really call that a smile?) as a jet of blood spurts from a split-open left ventricle; and at his feet are three skulls and two hounds and above him a few armless statues and a skeleton; and now Dr Freud, if I passed this microphone down to you, could you possibly say a few words to our listeners out there? What was that you said?

Mors ultima linea rerum.

Death is the bottom line.

In the middle of all sits Sun enthroned, ruling his children. The good father? Centre of the universe corresponding to the heart of man? I see a sun who looks down on some lost mountain and sees a child's face and on that face a look of intolerably familiar hurt, and what does he do? He holds his yellow belly and laughs.

You also laugh, Sigmund?

And you, Bella?

How dare you.

Round and round, Freudian lesson number one, it's in the canonic blood: holes, bowls, bagels, caves, tunnels, funnels – empty things that need filling up. Round and round, poor Judge Schreber conceiving a passion for the sun, imagined himself impregnated by those divine rays . . . *You are my sunshine, my only sunshine . . .* and giving birth to a new race which would be pure and redeemed – and so much for his father's binding and strapping and opening his heart with his big key – HAH! Oh isn't it FUNNY? No? Oh holy shit holy fear oh sun his face is crazed, he's not amused he's about to burst his gilt-bonds . . . sorry, Sunny, I can't help it, I've got my own tapioca pudding on the boil, swelling up, filling with magma . . . or gas . . . it's on its way, this is it, no, don't stop the drums, here it comes, keep on dancing, can't stop now, *hey*, this is the beginning and the end, *ho*, the act of creation, let her blow – relief is at hand. *Lighten our hearts, we beseech thee, O Lord.* The volcano roars, a stupendous fat rolling yodel of chest-thumping self-expression, oh nothing can stop her now and it's one of the great fireworks displays of the century. *The mountain is bursting!* shout the sailors from off-shore as she (Mount Pelée) blows her fumarole and the great coming is at hand. The dragon ejects her stuff through a V-shaped notch like a colossal gun-sight, a boiling red river which shoots down at a hundred miles an hour through the heart of the city, coating everything red, red rocks, red legs, red feet as if we'd been swimming in Beppo's Bloody Pond Hell. Terrible! Wonderful! Awe-inspiring! Nirvana! And how!

And now: out of my way: *hey heya hiya oh . . .* Scatter! Geronimo!

Judge Schreber, resurrected, experiences a feeling of something limitless, unbounded, *oceanic* – the heartfelt burp – while I on my last round, *heya heh*, shed my piece of flesh and coincidentally there she is, emerging in a shower of incandescent ropes: Donna Cautlin jack-knifing straight off the cliff, Evel Knievel style, and into the shimmering ocean below.

*

Fourteen

We are back at Bella's house. I am recovered though still shaken by all that sizzle and whoop-de-doo around the Sun Dance Pole. My eyes burn as from a fever and I am not inclined to budge from Donna's room, which is cool. It makes me think of wet jungly banana leaves wrapped round the head. I am soothed. Occasionally I lay my forehead against the white iced walls.

One thing I did do was jiggle open the cupboard with my Mastercard: a cracking open, you could say, all round.

The cupboard contained a burial urn with ashes. Donna's of course. Also some curious paintings done by her, and lastly a photograph.

Gourmet magazine people have been arranging the dining-room table in the Sun Room with a white cloth and pink tulips in jugs. I do not see how pink tulips fit the picture, but the designer mind has its own logic. Pink and grey napkins, two sparklingly empty wine glasses, two perfect white plates. The studio lights remind me of the operating room at Stanford. I think I'll venture out while they finish setting up. They are doing a feature spread about some gold skewers Bella has designed and executed herself.

By now the mountains are purple and hazy. I'm suffering from chapped lips. The air is not generous with itself. The Virginia creeper is creeping; the *arroyo* that was the river is so dry I can almost hear it cracking; or the sagebrush is going electric. The skin on my heels also has runnels and gullies. At sundown the lip of gorge further below us bleeds, then turns grape-black. Nature seems at odds with itself, exhausted, yet like a middle-aged woman still able to produce fruit, though you'd have to suck to find moisture. This is a landscape of starved souls.

It puts me in mind of one of your illustrious dreams, Dr Freud. You opened a book, there was a dried flower inside. What did it reveal? Guilt: you forgot to bring your wife flowers, you wrote a paper about cocaine, you once cleaned a herbarium, you had an obsession for buying books . . . and so on. That was how it was, you sat at your desk and analysed and analysed, endless litanies, dry associations.

Why is the flower in your dreams always dry? You stuffed your mouth with that fat cigar, your head with your own obsessive theories, your nasal passages with cocaine and your study with statues of naked ladies. You turned your female patients into dry texts to be deciphered. You sat at your desk and deciphered. Music, phooey. You stuck your nose in certain paintings and books but what did you see? Abnormal psyches, instinctive desire, masochistic submission, love based on pity . . . save it. The paintings I found were heavy with the colour red; only it wasn't paint, it was blood: her own.

The mountain post-eruption. What would you say about St Helen's for example? That it lost its head (ejaculated), leaving an erect white cone looking like a molar that needs filling? Or: cathartic relief, aaah?

Well, it depends. Take another example: the Virgin Islands volcano, turn of the century. In the wake of that one there came ash. The city was buried in it, the surrounding land stripped. A lot of people were barbecued. A three-ton statue of the Virgin Mary was sent flying forty feet from its pedestal. The area of devastation was roughly eight square miles, helical in shape, like the DNA molecule and the heart. Another twenty-four square miles were scorched and ravaged. So much for catharsis, eh Sigmund?

Let's look at a dream about men being whipped on the back, ringlets around their heads of wild rose-brier beaded with drops of blood, palms uplifted in supplication, headed for *Calvario* dragging a bloody cross between them? This was how Donna described it to me, except that I now know it wasn't a dream at all but an actual event which she witnessed:

It was when I was about twelve we were staying at Abiquiu. I couldn't sleep so I got up and wandered around and I heard this weird tootling noise and some lights heading up the valley, so I followed and when I got closer there were these shadows and then this guy came towards me with a black bag over his head and a huge wooden cross dragging over his shoulder — really freaked me out — then there was this other guy, he was hugging a cholla — one of those cactuses with needles like barbecue skewers — to his bare chest. The third one was getting whipped by the guy behind him. Really weird. I dropped to my knees and hid in a wild plum thicket, it was spring I remember, it smelled so good, but then there was all this whipping and moaning going on, it was hard to put it together. I followed them for a while then I fell asleep on the ground. When I woke up it was raining but it hadn't washed all the blood

201

away so I could follow the trail home, just like Hansel and Gretel. Then I found out they do it every year. Afterwards they hold a chipotle and sopapia breakfast around the crucifix.

What say you, Sigmund? Come on, let's have something original for a change. Repressed homosexuality? An old story, an annual performance, *Oberammergau*, we've seen it, the Passion Play dismissed in a puff of cigar smoke? Sometimes your Freudian slough fails to penetrate. Yes, *penetrate*.

The heart? It seems you crawled into the less salubrious nooks and crannies but you gave *it* a wide berth. And we followed, god help us. What was it you wrote to Jung? 'People find me strange and repellent, whereas all hearts open to you'.

The photograph in the cupboard shows a group of people seated around a dining-room table. Laughing, raising their glasses. The table is laden. In the foreground looking directly at the camera is a little girl with a face like a Queen Anne cherry and curly matted blond hair. She's offering an empty bowl to the camera. One leg is in front of the other and her mouth is screwed up to the side. The photograph is captioned: *Golden Bowl – Donna's birthday party*. It was evidently used in a feature article about Bella in *Arts USA* magazine.

Empty bowls notwithstanding, the only tree taller than me hereabouts, the cottonwood, is beginning to bear, in place of leaves, little heart-shaped fruits. According to a local author they come up burning like the bush in the midst of which was God.

Ahead of me is a wild plum with a bloom like that purple haze. There is also a mangled car tipped into the canyon. Take your pick. If you can accommodate both, good luck.

I drop down into the valley and walk along the road. There's the road gang from the *penitenciario* selling their wares – bits of tin in the shape of different body parts spread out on Indian blankets in the dust. Arms, hands, eyes, feet . . .

—What do you do with these? I ask.

—You got a friend who's broke his leg, you give him this foot. Your wife wants to have a baby, you give her this swelled belly. You want to quit smoking, you take this lung.

—What about this?

—You got a friend with a heart problem, mister?

—You might say so. What do I do with it?

—Okay, you take that to the *Sanctuario* and make an offering. You hang that around Santa Nina's neck. Any day you go you find her

202

loaded down, her little shoulders are draped with satins, lace, beads, crosses, pearls, baby shoes and a lot of these *milagros*.

—What does *milagro* mean?

—Miracle.

—Does it work?

—Guaranteed.

Sure. Bendy tin, a heart that looks more like a strawberry, a rip-off if ever I saw one.

—I'll take it.

When I get back I hang it by its red ribbon around the neck of the urn which I have taken out of the cupboard and placed in the *nicho*.

Excuse me, I think I'll just be off home now.

203

PART IV

Whether or not the heart, besides propelling the blood, giving it motion locally and distributing it to the body, adds anything else — heat, spirit, perfection — must be enquired into by and by.

William Harvey

The heart is what remains of me, once all the wit . . . is taken away.

Roland Barthes

One

I sit between them: Claire on the aisle, William at the window. *The face is pale but the ears are red as if about to hear all*, for in spite of grasping the rudimentary principles of aerodynamics, he is stricken with a flying panic. (My psychoanalyst's luck to have a phobic spook!) He clutches at the armrests, his knuckles more prominent than usual.

—What you need, William, is a drink.

He orders his usual tipple, a Bloody Mary. Lethal.

—I wish you'd have something civilized for a change, like a gin and tonic or a Martini or even a sherry.

The olive eye glints.

—I shall have it, Frear.

What does one say to such a bloody-minded ghost? Claire drinks Perrier water, I go for a whisky, William gets his.

We are flying to England for two – make that three – reasons: (1) It's time William went home; (2) It's time Claire had a look at the obscure Northern coast I hail from; (3) It's about time I revisited it myself. Last Great Journey Before Death? Let me be unoriginal.

Flying. You can imagine what Dr Freud had to say on the subject: to fly or to be a bird is a disguise for an infantile erotic wish. *Fly me, I'm Sarah . . . Georgina . . . Kate.* Those crude airline advertisements. Claire hates them. Freud would have crowed. *Hah! Who needs more proof?*

Getting above it all. I think of the Eagle Person, a.k.a. Sigmund Freud, who flying high looks down and sees death. No surprise there – the expected response from graduates of the Viennese School of Raptors. Outrageous! I shall have every neo-Freudian in the land down on me with the collected works (twenty-six volumes). I'll never survive the attack. Is this all he saw? No, of course not. He valued life as he did art, but in the end he reduced it to an alphabet soup of despair. D is for Discontent, E is for Envy (penis), S is for Sex, P is for psychopathology, A is for Anxiety, I is for Illusion, R is for Rationalisation. A real gagger.

What about the other letters that slide down, like J for Joy, O for

207

Oh! L for Love, L for Life, Y for Yahoo? It can't *all* be dross. I see him rolling his eyes to heaven. What am I going to do with you, Frear? What's happened to your head? You mean the erstwhile noble sphere, Sigmund? Gone. Replaced by a tomato. O ignoble beefsteak!

All right, he concedes defeat. You want to believe, so believe. The weak-minded need their illusions. I thought you were one of us but if you need to jolly yourself along to make the tail-end bearable then go ahead, who am I to stop you. But – so predictable, Frear! So unoriginal! Just like all the others. Of course I have learned to live with these ritual slayings, indeed I have so many holes in me I could pose as St Sebastian. He is weary underneath the *Weltschmerz*, the disgust is palpable. I hear you Sigmund, you're coming in loud and clear. But what about the other way round? I beginning to suspect that the feeling is mutual.

Oh my god, what have I said? Scratch that. Do I care? Of course I do! What do you think I am, a Tinker Toy boy? Somewhere amongst the wooden wheels and sticks there's a little hand-me-down motor that yearns for a fatherly pat. Hear that, Paper Freud? *Lup dub, lup dub.* Is it not music to thine ear?

Sigmund Freud thought music a bloody waste of time.

William, on the other hand, has been listening to Handel's Ode to St Cecilia, his smile rather gooey under the headset. Roll back the years, eh Will? Tell me, I ask, what do *you* see when you look down? (We're flying higher than the Eagle Person, courtesy of American Airlines.) He follows an imaginary plumbline, as it were, from the underbelly of the plane down to our womb-mother the Pacific. A great tub of ebullition, he says. We're still riding the coast.

About Claire I have my suspicions. Yes, she wants to see England and to 'get away' after an unhappy love affair with a certain Professor of Women's Studies – a rather Victorian response it seems to me – but the unspoken agenda is that she is here to look after me. The daughter as nurse-companion – yes, much as Anna was to Freud. ('Promise me,' she implored him, 'that if you should fall ill some day and I'm not there, you will write me about it immediately, so that I can come?'). The analogue is something we do not discuss. At least Claire is no breathless Papa's angel, his diminutive, his co-worker, his 'dear interesting creature'. How I should hate to get letters from her dripping as Anna's were with longing; hate to find myself writing to her, 'one misses you greatly' after only a week. Poor precious little Annerl. Well, poor Sigmund, helplessly entangled, intellectually and emotionally tortured by his need for her, by his need not to have such a need, and above all, not to have to be demonstrative about it.

But what was he to do, given his weakness for her, with that seductive maternal care; with letters *saturated* with longing for him: 'I think about you a lot and greatly look forward to a letter . . . when you have time to write'. The constant theme: oh, her father was *such* a busy man! How, in the face of all this, was he to maintain that surgical distance he insisted on for others? He didn't. He exempted himself, he ignored his own rules. He took on his own daughter as analysand and to hell with what the others thought. 'Keep no secrets,' he urged her, 'don't be bashful.'

Amazing how this avowed truffle-hound of sexuality managed to deny his daughter's sexuality. He behaved in relation to her like a man who had never read Freud. 'She does not claim to be treated as a woman, being still far away from sexual longings and rather refusing men.' Well, Sigmund, might you have had something to do with that, you old weasel? 'There is an outspoken understanding between me and her that she should not consider marriage or the preliminaries before she gets two or three years older. I don't think she will break the treaty.' You don't think, eh Siggie? Well, by that 'treaty' you made bloody sure she'd never marry. That Jones might come a-wooing you, but *not* your daughter.

No, my Claire is no one's creature. I'm lucky she agreed to come at all. But it's a chance for us to spend some time together, as she says. She means, of course, before it's too late.

Go fly, the arms are the wings of the heart.

Even after two months I still have Bella's voice twanging in my ear. I also have her gold heart, slowly revolving in its orbit, dangling from my earlobe. Claire says I look like a new man (or does she mean New Man?); Ruth, when she saw, covered her mouth and snickered. William called me shit-breeches, his stock response to the post-Paracelsians (roving hippie quacks, more or less) of his time. Not that this stops him toying with it in his childlike way.

Donna Cautlin? Her heart resides in my chest still. *The strong heart of its child mistress is mute forever?* No, Mr Dickens, not in this case. Or at least, its child mistress may be mute but the heart still *lup dubs* in the bosom of its recipient shrink, swelling and shrinking as hearts do. Just as it's about to shrivel and die it gives a mighty heave while thickening with blood and grows again, thus resisting its own demise.

209

For the time being.

How am I? I'm not sure. One hand asks the other, as William's patient John Donne said. Alive. The pulse quite healthy, if fast. The summer was cathartic. I am now prepared to entertain the following statement: my donor is dead, the heart is mine. The pen shakes as I write but there it is, something to strive towards, some foreign shore, if you like, where the heart and I may in due course come to take up residence together in a *modus vivendi* of sorts.

Pilots, ferrymen, guides at crossroads, forks in forests, at the base of boulders: the mythical figures who offer their services (on a wing and a dinghy) to the lost. Analogically, I suppose, I am ferryperson/ pilot to my patients: load up your gear and off we go, *hump hump, punt punt, zoom zoom*. You'd rather a stately stroll and the crooked arm of a gentleman? Delighted to oblige.

But who is going to take *me* across? How does the analyst/ transferencer complete *his* journey from child to adult to parent to old person to . . . Who shall be *my* guide? Any offers? William is making his way through a Dover sole which he complains tastes like boar's bristle. I nibble some fish and a roll, no butter. Claire is eating her vegetarian alternative and reading, as it happens, about guides and guiding.

—Tell me what it means to guide.

—In your language or mine? In the male sense it's to lead – push, shove, command. Drill sergeants, teachers, psychoanalysts, doctors – you guys who go around telling us what we should read, swallow, think, dream . . . Manipulators, secret agents, possessors of our minds and bodies –

—Claire, that will do, I get the idea. And in your language?

—Guiding is about inviting, she says, an opening-out not a closing-in. The guide gives permission, not orders. She doesn't stand by or look down on her victim like you guys do. She accompanies. To guide is to go on a journey with somebody, make cosmic connec- tions, enter the struggle yourself.

Ah.

The 'Fasten Seatbelts' sign is flashing: I think we have hit some turbulence here.

The problem is that the whole process has reversed itself and I am flying, as it were, backwards. *Before a man attains to maturity he was a boy, an infant, a foetus, an embryo . . .* I am a bean in the womb. By the time we arrive I shall have reverted to a twinkle in the eye. This is starting to sound like some kind of re-birthing nonsense.

My guides: on one side that weird seventeenth-century spook William, on the other my daughter Claire.

I have just started writing in my fourth fat spiral-bound notebook. The first and third were blue, the second and fourth red. How could I not think of the exhausted and vital sides of the heart.

William, now plugged into a raunchy-looking film called *Wild at Heart*, is into other things. Claire keeps getting seduced away from her book. And I from mine. A man is beaten to death; a young couple screw . . . and screw and screw . . . flames . . . a witch-mother. William is in a mild hypnotic state. Claire, revolted yet fascinated, can't tear herself away; though in the end – violence in its more subtle forms being so much more seductive – the fascination palls. Yuk, she gurks, pure sexploitation. Catapults herself out from under her food tray, and stomps off to the toilet.

The blasting, drilling, chiselling, boring, impaling, screwing of women – ah, the language of love!

—When the male is capable of intercourse, offers William, the hair on his throat and neck grows black, and the extremity of the prepuce becomes of the same colour and stinks abominably.

He quotes from *The Intercourse of the Hind and the Doe*, William Harvey, Exercise the Sixty-Sixth.

—Thank you, Doctor, that will do.

We'd been early at the airport, Claire and I, so we strolled around. The departure lounge sported an art exhibition called *The Right Foot Show*; shoes, feet everywhere. Giant papier-mâché clown shoes, tiny button-down doll-size boots, foot art galore. Claire stopped in front of a brass heart with a spike-heeled shoe, forties style, on top of the heart. Its title was, 'Stepping on Hearts'.

You couldn't do it with a real one. Picture a fist-sized organ, quite bumpy and slippery, no shapely slab of burnished brass but zig-zagged with stripped muscle fibres. It wouldn't balance, the beat would throw it off, the spike would make holes from which blood would spurt. Still, I said, it's quite a good iconic representation of the period, those padded-shouldered, platform-heeled forties toughies: Joan Crawford, Bette Davis and so on. No man would step on *their* hearts. And what, she asks, do you think made them so tough in the first place? Well, we know, don't we, how once upon a time, when their hearts were young and gay (okay, innocent), they gave them to somebody who mangled them. But never again. The boot is on the other foot, or rather the foot is on the other heart. Or better still let's all go barefoot and massage each others' big toes, which is only possible woman-to-woman according to Claire.

So have you managed to simplify your heartworld, my daughter? No more stepping on hearts, no more gendered violence, no more sex-linked power trips? She blew her nose, hard. What I object to, Dad, is your fucking cultural stereotyping. I mean, you guys are really heavy into making women look like the baddies again. Poor little boys being stepped on by big bad mommies, oh poor widdle woo, does it hurt vewwy much?

You see? They could not be more different, Anna and Claire. Freud got away with everything; I get away with nothing.

The movie is over. William, having conquered his flying panic, or anaesthetised it with Bloody Marys and Lynchean sadomasochistic sex, is now holding his glass up to the overhead light and with two fingers seems to be blessing it with the other hand – *Sanguis itaque est spiritus . . .* – while muttering murkily about blood and the spirit.

—William, what's coming down here?

—I speak of *this*, Frear, the prime and principal fluid, the celestial liquid . . .

Good heavens, is this an after-dinner drink or a bloody Eucharist? Through a glass coated with *ros primigenius?*

—Please, William, lower your voice.

—Frear, you do not understand.

—Too right. William, I thought you were a scientist.

His eyes are crossed as he watches my heart go round and round in its golden circlet. When it comes to rest he gives it an encouraging flick.

—Frear, so many before me have spoken of the spirit as an aerial or ethereal substance, something more excellent and divine than what is natural. They went so far as heaven to fetch down I know not what virtues from without the body – but I say it is not so.

Apparently his friend Fludd imagined a sort of champagne of the spirits making its pneumatic way through the bloodstream.

—No, Frear, he goes on, no more can it be expired than inspired. The spirit cannot be distinguished from the blood nor the blood from the spirit; for the blood *qua* blood, that is, by virtue of its nature and movement round the body, is identical with the essence of the stars and is endowed with animation and therefore divinity.

—William, this is sounding rather shit-breechy to me, if you don't mind me saying so.

—Then you do not listen to my words. Attend, sir. We are too much in the habit of neglecting things in front of our noses, in a manner of speaking, of worshipping specious names which seem to come down to us from some invisible source. The word blood which we have before our eyes and can touch has nothing of grandiloquence about it; but before such titles as spirits and *calidum innatum* we stand agape. No longer, Frear. The mask is removed from this idle division, this artifice of body and spirit. The two are one. And the first ranking seat, *sedes primaria* of that spirit – he flicks my heart again, sending it spinning – is most assuredly the Sun of the Microcosm, since it is mightily perfused with blood. The first to live and the last to die and all from a drop of blood . . . Betwixt the visible and invisible, betwixt being and not being, as it were, it gave by its pulses a kind of representation of the commencement of life.

Suddenly he turns to me, panic stricken.

—Am I flying, Frear?

And with that, before I can reassure him, he conks out, his greasy head on my shoulder.

The plane sleeps. Claire rests against my other shoulder. I put on a headset and twiddle the dial. The last Schubert Quintet: music, said Thomas Mann, one could die to.

I open the in-flight rag and read a review of a book called *A Wolverine is Eating My Leg* by one Tim Cahill. Here is a man who walks across Death Valley in high summer, scuba dives amongst poisonous fish and generally tries to scare himself to death because it makes him feel alive in an otherwise numbingly safe world. I compose a letter in my head: *Dear Mr Cahill, As someone who has recently undergone a heart transplant operation it strikes me as ironic to say the least that a perfectly healthy man like you feels the only way to get his kicks is to risk his life. Why not just live it? Yours sincerely, Dr Valentine Frear.*

I close my eyes. We're humming along quite nicely but for a snorer, an infant and a couple of aggressive whisperers just behind us. The woman is complaining to her seatmate about her daughter, a divorcee. *To tell you the truth, she's eating my heart out.*

Why do I have to hear these things? It's too late, the image won't go away now. Munch munch, mmnnn, heartmeat — delicious! I see the daughter making a meal of her mother's heart, sucking out the juiciest bits, aorta and other gristle pushed to the side of her plate. She sops up the gravy with hunks of sourdough rye. Heartblood runs down her chin. Yet, in spite of her nibbled-away heart, the mother still lives to tell the tale. A miracle.

I regard the sleeping William. Who is this man? What did he actually contribute to the sum of scientific knowledge? You might say nothing very much beyond what any intelligent schoolboy might have done given the mass of evidence already available. Apparently the circulation was all mapped out since the twelfth century. Leonardo da Vinci drew the heart with four chambers. It was no surprise really. He made no hairs stand on end nor any hearts flutter. Not like Galileo and his battle-cry of the enlightenment; or Darwin, shatterer of the faith of a generation; or Sigmund Freud, rootler around in the unconscious like a chimp with an ice-cream stick in an anthole. No, our William provoked a bit of grousing but no holy outrages. The blood goes round in circles and the heart is a pump. William Harvey, father of modern medicine. It all ends in a bump.

On the other hand our William remains as much a heart junkie as a pump pusher: a mystic, a poet, a cosmologist, an ooher-and-aaher before Nature; a fool's fool if ever there was one. (He was born on April the first, though his biographers tried to wangle it over to the second.)

One day, while examining a foetal chick, he discovered a thin web of tissue, and within a tiny pulsating drop of blood no bigger than the point of a pin. If he'd had a microscope he would have been able to identify, quite clearly, the first stirrings of the heart.

Einstein once likened the generation of a new idea to a chicken's laying an egg: *Kieks — auf einmal ist es da*. Cheep — and all at once there it is.

A chick is born: a new life, and all from a drop of blood.

The luminous egg. Between earring and aura and one more nightcap, yours truly is quite a flashy number.

Valentine Frear, the born-again Harveyan.

Crack, kieks, cheep.

The great stumbling block for psychoanalysts who work in the field of the imaginary is that strange word *reality*. At some point the ferryman or pilot, having patiently accompanied the wanderer into the lost land of dream and fantasy, begins to introduce the nontransitory (the found?), to encourage acting out, an involvement with everyday life: a trip, a birth, a new job, even death. It can be a painful moment, of course – after the crossing of seas and wild lands, adrift, at the mercy of the waves and the burning sun and so on and on – when the pilot deems the journey to be over and one bumps down in that foreign-seeming place which we may call the reality principle –

Ladies and gentlemen, we are about to arrive at Manchester Airport. Please keep your seatbelts fastened until the aircraft has come to a complete standstill. The weather in Manchester is mild and overcast . . .

It's six in the morning, grey of course. William and Claire have snoozed most of the night. I am surrounded by sleepy children. Claire rubs her eyes – Where are we? – curls back into my chest. I caress her hair. Shit, she whimpers, I need some OJ real bad. On my other side William intones, The sun ariseth, and the sun goeth down and hasteth to the place where he arose; the wind goeth toward the south, and turneth about unto the north, it whirleth about continually, and the wind returneth according to its circuits; all the rivers run into the sea, yet the sea is not full; unto the place from whence the rivers come, thither they return again.

Claire has drunk both our orange juices. William, bless his crimped hose, has polished off a good-morning Bloody Mary.

Time to disembark. I take William's sere old hand and lead him down the chute. He looks rather the worse for wear. Claire holds me by my other arm.

—Where are we, Frear?

—England, William. Home. Don't you recognise it?

215

Two

Let me tell you about the town where I grew up. Its main drag is about a three-mile strip of Edwardian and Victorian boarding houses – ours being the last one at the eastern end – across from a railed promenade overlooking Morecambe Bay. Beyond the bay are the fells of the Lake District which I could see from my attic window on a clear day. The backstreets were cheerless; they don't appear to be less so now, the new shopping centre notwithstanding.

How can I present such a place to Claire, who has experienced only North Berkeley hills gracious living and its counterpart, the ghetto slums of the flatlands? Morecambe, the English seaside joke town, its gypsy fortune tellers and its lights neither gross-glitzy like Vegas nor glamourously dangerous like Coney Island, merely dreary, derivative. The only thing you risk by going there is your aesthetic sensibility. Keep your eyes on the sea.

It may once have had a touch of the Chekhovian about it, but with a bloodless English twist. Its only real claim to fame is the Midland Hotel ('Hercule Poirot slept here!'), a white crescent-shaped excrescence at the edge of the sands. I remember an old lady who was like a miniature porcelain doll coming down the steps in her teensy-weensy high-heeled boots and white leather gloves with pearl buttons to the elbow, to walk her poodle. The sound of the waves ceased, or perhaps the tide was out. In any case, all I could hear was the *tap tap tap* of the dog's blue nails on the pavement. I remember wondering if the little lady's were equally long, and who cut them for her. My mother's I cut. Why didn't she do them herself? Toes and hedges, you got a boy to do them for you. Her eyesight as well as her heart were vague and unpredictable. It made sense. I was the one she leaned on, yes, even as I snipped.

To me as a boy Morecambe seemed as two-sided as the quiddity itself: one being a haven for the old and infirm, the other, beyond the rusty railings of the prom, the sea-pounding place where boys and lovers and occasionally suicides and rogues lost themselves amongst the detritus left by the tide's retreat. People did from time to time do themselves in. I watched them – almost all of them women –

216

standing at the rails with that faraway look in their eyes. The genesis of my vocation? Perhaps. I remember how once the waves came up forty feet, crashed over the prom and up our front steps. I leaned out of my attic window, exhilarated, terrified, letting the spray bathe my face while below my mother held her heart and made whimpering, save-me noises. For once I did not oblige.

Is it the people we most dispraise who in the end we most resemble? Morecambe and my mother had something in common, and it seems I learned their joint message well, which was to hide and to flirt at the same time; to fear danger but want to peer at it, if only from an upstairs window; to long to feel its spray while not getting soaked. My mother, waiting to be saved by a Valentino or a long-lost sailor boy, would entertain spooks rather than venture forth to collar some guy in the Midland bar. There were always the lodgers for that sort of thing.

Mother as safe base from which to go out and explore the world? It's a wonder I was able to open the front door. On the other hand, that rigorous training in armchair adventuring may have been of some use to me in my profession.

I warn Claire there isn't much to see but she is keen anyway. It's where you grew up, she says. So we go. What has come over her? She once said, Shit, you guys get pampered by your mothers, then by your wives and then you expect your daughters to take over – well, you're not going to eat me up alive, no way! And yet here she is with me now, I will not say hoveringly.

When we come opposite the house I stand with my back to it unable to face its dereliction, the grey-green damp, its bays higg-ledy-piggledy, its paint rough and scaly. It had been neglected then, leaning delicately away from its terrace-mate, but now it looks dissociated, beaten up. It seems to stagger.

We don't spend long, it doesn't seem decent. I tell her a few things about the house's history – evidently it once belonged to a sea captain – then we walk on along the front. The tide is high, wind (this is December, remember) causing the breakers to foam like wriggling white otters madly trying to reach the shore. None make it. Which makes me think of Freud and his famous line, 'The aim of all life is death.'

Poor broken-down Oedipus for our time, tirelessly pursuing what he calls the truth even though he knows it will all end in tears. I suppose he deserves a back-slap for sheer doggedness, even with his

217

ridiculous tragic vision and his death-drive and his urge to change and his desperate need not to change. Conquistador of the mind, reetard of the heart.

William, on the other hand, presents me with a fishmonger's eel. An animal, he explains, tenacious of life, by which he means its heart will continue to pulsate and palpitate even after motion in the auricle has come to a stop.

A boy with skinny legs and huge, multi-coloured trainers is walking along the railing, one foot in front of the other. If he loses his balance, he's had it. Christ! I yell, and go to scoop him up, but Claire restrains me. He's doing fine, you'll scare the shit out of him if you do that. Quite right of course.

My mother was tenacious of life but didn't know how to live it, or was too afraid. Donna Cautlin was not tenacious of life. Claire walks along in her Penney's workboots with such weightedness that I think even one of those forty-foot waves could come and go and still she'd be striding along.

When we look back the kid has gone. Flailing below? There he goes, says Claire. Running down the prom, home to his tea. Maybe he's training for the circus, she says.

I gather two million pounds has been spent on a sea defence wall and still it doesn't work. Every winter Morecambe pier gets demolished.

—Tell me, says Claire, what it was like when you were a kid. It must have been weird.

—Weird, yes, you could say so.

I was under the pier where I took shelter when the tide was out, mucking around with my jam jars and feeble nets. Mostly I got weed and sticklebacks and the sea wind blew in my face, but there were also the lucky days when I got a net full of shrimp which I took back to my room to examine and dissect. Then I'd make cramped but accurate drawings. (You see, William, I once had the makings of a scientist. What went wrong?) I had my books and my orderly studies and tide timetables on the one hand, and my mother's wonky heart and the now-you-see-'em, now-you-don't world of lodgers on the other.

Claire in her neat American jeans and her down jacket smiles and takes me by the arm. William in his billowing skirts trails behind. A north wind is blowing his words sideways. He's trying to tell me about a small shrimp with a transparent exoskeleton: a great boon since one can view its internal workings with great distinctness – the heart perceived as through a window. That shrimp, I tell him when we get into the shelter of Diamond Lil's Reno-type slot-machine joint, along with a great deal else along this coast, is now extinct.

It isn't easy, as everyone knows, revisiting the scene of one's youth. Naturally places change. But this, this transplantation of the monstrous, this *bad* copycatting – Marineland Oceanarium, Happy Mount Park, JR's Burger Bar, Mister Whippy, an American-style multi-million pound Bubbles Leisure Park and Superdome where the old pier used to be – this is . . . what can one say?

I'm thinking of William, who never allowed personal involvement to interfere with an opportunity of making an interesting observation in morbid anatomy. The fact is, he dissected his own father and brother. *A vast colon*, he wrote in his notes, *in my father*. And in his notes on the spleen: *Sorrow Thom: a spleen hanging like a letter V . . .* Of course it may be that he was merely present at the autopsy and didn't actually dig out the bits himself. We'll never know. Sorrow Thom.

Frontierland, the ultimate indignity. Only the English, as I tell Claire, could go for something so *fake*: the pale, droopy cowboys in chaps and floppy suede hats; thirty-foot cacti (O Sigmund!) poking up out of concrete; the stagecoach ('The South will rise again!' – Hackney Coach No. 506); the Ghost Train ride with its warning to 'Beware Ghouls' (William, stick close); the Runaway Mine Train ('The heart-stopping ride is now even more wild!').

The heart doesn't stop, it sinks, which is worse.

Something's going on down at the Haunted Silver Mine. Let's go watch, says Claire, who manages to be amused. Some old buffer with a sweaty red bandana around his neck and his belly hanging over his jeans is yelling at his skinny sidekick:

—Get in there and get that silver.

—He's got a gun.

—I don't care, get in there.

—He's got a big one (giggle).

—I don't care.

—You seen the size of it (double giggle)?

—Whatsa matter, you a coward or something?

Enough, Let's get out of here.

—Let's just look at this over here, says Claire.

It's an 'Original American Trappers Cabin'. The sign stuck in the loose chipping ground in its corralled front patch reads as follows: 'This original trappers cabin, showing the raveges of time and infestation of termites, was shipped from South Carolina in April 1990. Frontierland has now acquired a piece of American history.'

 . . . *the raveges of time and infestation of termites* . . . Claire, as well she might, is laughing.

—Raveges, she points out, is misspelled.

It has not escaped me.

—It's all so tacky, she says.

Yes.

Sorrow Morecambe.

!

Three

I have come to one of the small coastal villages to take part in a cross-bay walk, a fund-raising do for the British Heart Foundation. A fine spot, a place I used to come to on my pushbike. The sky over the estuary is the colour of my mother's eyes, the sands her cheek. Forgive me. I am suffering from reminiscences. What looks like a toy train with a yellow face chugs across the railway bridge. The clouds part, the rays from the finger of God radiate, a burst of sunlight makes it look like the opening shot of a Bible epic: the world is illuminated. Quick, close the blinds.

What am I doing here, looking for what? Answer: peace and tranquility, roots, smallness perhaps, comfort in the Dinky toy landscape. Oldness. Not just a few hundred years of façaded shacks but twelfth-century farmhouses, Roman walls, stone circles. The California desert needs no one. I want to be tucked away against a hillside. I want there to be light and air but also protection for one's back. A coal fire. I want the movement of the sea but not its ferocity. I am like one of those mongrel dogs who, loving and fearing water, stands up to its knees and howls. Sigmund Freud would have understood. William, that other mongrel, has gone to scrabble in the sands.

Claire has left her copy of Dorothy Wordsworth's journals behind and I have dipped into it. I like the way she writes. She makes the ordinary un-ordinary, a bed of potatoes as remarkable as a field of carnations; makes unexpected connections between disparate things the way poets and certain psychoanalysts do. She has the eye, nose and ear of a natural scientist: moon, stars, butterflies, flowers, the mountains – nothing escapes her. Listen to what she writes about swallows, how they ' . . . flew about restlessly, and flung their shadows upon the sunbright walls of the old building; their shadows glanced and twinkled, interchanged and crossed each other, expanded and shrunk up, appeared and disappeared at every instant'. It reminds me of Dr Harvey writing about the heart.

What I like is how she forgets herself, focusing instead on other things: deer, swallow, birch tree, strawberry flower, a star, even mists, ripples, spray, mountains, human creatures, all the wild and less wild things of nature. When she looks at daffodils she sees daffodils. Whereas brother William sees William seeing daffodils: his wonderful mind and his bloody human heart. Big deal. Dorothy merely states her case.

Let us take an example. When she gets the news that William is soon to be married (the crucifying event of her life), she writes about how every question put to her 'was like the snapping of a little thread about my heart'. *Ping ping ping*. We learn no more of how she felt but we see her turning eyes and pinking heart and a moon which 'travelled through the clouds tingeing them yellow as I passed along, with two stars near me, one larger than the other. These stars grew or diminished as they passed from or went into the clouds.'

Faugh! barks Sigmund Freud. Moon, clouds, phooey! A prize piece of neurotic sublimation! Headaches, swoons? Baloney, somaticization, hysteria! Sex, incestuous desires . . . sex!

Poor Dorothy, the very word would bring on a panic attack. No, don't look at me – she buries her face in her pillow – I can't bear it. She'd rather we look up there at the moon and listen to its brother and sister stars going twinkle twinkle. But somehow it has the opposite effect, and the *snap crackle popping* of her heart gets louder and louder until we have to cover our ears and move on.

I leave the front and climb a place called Church Hill, looking at posters on power poles as I go: lessons in birdwatching, folk dancing, yoga, chess, bridge, even marriage preparation. Here is graceful living. These are the great Zen masters of acceptance: farmers, doctors, builders, gardeners. They know. Life simply is, weather is, death is. They are rewarded for their pains with a paucity of pain: a low heart attack and divorce rate. People stay together until one of them dies: there is no point in doing otherwise. They plant fruit trees, ferry children to school and scouts, attend christenings and anniversary celebrations, and funerals of course. They make sloe gin, pick blackberries, sit round fires, have sing-songs, chop wood, weed gardens, make stripes with lawnmowers, make bonfires, collect holly. They knit jumpers that last a lifetime.

Forget it. I might as well be a Martian with fictional tendencies. Oh, I could tell you stories, impress you, tempt you with the metaphor that tempts me. I am wont to wax lyrical, as if the lobster that is my heart has cracked open revealing a meat as tender as a thermador and a world wrapped up in newly-elasticated coronary

222

arteries sighing with the very breath of life and love. But I'd be lying for this place is no different from anywhere else on this globe, which is to say at least as fraught with strife, corruption and unsatisfied longing as any other community. That cute little train with the yellow face carries plutonium to the power station over on the coast, polluting the beaches and causing an alarmingly high rate of leukaemia amongst children. Their sweaters wear out at the elbows.

Peace? Acceptance? Perfection? More hooey! More like a tacit agreement to keep the lid on, a *fin de siècle* return to pre-Freudian repression, suppression, sublimation, collusion – a high investment, *en effet*, in simply not knowing. A whole damn village of folk who haven't seen their own bellybuttons or each others' eyes in years. Too busy keeping watch on the tidal bore or the fells across the bay which beckon but keep their British distance. Families, hills, the tilted limestone: they have been here forever and will probably go on forever, the power station at Sellafield notwithstanding. For this hankering after the good life and its good old ways is none the less alluring for being chimaerical.

How are you? Fine. Are you sure? Stop asking so many damn questions. Go and chop some wood. Look at it this way, the heart pumps and the blood goes round, maintaining the body, as William tells us, in its vital and vegetative being, cherishing and warming the parts. Cells die and are replaced. Many wriggle out from the confines of their vessel walls but when they've had enough freedom come crawling back in again for a rest, *whew*. Molecules leap about and collide, any particular one may be replaced by a buddy, *choo choo*, a toy train on a circular track.

Along the high road and back down to the Station. The trains and buses are rolling in. I stop to pick up a snack at the health food shop which has a pair of curlicued hearts etched in its glass panelled door, and a sign in its window saying *I ♡ Cumbria but Sellafield breaks my ♡*. I make my way back to the shore. The walk is about to begin.

William is waiting in front of a sign reading: 'DANGER. Beware Fast Rising Tides/Quicksands/Hidden Channels'. In spite of its idyllic position and the shafts of light that make it look inspirational, the place is a real heartsinker. Since the last century hundreds have gone down in the sands, cut off by the tidal bore which comes in travelling, as the fishermen used to say, as fast as a good horse. It's like a low wall of water coming at you; you could never outrun it.

There's the tale of a boy, says our guide, doing his now-let's-put-

223

the-fear-of-the-sands-into-'em number, who was trying to cross on horseback and drowned. The following year his mother got carried off near the same spot. (My mother told me the same story.) More recently, a young man was sucked in because he wouldn't abandon his motorcycle. Takes all sorts, somebody says.

It's time. The guide raises his horn-handled walking stick and waves us forward. Families, dogs, children. The old, the young, the middle-aged with their gear: backpacks, cagoules, cameras. Everyone knows everyone else: a companionable, domestic affair. God bless, says a nun in trainers, and we're off, hugging the neck of the Knott, weaving our way around the estuary, trying to avoid the muddy rivulets. I take off my shoes and hang them around my neck; William has rolled his trousers Prufrock style. I think the wading birds, whose legs are skinnier than his, have come out in their numbers to watch. The cormorants, which he most resembles, keep their distance on a faraway sandbank.

The sand is corrugated and hard in places, in others it oozes between the toes. The worm-piles are like vermicelli. With nothing but sand below and sky above, it feels rather like crossing a rain-soaked desert. One loses one's bearings, looks for landmarks – Grange Over Sands, Humphrey Head, the Lakeland hills, Jenny Brown's Point – to be enclosed by the arms of the land.

William, gesticulating to the heavens, says:

—Are not the movements of the blood patterned on that *circulus* we find in nature; for example, the water that goes to form clouds, the clouds that drop rain upon the hills, the snows that melt and seek the sea once more. And the sun, if it is it that causes the evaporation of seawater and if it is the melting of this water's ice that gives back to the sea what the sun has drawn from it, have we not there something analogous to the action of that singular organ the heart?

Play it again, Will.

—Does not the heart receive the cold blood, warm it and then project it from the vessels that spring therefrom like the four rivers from Paradise towards all the organs of the body, which the blood then revivifies before it returns once more to warm itself in the heart?

The trouble with our William is that he talks in a combination of rather precise anatomical language and seventeenth-century blarney.

—William, what are you getting at?

The crowd have come to a halt before the river. Break-time, out come the sandwiches and flasks. Laughter is released, dogs run around scrounging for food. William the Good Circulator is in full flow.

—Recall, if you will, he intones, the title of my book, *De Motu Cordis*. Motion, life. Attend, sir. Attraction and expulsion, that is what I am 'getting at'. The beginning from which expulsion takes its start is at the same time the end-point of attraction. The disposition of the mover remains the same in its beginning and end, just as that which is called in Greek *gigglymos* or in Latin *cardo* or a hinge-like joint –

—I think you mean a ball and socket joint –

—Do not interrupt, Frear. In this, convexity represents the end and concavity the beginning, the former attraction and the latter expulsion. The convex is quiescent and the concave the moved. Beginning and end are divers in definition and yet the same, like the centre. The quiescent centre from which expulsion takes its start and in which attraction finds its end, the *ultimum membrum* from which motion starts and where it is completed – *ad quem pervenit* – is the heart.

—Dr Harvey, with all due respect, you're not telling us anything we don't know.

—My dear Frear, I am a student of medicine in its widest meaning. I am not bound, as my friend Scarburgh noted, by the laws of a single discipline but gather my knowledge from the fish market as well as the autopsy chamber, from marshes as well as –

On cue, he steps on a flatfish lurking in the sand. He pulls the thing up by its gills, pulls out his stiletto and slits the creature from nose to tail.

—Observe, he says, holding it under my nose, the creature's heart.

—Good heavens. William, please, you'll upset those poor children. Look, we're moving on. The guide is picking up his laurel branch, the whistle has blown. We don't want to be left behind – remember the bore.

—Frear, the principate of the heart – there's no stopping him now – is not incompatible with the truth of the movement of the blood. It is what you might call a partnership. True, it is through the motion of the blood that all parts are nourished, warmed and quickened; but eventually the blood in these parts is cooled down, thickens and becomes effete, for blood without warmth is crust or gore. Whence it returns to its principate, namely the heart, the fountain of the body,

225

in order to recuperate its perfection; here, through the natural, potent, fervent heat, as it were the treasury of life, it is made fluid again and pregnant with spirits; and the balsam is dispersed from here again; and all this depends upon the motion and beat of the heart. 'Tis the intimate hearth, the fundament of life, author of all. For you, Frear he hands me the fish's heart: perfection.

—Thank you, William. (What the hell do I do with it?)

It is time for the crossing. We are ordered to fan out in a single line lest we hit a soft spot. A great shrieking and exclaiming goes up. And will Mr Robinson now stretch forth his horn-handled walking stick and part the waters? I would not be a bit surprised.

And so the children go through in the midst of a sea not altogether dried up but nearly so. In fact the water comes up to our knees and we splash through, William trailing threads of fish-gore and oohing and aahing over a rainbow that has appeared while I, a man with a current surplus of hearts – one in his ear, one in his chest and one in his hand – gently let the fish's heart back into the river.

Four

Grasmere is surrounded by mountains small in size compared with American ones but large in intention. Fairfield, Helvellyn, Sergeant Man, St Sunday Crag – these were my boyhood prodigies, my companions, my subjects. I studied them like sculptures from all angles, hoping perhaps to absorb some of their solidity. They might suffer a touch of erosion but they'd be there. I got close, memorized their vital statistics, mapped them, learned their gorges and gullies, their rough shoulders and precarious edges from Wainright's first editions. I did everything but climb them.

I didn't have walking boots. My mother reported weekly, daily, minute-by-minute, disasters on the fells: a whole pile of scouts buried in a crevasse, brains dashed on Helvellyn, heart attack on St Sunday Crag, exposure on Crinkle Crags. And so on, and on. In my dreams I ignored her and bagged them, leaping from summit to summit. But when I left the house on a weekend morning the dream imagery gave way to my mother holding her heart and I got the willies. For her, for me. Where are you going? To the library. It was easier that way. I had a responsibility, I had a heart, a contamination.

Claire is sitting on a stone wall in the car park beside Dove Cottage, the house where William and Dorothy lived for a time. She's kicking the stones with her heels.

—So how was it? I ask her.

—How was Dove Cottage? You mean how was William fucking Wordsworth? William William, that's all they talk about, precious William. There's Dorothy rubbing her fingers raw and thanking God for the privilege of washing his dirty underwear, and wife Mary peeling potatoes in cold water for his lunch, and he's sipping daintily out through the garden gate. He had a separate entrance made through the garden so he didn't have to walk through the kitchen and get contaminated by 'women's doings'. She kicks so hard one of the stones loosens. More contamination.

—I think we'd better get out of here before the wall comes tumbling down.

—Sure. Fine. Anything, she grumbles.

—This road leads to a track below Nab Scar, I say. You can bitch about William as we walk, only keep it down. Anti-William sentiment must be received around here like marching through Belfast singing *Rule Britannia*.

She is unperturbed.

—What do I care? All those portraits of *him* and you ask if there's maybe one of Dorothy and this turkey just blinks and before you know it he's going apeshit again over William the Messiah. Dorothy is down on her knees on the cold flag floor washing his poet's feet and considering herself privileged –

—Female masochism: see Sigmund Freud.

—Very funny. They don't even see how *gross* it is. I was in the kitchen and this lady came in with a vacuum cleaner and I said to her, 'Is that Dorothy's vacuum?' and she just looked at me like I was from outer space.

—I expect to them you are, my dear.

—Thanks a bunch, Dad, that really helps.

We carry on, past another of William's relics, the Wishing Gate leading to a wood where I used to come to spy on the hills. Claire isn't finished.

—William's ice skates, William's watch chain, William's potty – she's winding herself up – two locks of William's hair on a pink satin cushion – all shrines to William. WHAT ABOUT DOROTHY?

All the farm dogs on Fairfield Fell are set barking. A cry of rage, I take it, for Dorothy Wordsworth and Anna Freud and Philip Sidney's sister and Freud's patient Dora and probably all the other daughters and wives she's read about and bled for. And herself of course. No one will do my daughter our of *her* voice.

—Feeling better? (She seems refreshed.)

—Go to hell.

I pray we have finished with the Wordsworths. With the whole business. We're above Rydal Mount, no other houses in sight, only Fairfield at our backs, the long ridge of Loughrigg in front. Claire puffs along in her padded jacket, sloshing straight through springs and waterfalls, still trailing steamy clouds of feminist wrath. Me, I'm watching a couple of clouds come together in slow motion, thinking how it would be on the tops, away from everything.

—Claire, look back at the light, how blue it is.

—Wow, you're right, I've never seen anything like it. It's like somebody dropped a bucket of blue paint.

It's gone, the blue, replaced by layers of pink and pearl. How would it be, I'm thinking, to move back, buy a derelict cottage half-way up a fellside, a Land Rover and a stack of wood? One would never be bored. I mention how I used to walk around here.

—Ever hike up in those big guys? (She points across the valley.)

—Those are the Langdales. They have good names: Pike O'Stickle, Harrison Stickle –

—Harrison's Tickle? That's a great name for a mountain.

—Stickle not Tickle.

—I prefer Tickle.

—Please yourself.

—I intend to.

—The answer to your question is no, not really. I skirted around the edges. I lost my nerve.

—Are they dangerous? I saw hikers all over the place yesterday.

—No, of course not. Everybody does it. Fewer back then, of course, but it was still perfectly safe.

—So why didn't you?

—I think we should be heading back. We can get some lunch, then split up for a couple of hours this afternoon and meet for a drink, okay?

—Sure. Was it because of your nervous mother?

—Something like that.

—Hey, look, a 'For Sale' sign. Let's go and see.

We follow the track. The gate is tied closed, the house looks abandoned. Claire climbs over, I hesitate. I'm not sure we should do this, it's private property.

—Dad, come on, there's nobody there.

I untie the gate, push it open, laboriously retie it. At the end of a long rhododendron wood is the house: a bungalow made of green slate looking out over Rydal Water and Loughrigg. Just the thing. No more conflict, ambivalence, tortuous anything. The simplifica-tion of desire. Just hang out, stare at the lacy hills, the sky turning blue and pink and gruff grey by turns.

—You could buy it, retire here, says Claire. You could probably afford it.

—It's a thought, I say.

And think, And you? Shall you come and live with me and darn my socks and feed me my cyclosporin? Cook the goose while I write the great psychoanalytic novel? Or shall we do it differently: you write the feminist novel while I cook the nutroast? And where is Ruth in all this?

Another gap, we're both staring out across the vale. Claire quotes Dorothy: *I lay upon the steep of Loughrigg, my heart dissolved.* I quote William: *The horizon's rocky parapet.*

—It isn't a contest, you know, I say.

—I know. There was a lot of weird incestuous stuff between them. It said in the museum that it was the loss of his mother and early separation from his sister that made William 'unusually responsive to nature'.

—Ah, the sublimation of desire – you see how you can't get away from it?

Five

After lunch and as soon as Claire's out of sight I get in the car and drive as fast as the car will go over the Kirkstone pass, head for Ullswater and park the car at the bottom of Deepdale. We've arranged to meet at our hotel bar not later than four, so I don't have much time. It's far too late to be setting out for the top in winter, and the weather is bad by now, heavy low cloud, wet and cold, and I don't have the right boots or ironmongery for the snow. But such considerations don't signify.

I walk to the head of the valley, follow the left-hand waterfall steeply up. At this point I'm not cold, in fact I'm rather hot and damp, giddy with my own folly. Are you with me Sigmund? William? Only the snow responds, chunks of the stuff coming off in my hands as I scramble up the gully. It's windy, getting dusk at three-thirty in the afternoon. I calm myself by thinking, This is only Fairfield. Dorothy Wordsworth, I noted, wrote in her journal: 'Attempted Fairfield but misty, went no further.' Perhaps I should have listened to her? No, this is silly, I'm more or less at the top already, no sweat, bearing right, down between where Deepdale joins St Sunday Crag. No problem. Back up to the summit. The light is gone by now but I'm still confident, moving briskly, heart working hard but obediently. Have I come up here to test a heart not worth testing? Trying to prove what? I hate to think. Subject perhaps for future speculation.

But the question at hand is more urgent: where to climb down? Every time I find or think I find a way down there isn't one, just a sheer drop. I make two, three attempts, then give up, decide to backtrack to where I emerged earlier out of the gully, try to make my way down the other side of the valley. I can just about make out my own footsteps, but it is very much a matter of wishful tracking.

Further along the summit, heading southeast. Dark now, also wet and blustery, also cold. So cold. My gloves are soaked through. No torch, slipping on ice patches. Can't waste time or energy. Close my eyes and see my mother. No. Raise my eyes to the sharp peak of Cofa Pike, where Sigmund Freud is tucked up in a sort of plastic bubble, watching me. And laughing. I hate you, I think, and keep going. My father, in a vortex of snow, rises up out of a gully and says, *Who the hell are you?* And kicks Freud out, then turns to face me at the bottom of his mountain. I can't make it, I'm too tired, my heart . . . *Yes you can*, he says, standing on that neat rocky upthrust waving me forward like Moses.

Freud did a demolition job on him, too. It's called *Moses and Monotheism* if you're interested, but I shouldn't bother. And may all our fathers who haven't drowned or disappeared or been deposed already go rolling down the fell like that lump of ice, *clunk*.

I can't.

You can.

On the top in the dark, the great vantage point is reduced to a matter of the imagination, nothing to see but hailstones. Nevertheless, I have done what I have done.

I must get down, must keep moving, hypothermia can cause fibrillation. No, not that. Pick myself up. Ahead, the remains of a wall: the heart is becalmed. Out of the snow now, muddy and wet. Still can't see much. Follow the wall which must lead back to Kirkstone. Begin to relax, thinking job done but it's bitter, wet. I feel heavy, silly. Hold to wall as best I can but ground keeps falling away. Mother says, *What did I tell you?* This is not helpful. Father . . . ? The wall is in places vertical, built on outcrops. Climbing blind, where am I going? I am distinctly in trouble.

Oh help, Sigmund – no, not you . . . William, everything is upside down, I am gasping at the cold and the madness of this chimaerical life, this chimaerical me. But then – no need to panic – things begin to right themselves and I think it will be all okay after all. I understand I am more myself than I have ever been in my life; and equally that I am composed of others – and bingo, I am free, this heart is mine. Hallelujah! William, is that you? Don't be alarmed, I am not dying. Verging on the disorderly or chaotical perhaps, but nothing serious.

My heart does one of its odd jigs. William, can you imagine how many names we have for the different sorts of arrhythmias? Ectopic beats, electrical alternans, *torsades de pointes* – rather beautiful that; high-grade block and escape rhythms; parasystole (atrial or ventricular, pure or modulated); Wenckebach (simple or complex); tachycardia and, finally, fibrillation. This naming of rhythms does for me what the organ itself cannot: allows specificity, brings some intelligence to bear on the problem. Like the naming of parts for you, William.

I put my hand to it: ectopic beats interspersed with sinus beats. Apparently if you count the numbers of sinus beats between the ectopic you find that in some people they are always odd: three, five, seven and so on, while in others the normal beats are always part of the sequence two, five, eight, eleven and so on. There is often some kind of regularity to these numbers, but as often as not irregularity also.

What did you say William? *It is when the heart is tense, moved, made vigorous, that we know we are alive.*

Then I am alive. Thank you, doctor.

Let me tell you how adrenalin works. (The head doctor regains his composure by explaining biological phenomena.) Individual drops of the stuff come from the sympathetic nerves and go shooting into the bloodstream. As it happens, I am without those particular nerves since the transplant, so in my case the adrenalin has to make its way slowly-slowly. When it finally makes it to the heart, *B-zoing!* Like a bunch of rolling sagebrushes hitting cactus. The drops thwack into receptors in the heart and set it off. The heart beats harder, the aorta walls give, blood gushes, eddies and whorls. Will the dam burst? A heart of whooshing and pounding, of fluid against fluid, fluid against solid, and solid against solid. Blood coursing from chamber to chamber, muscles contracting, walls stretching. Complex three-dimensional electric waves. Not a strip of wiggly electrocardiogram but a wild dynamical heart. Dynamical things are generally counter-intuitive – who said that? William? The counterintuitive heart, I like it. No, you wouldn't know of such things, William.

The heart in extremis constringes verily.

Oh aye. We call it fibrillation, doctor. The classic image for the fibrillating heart is a bag of worms. Instead of contracting and relaxing in a repetitive, periodic way, the heart's muscle tissue writhes helplessly. It cannot pump blood. Its heart waves are broken up. It cannot contract or relax. Constringes verily indeed. Some parts continue to work, yet the whole system goes fatally awry. An uncontrolled, ineffectual frenzy.

The only treatment is a massive jolt from a defibrillation device. Not currently available on mountain-tops.

Of course this is all the fantasy of a panic-stricken, benighted, relatively recent, still paranoid, hypochondriacal transplant recipient

233

who is not in fact experiencing fibrillation (he'd be dead by now.) He is numb and terrified but quite conscious and even mobile. He crosses the wall because he is too frightened to descend at this point; better to scramble across it. Then he sees lights in the distance. Oh. He keeps going, very slowly but trying to keep steady. His knees are jellified, his feet rubbed raw and flopping about like William's fish. In this condition it takes him ages to get down and when he does he is the other side of the mountain from where his car is. Eventually however (the heart may yet stop but the narrative plods bravely on) he makes his way on his ice-block feet down into Rydal and on into Grasmere to the hotel bar where he's promised to meet Claire and plonks himself down in front of a roaring fire. His glasses are steamed up, his hands too cold even to manoeuvre the zip on his jacket let alone find money in his pocket. His face nearly cracks when he tries to order a double whisky. With his still stiff hand he feels for his heart. *Mirabile dictu*, says William coming up behind him, it is still there. Walking towards him is his daughter.

—Dad, you're nuts. What are you trying to do, kill yourself?

Six

I seem to be alive.

—So my eyes reward me, says William. I congratulate you, sir, from my heart. But I observe you are rather unwell. You seem to live unmindful of your transposed heart –

—Trans*planted*, William.

—Frear, it is most distressing. Allow me to take your pulse. I am concerned by the cold blood pent up in the extremities.

—Nothing to worry about, doc, I'm fine, splendidly well in fact. All I need is another whisky.

—Not too quickly, Frear, one is in such states susceptible to phantoms and appearances.

One is also in danger of spluttering away one's precious mouthful of whisky in a burst of hilarity.

—Why do you laugh, Frear?

—Dear William, what else should I do in a world so heart-splittingly funny? The fact is, you see, I made it, I'm still here.

—I am delighted to note it. However, you will perceive, by the cold blood returning to the heart, with what celerity the current flows, and what an effect it produces when it has reached the heart; so that some who have travelled over snowy mountains are sometimes stricken suddenly with death, and other things of the same kind.

—Thank you, how encouraging. Not that it's death which concerns me so much as my toes. However, they are coming back. The blood pricks, causing such a welcome pain I could kiss each toe. I could kiss William's too, and Claire's; but perhaps fingers would be more seemly.

—Cheers, my very dears.

Claire undoes my boot laces while I hold my hands to the fire. Then she puts them between hers and rubs. Williams says, all living things need a site and source of warmth without which they will die. Chilled hands, toes, noses are thus restored to warmth and liveliness.

Shall we drink to the hearth inside and out? And why the hell not? Because one is afraid of looking foolish? But one is! One is *always* duped by some eternal-flaming nonsense or other – so why on earth not this? William, I raise my glass to you. I kiss the hem of your cock-eyed cloak and drink from the boiling red cauldron of your Simple Simon Science. What I like best about you, doctor, is how even after you have been cut down to size you are still there, the little imp with the hot feet and a taste for toying with hearts and blood.

—To you, Will.

—And you, Frear. He is looking rather misty-eyed.

—Dad –

—It's quite all right, I shan't embarrass you, my dear. I'm just thawing out here.

Claire, I appeal to you. Think on this splendid occasion of the absent-minded astronomer who, looking at the stars, falls in a ditch; of the absent-hearted psychoanalyst who, washing his car, suddenly sees stars; of Tom Thumb the mathematician who one day puts in this thumb and instead of a plum yanks out a straight line with a crooked heart. That is how it is, we haven't the foggiest idea of where we're going or we're we'll fetch up and in the meantime all we have is what we have. *Lup dub lup dub* and good heavens, what is the point of being good little psychopomps and cultural critics if we fail to register the full force of that 6.9 on the Richter Scale; if, when they open us up, instead of a heart they find nothing but some Freudian slough?

Mind-junk, heart-junk? Phooey, who cares. The thing about coming back alive is that suddenly you can feel: what William calls the evidence of the senses. Touchy-feely crap? Well, at least it's a change. Even though one's feet may be itching with confused blood (and incipient chilblains), one's bloodstream oversupplied with spirits (vital, alcoholic, etc.) yet everything is magically possible and that can be no bad thing. Round and round we go and have another Macallan's on me Claire, another Remy Martin? Feel that warmth!

Claire, have you ever seen the Watts Tower? Soaring steel and mortar columns graced with 70,000 pieces of coloured glass from 7-Up and laxative bottles, pottery shards, clam shells and bathroom tiles. What is it? To some it's like Gaudí's church spires in Barcelona, to others it's an architectural curse on the landscape. To me it's like the chambers of the heart.

No, I am not – to quote my friend William here – altogether feeble or insane. Or did he say foolish? Never mind. We must be allowed our phantoms even if they are weirdly dressed, and our dream spires even if they turn out to be made of Milk of Magnesia bottles.

Take our dog Willy. I feed him, take him for walks, and he wags his shiny black tail and slobbers into my groin. It's a little messy and embarrassing, but nice. So with the heart. It takes no prompting, just feed it and exercise it, and – hearken – there it is: *lup dub, lup dub.*

—Claire, do you know what St John said? *In the beginning was the word.* Well, I have news for you: he was wrong. In the beginning was not the word but the heart: *The first to live and the last to die.* I quote William Harvey.

—Who the hell is William Harvey?

—Never mind.

—Sure, as long as it isn't Wordsworth.

—It's not. A guaranteed original. It came into my head while I was up there on the fell. You ready? Here goes:

Silent imperceptible tiny writhings
Folding and fusion – how precise
Electric tension; quiver, twitch, beat
A subtle twist
It's easy – anyone can do it.

—That's real nice, Dad.

She's addressing a geriatric or a two year old. Or a terminal case. I look down at the bunch of plastic bags at her feet.

—Looks like you went shopping this afternoon, I say. Let's see what you bought, then.

—Sweaters – they call them jumpers around here. You really want to see?   I really want to see. So she opens her parcels and holds the sweaters or jumpers up to her front or mine and rehearses each one: this one for Ruth, that one for me, one for a friend, one for herself. Made from local Herdwick sheep of a colour not exactly brown but not grey either, in complicated bubbly designs.

—They're great, I say. Tough stuff, lasts forever.

—Do you think Ruth will like hers?

—Yes, yes I do.

—Will it fit her? The sleeves are so long.

—She can always roll them up.

—What about yours – do you like it?

—Give it here.

I pull off what I'm wearing, put on the Herdwick number, catch my earring, curse – it's all quite a performance – stand up and model.

237

The people at the next table say it's a perfect fit. By this time even Claire doesn't seem to mind if I make a spectacle of myself.

—You look great. She's smiling with all her teeth.

William is regarding me, the olive eyes more crossed than ever. What is it, Will? Have I been neglecting you, you petulant mutt? I have. Never mind. Here's to you.

—Claire, would you mind just getting us all another round?

—Dad –

—Just one more, I promise.

When she's gone I lay my hand on William's. It feels like a leaf from one of his first editions.

—Tell me.

—I am concerned, Frear, that if the heart has been chilled or affected by some serious fault, then the whole animal must suffer destruction when its chief organ –

—Relax, Will, I'm fine. Honest. I have the heart of a young girl, remember? Tonight I can never die. Listen to the music of that *lup-dubbing*.

But he is attuned to another music, one of those golden oldies one gets in English pubs these days. *If I give my heart to you, will you handle it with care?* He turns to me.

—Frear, he ventures, am I correct in thinking 'tis a song about a heart donor?

Oh William, William, you naive, bullet-headed, dandruff-ridden, Swiss-cheese-hearted old fool. His eyelids are drooping.

—You must forgive me, he says, for I am far stricken in years and I suffer indifferent health. Tonight I cannot match your ebullience of spirit.

—You're tired. We'll go soon, I promise.

—Dad, you need to eat something and get off to bed. I think you're suffering from exhaustion.

—Yes, yes, in a minute. Just a little stroll first, okay?

—They stop serving pretty soon.

—Okay, five minutes, I promise. Come, my dears.

Very dark, thick frost on the ground. We crunch our way down to the main road and the beginning of Rydal Water, then branch off to a quiet backroad leading to a hump-backed stone bridge over a stream. We are the only ones about in the dead quiet of a starry frozen night.

—Dad, where are we going? I can't see a thing.

238

—Don't worry, my love, I and the moon shall guide you for we are both numinous tonight.

—It hangs in the sky, says William.

—I'm freezing my ass off.

—Like the heart in its lunula.

—*Dad*, I'm starved, let's go.

So am I, I realise.

—Right. To the restaurant, men!

—*Men?*

Seven

We head north and east into the Eden Valley looking for an ancient stone circle known as Long Meg and her Daughters. Next to Stonehenge, according to Wordsworth W., 'it is beyond dispute the most noble relic of the kind that this or probably any other country contains'.

William says he once visited Stonehenge.

—I went with King James, whom I attended as physician at the time. The Duke of Buckingham had developed an interest in field archaeology and together we digged up the heads of bulls, oxen, harts and other such beasts, being the relics of such beasts as were anciently offered at that place in sacrifice. We did not however find human victims.

—I'm glad to hear it, William.

Claire switches on the radio, a programme called 'In the Psychiatrist's Chair'. Oh must we? I'd almost forgotten. The psychiatrist is asking his patient how he feels about being alone with his own thoughts, and the guy is saying, 'When you're alone with your thoughts they become circular and inimical to action, and frankly I'm not comfortable with that.'

—Frankly, I say, I know just what he means.

'Do you ever think about death?' The psychiatrist is Irish. 'As I said, I prefer thinking about things I can *do* something about. When you think about these things you only get depressed, you go round in circles.'

Which is precisely what we seem to be doing, going round and round a roundabout outside Penrith, looking for the right exit. Rather dizzy-making. I feel like the blood, having set out on its travels, has gotten trapped about my knees.

—Dad, what the fuck are you doing? Left! Here! This one! Get off!

She is keeper of the map and navigator.

When we get there I park on the grass verge and we just sit, gawping rather. Wordsworth called them 'the family forlorn'. They cast a weight of awe 'not easy to be borne' on his spirit. Well, I can see why.

Meg is an eighteen-foot-high sandstone monolith of a mother, and her daughters, I think, are limestone. They describe a huge circle and are surrounded by hills in the foreground and the great fells in the background. Earlier this century a farmer shot his driveway through the circle, thus cleaving about a third of the daughters from their mother and siblings.

Claire calls it a puny male joke. Typical. Always trying to sunder and invade. She turns to me and laughs. But it doesn't work, does it? You're right, I tell her. I also tell her how Big Mama Meg gave Wee Willy Wordsworth the willies. She strode after him, huge and mighty, in his dreams. Later on he repudiated her, said he'd overrated her importance as an object because he'd been taken by surprise. How's that for a nice bit of Oedipal denial? Shit, she says, more contempt of the mother.

She gets out of the car and slams the door behind her. I watch as she visits the daughters, appreciating their roughnesses and smoothnesses; spending time with some, acknowledging others and passing on. They seem to be as uniquely various as daughters can be: squat, lean, lumpy, leggy, toothy and so on; some commanding attention, others careless of it, still others laying low. Claire walks amongst them, a rabble-rousing younger sister; returns to Long Meg. I get out to pay my own respects.

Long Meg is of goddess proportions, but there is also a benevolence which her vast vertical bosom belies. When the weather was warm and I felt the urge, I would come up on my bicycle with a pile of books in my sack and lean against her spine, enjoying her protection. *The warm cuddle of mother rock.* I pretended I was hers as well. She showed no favouritism, I experienced no rejection. It could be that the daughters closest to her basked in a warmer maternal glow, but that only through the accident of proximity. On the whole she seemed capable of throwing the circle of her largesse, a great hoop of acceptance, round us all.

—Even you? asks Claire.

The question comes as a shock.

—To tell you the truth, I say, it never occurred to me – all right, call it male arrogance – that I didn't belong amongst them, that I was a cuckoo in the nest.

Claire looks up at Meg and quotes – good heavens – Wordsworth W: *Speak, Giant-mother! Tell it to the morn.* And why not? After all, if the Commendatore could do it in a flash and a boom, why not she?

Though frankly I'm not sure I wish to hear. Our giant mother is looking ominously flushed in the low sunshine – that warm red sandstone. *You turned us to stone. Left us out in the cold until we became fierce and mute and sick and cold. Then you looked and said, Hmm, and called us wise. Goddesses, muses, monoliths – you invested us with secret powers. The body, the heart, the earth, nature. Huh. Then you began suffering from Venus envy so you turned it around and invented penis envy. Our minds and tongues you took for yourselves. We babbled, stuttered, gagged. Don't worry, you said, we'll be your interpreters and translators and analysts and analysers. You became our psychopimps and poets. And then you carved your initials in our flanks.*

William is crouching on the ground beside her looking very small indeed.

—Frear, he says, something rather strange is going on in this place. Do you feel it?

Indeed I do. I'm busy picturing these lasses lifting their skirts and closing in, bent on sweet revenge.

I perceive a sort of booming.

—These are said to be magical places, Will.

—The monolith is transformed, he vows. Look, Frear, how she has become the fountain from whence a knot of veins causes the blood to move round the members.

He begins intoning as if in prayer: *Sarah, then John, then Thomas, then Eliab with whom I was closest, then Daniel, then Michael whose twin perished, then baby Amy* . . . He seems to be counting his own family off against the daughters. I see a sort of Dickensian line-up, with poor William, the oldest, having to fend for himself, losing himself in his books and bones.

—Can you see your mother in this great slab, William?

—I cannot see her, he says, for my father who was thus upright and of a stony disposition blocks my view. (He puts his hand up against Meg's front.) *Circulationis necessitas in rebus.*

Claire is sitting in the centre of the circle, the arms of Meg and her daughters around her. William and I join her. I sit between them.

—So, have you counted them? I ask her.

—Each time I went round I got a different number, so I gave up. Somehow I don't think they want to be counted. I get the feeling they're flowing and changing all the time. What about you?

I laugh.

—You don't really expect me to tell you after that.

242

—C'mon, snool, I saw you counting.

I look at her.

—Okay, seventy-two.

—That's what I thought too, she says.

—Bovillus conceived of the body enclosed by circles, one for the head, one for the abdomen, and one for the heart, says William.

We are becalmed.

Eight

Sand sucks but doesn't hold. The sound as I yank up my roots, thin as capillaries, and tuck them back into my socks, is something of a disappointment: no heart-wrenching cry of the torn vessels-of-life one hears about and perhaps wishes for. It is merely time to go.

Lancaster, this is Lancaster.

Claire is going straight on to London, William and I are stopping off in Cambridge.

It's raining. We stroll to the far end of the station platform where there's no overhead cover. Claire puts up her hood; William, immutably dry, is unsusceptible. The Castle looms above us. *Looms* indeed: that I should use such a word bespeaks my condition, one of gaining heart but losing depth of vision. A perceptual flatness takes over, as in a child's painting where a castle may perch with impunity on top of other buildings. Perhaps I need new contacts.

William is keen to the sizzle of overhead wires and the yellow computer screens hanging from the rafters showing train arrival and departure times. I have become expert in the ways of old men transformed into boys.

All passengers travelling to London and stations en route, we apologise for the delay of the 11.57 due to mumble mumble mumble . . . It is now running approximately fifty-five minutes late.

—Shit, says Claire, that's us. Nearly an hour to kill and there's only that smoky café.

—We could do a quickie tour round the Castle — it's just up the hill, as you see. It was the scene, by the way, of the infamous Lancashire witch trials.

She's interested.

—When was that?

—Sixteenth or seventeenth century, I think.

—Seventeenth century, second half, says William. I pass the information on to Claire.

It turns out we're just in time for the twelve o'clock tour. Our guide, a young man with an angry skin discolouration around his mouth, tells us that Lancaster Castle has been a place of punishment for the last nine hundred years. Hundreds were put to death in this very castle. It still – unfortunately – houses 250 prisoners. He can't however show us the witches' cell because that part of the building is closed off for repairs.

William is plucking at my sleeve, showing a morbid interest in the young man's face. I'm expecting a lecture on the pathology of skin pigmentation. Instead he says,

—I do believe he should have been taken for a witch, Frear.

—What on earth are you on about now?

He amplifies. Any mysterious red port-wine stains, in addition to anaesthetic patches and nipples and teats, were sure clinical signs of witchery.

—Well, Freud believed he would have been burnt as a witch in the Middle Ages; instead – this was in Nazi Germany, mind you – they burnt his books. A sign of great progress, he remarked in his wry way. But how do you know so much about all this, William?

—I know, Frear, because as physician to King Charles I was responsible for the diligent search and inspection of those women which were brought up from Lancaster to Surgeons Hall in London and charged with witchery.

—*Hundreds of witches were tried and condemned here.*

—What happened to your witches, then, William, did you condemn them too?

—I found nothing unnatural neither in their secrets nor in any other parts of their bodies, nor anything like a teat or mark, nor any sign that any such thing had ever been, but for the skin of the fundament, which was drawn out as yet will be the case after the piles or application of leeches.

—So what was their fate?

—They were all four of them pardoned, Frear, almost certainly due to an act of justice which was at least in part due to my enlightened views and prompt and energetic actions.

—Well, bravo, Will (champion of witches), that just about makes you an honorary feminist. My daughter would be proud of you.

And over there are the lunatic chairs, primitive versions of the straight-jacket. Anyone wishing to sit in one may do so.

William does. He is beginning to flag in a major way. We move on, up to the 'drop room', where prisoners were prepared for public execution by short rope.

Over there is Jane Scott's chair. She was wheeled in because she couldn't

245

walk. She had a withered leg due to her brother's violence. Then there was
Sarah Grimes who was reprieved at the last minute. It was proved she was the
victim of a frame-up. She got given her own coffin to take away.

—Oh terrific, says Claire, a story with a happy ending.

Next we have the grand jury room, where you will notice we are
surrounded by the portraits of twelve powerful men.

—Where are the women? comes a voice – no prizes for guessing
whose.

—I'm sorry, says our guide with a sigh, but I'm not responsible for
history. Any other questions?

—What were the witches' dungeons like?

It seems they were so deep underground, so perfectly sound-
proofed, that all the witches would have heard, chained to the floor
by iron rings, was the pounding of their own hearts.

Come Claire, William, our train is due.

Nine

Nostrils vibrating, palms pressed together, eyes closed and head inclined heavenward, I fear any moment a psalm will burst from his restive lips. (We are, by the way, not in King's College Chapel but in the Cambridge Coffee Co.) The next thing I know William has thrust his hand, in a rampage of intoxication, into a burlap bag marked 'Jamaican Blue Mountain'. Inserting a fingernail caressingly into a groove, he says, with a reverence I thought reserved only for the bean of the bosom,

—This little fruit is the source of happiness and wit.

I buy him a modest sackful to sniff now and again as we trot round town. We were both students at Caius College, albeit around 350 years apart.

—So, doctor, what is your considered opinion of the place – changed for better or worse?

He points to a Give Blood sticker in one of the old almshouse windows and giggles. Perhaps it is all too much for him, the architectural changes, the shops and lights and endless streams of cars, bicycles and students. Or he may be high on caffeine snorting.

I thought he would be eager to recollect his time here: his studies of pulses, urines and drugs, philosophy and physics and astronomy, not to mention the dissections of hanged felons, the post-mortems of fellow student suicides. But no, he prefers to go around in this daze or haze of pre-Freudian unconsciousness.

I suppose being a medical undergraduate wasn't all that much fun for either of us. For him there was incapacitating gout, or more likely malaria, which would explain that enlarged spleen of his. I suffered from migraines, complete with flashing lights, vomiting and diarrhoea. The heart palpitations I put down to an hypochondriacal heritability.

William has come to a halt in front of St Michael's Hall and is looking up at the statue in the niche.

—Who is that starched stovepipe, Frear, and what is he holding to his bosom?

The folly in question wears britches and flared coat and holds in his

247

left hand, against his chest, a heart. The brass plaque reads: *Dr William Harvey*.

—Victorian, I apologise, not our best period.

I hustle him along. This is getting embarrassing. It was to be a memorable farewell, a grand tour, a pilgrimage of the days of his youth, and what do we get but this inglorious farce of memories limited to salt and oatmeal and unheated rooms; and only these stone and painted apparitions which he seems to find so risible. Doctor, you are one of their honoured sons. But he seems unable or unwilling to appreciate his apotheosis. He is too far gone.

At the far end of the Senior Combination Room of the Old College hangs his portrait. He is looking distinctly derelict. His books are on display in the library. Look, William: *Falloppii Opera, Michaelis Savonaralae Med. Pract., de Mulier Morbis Spachii, Medic Tractatus* . . . He touches a spine or two but his heart is not in it. Look, there's your diploma . . . and there, your tongue depressor.

A sharp snort from the brown bag.

—Okay, what do you want, William? Would you like to find your old rooms?

He shivers.

—It was so cold, Frear, we had to run round for half an hour before bed to warm up our feet.

—Well, it was jolly cold even in my day – they were not exactly liberal with the central heating. What then? Evensong in the chapel? Speak, sir.

—I should like, he says at last, a hot bath.

Very well. Forty-five minutes later – I have been to evensong myself – I return to the basement and listen outside his bathroom door. He is in mid-flow of *Enter every trembling heart*. I open the door a crack and peer in. The place is billowing with steam, the tiles dripping sweat, the floor a–slosh, and the nose of a billowy William, pink with pleasure, peers over the water line.

Pink clouds over King's. Matins – with the sun pouring through the stained glass – is a heart-lifting affair. Afterwards we go, fulfilling my promise, for coffee. And then we must be on our way and an end to this picaresquing.

At the coffee shop he dissects the Cafetière plunger and makes a mess on the lace tablecloth. I too slosh coffee into my saucer (note: hand tremor worse today). What a pair we are. I apologise to the waitress.

He is not impressed with the coffee, which he says is not up to brother Eliab's standard.

—I have done my best.

An unusually thoughtful look crosses his face.

—Tell me, Frear, how do transplant recipient's normally die?

I suppose I must answer him.

—Well, doctor, acute rejection is the most likely scenario in this first year. Chronic rejection – a narrowing of the coronary arterial intima – is always a good bet, as are hypertension, cardiac effusion (an embarrassment, as they say, of the heart), arrhythmias and eventual heart failure. Then there are the infections. Loaded as I am with immunosuppressants, I am prone to all kinds of weird and wonderful, bizarre and opportunistic little bugs like CMV (cytomegalovirus), pneumocystis carinii, listeria monocytogenes, and so on. If one of those doesn't get me, a malignancy probably will. Indeed, they are finding increasing numbers of cancers, lymphomas especially, among heart recipients. What else? Pneumonia; and stroke – always a risk there. Renal failure – that's a probability. In fact I already have problems in that region. Then there are the minor side-effects of the drugs, some of which you will have noticed, doctor, like this tremor of the hands, the gum hyperplasia. But of course these things are hardly fatal. Shall I continue?

—That is quite sufficient, Frear.

He sips, puts down his cup, folds his napkin into a pyramid shape and regards it. The heart, he says, quoting Hippocrates, is in the shape of a pyramid. Have you ever thought, Frear, of making an end of it before the appointed time?

—I beg your pardon?

—An honourable discharge from this life, Frear.

—Oh I see. I don't suppose I would have gone through with the transplant if I'd been looking for a way out. You?

He sits back, closes his eyes,

—It was always my belief that it is lawful to put an end to one's life when one is tired of it or in great misery.

—And were you?

—Forgive me, Frear, if in recalling the irreparable injuries I suffered, I give vent to a sigh.

249

This he does.

—Whilst in attendance on his Majesty, he continues, during our late troubles, certain rapacious hands not only stripped my house of all its furniture, but what is a subject of far greater regret to me, my enemies abstracted from my museum the fruits of many years of toil, those precious papers containing accounts of dissections, autopsies and observations made on patients, not to mention those of humbler animals. Lost, all lost.

—His eyes fly open, the whites have clouded over.

—Twas the greatest crucifying that ever I had in all my life, Frear. Also, my twin brothers Matthew and Michael, dead in 1643. John, my second brother, in 1645. My wife shortly thereafter.

—I'm sorry, William.

I see him as he must have been – old, ill, childless, bereaved, *Crucified*.

—Was it then you made the attempt?

He nods.

—It was all arranged, Frear. 'Twas in my seventy-second year. Friend Scarburgh administered the deathly dose of laudanum on the appointed hour. Next morning he did accordingly come to take care of my papers and suchlike friendly offices upon which it was agreed he should perform, and did find me –

—Yes, William?

—He found me drinking a jorum of Yemeni.

—Coffee?

—Yes, Frear. Alive and well, and most excellently cured. (The old eyes twinkle.) The laudanum, instead of killing me, had brought away a not inconsiderable number of stones which effect caused such relief as to suspend any designs to destroy myself for some years. (He raises his cup.) To your health, Frear.

—Thank you. And yours, you old sonuvagun. William, I say (now it's my turn to sit back and wax philosophical), I suppose there are two ways of looking at this post-transplant life of mine: one as a death sentence, the other as an opportunity.

—In which wise, Frear, do you perceive it?

—I don't know. Both I suppose.

He is attentive.

—I do not mean to deny your sad affliction, Frear. The burden of unknowing is indeed a heavy one. However, I see that it is in some wise a gift; a chance, that is, to understand many things; to remove oneself, to digress from life and its rational structures and from that lost vantage point to ponder and wonder. For it has been found in almost all things that what they contain of use is hardly perceived unless we are deprived of them, or they become deranged in some way.

—As you say, William. But what am I to do with this understanding – which is not understanding at all but a kind of dumb witness?

He pats my hand.

—How am I to use my remaining years – or months?

He shrugs. His wispy hair is dry and crackly. At last he says – can those be tears filling his eyes? –

—Follow your nose, Frear.

His lip quivers.

—Dr Harvey –

—'Tis the palsy, Frear, nothing to be done about it. (Another twitch.) Have you made your will, Frear?

—Yes, as a matter of fact I have, but nothing like yours. I could never go through my property divvying things up so methodically, so diligently, the way you did.

I merely did what I thought best. To my friend Scarburgh, I gave my best velvet gown and all my little silver instruments of surgery – my sounds, probes, catheters and dilators and silver-mounted lancets, including the tongue depressor with the hallmark 1614 –

—Which we saw in the library –

—Do not interrupt, Frear. To my old friend Mr Tom Hobbes ten pounds as a token of my love. To my brother Eliab twenty thousand pounds and to my niece Mary West and her daughter I gave half my linen and all my silverplate. Except of course for my coffee pot –

—Also to your brother Eliab, yes?

He nods.

—A handsome object with a graceful spout. With all that warmth inside, it puts me in mind of the heart.

—Yes, William.

—And sex, he says.

—What?

One raised eyebrow, a leering cadaverous smile. He looks very like the British writer A. N. Wilson. And it just goes to show how wrong you can be about somebody: how at the last they can turn around and shock the pants off you. Which is what old Willy does right there in that maidenly teashop.

He moves closer and actually nudges me in the ribs. Then confesses to 'a pretty wench'.

What am I to do? Put him straight, say, 'Now look here, my man, we no longer use words like *wench, bird, chippy, floozy, bit-on-the-side* . . .

—I repeat, he says, half-rising to his pointy little feet and crowing – as if I hadn't heard him the first time – a wench. I made use of her – he pauses, looking pleased with himself – for warmth's sake, as Kind David did.

I have just taken a mouthful of coffee, which is unfortunate. My new sweater suffers.

—William, sit please. (I must make an effort after all – are you listening, Claire?) We don't *use* women like hot water bottles with convenient orifices, then discard them like –

He is looking most indignant.

—I beg your pardon, sir, but I took care of the wench in my will, as also of my manservant.

What does one say? Dr William Harvey, you are a revolting little suckseed, a hypercaffeinated mutt of a misogynist –

—What is it, Frear?

—Nothing, Will, forget it. We'll have one more pot of coffee for the road, shall we, and then we'll be off.

I order.

—And you, Frear?

—What about me?

—Will you continue to take your medicine?

—I suppose so. There are a few things I still want to do while I have the chance. I'm thinking about it.

I pour the water slowly over the grounds, stir, and now we wait. Two minutes. *Tick tock, tick tock.*

—Do not think too hard, Frear.

—You're right. What shall I do, then, sit quietly in a cave with my feet in an ice bucket? Soak in a hot tub? Go vegetarian, give up coffee?

—Certainly not, sir, 'tis the best medicine, as I have said on previous occasions. Learn from my own experience, Frear. To wit, I starved myself, neither eating nor drinking for twenty years, and still

252

suffered the gout. If to fast and have gout all be one with drinking and having gout, do as you have done.

He raises his cup.

—Drink up, Frear.

Ten

He lives at Eliab's house in Roehampton. He walks out in the morning combing the long threads of his hair in the fields. He sits down to dinner at a certain time every evening regardless of whether it is ready or the company assembled. He fills the salt cellar with sugar and eats from it.

William Harvey is nearly eighty and in spite of these quirks (manias) is probably in perfect control of his mental faculties; though what he calls gout-pain (erythromelalgia probably) might drive him to harmless foibles and/or despair.

He keeps an emergency ration of opium just in case.

He is no doubt aware, although he does not possess our knowledge of arterial degeneration and high blood pressure, of what he calls cerebral catastrophe, and may even notice his own distended temporal arteries – a sure sign of an approaching arteriosclerotic event.

June, 1657. The stout-hearted old man has for some weeks been confined to his room in his brother's charming retreat in the Surrey countryside. His grand-niece looks after him. His friends visit him and he spends most of his waking hours seated in a large armchair near an open window looking out upon the pleasing prospect of an English late spring and summer. He can still enjoy the colours and scents of the flowers, although his legs will no longer carry him to vantage points where he may observe the teeming life hidden amongst the plants and grasses.

It is the evening of the third of June. He has just been settled down at his look-out post when he complains that he can no longer see clearly. He requests his secreted dose of opium, but at this point his words become slurred and jumbled so that it comes out as a confused and indistinct utterance. He realises that he can have no further hope of recovery. He makes signs that his young relations should be sent for, and distributes the minute watch that he had sued in making his experiments, his signet ring and other mementos. As his paralysed tongue does not allow him to speak, he makes signs to Pembrose, the apothecary, to bleed him in the tongue, which operation the man manages to botch.

254

He loses consciousness.

The heart of the author of *De Motu Cordis* slows, then ceases to beat altogether.

His body is embalmed and laid out at Roehampton for three weeks awaiting burial at Hempstead Chruch. On 25 June a large procession of Fellows of the Royal College sets off from London by coach. It takes them two days to get there so the funeral service probably takes place on the 28th. On that day he is 'lapt in lead', a sort of mummy case that conforms to the shape of his body with a face crudely engraved on the surface. The case, on the other hand, is over six feet long, whereas our Wiliam was only wee. He is placed in the centre of a row of twelve Harveys with his feet towards a barred but unglazed window in the east wall. There he remains for more than two hundred years.

By the mid-nineteenth century the leaden shell has sagged around the limbs of its occupant revealing the bones of the skeleton within. Also, rain has begun to collect in the lid of the coffin and passes thence, through a fissure near the feet, into the coffin itself. The lower third is filled with a dark fluid, 'thick as melted pitch and having a peculiar organic odour' (probably a mixture of embalming fluid, decomposing matter and rain).

This will not do.

It is decided by a committee of eminent physicians to remedy the situation by making repairs. They do a patch-job which proves inadequate.

In 1882 there are further lengthy committee meetings. One suggestion is put forward: to transfer the remains to Westminster Abbey. Somehow it never happens.

At last – on St Luke's Day, 1883 at 4.00 p.m. – the mummy-shaped chest, judiciously restored, is carefully and reverently brought up from the subterranean family vault (he is risen!) and deposited in a sarcophagus of white Sicilian marble which is placed due north and south in the centre of the Harvey chapel. At the south end is cut: *William Harvey b. 1578, d. 1657.* Prayers are said. A handsome bound copy of his works is encased in lead and buried with him. The monolith cover is rolled onto the sarcophagus (sound effects, please) and after a number of pompous orations the proceedings are terminated.

William and I walk along a pathway from Audley End station to Saffron Walden. The way is bounded by great slopes to the west and the east, houses and farms and a comprehensive school in the throes of renovation. It is a fine Sunday, but still no taxis about, so we walk into town. Workmen are stringing up Christmas lights along the main drag. We are directed to an office above a shop. I ring a bell and a hugely fat man comes down wiping his nose with a hankie the size of a dishtowel. Where to? he asks. I tell him Hempstead Church, and at the sound of my semi-American accent he hitches up his belt. You're on, guv, he says, and ushers me to the passenger door of a battered American-sized stationwagon. He drives like a Greek and tells boring tales of Dick Turpin the highwayman.

—It's what all American tourists want to know about – we get a lot of 'em round about.

—Well, I'm afraid I know nothing about Dick Turpin, I say. (And couldn't care less.)

—What brings you to Hempstead Church, then, if I might be so bold as to enquire? (The man favours a fancy turn of phrase.)

—The remains of William Harvey.

—William Harvey . . . William Harvey? Oh *ye-eh-es*, now I remember, he's the heart and blood chappie. The Vicar knows all about him, history and the like.

—I just want to see his place of burial.

—If you'd like I'll have a word in the ear. A scholar and a gent, the Vic, he'll tell you all about it. Had quite a few visiting scholars hereabouts wanting to know about this Harvey, even a Frenchman once I can remember –

—Thank you, but it's a private matter.

—Suit yourself, guv.

He pulls into the church drive and parks on the grass verge. Sunday, he remarks. Service in progress, you'll have to wait a bit. He sounds pleased. You can have a snoop around the churchyard meanwhile, it'll be over soon. He looks at his watch.

—Thanks, I say. If you wouldn't mind waiting, we won't be long. (We?)

It's a fine day. The graveyard is filled with moss-grown gravestones and monuments, both upright and supine. William is holding his hand over his eyes, evidently trying to make out something over the horizon.

—What is it, William?

256

—Eliab's House, The Hall – I don't see it – it was right over there on that rise. He looks quite bewildered. I tell him not to worry, and walk back round to the front of the church. The taxi driver is propped against his machine.

—Excuse me, but do you happen to know anything about a manor house hereabouts called The Hall?

—Now you're asking, guv, there's a story in that. I can remember seeing it. Burnt down ten years ago, I'd say. It was over there, just over that hill. (He is pointing to where William was looking.) A right shame, fine manor house as I recall.

—I see. Yes. Thank you.

A forlorn William.

—Look at the sky, doctor, not a cloud.

—Eliab's house . . . (He is not to be distracted.)

—I'm sorry, William, I'm afraid it's –

He has disappeared into the Chapel. The service is over. I follow. There is the marble sarcophagus, so massive it necessitated building a pillar in the vault to support the floor. It is inscribed:

The remains of William Harvey
Discoverer of the Heart & Circulation of the Blood
were reverentially placed in this sarcophagus by
the Royal College of Physicians of London
in the year 1883.

So, there you are, William. He hoists himself up onto the sarcophagus facing the niche containing his own marble bust. His little legs dangle. From the bottom step I look up. His French biographer Chavois will have stood on this very spot, hand over heart, paying homage: *Grand Will . . . Survivant eternel, immortalise son nom!* Well meant, I suppose, in spite of the French twaddle.

—Frear, your taxi awaits.

—Let him wait. What have you got to say to me, doctor?

I stand between his legs.

—I remember well a certain Lord Clark who, it seems, had a retraction of the penis to such a degree that he illustrated the belief of some people that men can degenerate into hermaphrodites or women.

—I shouldn't worry about it, doc. (How do I keep a straight face?) I'm quite sound in that department.

257

He looks unconvinced. The church is filled with a strange light, a ticking noise.

—I once found a stone in the heart, Frear. My teacher found a scabby heart. Sir Robert Darcy, my patient, died of a heart disease and on post-mortem I found a ruptured ventricle with a rent of such a size that it easily took one of my fingers. *The gaping thing which is deep within man does not readily close.*

—I'll bear it in mind, doctor. Is there anything else you'd like to tell me?

—In the animal kingdom, Frear, one sees how those creatures that lack hands supply their needs either by a long neck and a beak, or by the tongue, as in bees and dogs, or by a proboscis as in the elephant and the butterfly, or by the feet as in monkeys, or –

—We call it overcompensation.

—My wife's parrot clasped things with its feet.

—The one you dissected?

—An excellent and well-instructed parrot, Frear.

—I'm glad to hear it, William. In what way would you say I have overcompensated?

No reply. He seems to be staring at the top of my head, or looking through it. He himself has become rather transparent. Dropping his gaze to armpit level, he reaches out and pulls me close.

—Dr Harvey, is this affection or what?

Closer still, his ear to my chest.

—'Tis how one listens to the heart, Frear.

—We have stethoscopes for the job.

—I am not impressed, sir, with listening through a tube. For I tell you, one gets closer to the thing this way.

Now he's percussing my chest.

—What do you hear, Doctor?

—An extreme cardiac dullness.

—Oh, terrific.

—Do not be foolish, sir, 'tis the sound all hearts make. Indeed, as when feeling for a joist in a wall, its solidity, as opposed to the spongiformity of the lungs, makes a dead or withal a flat sound. The heart beat itself, however, is quite merry.

—Oh.

—The ventricular tree is elastic and stretchable in youth; however, by middle age 'tis hardened and unable to handle the wilder gushes of

258

blood and yet still withal capable of exciting movement. If you live with circumspection, Frear, you may have a good life yet.

—I shall do my best. William . . .

—Yes, Frear?

—What happens then?

—The beat, which I believe is composed of many different rhythms, never stops entirely until the moment of death.

—And that is . . . ?

—When all things are becoming languid and the heart is a-dying, it ceases to respond by its proper motion. The left heart ceases to pulsate first of all, then its auricle, next the right ventricle, and finally, all other parts being at rest and dead, the right auricle still continues to beat. Life, indeed, lingers longest there until gradually, unwillingly, and with an effort it nods the head, as it were, and dies.

—So.

—'Tis an elegant and orderly phenomenon, sir.

—Thank you, William.

He regards his feet.

—Are they giving you trouble again, Will?

He looks away.

—A throbbing, Frear, an aching and burning, the like of which comes upon me so suddenly and intensely that the veins stand out in the feet and the temples as if a ligature had been applied, the feet becoming a dark purple colour, the arteries throbbing violently. The head, Frear . . . I believe everything has already gone dark. It seems to me, indeed, that I am entitled before this day is lived and gone properly into night, to ask to be excused.

—Let me admit, he adds, I am a little weary. (He has closed his eyes.)

Yes, William. And what am I to do now? Hand on heart, a fond farewell, a few more corny platitudes and we shut the covers of our tomes and tombs?

I stand and look at him. I find I am smiling not a little absurdly. He seems, even with his eyes closed, to smile back – or is it a final twitch of the palsy? And do we now say *sic transit* – or in Claire-speak, *sick transit* – as another snoolish old patriarch crawls back into his tomb-womb and good riddance?

—Frear.

—Yes?

The hand flaps.

259

—I congratulate you from my heart, and I pray that you may go on as you are doing, with grace and –

—William –

—Go, most worthy sir, and whatever you do, still think kindly of your anatomist.

—I shall.

A fleeting touch of the hand and he is gone, disappeared into his cold bed according to the laws of discriminating chimaeras – without the accompaniment of trumpets or trompe l'oeil angels, and certainly no Don Giovanni-ish wails; leaving me stranded, the knees of my heart, as it were, quite bent.

—Had a profitable time, guv?

—Yes, thank you.

He opens the door for me and haply, as William would say, we ride in silence back to the station. Only after a time do I realise that I am clutching something rubbery and rather slimey. I open my palm. Good heavens! Where on earth did the little bugger get such a thing?

—Care to share the joke, guv?

—That's all right, I say.

A balloon, red, in the shape of a heart.

Eleven

My teeth and wrists ache. I'm getting to the end of this notebook and am not inclined to start another. London is wet and windy and our plane leaves in a couple of days. Claire has to get back to work, Ruth thinks I'm overdoing it, my cyclosporin prescription is running out and I'm due for my one-year tune-up at Stanford. Generally the message seems to be that the smoke has cleared, as after the Civil War. With William and the last of the ghosts gone, I too can go home. Not that I am inclined to move just yet.

I am in the William Harvey Library of the Royal College of Physicians, erected 1964, just across from Regent's Park, which will have been open farmland in William's time. It's quite central, well placed for the tube. I'm to meet Claire at the Leonardo da Vinci exhibition over on the South Bank in a couple of hours. Meanwhile I sit amongst a number of well-preserved volumes of William's first editions, his portrait with the knitted brows above me. William, tell me, where did you get that absurd balloon? But he is mum, embalmed in varnish, and however much I pester, cannot answer any more of my sophomoric questions. Even after years of analysis, largely devoted to separation anxiety, I do not cope well with sudden disappearances.

De Motu Cordis is a mere seventy-two pages long, a small, stumpy book bound in leather, stamped with gold. It was printed by a second-rate publisher by the name of William Fitzer in Frankfurt in 1628 – an unfortunate choice as it turned out: William Harvey never saw the proofs, there were 126 inaccuracies, and the paper, poor and thin, soon turned brown and friable. Of course all that has been taken care of. Each page is now preserved in a sort of pericardium of thick plastic laminate which will mitigate against if not stop further deterioration due to rough handling, or any handling at all.

A book about the movement of the heart that has had all movement checked. What would you say to that, William?

Mine has had some rough handling. My heart, that is. It may be deteriorating or worse inside its plastic wrap.

Yesterday's *Times*, which I read on the tube this morning, had a

261

special health section, including a report from the 39th Congress of the European Society for Cardiovascular Surgery in Budapest on heart transplant recipients. I quickly turned the page and read about the effects of passive smoking on children. Dreadful. I flipped over to see what was on TV. 'Heart of the Matter: *No one who objects to war has to join the British Army.*' How interesting!

Don't talk to me about avoidance behaviour.

According to the report giving female donor hearts to men could turn out to be a big mistake.

Female-to-Male Heart Swap Risky

According to Professor Yves Logeais of the La Pitie Hospital Paris giving female donor hearts to men appears to be a strong independent risk factor for lethal right heart failure and a major cause of death after cardiac transplants, a cardiovascular surgery conference has been told.

Five died of right ventricular failure shortly after surgery. Four out of five of the heart failure deaths were men given female hearts compared with 13% of the control group. Preoperative pulmonary pressure was around 30% higher in the heart failure group than in the controls and their cardiac output was also slightly lower.

Professor Logeais suggested that female donor hearts were risky because it was easy to overestimate their size and hence give a heart too small for the recipient. Size was usually estimated on body surface area and weight but this did not allow for extra fat around female hearts, he said. Professor Logeais suggested that echcardiography would assess more accurately the size of female hearts.

My first reaction was panic. I shall be murdered by my own material. I clutched at my heart pocket and searched the faces of the people on either side of me on the Tube, but nothing seemed to be amiss with them. That is how it is. The world tilts but only you fall off.

Now that I have had time to adjust I can appreciate the irony of the thing – a major ha ha in fact. Just desserts (bitter mousse) to the guy who has objectified, subjectified, fictionified and Freudianified women from the safe depths of his super recliner. I can hear Claire's voice: Hah, I'm glad! Just what you deserve! Perhaps I'll write a novel, call it *Revenge of the Female Heart*.

I refold the article. Already it's starting to tear at the folds. Perhaps I should have it encapsulated.

I put it back in my wallet, thank the Harvey librarian and make

262

my way out to the street. Regents Park is across the street – perhaps a walk will do me good. *If you please to spend some of the parings of your time to fetch a walk in this grove you may haply find . . .*

The parings of my time?

My legs are not doing what they're supposed to do. I cross over to the station at Portland Place, trying to line up my features correctly. My cheeks are going in one direction, my ears in another; the nose is turned sideways. I ought to be going to a cubist exhibition. Do I tell Claire, or not?

According to my heart I am three years old. At that age it beats at a rate of ninety per minute; after that, for most people, it begins to slow until it gets to around sixty or less at death. That is not how it will be for me. William was wrong. For me it will be more like a beheading than a nodding of the head. My garrotter, needless to say, will be a woman.

His politics of the heart was also wrong. All mankind (sic), he said, is reduced in the matter of the heart to a most perfect democracy. Is that so? How does that square with your other line: the heart is the father, the prince in the kingdom, the fountain whence all power, all grace doth flow, etc?

Claire, I have tried. But it may prove after all to have been inadequate, size-wise. A purely physiological discrepancy, you understand, nothing sexist in it.

So much for perfect democracy.

—Dad? Hi.

—Claire. Ah. There you are. Where've you been?

—I spent the morning at the National Gallery. Looked at lots of pictures of Madonnas.

—Affirmation of the mother principle?

—Something like that.

—Isn't it all a bit iffy? I mean, the exemplary Mary, meek and mild, walking oven for the Lord's little bun? Isn't that precisely the image of womanhood you've been trying to demolish?

—Dad, Christ, you're way behind on this. There are other ways of looking at the Mary figure than as bearer of a male god. That's the whole point. But you wouldn't understand so forget it. Did you rest this morning?

—Of course.
—How are things?
—Things?
—Yeah, things.
She's staring at the spot where, according to William, heartburn and heartbreak are felt.
—Oh, fine. Fine.

Twelve

The Leonardo exhibit. We have been queueing for half hour in wind and rain. I am no longer worried about the heart-swap report. After all, it's only a preliminary finding, the size of the sample is unclear and the greatest danger period is just after surgery. At this point, it is statistically unlikely that I will keel over into the Thames. With any luck.

Claire tightens her grip on my arm, holds the umbrella over my head.

—Dad, she wheedles, why don't you go wait inside . . . what if you get a cold . . . it could turn into an infection . . .

It's flattering, unflattering, comforting, frightening. She mustn't know; I want to tell her. I want her to intuit the danger; I want to be spared the indignity of telling her. I want her to be sorry. I want to spare her. I want her to be my guardian angel – my one-woman feminist protection racket.

She pulls me along.

—C'mon, Dad, we're moving.

The queue snakes through the museum, its tail-end emerging through a side exit. A sort of Harveyan movement. It is not true, by the way – contrary to what has been claimed – that Leonardo discovered the circulation of the blood. It was our Will, of course.

How could I not think of Freud and Anna after he became seriously ill? She began tending him round the clock. It was she rather than his wife who stayed with him through the night after his operation, who nursed his wounds, who held his hand, who changed his dressings. And the more dependent on her he grew (eventually it was a pretty comprehensive thing – he had cancer of the jaw), the more screwed up he got because he detested dependence. And although he sought desperately to keep his analytical cool, in relation to Anna he was about as restrained as one of Leonardo's turbo engines.

We buy our tickets, check our coats. The gallery is thick, traffic moves slowly from drawing to drawing. We linger before 'Skull compared with an onion', letting people go round us. It shows a man's head in profile, the top of it layered diagrammatically. Claire

265

thinks it ugly. I don't care if it is Leonardo, she says in her best *nya-nya* tone of voice. Actually, I agree with her: the heavy line, heavy features in profile, and the bulging circumscribed eye are unpleasant. Next to this, he's drawn a more delicately executed onion, cut through the middle, revealing its layers or rinds which he compares with the layers of the cranium, starting with the hairs and flesh, peeling off down to the 'fundamentum'.

His prime objective, according to our notes, is to seek out the '*senso commune*', the seat of the soul. He locates it in the *optic foramen*: 'the place from which the tears rise up from the heart to the eye, passing through the canal of the nose.'

From senso to sex. Before us is the infamous 'Coition of hemisected man and woman' which Freud spent so long analysing.

—What do you make of that? I ask Claire.

—Yuk. He's made the woman a hag, all contorted with a poochy stomach and hangy boobs. Whereas the guy sticking it to her is like a Greek god – not that he looks like he's having a lot of fun either.

—As noted by Freud, who also pointed out that he couldn't draw female sex organs. Look at the uterus – it's completely confused.

—What else did Freud say about Leonardo?

—A lot. Too much. He developed a theory about the origins of his homosexuality. His asexuality. His art as neurosis. His science as regression. It makes me tired just thinking about it. If you really want to know, go read his case study. Right now I'd rather just enjoy Leonardo's drawings.

She points to an erect penis aiming at a male anus.

—He didn't have any problem with the male anatomy, that's for sure.

—Hmm, interesting. Freud did *not* notice that, as far as I recall.

—Great, go publish a learned article. You can acknowledge me in a footnote. Oh look, she says, moving on, the female genitalia. The opening of the vagina is like a giant doughnut.

—Or the letter 'O', I add.

—Or the entrance to a cave: a deep *deep* cave.

She makes a monster face.

—With horrible clawed female creatures inside waiting to –

—Stuff it . . . What are those?

—Anal sphincters.

—They look like flowers.

We move on to the next room.

266

—There's one thing I don't understand. How does all this anti-woman stuff square with the Mona Lisa and the other Madonna pictures?

—Ah, that's different. Those are idealisations – that he could handle. Unless you subscribe to the theory that the Mona Lisa is really a man disguised as a woman.

She shrugs, I move on.

—Come and look at this, I say.

She reads the label: 'The heart (with bronchial tree'.)

—It looks like some kind of rootball.

—So it does. Apparently he did more drawings of the heart than any other organ.

—What's this, it looks like a piece of manicotti.

—The aorta, dummy.

—And this one that's like the inside of a church?

—Columns and vaulting – those are the ventricles.

She stares at it, at me.

—I've never thought about what it looks like inside. It's beautiful.

—It isn't quite so aesthetic in the flesh, but yes. He was very interested in the heart. He even proved that the valves allow the blood to pass in only one direction. There, that drawing shows a detail of the valves. They're very delicate when you see them opening and closing.

—When did you see that?

—You forget I once studied medicine.

—You're right, I did. I really did. It would be nice to learn about the body. Think I'd get into medical school?

I don't know. You'd have to graduate first.

—What about money? It costs a fortune.

—We can see about that if you're serious. Are you?

—I don't know.

—The foetus; curled up on itself, legs crossed, head heavy, like it's already got the woes of the world weighing on it. What do you think of that?

—Real sweet, she says, and smiles. (I see her in a white coat placing a newborn baby on its mother's tummy.) What would you do, obstetrics?

—I haven't got that far, it was only a thought. Don't push.

The woman behind thinks she's talking to her.

Motion and flow: of water and its vortices. Leonardo is obsessed by

267

movement and force: spirals, the growing plants, the configuration of hair. Leda's wig is like a pair of ram's horns; even the limbs of his babies are tornado-like. His deluge study looks like a woodworker's studio with the blower turned on.

—See any connection here with the heart studies? I ask.

—Sure, she comes back, the heart moves too.

—Exactly. He's interested in turbulence, perpetual motion. The heart works in harmony with the turbulent action of the blood, like water and its vortices. It never stops.

The heart should be perfect; like Leonardo's perpetual motion machines, it should never stop. But eventually it must, it does. Machines rust, pen bladders run dry, pumps give up. *When all things are languid and the heart is dying . . . it seems, as it were, to nod the head and die.*

—Are you all right, Dad?

—Yes, fine. I feel like I'm inside a blender with the switch turned on.

—Come on in here.

She motions from the next room. Studies of hands, rocks, more genitalia, flower petals. In these there is stillness and peace, the rhythm of repetition, but also of a gentleness that speaks of closure.

—Claire, I think I've had enough. You about ready to go?

—Sure, I just want to take a quick look at the flying machine – they've reconstructed it from his drawings.

It fills the whole room.

The great bird will take its first flight from the back of its Great Swan; it will fill the universe with stupefaction, and all writings with renown, and be the eternal glory of the nest where it was born.

—I just remembered we take off tomorrow, she says.

So we do.

268

Thirteen

Our last night. The Ramaswamy, according to their own legend, is the oldest Indian restaurant in London. We enter what looks like an office lobby off Regent Street and ring for the lift. It spills forth a character in baggy trousers, moustache, turban and scabbard who bows and ushers us in. As we ride up to the restaurant Claire, who is dressed herself like Nanook of the North, starts giving him a hard time. Hey, do you really get off on wearing that weird outfit? Don't you get tired of going up and down in this elevator? Doesn't it piss you off having to bow to a bunch of fat slobs? And so on. I tell her to lay off, the man is only doing his job. She says that's what the Nazis said.

Once up in the restaurant, he tries to take 'Madam's' down jacket. I can manage myself, she says, but with a mollifying smile that sets him off to even deeper salaaming. On the way to our table she *pssts* in my ear,

—Hey Dad, I figured I wouldn't embarrass you by telling him to fuck off.

—I really appreciate that.

She allows herself to be seated. A waiter spreads a napkin on her lap.

—Jee-zuz, she appeals to the ceiling, are they gonna offer me Beechnut baby food next or what?

While she studies the menu, I study her. How is she? I don't know. Shame on me. Shame, the Cinderella of the emotions. Fear of ridicule, failure to live up to one's ego ideal. Never mind me, this is about Claire. How do I find out? Do I wiggle my eyebrows up and down like Groucho Marx impersonating Sigmund Freud, stick my cigar in her face? *Tell me, tell me all, don't hold anything back.* I have been waiting, you see, for the right moment. At this rate we could wait forever. We don't have forever.

—Claire, I'm not trying to pry but if you want to tell me what happened back home, with your friend – lover – this summer, I'm here.

—What do you want to know? She breaks a papadum in two.

269

—I don't want to know anything, I'm just trying to find out in my delicate way if you're all right.

—I'm all right. *Crunch*.

—I gather there was an age gap.

—That wasn't the problem. It was that she didn't want to be tied to one person. I couldn't handle it.

—Object-inconstancy; in other words, promiscuous.

—That's a gross word, Dad.

—But accurate?

—No, it's a typical male put-down. Tell me, who calls men promiscuous? It's not a matter of her 'sleeping around' or whatever is the dumb expression you guys use, it's that she wasn't into one-to-one relationships. She's open to a lot of different people. Which makes getting involved with her risky. She warned me, but I took the risk. So there's no one to blame but me.

—Aren't you taking rather a lot on yourself? It doesn't sound that simple to me.

—Nothing is simple to you. Stop trying to protect me, it's my problem.   —I still feel responsible.

—Responsible for what?

—For everything. I'd like it to be different for you.

—You mean you'd like me to go straight. Listen, you goddam phallocrat, my sexuality is more than your pat Freudian bullshit, it's who I am and I like it that way, so you can just fuck off.

She reaches across the table, nearly knocks over my wine glass and pokes her fingers into my chest.

—I'm sorry, Dad, I didn't mean to go over the top like that. I know you're trying to help, but really there's nothing you can do. I'll get over it in my own way. But it isn't about being gay.

—Then what's it about?

She stops chewing.

She doesn't need to say it.

She's smoothing the clean linen with her thumbs, I am doing it with the flat of my hand. A father-daughter double act: the needy-placatory gesture symbolically demonstrated. For my part I am jealous of the bit of tablecloth underneath her thumb.

Loss. What will they say at Stanford about the heart-swap report? A bunch of hogswallop? Not worth the paper it's written on? Forget it: go home and get on with your life, Dr Frear. Or: *We-ell* (cough cough, shuffle shuffle) there may be some indications in that direction but at this stage it's still too early to say anything conclusive. If I were you, I'd put it out of my mind. In other words, it's too late now to give you a guaranteed compatible, user-friendly *male* one, so you'd better just make do with what you've got.

—Dad, you okay?

She takes my hand. What do I do now? Look where? Say what? *My dear, your timing is timely.* Somehow I have contrived to hang on. So has she.

—I'm fine. (We manage to let go.) Very well in fact. It's been a good trip. Thank you for coming.

—Dad . . . she says, but can't get any more words out.

—Yes?

—This eggplant stuff is terrific. I need some more water, it's real hot. And could we have some more wine? I feel like getting drunk.

—Of course.

I order another bottle and some water and we're off, reverting to what we know best. I begin in lecture mode (the snool-bore's favourite form of communication), telling her about how Freudian theory could be useful to feminists, lesbians in particular. He believed, you see, that we are all naturally disposed to be bisexual.

She looks doubtful, says it's a good try, calls him Dr Fraud. Feminism, she explains in her old trying way, is about politics, social determinants, economics – the real world. According to her, my friend Fraud and I are living somewhere else. Where? NW3?

—Claire, I tell her, you may think I don't know anything about feminism, but equally you know beans about Freud. The point is that Freudian theory – not Freud himself necessarily – can be used, extrapolated from.

—Okay, so tell me: what's your stuff got for us?

—Well, for one thing, women can't step out of being sexed or gendered. There's no clear dividing line between the psyche and society. I mean, understanding the Oedipal stuff, for example, allows you to understand the reproduction of male dominance, the contempt for women as poor penis-less creatures, their consequent self-devaluation, and so on. If feminism wants to change things it needs a *theory* of how we become sexed and gendered in the first place. You want a shift of focus, and power, from the father to the mother, fine. Go read Freud on the psychological price most women pay for giving up the mother as love-object. It's about basic drives: dependencies, feelings of helplessness and so on.

271

—Yukko bullshit.

—Yukko they may be, but bullshit, no. Look, Claire, gendered behaviour can't be dropped at will. We need to understand, observe the complexity of it all. I'm not saying become a card-carrying Freud, just don't throw the baby out with the bath water. It's about understanding *why* it's difficult to change. Looking at things like ambivalence, attractions to the wrong people, the need to please, the temptation to get hurt. Why, for example, so many women keep taking the blame, keep putting themselves down.

—Because they're being oppressed by men like you in positions of power. You're saying we're determined, we can't change – good reactionary stuff, dogma of the sadostate. Keep things as they are, thanks a lot.

—Claire, you haven't been listening. The theory doesn't deny that change is possible. And whatever else, you can't have a social or political theory that talks about change without a psychological one – it's too split off, they have to work hand in hand. You can't stuff away all the mess – the fantasies, the desires, the sexual drives – they keep tumbling out, it's all part of it.

—Okay, what about the other way around: how can you divorce yourself from the political stuff?

—Because, unlike you guys, we have no axe to grind. We are value-free: we simply record the truth about human development and life –

—What crap!

—What would you like for your main course, my dear?

—Vegetable vindaloo, the hotter the better. I'm in the mood for it. What about you?

—Saffron chicken, I'm slimming.

—Dad, you're a stringbean.

—Well then, I'm being kind to my heart.

—You're drowning it in wine. Go easy.

—Claire, Sigmund Freud was not wholly consistent, especially in his later years, about just what powers to assign to the ego and the id; but he rarely got it wrong that in most cases the id holds the upper hand.

Id grabs the neck of the wine bottle and pours.

—To your health.

—And yours, Dad. How is it, by the way? She focuses on the relevant spot.

272

—Ticking up a storm. O'erflowing.

—Oh yeah? With what?

—A yeasty brew. Cheers.

—Dad, you're drunk. And you didn't answer my question.

—What was that, my dear?

—About how Freudians can justify being apolitical. And stop my dearing me.

—Yes, my dear. As a matter of fact, you guys may have a few titbits to offer us too.

—Dad, you're a creep.

—Actually, I think the feminist shake-up has been no bad thing for us. It's allowed psychoanalysis a re-birth, transfusion of new blood, et cetera, et cetera. Entirely salutary. The shift of emphasis to the plenitude of the pre-Oedipal is a heartening project indeed.

—Blow it out your nose.

—Ah, the nose. Did I ever tell you about Freud's obsession with the nose?

—About a zillion times and I don't want to hear it again. Dad, what are you going to do when you get home?

—I don't know.

—What about your practice?

—What practice?

—Aren't you going back to work?

—I don't think so.

—Not even part-time? What will you do?

—I told you, I don't know. I need time to think about it. I'll tell you a joke instead.

—Oh no.

—You'll like this one, I promise. Anna Freud, having reached puberty, is beginning to show a precocious interest in her father's work, so Freud gives her some of his writings to study. About a month later he asks her if she has any questions about what she's been reading. 'Just one,' she replies, 'what is a phallus?' Being a man of science, Freud dutifully unbuttons his trousers and shows her. 'Oh,' Anna exclaims, thus enlightened. 'It's like a penis, only smaller!'

She runs off to the toilet. When she gets back she says she hates me. I made her pee in her pants.

—C'mon, it wasn't *that* funny.

—Dad, I almost think I'm glad you had a heart transplant.

—That is an indecent thing for a daughter to say to her father.

273

She considers this, then says it's her turn to tell a joke. I put down my knife and fork, fold my hands in my lap.

—Okay, so this lesbian comes into the gynaecologist's office for a routine check-up, takes off her boiler suit, plops herself on the rack and sticks her feet in the stirrups. The gynaecologist checks her out and pronounces it clean as a whistle in there. Lesbian says, 'Oughta be, I have a woman in three times a week.'

One joke each at our own expense, I'm thinking, not bad going. I say I like it. She looks pleased.

—Now tell me about your plans. Will you go back to the restaurant or what? After a thoughtful chew, she comes out with a piece of news nearly as gob-smacking as William's wench.

She's thinking of studying psychoanalysis.

I look at her. She must be drunker than I thought, or I'm suffering from a perceptual delusion.

—Explain please.

—It happened over the summer. I began to see the possibilities of the psychoanalytic thing, only from a different theoretical perspective than yours of course.

—Of course. But even so – Sigmund Freud, the feminists' friend?

—Something like that. I don't know. It's weird isn't it?

—In a word.

—I'm scared about the medical part too – it's such a long slog. But I feel sort of excited about it.

She sucks a greasy finger.

—What about our fence? How can we sit on different sides of it? What about politics versus psychology, all that stuff we were just arguing about?

—I was playing my role, it's an old line. Like yours is. I still meant the things I said, but I also see what you're saying. The personal/ political polarisation needs to be looked at. I think there are things we could learn from one another, maybe we could even work together.

—Claire – you mean us, you and me? Look, what is this, a barn dance or what? Okay everybody, get ready for the doh-si-doh . . . and swing your partner round and round . . . At this rate, we'll end up on opposite sides of the room. It's mad. Here I am delicately poised to pronounce it all a bunch of expensive humiliation, a patriarchal prosthetic friendship and a few more where that came from, and she's ready to go for it.

274

Sigmund, help me. I know that children want to grow up fast, desirous of our adulthood, our sexuality, not to mention the professional patina of our prestige; while we want the simplicity and so-called innocence of their childhood. But work together? Like Freud and Anna? Why? Claire, I want to say, is it because you think I haven't long to live and you're feeling helpless and it's the only way you know to heal the rift? Or is it some crazy idea of picking up where I leave off? Or is it the only way you know to say you care about me? A long slog indeed. Claire, has it not dawned on you that by the time you finish your degree I won't even be here?

—First get your medical degree, I say, then we'll see. (Meanwhile I shall be busy preparing for my Honourary one.) Now, what would you like for desert?

—Rasmali with pistachio nuts and cream – she licks her lips – my favourite. You?

—I'll nurse my brandy.

—Dad, what would you do instead?

—Instead of what?

—Your *practice.*

—Oh that. Let's see. I shall burn my books and take to the High Sierras. Buy a cabin and an old Jeep and go fishing. Meditate. Chop wood. Bake bread. Become a Buddhist. Or a Sufi. I believe they locate the unity of mind and body hereabouts (quick jab to the sternum). Commune with nature. Go eagle-spotting. Explore the bliss technique.

—The *bliss technique?*

—Bliss is the basis of the Ayurvedic mind-body healing method. If you place your fingers over your heart you can feel the source of time and space.

—I don't believe this.

—I shall sit contemplating not a whole lot in front of a well-stoked fire. I might revive the ancient idea of the heart as a sort of furnace, rather like one of those Swedish wood burners. Too little air and it smoulders, too much and *woomph* – a feverish heat; a great deal too much and *clang* – just listen to those cold, cast-iron doors go clang! The hot heart. A myth authored by a bunch of cold-hearted old fools but rather a nice metaphor all the same. Symbol of both the perfection as well as the iffiness of the universe, and a reminder of the power of love.

—Dad, are you going soft in the head or what?

—You could put it like that. Let's just say I'm sinking into my ripe cheese-hood.

I can almost smell it. I picture the provolone that hangs in our kitchen. When Marat died after the French Revolution his heart was transferred to the Cordelier's Clubroom and suspended in an urn from the roof. *O Coeur Marat*, they cried. I see mine dangling beside the provolone twisting and turning as the heat rises. *O Coeur Valentine*.

—Dad, are you sure you're all right?

—Yes, of course. Did you know that Harvard and Princeton are fighting over who should get Einstein's brain?

—No. So what?

—So simple. No bidders for his heart.

—Dad, have you been reading Buddhist stuff or what?

—No, but I may do. And while you're steeped in Freud I shall entertain myself with Jung. Get in touch with my anima.

—You sure you don't mean enema? Dad –

—Yes, my dear?

—You're starting to sound like some kind of Billy Graham of the heart world. What is all this?

—Billy Graham: inspiration! I shall become an evangelist of the transplant world. Spout St Augustine on the affirmation of the whole person, body and soul. In an instant . . . it was as though the light of certainty flooded into my heart and all the darkness of doubt was dispelled. Hallelujah! I shall appear on talk shows. Advocate universal heart transplantation. Write a conversion pathography.

—Huh?

—*I Found My Heart in San Francisco. Confessions of an Ex-Psychoanalyst Turned Cardiac Patty-Melt.* Freud said people found pathographies unpalatable but today not so, we are living in the age of bring-'em-back alive experiences and terminal visions – real bestseller stuff. I shall write a drama of the heart, full of palpitations, hovering angels, ghosts, disembodied voices, unearthly light. I could probably sign a contract with a publisher tomorrow. Or, on a more academic note, how about: 'The contemporary pathography as twentieth century update to the early spiritual conversion autobiographies'. I shall submit a paper to *Cardiology Today*.

—Dad –

—St Teresa – she had what she called transverberations, raptures of mystical union with God. She described it as an erotic encounter

276

with an angel in which her heart was pierced by a fiery dart of gold. Great Freudian stuff. I shall explore the surgical correspondences.

She's rapping on the table.

—Dad, we're going home tomorrow. Back to California. Have you thought about that in between all this New Age boy scout baloney?

Oh god, the reality principle. To be reminded of it by my own daughter. Clunk.

—Claire, according to Sigmund Freud, reality and fantasy are brothers if not twins.

—Fuck Freud. And you're talking to the wrong person about brothers. What about Ruth? Where does she fit into all these plans of yours?

—Your mother and I will live happily ever after – as ever.

—Balls.

—What balls? You don't believe we were happy or that we will be happy?

—Dad, you guys live in two different worlds.

—What would you have us do? People who expect romantic bliss from marriage are stuck in some oral phase of expectancy which dooms them to inevitable disappointment. Such things don't last – as your mother and I both know. But we worked hard and we have our modest successes to show for it. That includes you, by the way.

—Gee thanks.

—So call it a happy ending by default, then. I'm too ill to leave your mother and your mother is too responsible to leave me. We shall probably go on living together the way the American and Pacific land plates do, according to earthquake experts. Where the plates meet, each moves off in a different way, causing them to shift their positions. They slide past each other and occasionally pull apart or press together: *pulsus, tractus*. In other words, we'll make do. What do you think of that?

—I think we should pay the bill and get out of here.

277

Fourteen

Next morning. We load our bags into the taxi. I explain to the driver that we'll be making a small detour on the way to the airport. Claire's afraid we'll miss our plane.

—Where to?

—It won't take long. A quick visit to see Sigmund Freud.

—*Sigmund Freud?* He's been dead for fifty years.

—His statue, I mean.

—I don't believe this. Where the hell is it?

—I'm afraid I don't know exactly, but it's somewhere near the Freud house.

—The who house?

The driver is lost. This could go on all morning. I tell him the name of the street and we're off, Claire mumbling about a wild goose chase.

—Not a goose, my dear, but the father of psycho . . . stop! There he is! Behold!

A life-size bronze of Dr Sigmund Freud.

Claire giggles. I ask what is so hilarious and she points.

His head is covered by a black plastic rubbish bag.

Nevertheless, I shall get out and pay my respects.

—Don't be long, she yells after me.

So, this is what it has come to. Poor Dr Freud: born in a caul, hushed up in black plastic. How dare they. Such a desecration! Who did this to you, Sigmund? Come, tell old Big Ears. Is it the work of a disaffected follower re-enacting the ritualistic killing of the father – a colleague of mine perhaps? A vandal with a sense of humour? An analysand wreaking his revenge? Or some sister-terrorist of Claire's?

You have to admit, Sigmund, it's a brilliant move: the justest or the cruelest punishment, depending on your point of view. But then no one is better placed to appreciate the humour of it than you. Are you not amused? I'd like to think of you chuckling inside your bespoke headgear.

What's that you *pfumphed?* Hot, dark, smelly, cavelike . . . *womblike?* Well, there you are. What could be more apt?

278

No, it can't be pleasant for you. You who thrived on insight. Come again? Oh, I see. You want me to remove the offending object, strip it off the way you stripped us of our self-deceptions? *The drama in the human heart is really tragic and ends only too often with the total disintegration of the personality.*

Poor Sigmund, befogged and befuddled. However, it's no use you whipping up a storm of resentment in there. I'd save my breath if I were you. Did you bark something?

Get this damned bag off my nose!

In due course, *mein Goldener.* I suppose Mrs Harvey's parrot must have slept with a covering over its head.

It's long past my bedtime, Sigmund. I've drunk too much, my mouth burns, my eyes prick, Claire is knocking on the taxi window, pointing at her watch. And you? Just look at you. How dare you talk about self-deception? What about your daughter, for instance. Now, now, Siggie, control yourself. You'll just create a lot more humidity in there. It must be like a butterfly house. Anyway, you know very well what I'm talking about: the pandering scheme of yours to find her a worthy woman. *Anna has a thirst for friendship with women . . .* Hah! Oh she had a thirst all right, which you watered you old pimp, and once she was safely yours you complained to anyone who'd listen that she hadn't met a man fit for her. Or was it not rather – just between us – that you were afraid she might meet one quite fit enough, hmm?

Hatchet job! Infantile rebellion! Professional jealousy! More illusion!

On second thoughts, I might just let you stew in that bag.

Patience, doctor. You might even, in time, grow to enjoy your befogment. No? You despise not being able to see what's in front of your nose? I think we'll leave the nose out of it for now, if you don't mind. Personally I plan to cultivate my bufuddlement. In fact, I'm quite looking forward to it. With all due respect, Dr Freud, I have had enough *Todesangst*, enough truth, enough messianic obsessions, enough of civilization *and* its discontents, enough sexual disablement, enough insight and avoidance of illusion and enough rotten weather reports of the psyche. It's not that I think you were bad or mad or led us up the garden path. Let's just say I'm tired of you and your Sigmoidal *circumbendibus.* Let's just say I'm tired.

Don't think I don't know. Like you, I'm haunted by the ghosts of ideas. Like you, I have a daughter and every time the shutter of her eye clicks I feel my heart beat. Like you I am bored with my wife but make do. At the prospect of going home I feel like one of those umbrellas that turns itself inside out in the wind. All manner of bodily things that can ache ache, all that can twinge twinge. As a matter of fact, I'm thinking it's time to put this singing bird (Rosetti), this irritable but not ossified organ (C. Bronte), this outworn rag-and-bone shop (Yeats), this limp blimp (Nabokov), this neither gentle nor entirely manly heart (V. Frear) – to bed. *How long will my heart last?* You asked the question often enough. I shall try not to. Fortunately, the heart at its end doesn't rot like cancer of the jaw, so with any luck I shan't smell as bad as you. My dog William may still want to know me. And my wife Ruth. But come, cheer up, the end is also the beginning. Sorry, that was Jung, was it? Actually, I was thinking of my friend William Harvey.

Dr Freud . . . hello? Can you hear me in there? Good. Do you remember that brief paper of yours, 'Theme of Three Caskets'? No one reads it much these days. A sort of meditation on death and the love of women, with particular reference to the daughter figure in *King Lear*. You talk about Lear as an old man, a dying man, a man who is doomed but still not willing to renounce the love of women and therefore stubbornly insists on hearing how much he is loved. But then you recall the final scene in which he carries his daughter's dead body on to the stage (Cordelia, according to your paradigm, is death). 'Eternal wisdom . . . bids the old man renounce love, choose death and make friends with the necessity of dying.' One of your clever twists here: Cordelia is dead but it's Lear with whom we identify; Lear who yearns in vain for the love of woman as he had it, or would have had it, from his mother; but it is only the silent Goddess of Death, his daughter, who will take him into her arms.

—*Dad!*

You hear that? My daughter, unlike yours, is no paragon of feminine patience. She's losing her rag. I must leave you.

By the way, did you ever run into the physicist Hermann von Helmholtz? A countryman of yours. He also wrote about how the universe is dying, choking on its own entropy, dissipating into useless waste heat, squandering its resources. Many thinkers have balked at the ghastliness of the prediction, while others, like Sir Arthur Eddington, have gone along with it. 'I can give you no hope;

there is nothing for it but to collapse in deepest humiliation.' Is that a vigorous nod? You agree, Sigmund?

The more I look the more I think that black bag suits you.

—Heathrow Airport, please.